"I really enjoyed it...and there's so much going on that there's something in '12 Miles to Paradise' for every reader to grab a hold of. I learned a lot, too." - **Mary Lou Lynch**, aircraft production assistant, Port Orange, FL.

"I'm a very avid reader and *"12 Miles to Paradise"* is a MUCH better story than "Big Trouble!" -- and "Big Trouble!" was a bestseller. There is something about *"12 Miles"* that just grabs you. I couldn't put it down and hated to see it end. I recommend it to everyone. It's an absolutely perfect 'airplane' book and one of the best stories I've ever read." - **Jake Burns**, recent UVA grad and engineer, McLean, VA.

"I loved the story – and all the interwoven messages within it. *"12 Miles"* is everything a great book should be – and then some. I hope some day somebody makes it into a movie. I recommend it to anyone who loves horses or anyone who's ever been in a relationship!" - **Lisa Johnson**, administrative assistant, Denver Nuggets basketball team, Denver, CO.

"I thought it was great – I absolutely loved it. I literally couldn't put it down. It's kind of like a love story, written by a man. I don't know if that sounds right, but the whole time I kept reading I kept wondering who Hollywood would cast in the different roles." - **Jay Tucker**, real estate title executive, Austin, TX.

"12 Miles" won't help you win the third race, but our readers out here will really like it." - **Christine Crocker**, manager, *Champions!* gift shop, Santa Anita Park, Arcadia, CA.

"I read *"12 Miles"* in two days. I took it everywhere I went and every moment I just kept reading. It's a real page-turner and I was sorry to see it end. This is a very, very good story." - **Jay Clark**, business executive and avid reader, Englewood, CO.

"There are only two writers who make me laugh out loud: Mark Twain and Ted Simendinger. Simendinger is so descriptive, and so visual, and so true to character development that he could never be a ghostwriter and get away with it. You'd know it was him within minutes." - **Dave Murray**, retired engineer, Beltsville, MD.

"I read this wonderful book the day I got it and I could not put it down until I finished! It was an entertaining, warm, belly-full of laughs!" - **Linda Maxwell**, Stable Manager, Palm Meadows Training Facility, Boynton Beach, FL.

"I thought it was great – I loved it! And the descriptions of New Zealand were so vivid, it makes me want to go there!" - **Cindy Hensel**, two-time defending women's golf champion, Hidden Hills Country Club, Jacksonville, FL.

"I loved it – from start to finish – I loved the entire story." - **Mike Howland**, CEO of Noble of Indiana, Indianapolis, IN.

"What a great book! I could not put it down. It is perfect for a movie!" - **Gene Ahlhorn**, business executive, Pearland, TX.

"I LOVED IT! What a great story! And what great characters! I could not put it down!" - **Laurie Piscitelli**, nurse, Jacksonville, FL.

12 Miles to *P*aradise

A people story about horses & horseracing

by Ted Simendinger

Second Edition

Book cover design by Karen Saunders, Denver, Colorado USA

Book cover photographs by Skip Dickstein, North Chatham, New York USA

Editing by Barbara McNichol, Tucson, Arizona USA

Library of Congress Cataloging-in-Publication Data

Simendinger, Ted
    12 miles to paradise
Ted Simendinger. – 2nd edition.

ISBN 0-9702405-2-X

1. Humor   2. Fiction   3. Title

Library of Congress Control Number: 2001119647

10   9 8 7 6 5 4 3 2

Published by: Airplane Reader Publishing
                      Denver, Colorado U.S.A.

Notice of Fictitious Content: 12 Miles to Paradise is a purely fictitious story. The storyline blends existing venues with fictitious characters for the sole purpose of entertainment storytelling. By permission, and with the author's gratitude, several existing characters are identified as themselves.

Printed in the United States of America

Thanks

12 Miles is a wonderfully funny make-believe story—a people story—that sits in front of horses and the horseracing industry. It features a culturally diverse and tightly interwoven ensemble cast, with the principal characters being blended hybrids of scores of oddball friends from all around the world.

The vivid images of the described venues blossom from some of my all-time favorite places: sprawling, frenetic South Florida; tiny nearby Bimini, Bahamas; and both the half-a-world away picturesque North and South Islands of New Zealand.

On the home front, thanks to Mary Ryan, Doug Donn and Victor Sanchez at Gulfstream Park. I remain gratfeul to the American horseracing experts who helped shape the story, most specifically Donna Brothers, Damon Thayer and my brother Mark. A tip of the cap, too, to Rich Cardillo, the funniest man in xerography.

I offer, too, a toasting click of Kalik to the wonderful people of tiny Bimini, my favorite Bahamian refuge with more magic per square inch than anywhere on earth.

And extra special thanks to my pals in New Zealand: Aucklander Lloyd Hill, Christchurch's Don Brown, James Jennings at New Zealand Bloodstock, Ross Hawthorn at Ellerslie Race Course, and the nation's famed Thoroughbred breeder, Cambridge Stud's dynamic leader, Sir Patrick Hogan.

A cheery hoist of Speight's, too, to all the people in the tiny South Island hamlet of Glenorchy. Glenorchy is the Hope Diamond of geography. If you've watched New Zealand director Peter Jackson's film *Lord of the Rings,* then you've already seen where a couple key parts of this story take place.

Thanks most of all to the real sparkling jewels of my life – Bonnie and Gracie—both of whom encouraged me to write the story I really wanted to write. Thanks to their support, I did—and I sure hope you enjoy it.

Table of Contents

The Swap Shop

The great filly and Kentucky Derby winner Sweet Affirmation had only three foals during her lifetime. A champion runner during her racing days, Sweetie wasn't so lucky off the track and had breeding struggles her whole adult life. She produced but a trio of sons in 20 years of trying: Thunderbeetle, Eagleman, and Whodathunkit. None ran much faster than the men who bought them and Sweet Affirmation was finally retired from breeding at the age of 23.

Her sons never achieved much on the track. Thunderbeetle finished third in a race once, but it was only a six-horse field. And Thoroughbred history also reveals that shortly thereafter Thunderbeetle sort of pointed himself toward retirement after a mere four career races.

Prior to the start of Thunderbeetle's final effort—that day's ninth race at Churchill Downs—the horse screamed and hollered in the paddock during saddling, which was a bit of an annoyance to many. He followed that up ten minutes later by trying to mount the outrider pony in front of him during the post parade.

The man riding Thunderbeetle—jockey Gaspar Zas—angrily hopped off the racehorse, yelling in Spanish something to the effect that he wasn't getting paid enough to ride shotgun in such a bizarre threesome.

After Thunderbeetle's abrupt retirement from racing, his pedigree afforded him a shot at a modest breeding career. Thunderbeetle adapted well to his new sex-for-hire responsibilities but demand for his services was minimal. In most years, he was bred to a modest 15 mares or less.

Five of his offspring won claiming and allowance races of varying degrees. Thunderbeetle would never match the great Secretariat's clan of 2,282 kids, but for a tall turtle at least he had a safe job he enjoyed and was quite happy pursuing.

Eagleman, meanwhile, never even made it to the races. He cracked the condylar bone in his left foreleg as a two year old in training and was retired without a start. His pedigree didn't help much after the injury since, against all odds, Eagleman proved sterile. He shot nothing but blanks.

Ever since, Eagle has since been an anonymous outrider horse at Belmont Park—a "pony," the industry calls him. He squires horses to and from the track that on their best days couldn't have outrun his mother even if she moonwalked the final furlong.

Sweet Affirmation's youngest son—Whodathunkit—was sent to train and race at Gulfstream Park in South Florida. He, too, never made it to the starting post. In a freak accident the very first time the horse was closed inside a starting gate to practice breaks, one of Gulfstream's million swooping seagulls zoomed right past Thunk just as the gate flashed open.

The bird's sudden, erratic mid-air redirection and pull-up caused its wingtip to brush Thunk's face, slightly lacerating the corner of his right eye and eyeball. The terrified horse reared on his hind legs, tossed his rider, then leaped awkwardly to the left. As he did, Whodathunkit immediately got slammed and knocked to his knees by a loose horse who'd dropped his rider, was running free on the track and chose the exact wrong time to cut in front of Thunk's starting gate chute in its panicked search to return to the barn.

Thunk ended up with two types of injuries: physical *and* mental. The outside physical scars healed first. The emotional scars inside proved much, much deeper.

While recovering from his eye and leg injuries, Whodathunkit had a severe allergic reaction to some medication, developed a fever, and nearly died.

It was well over a year before he could resume training. When Thunk finally did return to a strict workout regimen, he didn't seem particularly thrilled about training in general or starting gates in particular. He remembered the gates. Whodathunkit knew he was safe *in* one, but not *leaving* one. Nothing good happened when a gate opened and Thunk felt no compelling need to move forward even an inch.

Time after time the trainer loaded the horse into the starting gate to practice starts, and every time the starting gates flashed open, Whodathunkit just stood there as immovable as Sherman's granite horse statue carved into the face of Stone Mountain, Georgia. Most days Thunk simply sat down, on the spot, and refused to move. Thunk's strategy was simple: Nothing bad would happen if he never inched forward.

One rainy, sodden morning at the training facility, Thunk even plopped down, rolled over, dropped his exercise rider in the mud, and thrashed around on his back in the slop like a cat trying to get comfortable on a living room carpet. Thunk froze there, in the coffee-and-cream-colored mud with a steady rain falling and all four hooves pointed straight to the heavens. For five full minutes, Thunk blissfully relaxed, his tongue flopped out the side of his mouth, catching big splattering raindrops eight or nine at a time.

His exasperated owner finally gave up when the horse stubbornly refused to leave the starting gate for about the 500th time in a row during early morning training exercises. Once burnt, twice learnt, and it seemed as though Thunk liked starting gates about as much as poor folks liked paying taxes.

Racing, clearly, seemed *not* Thunk's calling.

A fellow by the name of Farley Tribble owned Whodathunkit then and, facing an ugly and expensive divorce, Tribble decided to dump the horse so his wife would have one less lawyerly in-flated asset to argue over in court.

Farley even had the horse gelded, figuring the surgery re-moved the possibility his wife's lawyer might argue the stubborn son of a Kentucky Derby winner was worth a hypothetically pre-posterous amount at stud.

The day after surgery, Tribble traded his gingerly stepping gelding to a Boca Raton horse vet named Rosenfill to clear some past-due bills—many of which Thunk had created. Rosenfill, who needed a doorstop of a horse like a dairy farmer needed cheese, turned around and sold Thunk for $500 in crumpled cash to a young trainer from Hialeah named Carlos Rosa.

Rosa tried for two months to get Whodathunkit to break from the gate and you had to give Rosa credit—Carlos had the patience of ten men. He tried everything except stuffing Whodathunkit into a circus cannon and shooting him out. Once Carlos even had a lead rope tied between Whodathunkit's bridle and a small Toyota pickup. But all that innovative training tech-nique managed to do was piss off the horse, bury the pickup in soft sand all the way up to the rear axle, and infuriate track presi-dent Donny Ray Douglass.

Thunk didn't like that towing tactic one little bit. He simply dug in, held his ground like a snarling cougar pushed to the edge of a cliff, and stubbornly anchored down until the Toyota spun itself into an immovable mess.

Nope. When it came to launching this horse from a starting gate, nothing worked and the stubborn gray gelding made Francis the Talking Mule look like Secretariat. It was maddening, espe-cially to everyone who remembered what a great and courageous athlete Thunk's mother had been.

Carlos Rosa finally surrendered and gave the horse to his next-door neighbor Pipe. Pipe was a plumber and liked being called Pipe better than his Cuban name Pipino. He'd never owned a horse and relished the opportunity. Pipe kept the horse in the chain-link-fenced back yard of his little home in Hialeah.

In two weeks, all the grass was gone, piles of hay-and-grass-based post-digestive byproduct were baking in the Florida sun (and stinking up Pipe's neighborhood), and all 12 sprinkler heads were broken. When Pipe turned on the sprinklers to grow more grass, a dozen plumes of water blew skyward like a synchronized missile launch.

One Friday, Pipe's wife informed him that his career as a horse-owner was officially over and that he had 24 hours to get rid of Thunk or she would get rid of them both in a bargain-priced package deal. And, like all dutiful Cuban husbands, Pipe realized that hell, in fact, hath no fury like a Latin woman scorned. It was time to get rid of the horse.

So that was how Whodathunkit came to be standing, just after sunrise on a Saturday morning, in the parking lot of the Fort Lauderdale Swap Shop, wearing giant lime green Elton John-styled sunglasses with a crudely made cardboard sign hanging from his neck. The sign had a very simple message. In block letters, it said: "HORSE 4 SALE. CHIP." Pipe sat nearby in a folding lawn chair with one of the plastic support bands under his seat broken and missing. A fat guy would've fallen through, ass first, but Pipe was a little fellow so the seat held him OK. Just barely, but OK.

The Swap Shop was a sprawling monstrosity of pureed confusion located a mile-and-a-half west of Exit 30 off of I-95 near Fort Lauderdale and a half-hour north of Pipe's home in Hialeah.

Pipe drove Thunk to the Swap Shop in a rented a U-Haul truck. He paid $30 a day, plus a quarter a mile. It had been one hell of a ride, at least if you judged by the clattering, banging, and commotion that dented the crap out of the truck's thin metal walls as the horse lurched and ricocheted from side to side. Pipe had no intention of returning home with anything heavier than cash—except for maybe some mangoes from the large co-op farmer produce stand near the eight kiddie rides bordering Sunrise Boulevard.

The Swap Shop was a South Florida institution and deservedly so. At night, the site doubled as a 15-screen drive-in movie theater, but its fame came as a colossal flea market.

Everything you could buy from a slow-moving car in Little Havana—and much of what you couldn't—could be bought for bargain prices at the Swap Shop. Hundreds of vendors blanketed the campus, selling everything China ever invented.

Thousands of bargain hunters swarmed the place from sunrise when it opened to sundown when it closed. His cardboard cup of coffee steaming in the morning mist, Pipe was already in position when the Swap Shop opened, determined to sell his horse as quickly as possible.

And, as luck would have it, an angular fellow in his late 20s named Truck Roberts stopped by the Swap Shop that morning to buy some fruit and vegetables. From a hundred yards away, Truck spotted the gray horse wearing the lime green Elton John sunglasses and the cardboard "Horse 4 For Sale. CHIP" sign dangling from his neck.

Truck angled over to investigate. He cut catty-corner between a heavily perspiring beet-faced man with a dozen old vacuum cleaners and a weather-beaten gap-toothed fellow offering warped old record albums that no one would ever buy.

Approaching the horse slowly, Truck stopped six feet away and looked him over. The horse looked physically OK—like a well-bred one and not an old slouch-backed plow pony.

Truck read the cardboard sign around the horse's neck.

"Chip?" Truck asked quizzically of Pipe, who hopped up out of the half-busted lawn chair. "Who's Chip?"

"One thousan' dollah—tha's chip," said Pipe.

"A thousand dollars? A thousand dollars? *A thousand dollars* for a horse standing in the middle of a flea market?"

"For you, I give bess price. Five hunnah dollah. Bess price. Five hunnah dollah. Great horse. Fass horse. Very fass. Run at track. Guffstrim." Pipe was anxiously putting on the close. He needed to move this equine pig. The sooner, the better.

Truck notched an eyebrow, his left one, and replied, "Really? He ran at the track? If he ran at the track he's got to have papers." Truck stepped over and muzzle-rubbed Whodathunkit. Thunk decided not to bite him although he had an easy open shot since Truck was looking at Pipe and not paying the horse any direct attention.

"Yes. Papers. Yes. Papers," nodded and smiled Pipe. "I get for you." Pipe pulled out his wallet, took out four sheets of well-folded papers, and handed them over.

Truck looked at them. "Jockey Club papers," he mused to himself. "Son of a gun, a Thoroughbred." He scanned further. "Sheesh almighty." His eyes bugged out at the recognizable name of the horse's dam: "Sweet Affirmation." *Son of a Derby winner?* Truck furrowed both brows and possum-acted like he'd just read this horse was an illegitimate son of Mr. Ed.

Truck looked at the tattoo identification on the papers.

"That's it," he wryly thought. "That's the scam."

Truck, still rubbing the horse's head, peeled its lip back. "Son of a another gun," he thought. There it was. The tattoo markings matched the papers. This *was* the son of a Derby winner.

Pipe could sense a decision being made. He needed to hook this fish and he needed to hook him now. "Five hunnah dollah," he repeated confidently to Truck. "Bess price."

"Three hundred," said Truck. "Three hundred cash, take it or leave it."

Pipe, never one to look a gift horse in the mouth—especially when trying to get rid of it—smiled broadly and stuck out his right hand, vigorously pumping Truck's up and down. "Three hunnah dollah," Pipe beamed. "*Sole! Bess price!"

It was about 100 yards to the office building where the five-languaged MiniBank 2200 autoteller stood between a cotton candy machine and a clown-faced helium balloon inflator. Truck and

Pipe walked over together, with Whodathunkit clip-clopping along behind. Truck withdrew the cash and handed it over. Pipe traded back the Jockey Club papers plus the short lead rope with Whodathunkit tethered to its southern end.

Truck now owned a horse. Pipe pivoted to leave.

"Hey! We need a lift in your U-Haul," called Truck.

"Where you live?" asked Pipe suspiciously. The rental truck cost 25 cents a mile and Pipe had no plans to waste even one of them on this gullible gluepot-owning fruitcake of a stranger.

"We need to go to Gulfstream," said Truck. "Just drop us off down there."

Gulfstream Park was in Hallandale, about 15 miles south but not too far off I-95. It was pretty much directly on the way back to Hialeah. To Pipe, it was a mere two-dollar detour.

"Guffstrim? Guffstrim?" Pipe slowly pondered aloud. "Fiffy dollah," he finally decided. "Bess price."

"Twenty," countered Truck.

"Sisty dollah," said Pipe. "Already tole you fiffy dollah bess price."

"Fifty, dammit," said Truck.

Truck pivoted around, went back to the autoteller, picked English instead of Spanish, French, Japanese or Korean, and withdrew more cash.

He caught up with Pipe and the horse as they headed down Aisle 4 back toward the U-Haul. "Another cash machine service charge," he groused to himself. "But," he reasoned, "I have a home for this horse—and *boy*—will the new owner ever be surprised!"

Pipe and Truck loaded Thunk clip-cloppingly back up the tailgate ramp and into the U-Haul. Pipe drove, turning left onto Sunrise Boulevard and then right onto the Exit 30 entrance ramp onto I-95 South. They rumbled slowly without incident 11 miles to Exit 21, Hallandale Beach Boulevard.

Twenty-five minutes after leaving the Swap Shop, the U-Haul pulled up by track security at Gate A on the south side of

Hallandale Beach Boulevard, just east of U.S. 1. The guard, who recognized Thunk when Pipe and Truck slid open the cargo door to show the horse, shook his head and said nothing. This slug of a horse was a local legend. And here it was, back again. Nothing in racing surprised the guard, who'd worked at the track for the last 31 of the 50 years the place had been open.

The guard gave the guys a temporary access permit and in they drove to famed Gulfstream Park—through the very same gate Whodathunkit exited not too long ago, seemingly destined for a starring role in an Alpo commercial. The guard shook his head and mumbled "Good luck, pal" under his breath as Pipe and Truck rumbled off slowly through the track's backside entryway.

Pipe parked the truck in the shade and Truck stepped quickly and purposefully into the small white receiving office to the right. Pipe waited in the truck. Truck spoke with a track official, filled out some forms, coughed up some money, grabbed a couple of extra forms, and stuffed them in the left butt pocket of his faded jeans. He emerged with a confident bounce in his step and hopped back into the passenger side of the rental truck.

"Right there," he said to Pipe, pointing toward the hedge-lined unloading paddock 40 yards away. "I've got two nights in the Receiving Barn."

Pipe dropped off Truck and unloaded the horse, then immediately dirt-clouded both with dust and hay particles in his spinning-wheeled haste to speed away. Pipe had already planned what to do with the money. He decided to tell his wife he got $70 for the horse. He'd give her $50 and keep the rest.

Truck walked the horse over to its assigned stall, then quickly strode a hundred yards to a pay phone on the outside wall of a tiny faded-white-paint backside eatery called the Snack Shack. A skinny little Cuban counterman with a name tag reading "PISO" gave him a couple of bucks worth of phone change.

Truck made three quick calls, then tracked down a groom and peeled off $20 for him to feed and keep an eye on Thunk.

For $20, the groom promised to keep *both eyes* on him.

That accomplished, Truck then caught a lift in one of the golf carts that waterbugged Gulfstream's backside. The cart's driver, famed racing trainer Frank Brothers, drove Truck around near the front of the track, where Truck hopped out and shagged a cab back to the Swap Shop to retrieve his car.

It had been a fun day already, and it wasn't even noon.

Meanwhile, back in the Receiving Barn, the gray gelding was leisurely chomping on his room-service fresh feed lunch with an occasional slurp from the side-walled water bucket. This was one of his final meals as Whodathunkit, the stubborn horse who always sat down when the bells clanged and the starting gate doors flew open.

Very shortly, he'd be known simply as "Bonefish." And Bonefish, the first son of a Derby winner ever sold for $300 in the parking lot of the Fort Lauderdale Swap Shop, was soon to be heading for the ride of his life.

Bonefish Goes to Bimini

Two mornings later, the horse headed to the Bahamas.

Bonefish arrived in Bimini in style—posing proudly on the newly astroturfed rear deck of a 48-foot Hatteras sportfishing yacht skippered by a close friend of Truck's named Mountain Trombley. Mountain was an enormous fellow—about 6'7" and 350 pounds—with a full light red beard and dirty, scraggly, matching hair.

He and Truck had met eight years before on a country highway in rural, mountainous western Pennsylvania—just outside the tiny burg of Tidioute. There, Mountain had loaded all his worldly possessions inside his converted school bus—his home on wheels—then tried to drive it up the steep, winding Allegheny mountain hillside.

Unfortunately for several trailing motorists, Mountain was over-caffeinated at the time and forgot to latch the back door to the bus. When Mountain drove up a severe incline, the rear bus door swung wide open and all of the stuff Mountain had carelessly tossed inside suddenly came tumbling back out—bouncing and scattering heartily downhill behind him.

Mountain drove almost a mile out from under the last of his furniture before he heard the car horn symphony behind him and realized he might have a problem. Not even the loud clattering of his pots and pans had cut through the blaring stereo enough to make him look in the bus's jaggedly cracked rear view mirror.

"Damn, Man!" Mountain cried. "Not all my shit, Man! *Oh, Man!*"

Mountain pulled the bus onto the shoulder of the narrow road and walked to the back of his now-empty bus. Hands on hips, Mountain stared downhill at the trail of life possessions. If the bench seats weren't bolted down, they'd have fallen out, too. Mountain's non-bolted-down stuff was haphazardly scattered along two miles of winding country roads.

Truck had been on vacation fly-fishing for big brown trout and was driving a rental car second in line behind the bus. He pulled over, spent two hours helping Mountain clear all of the crap out from the roadway, and a friendship was born. The two were an incongruous pair but were about the same age and got along instantly. In fact, within a couple of weeks, Mountain pointed his rickety old bus south to Florida—downhill all the way—and moved near Hallandale. He quickly found work at a big Fort Lauderdale marina and soon became the caretaker of several nice yachts.

Truck's first call from the Snack Shack pay phone was to his giant friend. Mountain went to Home Depot, bought a rolled-up green astroturf carpet for three bucks a square yard, and cut it to fit the rear deck of the Hatteras. The yacht owner, a stockbroker from New York named Michael Tightslax, wasn't due back down in Florida for another month or so. Mountain figured what Tightslax didn't know wouldn't hurt him.

The morning of their impending Bahamian cruise, Truck pigged out on a monster omelet and grits at the Verandah on Las Olas in Fort Lauderdale and, after eating, drove 15 uneventful minutes in light traffic down to Gulfstream.

Truck drove onto the track's backside campus and took the immediate left inside Gate A. He parked by the Receiving Barn where he shook hands with Shedrow Jones, who loaded Thunk into a real horse van.

Shedrow, Truck, and Thunk then drove south down U.S. Highway 1 to 135th Street in North Miami, turned left at the light, and pulled into little Keystone Point Marina. They met

Mountain dockside at 8:30 a.m. sharp, just as noted fishing guide Minnow Thomas prepared to cast off his lines and head offshore for another day of miracle working for two well-heeled, pasty-thighed, ill-dressed tourists.

Minnow, who was nearly Mountain's size, did a double take when he saw the horse. "If that's the bait," he hollered to Mountain over his twin idling outboard engines, "I'd rather go with you! What the *hell* you fishin' for?"

"Bait, nothin'!" roared back Mountain. "Doin' a Lady Godiva photo shoot today with a half-dozen South Beach models!" With that, Minnow's eyebrows arched, his jaw dropped, and his shoulders visibly sagged. At that precise moment, Minnow would've traded three world-record fish for one Lady Godiva photo shoot—and both big men knew it.

Truck loaded on board a saddle, blankets, and other assorted paraphernalia Bonefish would need in his new home. It was sort of a "do-it-yourself horse kit" assembled from the kindness of various backside contributors.

Shedrow even had the backside leathersmith tattoo a quick brass "Bonefish" nameplate onto a new halter. That was an optimistic presumption on Truck and Shedrow's part, since Truck had mailed in the name change request to the Jockey Club just eight hours before. They wouldn't know for another couple of weeks if the name was already taken. But, where the horse was going, it wouldn't really matter.

The trip across the Atlantic from Miami to the closest of the Bahamian Islands was only 50 miles and the cruiser handled it smoothly in calm, forgiving, gently rolling seas. The Gulf Stream, which flowed north at four miles an hour like a river within the sea, made the crossing a tricky one for smaller boats. Outboards under 25 feet rarely made the trip except in perfect conditions, but a yacht like the one Mountain was skippering handled these seas like an aircraft carrier.

Mountain, Truck and Bonefish arrived at the customs dock on the lee side of North Bimini in less than five hours. They cleared customs quickly, since few foreign boats arrive on Mondays.

Most vessels from the mainland arrive Friday and chug home Sunday after their occupants had sunburned their way through a weekend of fishing, diving, and booze-fueled carousing. Some would call it white-collar debauchery.

Since a horse had never arrived on a yacht in Bimini Harbor before, there apparently was no customs law against it. "What luck," Truck said to Mountain after emerging from customs and hopping back on deck. "Monday is *Horses Get In Free* Day."

Bimini was a tiny little speck of a sand dune on the opposite side of the Gulf Stream from Miami, about four miles long but just a Tiger Woods 1-iron wide. There were actually two islands—three if you counted little uninhabited East Bimini—but the majority of the 1,300 islanders lived on North Bimini. The island served as the film site of the final dramatic scene in an Academy Award winning movie "The Silence of the Lambs" when actor Anthony Hopkins, portraying Hannibal the Cannibal, said from an island pay phone that he was "having a friend for lunch."

That scene was shot from the precise spot Mountain and Truck stood after disembarking customs with the horse—just 200 yards down the hill from a long stretch of sand Ernest Hemingway once called his favorite mile of beach in the whole world.

The Gulf Stream paralleled the Bimini coast all along its western shoreline and the giant fish of the sea—the tuna, marlin and sharks—swam up and down that coast year-round. Big wahoo teemed in these waters, too: 50-, 60-, even 70-pounders. Wahoo were big, powerful, toothy barracuda look-alikes that rocketed all over the ocean at speeds of up to 50 miles an hour the instant they felt the sting of a hook. People came from all over to chase this popular game fish in big-money tournaments.

But to the east of Bimini, expansive shallow sandy flats teemed with small dancing crabs, shallow-water fish, and sharks of all colors and sizes, wing-flapping skates and sting rays, delicious conchs, and spiny black sea urchins. During high tide, larger game fish often glided the flats in a tail-swishing hunt across the food-rich shallows in search of a fresh seafood lunch or dinner. The predators then left the flats, retreating to the deeper water of the surrounding sea, when the tide turned back from high to low.

Bimini was a jewel of a place, insulated from too much confusion by its tiny size and relative inaccessibility. Most visitors hopped over at 3,000 feet from Miami's Watson Island on a small seaplane that splashed down in the harbor and roared its way up and out of the water. A lesser number made the 50-mile ocean crossing by boat. Either way, it required a commitment just to get there.

In Truck's view, Bimini was 25 minutes and a million miles away from Miami. After landing in the seaplane, it took but three or four minutes to pass through a little green customs hut and become an official tourist. Once processed, you then could take a taxi 300 yards up dusty King Street to the Compleat Angler Hotel. First-timers to the island took the cab; second-timers walked.

Truck's first visit to Bimini had been four years before and he instantly fell in love with the placid peace of the tiny oasis hideaway. He was happy and comfortable here, so much so that he'd twice brought friends over from the States and challenged the islanders to baseball games.

The first game ended in a 3-3 tie when the monsoon rains of a tropical depression arrived during the bottom of the fourth inning. A sheer wall of charcoal black clouds blasted its way across the open sea, heading straight for the players. A lot of guys took one look at nature's accelerating sheets of angry winds and waterfall rains, and began swinging at the first pitch.

"Everybody won," Truck said at a special school assembly the next day. He very much felt that way, too. At the end of the assembly, three dozen young children, dressed in their best, sang four songs. He thought they sounded better than Streisand.

So for Truck, coming back to Bimini was the happy return to a little slice of home and a chance to see some cherished friends. Mountain had been over but once before and was working. He was glad to tag along now and have a little fun.

Once through customs, with nothing so trivial as quarantine to deal with, the two men and gray horse began their 20-minute ambling procession up King Street.

While Mountain rode the horse supply stuff alongside in golf cart #21, which had no brakes and was rented from Cap'n Pat, Truck walked Bonefish up Bimini's dusty narrow main road the mile he needed to reach the part of the North Bimini called Bailey Towne.

There, they stopped near a small brown frame house next to the Bay Front Park ball field. Truck handed over the horse's lead to one of the 19 kids they'd collected along the way, complete with smiling instructions to stay out of sight for just a minute or two.

Truck walked up, knocked four times quickly on the screen door's painted wood frame, and waited. Impatiently, he pounded again.

From within the house, Truck suddenly heard a loud and familiar voice call out, *"Just a minute! I'll be there in a minute! Hold your horses!"*

Truck wasn't holding his horse—a little kid was—but he looked over his right shoulder just to make sure. All the kids were giggling.

The screen door swung open and an old friend, Bahamian fishing guide Anvil Sanders, smiled when he saw Truck. Quickly Anvil looked puzzled, though. "Truck, what are you doing here? We supposed to fish today? I thought it was tomorrow. Didn't you call and say Tuesday?"

"Yep," smiled Truck. "We fish tomorrow. But I came in early. Got a special delivery. Today I need you to sign some papers. Customs rule, from what Basil told me down at the dock when we checked in."

Anvil looked at Truck suspiciously. "What kind of delivery you talkin' 'bout?" Anvil asked.

"Don't be so dramatic, Anvil," Truck replied. "I came all the way over a day early just to bring you something special and here you are—bustin' my chops."

With that, Truck stuck out some papers. He had folded them over so Anvil couldn't see what he was signing, which was actually unnecessary since without his reading glasses he couldn't see a whole lot better than Mr. Magoo.

Anvil took Truck's white plastic Marriott Hotel pen, scrawled his name in black ink where Truck pointed, and handed the pen back.

But Anvil got suspicious when Truck flipped open an inked stamping pad and quickly rolled Anvil's thumb print inside a printed box on one of the forms.

"Customs," assured Truck. "No big deal. Blame Basil. He said he needed it for customs in Nassau. I promised him I'd bring it back after I delivered your present." Clerical mission accomplished, Truck folded his papers longways and shoved them into the back left pocket of his khaki Dockers shorts.

"Present?" asked Anvil suspiciously. "What kind of present you talkin' 'bout?"

Truck pointed around the side of the house where Bonefish stood. The horse was completely surrounded by a circular squadron of happy, hopping kids. The 19 had expanded to 30 or more as the ones with the shortest legs finally caught up.

"Anvil," Truck said with a dramatic sweeping underhanded wave toward the horse, "meet Bonefish."

"And Bonefish," Truck continued, sweeping his arm from the horse back toward his pal, "meet Anvil."

Following that flowery introduction, Bonefish lifted his tail on cue and plopped a three-bombed "hello" on the sparse and sandy grass. The barefooted kids closest to the action leaped back for safety.

Anvil's eyes widened like almond-colored ping-pong balls. His whole life he'd dreamed of owning a horse—he and Truck had talked about that a few years back while fishing—and now he had one. Counting Bonefish, there was now exactly one horse in all of North Bimini. And Anvil Sanders was its very proud owner.

Predictably enough, Bonefish became an instant island celebrity and pretty much everyone adopted him. And, quite frankly, they had to. There wasn't a lot of grazing for him unless he had free run of the whole four miles of sandy soil. So, Bonefish became North Bimini's official wandering lawnmower and portable fertilizer dispenser.

A couple of dozen kids took turns riding Bonefish to and from school. They brushed him, bathed him, and saved up nickels and dimes to buy him candy. Bonefish had a sweet tooth—especially for peppermints and red Twizzlers licorice—and happily inhaled both. Quickly he developed a nose for kids and candy, in no particular order.

Six weeks after arriving, Bonefish finished eating breakfast at the white-and-green-trimmed Wesley Anglican Church front yard, and wandered in to Queen Street Elementary School. Clopping 30 feet down the gray-tiled hallway, Bonefish stuck his head inside the third-graders' door, searching for kids and candy—and not necessarily in that order. Mrs. Browning shooed the horse back outside while the kids all cheered and hollered his name.

Anvil's son, T-man, rode Bonefish every morning before school, loping up the sandy northern shoreline beach to its farthest point and then back home again. For the first two or three months, T-man fell off into the deep white-crystal sand half of the times the horse broke into a gallop.

Bonefish's regular responsibilities soon came to include mowing the island's baseball field and dragging the infield each Saturday morning before games. T-man tied two ropes between Bonefish's saddle horn and a small section of chain link fence that Bonefish dragged to smooth out the dirt behind him. The makeshift horse-powered rake worked beautifully.

Anvil lent Bonefish all around town as needed. He mowed both island cemeteries and his post-consumptive byproduct was used to help grow vegetables in several church gardens. Those vegetables sold for a premium since they grew the best of all on the island. Bonefish's poop became a marketing tool and sign of quality. Buckets of big fat tomatoes and stacks of large heads of leafy lettuce were sold under hand-printed signs that read: "Grown with Bonefish Fertilizer—God's finest!"

Anvil quickly grew to love his horse and enjoyed the celebrity that went along with being Bonefish's owner. Being a horseman was far more noble fame than the way he'd earned his nickname decades before. Back then he was Anthony Sanders, a skinny 15 year old, until one day he got mad at his friend Leonard "Weevil" Stuart. Weevil was moving in on Anthony's girl and Anthony didn't like it.

Young Anthony—all 132 pounds of him—somehow managed to lug a 90-pound blacksmith's anvil up two flights of stairs to the top railing above the King Street grocery store. Anthony struggled mightily but finally managed to perch the heavy iron on the very edge of the railing. Once he had it positioned, the exhausted youngster paused for a few minutes to catch his breath, then took careful aim at the street below.

Anthony Sanders then shoved that 90-pound anvil off the railing and seconds later smashed Weevil Stuart's bicycle to smithereens. He trudged back downstairs, lugged the anvil all the way back up again, pushed it off the railing again, and smashed Weevil's dive sack full of fresh live conchs into a billion bits of useless shell fragments and pulverized goo.

Weevil got the message and quit calling on Anvil's girl. Five years later, Anvil married that girl, Miss Alma, and they've remained happily married ever since.

By the age of 18, Anvil Sanders followed a family legacy and built by hand his first wooden boat—a 15-foot skiff for fishing the flats. When the paint dried, he'd become a fifth-generation boat builder. Like his ancestors before him, Anvil built by sight and feel, using native island woods and few automated tools.

From that point forward, Anvil built two boats each year. When finished, each one merged utility, durability, and art with near-perfect craftsmanship.

By the time he turned 21, Anvil's reputation had spread to the mainland, so he was able to presell every boat he built to Americans. His boat-building earnings surpassed his income as a bonefishing guide and afforded the young family man a good, hard-earned lifestyle.

But owning this horse—this gelded gray son of a Kentucky Derby winner—suddenly made Anvil an even more notable island figure than smashing conchs, fishing the flats, and building boats by hand.

Anvil's biggest hope now was that keeping this long-dreamed-of horse wouldn't drain him financially. Anvil's wife Alma, with whom he scored thousands of points decades before by crushing Weevil's bicycle for romance, was a loving, caring woman. She clearly understood what the horse meant to her husband, their son, and all the other island kids. Alma hoped things concerning the horse would work out, too. If necessary, the family would cut corners to make ends meet and keep Bonefish around for everyone to enjoy.

Truck realized he was forcing this animal on a family whose life was good but money was tight. He'd known them long enough to realize that if Bonefish became too much of a burden, they'd call and tell him. So, before he climbed back aboard Mountain's cruiser for the ride back home, Truck and Anvil shook hands on that very commitment.

That's how Bonefish—the gray, four-legged squire of Bimini—happily settled into his new home. He was free of starting gates, dive-bombing seagulls, guys with whips, Toyota pickups, and a little stall with a lousy view. Here, he pretty much had run of the island and spent hour after hour contentedly watching kids play baseball and basketball at the park.

He got plenty of exercise and whenever a neighbor needed him, Bonefish reported for duty. Since the island was a mere 300 yards wide, Bonefish soon learned to find his way back home from anywhere. And, as most islanders continually crisscrossed North Bimini by foot, bicycle, or golf cart, finding Bonefish was never a particularly difficult thing for Anvil or T-man to do.

While Bonefish was the only horse on North Bimini, seven others lived across a 200-yard channel in South Bimini—a larger but less densely populated island than North Bimini. Every once in a while, during slack tide, T-man or Anvil would swim Bonefish over to South Bimini to hang out with the other horses or make a routine visit to the vet. If the current was strong, or strengthened while they were over there, they boated back across on a wide-bottomed flat-decked water taxi. The first couple of times he stepped aboard and made the five-minute trip, Bonefish didn't like it. But soon enough he learned to just clatter down the ramp and climb aboard.

Since Bonefish was gelded, his South Island visitations created no major social or ego problems among the other horses. The visits were nice but, generally speaking, Bonefish was quite happy at home—The Master of His Domain—spending his mornings running on the beach and afternoons watching Anvil craft small wooden boats by hand.

Hour after hour, Bonefish listened to calypso and reggae on the radio, grazed when he got hungry, and watched the children noisily play at the park after school.

He had never been this happy at Gulfstream. And the people at Gulfstream had never been this happy to have him around, either.

What Are Friends For?

Earl Chester Isaac Malcolm Roberts was named after all the guys on his dad's bowling team. Had they not won the league title two days before Truck was born, he probably would've been named Joe.

Earl was Truck's dad and claimed top billing because he converted a clutch 4-10 split in the tenth frame to snatch victory from the jaws of a second-place finish to the dreaded team from Pappy's Grill. After Earl, the order of Truck's legal names was dictated by the final game scores of the teammates—from Chet's 206 down to Malcolm's 128 gag-job.

Although born with a hatful of names, Truck received his lifelong nickname from his mom the morning of his first playpen jailbreak. Mrs. Roberts had heard a noise, rushed into his room, and found her pint-sized son happily playing with his yellow dump truck on the bedroom floor. The toddler had looked up, smiled like a happy-face cartoon, and gurgled, "Truck, Mama, truck." From that morning on, he and the truck proved inseparable and it's made every move of his life ever since.

Truck Roberts was born and raised in Denver, Colorado. Like pretty much everybody who lived there, he spent as much time as possible in the mountains.

Spring was a three-month melody when God and nature danced a glorious waltz of color and life. In the wild, baby everythings hopped and wobbled everywhere and the young boy with a love of the outdoors hiked the hills to learn the secrets of the valleys.

Summer in the Rockies meant horseback riding and trout fishing and Truck caught his first trout at the age of four. He remembered it being a monster—a giant fish as long as he was tall. Scrapbook photos show it a wee bit smaller, at best perhaps a pound.

Fall's chilled mornings triggered the painting of the palm-sized green leaves on the smooth white-barked aspen trees a flame-colored yellow. Mountainsides dappled with splotches of gold and, to Truck, life was never better than a crisp autumn morning threading his 5-weight Sage fly rod alongside the trout-filled waters of meandering Tarryall Creek. There, he spent time with some of his closest friends: Rocky Mountain sheep, mule deer, antelope, and elk. They scattered throughout the surrounding plain and craggy hillsides, taking turns wandering down to take a drink and watch him fish.

Winter, of course, meant skiing, skating, hockey, and snowball fights.

Hidden in these picturesque hills, Truck learned about the cycle of life and death from voiceless creatures that ranged from a few inches long to more than one thousand pounds.

The coyotes, hunting in packs, were especially savage teachers. At the age of 11, Truck saw his first elk fawn slaughtered by the careful stalking of an alpha male and four females. Two years later, he saw another. Helpless to intervene, he witnessed both from less than 400 yards away. Nature culled the weak, however sickeningly brutal its methods appeared.

The Roberts family lived in a tidy neighborhood of middle-class homes. Earl Roberts was a plumber, his mother Janine an eighth-grade teacher.

Truck's first social interaction with members of the opposite sex came at a party during seventh grade. It was at Arnold Velour's house, but nobody called Arnold by his given name. Everyone called him Stinky. For some mysterious reason, Stinky decided to ruin the party by inviting *girls*, too. And then somebody—Truck didn't know who—got the bright idea to play spin-the-bottle, a game complete with melodic sound effects that only a circle of itchy-lipped seventh graders could create.

Truck didn't mind playing until Angel Fleaton spun the empty Coca-Cola bottle round-and-round and it slid to a terrifying slow-motion halt pointing directly at him. His heart skipped a beat. Two beats, actually. Angel's random love spin presented two very real and immediate problems.

First of all, Angel was a nice person but no way—definitely *no way*—would Truck Roberts ever in his lifetime *want* to kiss Angel Fleaton.

Secondly, every window in the place was locked. He saw no chance for a bold, dramatic flying-Superman escape through an open window.

As Angel patiently waited, blindfolded with lips puckered, Truck was miraculously rescued from this living nightmare by a wiry little brown-haired kid named Ben Bentley. Ben swooped in, intercepted Angel Fleaton, and nearly choked her to death with his tongue. The circular gallery watching gasped.

Well, the guys gasped. The girls "oohed" and "aaahhed."

Oddly, Angel seemed to like it. She rolled Ben over on his back, pinned him there, and kept right on kissing until Skip Wagner broke it up because he thought their braces were stuck. And so, from that moment forward, Truck Roberts and Ben Bentley became blood brothers. All because one didn't have the hots for Angel Fleaton and the other one did.

The two remained fast friends from that day forward.

By high school, Truck was working the typical array of jobs teens leapfrog around doing. He worked sporadically with his dad, but Truck hated plumbing and moved like a sloth to prove it. Earl got more work done without him than with him and finally gave up bugging Truck about taking over the family business. At the age of 16, Truck retired from plumbing for good.

Still needing spending money, Truck decided he'd try construction work on a high school expansion project. He tracked down the project foreman and signed on as a carpenter's helper. The work was outdoors, good exercise, and paid well—in cash on Friday afternoons. Truck regarded construction as far superior to unclogging toilets or standing calf-deep in a flooded basement.

Truck lasted five weeks, then got fired for not showing up after lunch one Wednesday afternoon. Technically, it wasn't his fault. He *wanted* to return after lunch, but ended up trapped, face down, in a tipped-over port-a-john, thanks to his Angel Fleaton-kissing pal Ben Bentley and another buddy named Rich Bellis. Truck never saw the pair sneak up from behind and tip the damn thing over while he peacefully sat inside but distinctly heard them laughing as they ran away.

Like all kids, by the time Truck Roberts finished high school, he knew twice as much as both parents added together. He decided to strike out and see the world—at least the Florida part of the world. He ended up working his way through a small private school and spent his college years immersed in the exact same things all red-blooded American college boys had done for centuries: He smoked, drank, fished, and primarily "dated" himself.

Well, that's not quite right. Not every freshman boy smoked, drank, and fished. But in his junior year, after three years of trying, Truck finally lost his innocence. His deflowering didn't last long—about as long as a top-fuel drag race. Once finished, Truck gazed starstruck into the furrowed brow of his partner—a short, sandy-haired, bespectacled freshman from White Plains named Lorraine Peabody. Gently, romantically—and quite gratefully—Truck whispered softly to Lorraine, "Was that good for you, too?"

Lorraine looked at him and seemed annoyed. "That wasn't good for *anybody!*'" she snapped disgustedly. "That was awful!"

Her assessment disappointed Truck, who had vigorously attacked this freckle-faced little angel like an octopus playing racquetball. He'd even suavely used an upper-classman's finesse by removing her bra without scissors.

Their relationship ended shortly thereafter. Ten minutes, according to his wall clock.

From that point forward, when it came to female interactions, Truck Roberts lacked a whole lot of confidence. Part of the problem was that he never learned how to communicate. While growing up, all his folks ever did was grunt and snort in some sort of marital code.

Ben told him that married life did that to people and that, after a few years, all married people quit speaking and started grunting. Grunt-coding, Ben said, was the marital way. Married people used it to communicate since grunting was faster than uttering complete sentences that got interrupted anyway.

Midway through his senior year, Truck met someone special and actually *did* try to communicate. He fell butt-over-tincup for a tiny raven-haired gymnast from Montreal who talked dirty in French.

Truck thought that lingo was the coolest thing he'd ever heard—even cooler than a coyote howl or elk snort. Animal sounds were good, but a dirty-minded French girl poured from the mold of a gymnast was something else entirely.

Even her name was sexy: Dominique Dominescu. He'd never been in love before, so he figured gut-spilling was the right thing to do. He decided that the more emotional blood he shed, the more Dominique would like him. Within weeks, he'd bathed in it.

Ben thought Truck was nuts and told him so. "Man," Ben moaned, "you *never* tell them that stuff! Spider and fly! Spider and fly! You're trapped in cobwebs once you start sharing that stuff."

Well, unfortunately for Truck, Ben proved to be more right than wrong. Dominique thought he was too insecure—too much a little boy, not enough a man, and dumped him for a guy who spoke Italian. Since the only Italian words Truck knew were spaghetti, ravioli, and lasagna, he was burnt toast when Dominique abruptly decided to unplug his little toaster.

When Dump Day came, Dominique came up short on finesse. When Truck didn't quite get the message, she belittled some of his insecurities.

Later, Truck told Ben that he didn't really mind getting dumped. "My mistake was telling her my feelings," he told Ben over the phone. "When you do that—when you trust them with your inner-most feelings and thoughts—they use them to rip your heart out, toss it on the ground, and stomp on it 'til they get calf cramps. When they know what you're thinking, they know how to get to you.

"And I can tell you this," Truck added with a loud emphasis, "I am never, *ever,* going through that again. Ain't no way. Never."

"Not even for Angel Fleaton?" Ben kiddingly teased his pal. "You *know* she wants you. You *know* she's still hungry for a nice juicy piece of the Truckster."

"No," laughed Truck. "Not even for Angel Fleaton."

Truck was slow to rebound from the scars of lusting for small things gymnastic. In his mind, Dominque hadn't just stomped on his heart—she'd trampolined it. Aerial flips, twists, somersaults—you name it, she did it. Squished his heart beyond repair. If he'd lacked self-confidence before, Truck was now of the studied opinion that women were nothing more than sweet-smelling soldiers of the emotional enemy.

Quite frankly, Truck didn't know what he was supposed to do. He certainly wasn't going to grunt in code to his parents about it, and he damn sure couldn't say anything to the guys. He felt haplessly puzzled. He'd heard that falling in love was good, not bad, and the stomachaches you got from girls were the best kind to have. They had a magic power that made you smell flowers, hear birds chirp, and listen to the lyrics of love songs on the radio.

Maybe for some guys they did, but certainly not for him. "Enough of that foolishness," he decided. "Drinks, yes. Dinner, maybe. But I ain't lettin' nobody in."

So, after Dominique hammered his heart into a thousand shards of sadness, Truck opted to internalize everything. Sharing and caring was too painful. What was the point? What did it get you? Nothing. Not a damn thing.

Nope—he'd made that mistake once and wouldn't make it again. By the time college ended, Truck had firmly twisted shut all the valves to his inner self.

It proved to be a dumb, and typically male, decision.

Hi Mom, Hi Dad

Truck earned a business degree and decided to return to Denver. Abandoning his major, he wanted to become a famous newspaper columnist and hired on as a newsroom flunkie. He was paid peanuts. The first day at work, he introduced himself to the sports editor. The editor looked over the top of his half-rimmed reading glasses and limply shook his hand.

"Read the classics," the guy said, paraphrasing H. L. Mencken. "That way you can see who you're competing against." With that, the editor looked down at his work and resumed doing whatever it is editors pretend they do.

Truck's uncle warned him about the newspaper business when Truck phoned to tell him about his new job. "Remember, Truck," his uncle said, "you can't eat a byline."

He proved quite right, as uncles often do. Working at the paper was glorified slave labor that paid nothing and, after 18 months, Truck was more broke than a plastic alarm clock twice run over by a tractor-trailer loaded with floor safes.

He also learned another important lesson about life in general and his in particular: You can't go home again. His job paid so little he'd never escape living with his parents. They said nothing, but everyone knew the fuse was lit, sizzling, and burning quickly toward the inevitable ka-*boom* of permanent separation.

Bored and busted, Truck itched for a change. One winter night, Ben called and they talked for 20 minutes. Ben was in Fort Lauderdale, working for Toyota. The money was good. The job was good. The weather was good. The babes were great.

Ben urged Truck to move back to Florida, but this time down south. To hear Ben describe it, the place crawled with girls and the beach was paved with bikinis. Every day, Ben said, hundreds of girls were begging for tanning oil help for those hard-to-reach places in the middles of their backs.

That was good enough for Truck. When it's time to go, it's time to go. And it was time to go. Truck quit the paper and, with both parents' eager help, jammed his stuff inside a boxy little U-Haul single-axle trailer. He headed to South Florida.

Three days later, Truck Roberts tugged his little U-Haul into Plantation, a Fort Lauderdale suburb, and moved in with Ben. They lived in a good apartment complex where a lot of girls hung out by the pool. None of them seemed eager to have oil rubbed on them by a broke, unemployed guy who reeked of cheap cigars, but Truck shrugged it off as an aberration. They'd learn soon enough.

A couple of weeks later, Truck landed a job. It was hardly the most glamorous of occupations—photocopier sales—but the money was great. He had to wear a tie so he figured the job must be important. Best of all, he could see the beach from his office window.

Within a month, Truck wished he'd moved to South Florida years before. Life was good and getting better. Years later, that necktie-wearing job of his would take him all around the country, then halfway around the world.

And one day, in the not-too-distant future, that tie-wearing job of his would even afford him the chance to go buy a horse at a flea market.

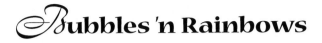

Bubbles 'n Rainbows

Turangi, New Zealand

Truck recognized the hat when it floated by. He should have—it was the third time this morning he'd watched it bob past. A quick glance at his black-strapped Timberland watch showed four minutes before nine. They'd been fishing less than two hours.

Gracefully, Truck lifted the olive-colored Sage 8-weight fly rod and flicked his line back and forth first once, then twice, before settling his dry fly—a size 14 Royal Wulff—barely a foot in front of the half-submerged green bucket hat.

With a gentle upward flip of the wrist, Truck hooked the waterlogged hat and began dragging it out of the mighty New Zealand river's swift current and toward the calmer knee-high pocket water where he stood.

Dripping hat in hand, Truck splashed over toward where his Kiwi friend, Lloyd Hill, was draped over a boulder, gasping for air.

"See any?" Truck called out as he waded upriver and got close to his half-drowned friend.

"Dammit, Mate!" gasped Lloyd with a belabored exhalation. "I was surrounded, man! There I was, minding my own business, and one of the bloody things untied my boot laces, knotted the bastards together, and a whole *school* of trout pushed me in! The buggers bloody attacked! It's a bloody miracle I escaped!"

Lloyd was soaked from head to toe and back again. His name-engraved pewter flask was still safely zipped inside his upper waders. Lloyd unzipped the pouch, grabbed the flask, unscrewed the top, and tilted it to his lips. Then he tasted a warm mouthful of the 15-year-old scotch. Thank God, the Laphroig was safe.

"Aaahhhh," Lloyd winced then smiled after the quick nip. "Nectar of the gods. We may now safely resume fishing."

And with that, Lloyd struggled to rise, waddled ashore, plopped down on the bank in a splashy explosion of spilling river water, and proceeded to begin the process of emptying his waders yet again. Whatever trout had been in the Tongariro River's famed Major Jones pool were now long gone or lock-jawed.

Truck watched, shook his head, and said nothing. Truck had fallen in before—every river fisherman has—but he'd never seen anyone do it like Lloyd. Lloyd fell in at least once every single time they'd fished together. Truck long ago lost count how of many aquatic breakdances he'd witnessed.

Once Lloyd bravely attempted to ford a river at least six feet deeper than Lloyd was tall. He simply marched in, braved the strengthening currents, confidently kept marching—and disappeared. Simply put, his hat ran out of Lloyd before drifting its lonely, peaceful way downriver.

Another time, Lloyd slipped on a mossy stone after pivoting around to fight a willow tree that leaned out from the bank and ate Lloyd's airborne #10 black Wooly Bugger. He fell in water four inches deep.

Make no mistake, Lloyd Hill and good sippin' scotch were made for each other and for this sport. In each case, all one had to do was add a splash of water, sit back, and enjoy.

Once Truck was sure Lloyd was safely on the bank, he worked his way well below the elbow bend of the Major Jones pool and tried to coax another football-sized rainbow to leap out of the water to say hello. The New Zealand trout were big and strong and powerful—the stuff of legend and well worth traveling halfway around the world to pursue, which Truck was doing for the third time. He loved everything about New Zealand—including the friend who always seemed to spend more time drifting downriver than his fly did.

Nature had bestowed wonderful differences in wildlife between America and New Zealand. There were no snakes in New Zealand, just as there were no bears or cockroaches, squirrels, or foxes. Instead of large, toothy predators, New Zealand was overrun by millions of fined-haired opossums, endless mountain ranges full of red deer, and ten trillion happy rabbits.

The skies were full of ducks and flocks of mischievous birds named keas that broke into cars just for the hell of it. Keas are the only birds known to have a society in which the higher-status individuals force the others to work for them—a trait left over, perhaps, from previous generations of British rule.

New Zealand sported 12 sheep for each of its 3.8 million people. Sheep were everywhere, even in hallway broom closets. Truck often wondered how farmers thought up names for 45 million sheep and why they didn't shrink when it rained. Surely there was were logical answers.

New Zealand spread out along an 1,100-mile vertical length of two primary islands, North and South. Most folks lived in one of four cities, two up north and two down south. Auckland and Wellington were the two largest cities on the North Island. Truck and Lloyd were in the heart of big trout country, a bit north of Wellington.

The fishing that day, as usual, was magnificent. The two men caught a dozen fish—11 rainbows and one brown trout, at four pounds, the smallest of the lot. The fish averaged a whopping six-and-a-half pounds, spectacularly huge by American standards and very good, too, for New Zealand, since the average trout here went three-to-four pounds.

About two-and-a-half million pounds of rainbow trout were extricated from these world famous waters each year.

Later, as this warm late-spring early-November day chilled with the sundowning arrival of evening, Truck and Lloyd decided to head back to the Tongariro Lodge. A hot shower, a piping-hot feast of fresh lamb, and melt-in-the-mouth steaming venison medallions would serve to usher the fading daylight well into the brisk, clear star-filled night.

His hot shower proved too tempting for Truck. Belting out a rousing chorus of *"There's No Business Like Show Business!"* he lathered away with too much zeal his lower half. In a stage of obvious happiness, Truck got caught oversoaping when Lloyd stepped in the small bathroom, shaving kit in hand.

"Whoa, Mate!" recoiled Lloyd, noticing his friend's joyous condition. "I never realized you so thoroughly enjoyed those old Broadway show tunes!"

Embarrassed, Truck wheeled around away from Lloyd so only his butt was visible, but it was too late. Caught oversoaping by the Shower Police dampened Truck's enthusiasm for the rest of the song, which ended rather abruptly.

Fittingly enough in this wool-growing nation, Truck emerged sheepishly from his shower and quickly dressed for dinner. After all, he was on the road—and sometimes a man on the road finds a nice hot shower among his best of intimate friends.

"Ah!" smacked Lloyd, hoisting a generous scotch aloft as Truck prepared to sit down for dinner. "Here's to big trout, the nectar of the gods, and oversoaping in rhythm to Broadway standards.

"Cheers, Mate!" he concluded, beaming broadly. And with that elegant toast, Lloyd Hill closed his eyes and savored a mere lip-glossing sip of Laphroig.

Truck opted for a pint of Steinlager, the award-winning New Zealand beer. Steinlager sponsored New Zealand's world champion America's Cup yachting team, which made the company a titan of righteousness throughout this long, slender, sailing-crazed country where one could never be more than 100 miles from the sea.

The men sipped their drinks in the wood-stained bar of the famed Tongariro Lodge, surrounded by photos and wall-mounted piscatorial goliaths. The trophy trout represented just a sliver of the flyfishing dreams sometimes fulfilled in this trout angler's cradle of heaven.

Most of the dozen or more giant trout hanging on the walls were rainbows. A few were browns. All were absurdly large—larger and fatter than mailboxes with fins.

The Tongariro Lodge sat on 22 manicured acres along the same-named river near the southern tip of trout-filled Lake Taupo. A lot of legendary people had fished there, including avid flyfisherman and former U.S. President Jimmy Carter.

During spawning season, thousands of giant trout leave the lake to swim up the Tongariro to spawn. Most of the giant fish displayed on the walls of the lodge had been caught during those spectacular spawning runs.

The roaring river was within sight and earshot of the lodge and had a romantically powerful magnetic pull—not just because of the trout, but also because of magical scenery and surprise extras like floating pumice rocks bobbing their way downriver.

The Tongariro's famed river mouth delta, itself an excellent spot to fish, poured into the enormous Lake Taupo just a few miles down from the Lodge. And that lake, Lake Taupo, was the cradling mother and breast milk of one of the earth's truly magnificent trout fisheries. People came from around the world to see it, fish it, pose for photos by it, and commit its nuances to memory and soul.

Taupo was a magnificent piece of water—a former volcano head now filled with water and colored a shimmering Lake Tahoe shade of sapphire blue. The lake was huge, roughly 25 miles long, 19 miles wide, and, from north to south, shaped like the African continent.

Taupo averaged 400 feet in depth, with its deepest hole carved still another 100 feet down. It was also full of baitfish on which the trout gorged themselves to gargantuan size.

The friends had a loud and boisterous night that finally ended after mounds of great food, several cocktails, and thousands of laughs. An outdoorsman's kind of contented fatigue ushered both back to their cabin just before midnight. Tomorrow's four-hour drive back to Auckland—a northbound journey bisecting the central portion of the North Island—would come soon enough.

In the morning, Truck and Lloyd attacked a full breakfast and left the Lodge under a bright sunny sky at just after nine. The men traversed north along the scenic two-lane Highway 1 the length of the lake's eastern shoreline, passed through the town of Taupo at the tip of the lake shortly before ten o'clock, then continued on, soon passing the Wairaki Golf Club.

Lloyd drove another 20 minutes, then stopped the car briefly for a leg-stretcher at Huka Falls—a narrow, powerfully roaring Kiwi version of Niagara. The men then headed up past sulphur-smelling Rotorua and its boiling mud pools, geysers, and steam-spouting thermal fields. The acrid stench reminded Truck of coastal Georgia's stinking paper mills, but he said nothing since Lloyd had never been there.

Rotorua, too, had great fishing—the lake was continually stocked throughout the year with catchable trout—but the men chose not to stop. The area was best fished by small boat and, given a choice, Lloyd much preferred falling into a river than falling out of a boat.

An hour or so north of Rotorua, they motored through the quiet, beautiful horse farms of Hamilton and Cambridge—the heart of New Zealand's famed Thoroughbred breeding country. Jet-black soils grew thick, broad-bladed emerald green grasses rich in nutrients. To Truck, the area looked even lusher than the famed grazing pastures of Kentucky.

Ninety minutes later, in mid-afternoon, the two men rolled into Auckland. As they approached the huge arcing bridge into town, Truck studied the view out his passenger window.

The City of Sails, Auckland was called, and it was easy to see why. A thousand boats under sail were figure-eighting their way around the Hauraki Gulf, the same water the America's Cup yacht races traversed. Back in the States, Truck had often visited Annapolis, another sailing town. He understood the water, the wind, and the silent determination of people who thrived on tiller-tugging one-upsmanship while chasing each other in quiet boats with no motors. Kiwis were born to sail and loved to prove it.

Lloyd continued to drive home to Remuera, one of Auckland's nicer suburbs. Nearby lived Sir Edmund Hillary, the beekeeper-turned-climber who first summited Mount Everest. Since his famous climb, Hillary devoted most of his life to helping the Sherpas of Nepal. Hillary was a selfless, caring man, and Truck admired him enormously.

So did Lloyd, who never tired of admiring Sir Edmund's portrait since it adorned the face of New Zealand's five-dollar note.

Once arriving at Lloyd's house, they unloaded Lloyd's stuff and reloaded the car with Truck's luggage for his long flight back to America. When they finished, the pair had two hours to kill and made the only sensible decision—a foray 15 minutes through Epsom's beautiful trees and gardens to the edge of the Mount Eden business district. Once there, they would ascend a few stairs, step inside, and say hello to a couple of comfortable barstools at a neighborhood pub named the Horse & Trap.

And as the two men tooled along in Lloyd's old gray BMW, neither had an inkling that a whole lot of confusion was already sitting in the bar, sipping beer, chatting, and waiting for someone new to talk to.

Ready or not, Truck's life was about to change.

The Horse & Trap

The Horse & Trap was a well-kept neighborhood pub on Enfield Street, perfectly snuggled into a sloping hillside on the periphery of Auckland's business district. It was a relaxing, high-ceilinged place to enjoy cold drinks from tall glasses. The Trap exuded neighborhood warmth and friendly, unpretentious, and loyal customers.

When Lloyd and Truck walked in that day, all 12 high-stooled chairs at the bar were empty. They selected two just right of center and ordered a pair of fresh drawn Steinlager pints. It was still early—mid-afternoon—and the place was empty compared to how it would be once the downtown business workday was over.

Nearby was a table of four girls in their early 20s—too young to bother with. Three of the four were attractive in differing ways. The fourth had short green hair and wore a small silver nose hoop, which both men found as appealing as a gum scraping by a hung-over dental assistant. Two of the women smoked, including Green Hair.

Lloyd had just started summarizing, fish by fish, the events of their Tongariro adventure when Green Hair got up from the table and approached the men at the bar. She stopped next to Truck and said but one word: "Darts."

"Darts?" he repeated back, not understanding.

"Darts. Would you care to play darts?"

Since Truck already knew how Lloyd's trout stories turned out, he looked at him for permission to play. "Give it a go, Mate." Lloyd encouraged him with a wave-away of his right hand. "Represent American men in the tradition for which they're known."

Truck nodded and turned back to Green Hair. "Depends," he said. "I'm *very* careful about who I play darts with. I don't play darts with just anybody."

"Oh?" asked Green Hair curiously.

"Oh, yes," Truck replied. "Let me first ask you a qualifying question."

"Qualifying question?" Green Hair repeated with furrowed eyebrows. "A qualifying question to play a bloody game of darts?" She paused for a moment, looking at this odd American, then smiled. "You Yanks are buggers, aren't you? Go on then. Give it a go. Gimme a rip on your *qualifying* question."

"OK," said Truck with a smile. "If you were one word in the dictionary, what would you be?"

Green Hair smiled broadly. It was a great question, far better than she had expected. This chap seemed to have a shred of a brain hidden somewhere under his badly cut hair.

Green Hair scrunched her face and pondered an answer. Leaning forward, her nose just six inches from Truck's, she puckered her lips and licked them with her tongue. Truck didn't notice her lips. He was staring cross-eyed at her nose ring.

"Mysterious," she whispered softly.

Satisfied with her response and not wanting to let him off the hook just yet, Green Hair then asked Truck the exact same question. What one word in the dictionary was *he?*

"Flaccid," interrupted Lloyd. "Unless, of course, you've got some Broadway show tunes on the stereo somewhere."

Both Truck and Green Hair broke up laughing at Lloyd's answer.

"OK," said Truck with a smile as he stood up, waving his arms high in surrender. "I give up! I give up! I'll play."

So Truck adjourned to the side of the room where the dartboard was hanging. He hadn't played darts in years but he liked being asked.

"What are we playing for?" Green Hair asked as she held out six nearly new goose-feathered darts. She told Truck to pick three of them.

"A beer?" she said, answering her own question.

"OK," said Truck. "A beer it is. You go first. Ladies before gentlemen."

Truck's opponent politely turned to him, stuck out her right hand, and firmly shook Truck's. "Good luck," she said politely.

"Good luck to you, too," laughed Truck.

With that, Green Hair put her two feet parallel to the painted line on the floor, squared her shoulders to the target, weighed the dart in her right hand, and once, twice, then three times cocked it back and forth in front of her face.

Suddenly, she paused. Turning to Truck she asked sweetly, "Um, bull's-eye to win or a whole game of Cricket or 501?"

"Bull's-eye to win sounds simpler," Truck replied. In truth, he had no foggy clue what Cricket or 501 even was, so Truck opted for the familiar game. He knew there were two kinds of bull's-eyes but was unsure of the difference between the two—and too proud to ask.

"OK, Mr. Broadway Show Tunes," she said with a laugh, turning toward the board. "Bull's-eye to win."

Green Hair squared her shoulders again to the target, aimed intently, furrowed her brows, resumed her thrice-levered arm-rocking motion, and let her first dart fly.

"Oh my God! Look! How lucky I might be!" she squealed happily. There, right dead square in the center ring of the dartboard, stuck her first toss. It was a perfect shot.

Andrew! she called out loudly with an arm-wave to the bartender. "Could you draw me a pint of Monteith's? You won't believe it! I got a *bull's-eye!*"

"Congratulations!" called the bartender. "A pint of Monteith's for the lucky little lady!"

With that, Green Hair turned to Truck and smiled with the grin of a candy-laden child at Easter. "Thank you," she beamed as she stuck out her right hand and shook Truck's again. "Good game! You are *so* nice!"

As they shook hands, Truck eyed her closely. His left palm still cradled all three darts. Somewhere behind that mousy green hair and God-awful nose ring might be hiding a pretty young woman, he thought. But she sure made it hard to tell. Green Hair wore a sleeveless lime green spaghetti-string top without a bra and caught him peeking at her small chest. "I forgot it," she blushed about the bra as she ended the handshake. "Not much of a reason to remember, is there?

"Can we play again?" she eagerly asked, changing the subject and segueing quickly back to the game at hand.

Truck, who'd already bought one beer and had yet to throw a dart, hesitated before replying. "Depends," he finally said.

"Depends on what?" Green Hair asked, feigning a pout.

"Depends on whether you can answer a Let's Play Again qualifying question."

"OK, let's go. I'm game," Green Hair replied. "I'm sure you stay up all hours of the night thinking up these bloody questions in case you end up in a bar throwing darts for beer with a braless little green-haired Kiwi girl."

Truck ignored the jab and continued, unimpeded. "In the Olympic Games," he began, "according to the rules, *if*—and this is during the actual competition, mind you—*if* one synchronized swimmer drowns, do all the others have to?"

"Yes, absolutely," Green Hair replied assertively. "And they are *not* to be removed from the pool until the completion of the high dive competition!"

"Close enough!" laughed Truck. "Let the game begin."

"Ladies before gentlemen?" Green Hair asked. "Or would *you* prefer to go first? It's OK with me if you want to go first. Oh!"

she clapped as Truck weighed the question, hopping up and down like a green-mop on a pogo stick. "I just can't *believe* I got a *bull's-eye* on my very first throw!"

Truck figured either she got really lucky or she was hustling him. He bought the act and figured she got lucky.

"Ladies before gentlemen. Absolutely," said Truck. "Forever and always."

"Aren't you sweet?" she beamed. Green Hair stuck out her right hand and firmly shook his again, pumping it firmly up and down four times quickly. Then she turned her attention back to the dartboard.

Well, Green Hair blitzed Truck four games in four throws and, in less than ten minutes, had won a round of drinks for her and her girlfriends. Mission complete, she decided she didn't want to throw darts any more and sat back down at her table.

Truck, still holding all three of his never-thrown goose-feather darts, stood alone in front of the dartboard like a man who'd just lost his pants in a poker game. He was 29 and if he kept playing, he was likely to be 59 before he ever had a chance to throw one.

The four girls all turned to Truck, hoisted their still froth-topped pint glasses, and let out a resounding chorus. "*CHEERS!*" they shouted. Then they clinked glasses of congratulations to Green Hair.

Green Hair waved Truck over to join them. "C'mon, c'mon," she said. "Don't just stand there and pout. C'mon, sit down. And bring your mate."

Truck sat between Green Hair and the prettiest of the bunch, a beautiful girl with a buxom hourglass figure and a huge mane of long light-brown frizzy hair. Her name, he learned, was Mitzi.

After Lloyd drew up a chair between the other two girls, introductions went around the table. Mitzi introduced all of the girls. Apparently she had done this a thousand times.

Lloyd sat between Phoebe and Bird, who was apparently Green Hair's best friend. Bird was cute and petite with dark eyes and short jet-black hair. Phoebe was a big girl, 5'10" or so, and a bit ordinary looking. She wore her dirty blonde hair shoulder length and had freckles, but not a busy amount.

Green Hair had a real name and Truck asked what it was. "Cushla," she replied. "Cushla Wimsett. Pleased to make your acquaintance." She expectantly stuck out her small hand. Truck shook it for the ninth time in 20 minutes. "Truck Roberts," he replied. "Pleased to make your acquaintance as well, Miss Wimsett."

"So," Truck continued, "what kind of name is Cushla?"

"The 'ell with my name," she laughed. "What the 'ell were *you* named after?" She put down her beer glass from her lips and smiled. "Assumed," she continued without waiting for his answer. "Cushla's an assumed name. My real name is Jeffrey Franklin Wimsett. My father wanted a boy."

Truck couldn't tell if she was serious or pulling his leg so he looked at the other girls for a clue. They stared back with blank faces. These four had the practiced choreography of a veteran theater troupe.

Turned out she was telling the truth. Cushla told Lloyd and Truck how her father had wanted a son and named her accordingly. Cush had a younger brother, Graeme, but he caught a deadly virus and went deaf at age six, blind at age seven. He never recovered and died the night before his ninth birthday.

Truck knew how tough that must've been to deal with since one of his best friends suffered a similar horrible fate before passing away at age 22. It was a miserable thing, scarring to everyone touched by its sadness.

But the talk immediately turned back to happier things. Truck spared Cushla the exercise of beating him four more times at darts and simply ordered a second round of beers after their first round ran dry.

The Posse, as the girls called themselves, were well practiced at chatting up men in bars and the machine-gun laughs were endless. The girls took turns peppering Truck with questions about American men while Lloyd, remaining silent, stole glances at Mitzi's impressive figure while she pretended not to notice.

None of the girls had yet visited the States, although all four wanted to. Cushla said she wanted to go to the World Dart Federation tournament at the Opryland Hotel in Nashville. Bird opted for Orlando and Disney World. Phoebe wanted to go to Hollywood and Beverly Hills to see the movie stars' homes. Ideally, she said, she'd like to see Kevin Costner's jacuzzi. With Kevin in it.

"You'd love Malibu Beach," Truck told her. "That's where the movie stars meet their wives and girlfriends. The girls lie on their towels, in bikinis and glistening with oil. The rich Hollywood actors and producers walk up and down the beach saying hello. Sort of like window-shopping.

"Lots of girls," Truck continued, "see a star they want to meet so they pick up their towels and run farther down the beach, lie down, and wait for the star to walk by again. Sometimes there are 20 girls in bikinis running in both directions, picking up and putting down their towels—like human dominoes."

"Wow," said Phoebe wondrously. "What a smart idea."

Truck nodded and turned to Mitzi. "How about you?" he asked. "Anywhere you'd like to visit?"

Mitzi opted for Aspen. "I think I would like Aspen," she said. "Especially during ski season. And Miami. I think I'd like Miami."

Truck then told an Aspen joke. Every Colorado native knew at least four Aspen jokes and he innocently quizzed the girls with one of his. Smiling, he asked, "What do a condom and an Aspen woman have in common?"

"Dunno," said Mitzi. "What *do* a condom and an Aspen woman have in common?"

"Both spend more time in your wallet than on your, um, pinkie!" said Truck.

"Pinkie?" cried Phoebe. "Is *that* what you call it? A *pinkie*?"

"This is what we call a pinkie," said Cush, holding aloft the short, thin little finger of her right hand. "Is that what you Yanks 'ave got? Little boogers, are they?"

The girls laughed like crazy and even Truck started laughing. He'd tried to choose his words politely and still ended up with the wrong one coming out. Maybe the Aspen joke wasn't such a good idea after all.

Lloyd tapped his watch, signifying that happy hour was over. It was airport time. The two guys stood up, shook hands around the table, and said goodbye. Truck shook Cush's hand last, gently sandwiching the top of her tiny right hand with his left. He held on as he looked at her and smiled, consciously reminding himself not to stare cross-eyed at her nose hoop.

"As for you, Miss Wimsett," he began, "I shall miss *you* the most of all. While I gather the past hour has been ritualistic child's play as you vanquish yet another beer-buying rube, well, from my perspective, permit me to say, Miss Wimsett, that the minutes with you are diamonds and emeralds to me."

Cush blushed as she looked around at her girlfriends. "My word. Didja hear that? Diamonds and bloody emeralds? How romantic! You're almost making me feel guilty. Not entirely, but nearly.

"Time to play best 5-of-9, have you?" she added with a mischievous grin.

"Next time, OK?" said Truck. "Not now. Gotta run. Best to you all. It's been fun."

Truck released Cush's hand, said goodbye, and congratulated her on being such a fine dart player. "It's never a disappointment to lose to a wonderful talent," he said. "And camouflaged under all that green coloring is one heck of a wonderful talent. Clearly the finest leprechaun dart-tosser I've ever been defeated by."

"Why, thank you, sir!" she replied with a broad smile. Cushla didn't get a lot of compliments unless it was closing time and few of those were this sincere. And no one had ever compared her to expensive jewelry before. "Where are you headed now, Truck Roberts?" she asked curiously.

"Too far to travel just to win a beer," he answered. "Back home. Got to head back for work and Halloween. The work I don't mind missing, but I would never miss a Halloween. An American tradition. Kids and costumes.

"All year long, kids are warned to never take candy from strangers. Then, one night a year, they're sent out with orders to get as much candy from as many strangers as possible. How can you not love it?

"Here," Truck continued, handing a business card to Cush. "Here's my card. Call if you—any of you—are ever in the area. I'll practice my darts. I'll be up for a rematch," he said with a smile, crossing his heart with his right index finger. "Promise!"

Truck sketched a brief note on the back of his business card. On the spur of the moment, he drew nine separate characters, in dot patterns like dice.

Cush studied the dots for a moment, then smiled as she recognized the markings. "Dice? No, not dice. Braille is it? It *is* Braille. But what's it mean?"

"Cosmic secret code," teased Truck. "And you're right. A little message in Braille. You're smart—I've little doubt you and the Posse will figure it out. If not today, then certainly some other time. Goodbye."

With that, Truck and Lloyd left the bar, piled into Lloyd's old gray car, and stick-shifted their way toward Auckland International.

"Green hair, eh, old boy? Wonder if it matches," Lloyd snickered slyly as he finger-rolled a left turn from his one-handed grip on the wheel. Lloyd was looking straight ahead with a smug smile on his face.

"I've got 18 hours of airplane time to ponder that very thought," replied Truck. "Drive on, old bean."

After the guys left, Cush and her friends spent ten minutes talking about Lloyd and Truck, but soon got bored and went back to playing "Who Would You Rather Be With?"

Cushla slid Truck's card in her jeans pocket and tossed out a hypothetical matchup for the girls to argue about. "Who would you rather be with," she asked, "Brad Pitt or Mel Gibson?"

"Brad Pitt!" shouted Phoebe. "Mel's too bloody old!"

"Brad Pitt," agreed Bird, nodding.

"Mel Gibson," cooed Mitzi. "If I got my hands on Mel Gibson, I'd make him bark at the moon. And he'd prob'ly do the same to me. *Oooohhh*, I *lo-o-o-o-ve* Mel Gibson!

"What about you, Cush?"

"Brad Pitt. Mel's so old, he needs two birthday cakes to hold all the candles.

"The Baldwin brothers or Sean Connery?"

"More is better!" screamed Phoebe. "Baldwin brothers!"

"Mitzi?" quizzed Cush.

"Mmmm . . . ," Mitzi replied, "Give me the golden oldie. Bond, James Bond. Bond is short for bondage, you know."

"OK," Cush laughed. "Here's a toughie: Who would you rather be with, Kevin Costner . . . or Prince William?"

"Whoa!" hooted the girls loudly.

"Cush! You're too cruel!" hollered Phoebe.

"Welcome to the real world, little Willie," said Mitzi.

Cush laughed and took a long gulp of beer, finishing the last of Truck Roberts' defeats with a smile.

—◆—

Later that night, at home, Cush decided to keep Truck's business card. She flipped it over and glanced again at the Braille letters on the back and thought about his diamonds-and-emeralds goodbye. She smiled, then tossed it in her hand-carved teak memory box from Indonesia.

A year later, that card would come in handy. By then, Cush had grown through the green hair and afternoon beer-drinking phase of her life and had decided to get a real job. Coincidentally, she saw a newspaper advertisement from the same giant international company Truck worked for. Cush remembered Truck's business card, fished it out of her memory box, and used it as a reference during her interview. Cushla gave the card to the hiring manager who remembered Truck well. He stapled Truck's card to her application after circling Truck's name in red ink.

If this polite, well-dressed brunette was a friend of Truck Roberts, then that was good enough for him. The next day, Cush had a real job, in a real company, largely thanks to a guy she flim-flammed out of some beers in a bar one year before.

As it turned out, fishing that innocent little business card out of her memory box and following it into the world of big business would totally reshape the rest of her life.

he Posse

Growing up, Jeffrey Franklin Wimsett lost her mother to cancer three days after her eleventh birthday. Having just lost her younger brother, Cush was devastated when she lost her mother—her very best friend and constant companion. Cush's father was no help and a lousy parent. He drank like a Muscovite, a gallon of vodka a week, and was rarely around. He knew little about child-rearing and cared even less.

After her mother's funeral, Cushla barely spoke to anyone for nearly a year. Finally, a caring neighbor nominated Cush for admission to the Wentworth School, a private school for kids whose parents were financially disadvantaged or without a marital partner. Provided it didn't cost him anything, Mr. Wimsett didn't mind Cush leaving home.

Entrance to Wentworth was competitive and only the most talented of the disadvantaged were fortunate enough to be accepted. Cushla Wimsett posted the third highest score among over 200 tested nominees.

Entering Wentworth proved to be a life preserver for the little seventh-grader. It was there Cush met and bonded with her closest friends: Bird, Phoebe, and Mitzi. The four stuck together like freshly chewed gum stomped onto a sidewalk. By eighth grade, they called themselves "The Posse."

Wentworth produced leaders—and lots of them. A solid education, coupled with a hefty dose of street sense, enabled many graduates to carve out lucrative, successful careers as surgeons, lawyers, and members of parliament. One former pupil even became governor general of New Zealand.

As Lloyd would tell Truck later, "At Wentworth, they get a good education and go on to screw the establishment kids who learn their tricks less than a mile distant."

A mile distant, in the heart of the eastern suburb blue-blood country, stand the old-bricked buildings of Regal Preparatory School—the private school where society kids learn the ways of the upper-class world. The Posse never could have stepped foot on Regal Prep property unless they used a flashlight and a very tall ladder to sneak their late-night way across its ivy-covered, brick walled perimeter.

Lloyd also had a blunt opinion of Regal Prep. "Regal Preparatory School, for grades 5 through 12, is where the little 'establishment darlings' are taught all about 'fair play' and other cunning behavior traits to ensure they continue to rule the great unwashed."

In Lloyd's view, the Kiwi populace sported two types of folks—the washed, and the unwashed—and each had its own leadership factory. Regal Prep scrubbed the washed; Wentworth housed the unwashed.

The two schools, understandably, were the bitterest of rivals. And a few years after arriving at Wentworth, Cushla Wimsett herself contributed mightily to fostering that tradition.

Wentworth had a reputation for being tough academically but school came easily to Cushla. She read quickly and retained virtually everything she saw, read, or/and heard. Cush could accumulate, process, and apply knowledge quickly and easily.

Cush also had a lot of the street in her. In some circles, like Regal Prep, common sense was often in short supply.

Not so with Cush. The brightest member of the Posse, Cush seemed to navigate reality easily. She lived for the day, and maybe tomorrow, but rarely looked too far beyond that. She had a tremendous ability to focus and wasted little time looking over her shoulder at the past or daydreaming about a hypothetical future.

Wentworth was also where Cushla learned the game of darts. She happened past a tournament one time, stopped, and stuck her head inside the pub to watch. She was instantly smitten with the game's ultimate fairness. Darts required concentration, execution, nerves, and confidence. Luck had little to do with it. It was her kind of game. Skill mattered.

Cush loved her friends, loved to throw darts, and quickly learned to throw them with uncanny accuracy. Whenever an important shot came up, she whisked away her shaggy hair, squinted her bright green eyes, and invariably rose to the occasion. A naturally ambidextrous athlete, just about every sport came easy to her but, far and away, Cush loved her darts the best.

Cushla won Wentworth's dart championship tournament for the first time as a seventh grader, and defended her school title for five successive years, graduating undefeated in league play over her final four seasons. In eighth and ninth grades, she won the title left-handed, just to show off. She was the New Zealand prep champion all through high school—through to twelfth grade—and defeated a different Regal Prep student in the finals four of those five years. It was a feat that made her as popular at Wentworth as an America's Cup sailing champion.

Cushla took great pride in the fact that she threw as well left-handed as she did right-handed. Around Auckland, she would play—and beat—every competitor. She entered the New Zealand Open as a 14 year old, finished fourth, and cried all the way home. At 15, Cush narrowly lost in the finals. The following year, she won the Open two days before flunking her driver's test for the first of five successive times.

Cushla kept failing the test for two primary reasons. Her borrowed car—a terribly rusted-out, ill-tuned, and smoke-belching disaster that barely kept running—certainly didn't help. But with Cush impatiently popping the clutch before depressing the gas pedal as she shifted gears, the resultant spastic lurches conked out the motor every single time. Her test examiner told Cush that, regardless of what else she'd learned at Wentworth, she'd finish school with a doctorate in whiplash.

On her first licensing attempt, Cushla stalled seven times trying to back up and parallel park. After she finally fit the car between the cones, she beamed triumphantly at the examiner, a potbellied, balding old man named Cyrril Powell, and asked, "How was that, Mr. Powell? Did I pass? Have I now earned the right to traverse the highways and byways of our fair lovely town and wonderful nation?"

"Dramatic, Miss Wimsett," Mr. Powell replied. "Dramatic, yet unsuccessful.

"Perhaps on the next go-round, Miss Wimsett. Better luck next time." Five tries later, in a different car, she finally passed.

Young Cushla realized she couldn't depend on her father for much in the way of emotional or financial support, so she searched for ways to earn spending money to help pave whatever roads life's travels would take. Cush took on odd jobs wherever she could; she babysat, washed cars, and finally, at 15, lied about her age to get a job as a waitress in a hole-in-the-wall diner.

Named Eggstraordinary, the restaurant served only breakfast and lunch. Cush lasted one day and was fired. She burned everything she cooked, dropped everything she carried, and got distracted and poured hot coffee on a fat man's zippered pants.

In a stroke of great fortune, exactly one week later, Cush began working at Ellerslie Racecourse. Ellerslie was a beautiful horse track about three-and-a-half miles from Wentworth. Cushla ran to and from work each day. She could run like the wind and loved the fitness it brought her. Indeed, she loved the rainy days best of all. When she ran in the rain, Cush swore she could hear the flowers grow.

On race days at Ellerslie, Cushla did just about everything from working back in the holding stables to polishing saddles, selling programs, or flipping rump steaks and pouring sodas at The Winners Circle Café. As the home of the Auckland Racing Club, Ellerslie and its race meets were pure magic for a motherless girl in search of something beautiful to love.

Cush enjoyed riding the great animals and volunteered to exercise the horses whenever the track people needed help. As a racing track, not a training track, Ellerslie had but a half-dozen overnight stalls. The rest of the enormous barn temporarily housed horses shipped in to run that day. Ninety percent of the racehorses running at Ellerslie vanned in on race day from within a 50-mile radius.

Many of the horses were trained in at Takanini, 13 miles south, and Cush worked there every weekend except when Ellerslie was racing. Typically, Cush left the school grounds running in the darkness of the early Auckland morning, usually between 4:30 and 5:00, just to work the horses. Her petite size and wiry, fit form made her perfectly suited for the job. Plus, Cush had soft hands and communicated well with the animals.

At the end of each 12-hour day, Cush caught a ride back to school with one of the barn hands.

At Takanini, Cush only tumbled once—when a filly she was galloping made an uneven step and snapped a foreleg. Cush took a terrible fall but managed to cover up in a protective duck-and-roll and avoided serious injury. Fortunately, the horses behind her swerved past and she escaped being trampled. Her mount, a three-year-old filly named Girlarrific, had to be put down.

The accident haunted Cushla for months. She felt responsible, even though everyone at Takanini realized the tragedy was a random lightning bolt that struck down an occasional animal at every oval the sport was pursued. Injuries were, far and away, the ugliest part of an otherwise beautiful business.

Because of her love of horses, one of Cush's favorite days each year was Ellerslie's running of one Australasia's greatest horse races—the Group One Auckland Cup. The Cup was a big-money race and massive social spectacle. Cushla always complained about the fuss and crowds but, deep down, she enjoyed dressing up to work the stylish event. She adored the hats and dresses the rich women wore. Although she couldn't picture herself ever owning such finery, she loved the electric excitement the big event created.

The Auckland Cup was also a day the other Posse members never missed. The girls dressed up, circulated, and swooned over the men. Mitzi, in a normal year, would give her phone number to a dozen requesting suitors. Depending on the inquirer, she transcribed the digits in either the right or wrong order.

Bird normally skipped the phone number gambit and simply tried to zero in on, and pick up, one new dating prospect each year. For some reason, she fared better in the odd-numbered years than even. None of the Posse could figure out why, but it sure seemed as predictable as spring rain.

Phoebe skipped such foolishness. She lived for gossip. The girls teased her that she should have been born with radar dishes on the side of her head instead of ears. Cush even called her "The Neighborhood Busybody," a title that fit like custom tailoring.

Phoebe considered it her personal responsibility to garner as many gossipy tidbits as possible. Factual verification didn't matter; *quantity* mattered. Rumor and innuendo were her breakfast and lunch.

Phoebe's job was to assemble, then report to the Posse, whatever dirt she uncovered. The Posse would then piece together the mosaics of truth. The girls considered this a fair and democratic way to properly dissect the lives of other people.

— ◆ —

As the Posse's senior year at Wentworth rolled toward its inevitable end, all four girls faced a stark reality. The safe haven of the school's motherly bosom was about to dissipate and each was faced to make some big decisions, yet none seemed particularly eager to make them.

Wentworth put a lot of pressure on all of its students to attend college. After all, they were groomed for college and careers, in theory anyway, from the first day they arrived on campus.

For Cush, college was a natural extension of her life—"13th grade," she called it. She could choose where she wanted to go. Cush had grades and athletic prowess, so every major school in New Zealand recruited her, plus four from Australia. The hard part would be deciding where to spend the next four years.

The options weren't as clear-cut for the others. Bird, who along with her brother was a foster child, wasn't sure whether to go to college or simply retire from education, get a job, and earn a living. Bird didn't want to leave Auckland unless Cush decided to go to school out of town. Bird and Cush were close, very close, and Bird decided she'd worry about what she would do after Cushla decided what *she* would do.

Mitzi, meanwhile, had money—a giant trust fund—which meant she had options. Both parents died in a fiery automobile accident when Mitzi was seven years old. Mitzi was in the back seat when her father swerved to avoid a red deer crossing the road in the deep darkness of a moonless night south of Turangi. He lost control and the small car slid off the pavement, slamming into a centuries-old oak at near-highway speed.

Mitzi's older brother and younger sister were also killed. When the emergency crew arrived on the scene, young Mitzi was kneeling on the floor of the back seat, wedged under the crushed metal roof, shaking her dead mother's shoulder and telling her to wake up.

Mitzi's trust matured on her 18th birthday, putting her in the enviable financial position of being able to do whatever she wanted.

Phoebe, meanwhile, wasn't so lucky. Her Wentworth grades would probably slide her into the freshman class at the University of Auckland, but that was about it. Post-Wentworth, Phoebe's lone goal was finding a husband—the sooner, the better. She knew a college campus was a great place to search, so Phoebe intended to major in boy-watching and husbandry research. She didn't care about sports, couldn't even hula hoop or rollerblade, and was somewhat ordinary looking. But Phoebe was also determined, and that covered a lot of other shortcomings.

For four different reasons, the Posse all ended up at the University of Auckland. New Zealand's largest university, U of A was a venerable center-city college, founded in 1883. Bordered by the beautiful and historic Albert Park to the west, the university sported a large campus, three square blocks and parts of three more, sporting beautiful views overlooking the harbor.

Steeped in generations of tradition, the university had 26,000 students—about 20,000 full-time. Close to 6,000 graduated each year, so clearly the Posse had gone from being big fish in the Wentworth pond to zooplankton in a sea of student diversity.

Cushla decided to accept an athletic scholarship and stay in Auckland, primarily basing her decision on the feeling that the only real family she had was the Posse and she wasn't going to be the one to split them up.

Bird was thrilled that Cush was staying in town, so she immediately announced she, too, would enroll at U of A.

Clueless about what to study, Bird enrolled in a general program designed to help students figure out which direction to take their college careers.

Mitzi, meanwhile, figured that, with thousands of males in the upper class at U of A, she'd have a sufficient inventory of potential suitors. Mitzi was a good student and planned on some day owning and running her own business. She enrolled in the School of Business and Economics to learn about international sales and marketing.

Phoebe was overjoyed that her friends were going to U of A and selected Accounting and Finance as her major, since nearly all the program-goers in those disciplines were men. She fully expected, four years hence, to emerge from the University of Auckland with two things—a diploma and a husband—and preferably not in that order.

Over the next four years, the Posse churned through a blizzard of fellows for a variety of reasons. Bird had the two most stable relationships, both lasting two years. She had lined up the second fellow before dumping the first and missed zero Saturday nights making the changeover.

Mitzi dated early, often, and had no extended relationship worth mentioning. She seemed to be maturing quickly beyond her years and the college guys—though eager and enthusiastic— lacked the earthy cool, surety, and financial wherewithall of older, more confident men. By the time Mitzi was a junior, she was dating men five to 15 years her senior almost exclusively.

Phoebe stayed busy falling in and out of love as quickly and as often as possible. She had a bubbly, happy attitude that radiated niceties about anyone who asked her out. In her view, anyone nice enough to ask her out automatically had marriage potential. Phoebe staunchly defended every guy she dated, no matter how he looked or what the rest of the Posse thought. Her longest relationship lasted five months.

Cushla specialized in short-term relationships, too. She never celebrated the same holiday twice with anyone and wouldn't date for the sake of simply having one. "I don't know why I'm like this," she told Bird one night after their umpteenth forgettable double date. "Maybe I'm just scared to get a guy *two* birthday presents or *two* Christmas presents or *two* Valentine's Day presents. Maybe it's some deep-rooted hang-up I've got."

"It's going to be hard for you to live happily ever after if you can't even make it through two Christmases," Bird countered.

"The 'ell with the *ever after* part," replied Cush. "The *live happily* thing would be good enough for me. And my experience has been that men simply become rather boring and aren't worth the maintenance.

"If I have car trouble, I can date a mechanic. No need to keep him 'round all the time—just 'til his usefulness is served."

Clearly, Cush lived on a different social planet than husband-hungry Phoebe. But she was attractive, outgoing, and curiously friendly, so she met a lot of fellows. Cush didn't have anything close to a steady boyfriend until the summer before her senior year.

Then, one night, she met a guy named Gavin Jallacy in the pub. She beat Gavin six straight games in darts and, after every loss, he became even more thoroughly convinced each one was a freak accident.

Gavin was such a shallow rube, Cush decided he might be worth keeping around. She dated him for a while, even though it was obvious he lived a paycheck-to-paycheck life and probably always would.

Gavin also put zero pressure on Cushla to do or be anything whatsoever. He was what Mitzi called a "wizzy-wig"—spelled "WYSIWYG"—an acronym for "What You See Is What You Get." It was not a flattering term since Gavin most certainly was what he was and Mitzi held little optimism that he would ever outgrow it. But if Cush wanted to spend her life dancing on stilts, Gavin couldn't have cared less.

Cush found this Bohemian attitude refreshing and, soon, her outlook on life, fashion, ambition, and values began to change.

She chopped off most of her hair, dyed the pixy remains a shade of wicked-witch green, and spent four hours in a piercing parlor before emerging swiss-cheesed and sore. Cush also became a fiercely loyal devotee of a loud local punk rock band named Stinky Fingers, whose best song was a catchly little ditty called *Phlegm of the Night.*

But through it all, Cush had her darts and her running. And, braless, green-haired, body piercings and all, Cush made a regular habit of beating just about everyone she played darts against, either left-handed, right-handed, or alternating one with the other.

But one night Gavin started a bar brawl that Cushla quickly found herself face-first in the middle of. Literally. The barkeep called the cops and Cush's father had to come down to the station to sign her out since she had no money.

Cleater Wimsett arrived at the station clean-shaven, well heeled, and smartly dressed. He looked very dignified, and very sober.

Mr. Wimsett bailed out his dirty green-haired, nose-ringed, troublemaking daughter and chose not to ask about the coin-sized welt mousing nicely under her left cheekbone. He assumed whomever put it there had a very good reason.

Father and daughter drove home in silence. Both realized life's pendulum had swung in opposite directions for each of them. Cleater Wimsett's sober new life featured a quiet and dignified behavior surrounding his new job at the Art Museum. His energies now poured into the study and research of Italian Renaissance masters like Piranisi, Tintoretto, Canal, and Titian. Water now poured where vodka used to tumble into a never-empty glass.

Cushla's life, meanwhile, had gone the other way and was now comprised of bar brawls, dirty green hair, no real job, and no bank account. Yet she knew it all would sort itself out in due time and that time was rapidly approaching.

Gavin tried to make up for the brawl by buying Cush a pair of good rollerblades from Smilin' Jay's Pawn Shop in Ponsonby.

He also gave her a single rose, which Cush loved and thought was romantic until Mitzi heard about it.

"Say it with flowers," Mitzi sniffed. "Used skates and one flower says, 'I'm *cheap*.' He'll never buy you a diamond, Cush," Mitzi added bluntly. "Instead of a shiny engagement ring, you'll be lucky to get a big foam puffy hand saying 'You're #1'."

Mitzi thought Cush could do better, much better, and simply had to raise her sights out of the gutter to do so. Cush didn't argue, and Gavin did have one annoying quirk that bothered Cushla quite a bit.

He refused to wear underwear. "Swingin' free, goin' commando," he cheerfully called it.

Phoebe warned Cush the neighbors would gossip so she gave her a brand new pack of ultra-white men's underwear to hang on the clothesline. The briefs were just for show but the spying and gossipy neighbors were talkatively impressed by Cush's ability to wash and hang whiter whites on the clothesline time after time.

Cush was glad Phoebe was around to think of things like that—slathering mortar between the bricks of reality. Sure, Gavin had his faults. But he was OK. Plus, she liked the skates. So, he would do for now.

A few months later, those same bricks of reality began building a wall between Cush and Gavin. The more she listened to Mitzi, the more convinced Cush that Mitzi was right. Gavin would never be much more than what he already was—an unmotivated underachiever. She finally tired of his slovenly ways and kicked him out, giving him all three pairs of the really white undies as a farewell gift.

One week later, on the Posse's final afternoon before college graduation, the girls decided to go out for a celebratory lunch and drove over to Hammerhead's on Tamaki Drive. They sat upstairs on the veranda and watched as streams of rollerbladers wheeled along the broad sidewalk tracing the curving waterfront edges of Okahu Bay.

From behind her sunglasses, Cush imagined herself rolling along among them.

As the falling sun matched the falling tides of their iced-tea glasses, the girls reminisced about their college years and then predicted what would happen in the four years ahead.

Everyone predicted Phoebe would get married because that was what Phoebe wanted to hear.

Cush predicted Bird would marry a wealthy husband, have twins, and never have to work a paying job for the rest of her life.

Bird predicted Cush would win the World Dart Federation title, defeating Trina Gulliver of England in a match shown on pay-per-view around the world. She also predicted Cush would sign an autograph for Prince William, but forget to write down her phone number.

Mitzi predicted that Cush, Bird, and Phoebe would all come to America for a visit once she set up her new company in Miami. She also predicted that bronzed muscle-bound he-men would be waiting for each at the airport. This prognostication caused the loudest glass-clinking cheer of the afternoon.

Mitzi then hoisted her glass and proposed a toast:

"One for one and all for all,

"Together we win, together we fall.

"Forever and ever, always friends

"The Posse shall ride together again!"

"Cheers!" they all cried out as they spanked their glasses together.

"Hey!" Bird cried. "We graduate tomorrow! We need to go somewhere that Cush can win us a beer!"

"The Purple Kiwi?" asked Phoebe, referring to a tavern near school.

"Too low rent," replied Mitzi. "Nobody there has money. Let's go to the Trap."

The girls prepared to leave and, after Phoebe broke out her calculator to cut the bill four separate ways, the girls piled in Mitzi's Lexus. They drove the scenic route toward Mount Eden, passing Cornwall Park and the beautiful obelisk perched high atop One Tree Hill.

One Tree Hill was to Auckland what the Eiffel Tower was to Paris or the Golden Gate Bridge was to San Francisco. The sight of the singular tree, high on the hilltop protecting the city, was an image Mitzi freeze-framed to take on her impending scouting trip overseas. This beautiful spot, the highest around, offered a magnificent circular view of the city.

Tour buses followed each other all day long, snaking their way up and down the narrow winding road to reach the summit. After sundown, cars replaced the buses and in these cars were lovers driving up to share the view of the glittering lights in between long, unhurried kisses.

Five minutes after passing One Tree Hill, Mitzi's car turned the corner onto Enfield Street. The girls pulled up to the Horse & Trap just as another bloke in a big old beat-up station wagon was pulling away. The car had plenty of room and parked in the spot second closest to the front door. Cush started exercising her right wrist. She needed to find somebody who wouldn't mind losing four straight games of bull's-eye.

It was here, ten minutes later on an otherwise forgettable afternoon before graduation, that the Posse stumbled across Lloyd Hill and Truck Roberts stopping in for a quick beer on the way to the airport.

The Black-Eyed Bunny

Not long after Truck accepted a big promotion and moved to a sprawling corporate training center in northern Virginia, he soon realized he'd spend the next two years as featured soloist in a one-man band.

At new teacher orientation, Truck sat next to a slender bleached blonde named Patricia Thayer who smiled, turned, stuck out her hand, and said, "Hi. I'm Party Patti." Patti was about 5'6", quite single, and from the suburbs of Kansas City.

The pair spent the next week learning how to recognize personality types and managing adult behavior in a classroom setting. The personality typing especially intrigued Truck. To Party Patti, it was no big deal. Patti said women's magazines typecast men all the time.

Party Patti quickly became Truck's best friend and, as emotionally protective as Truck was, Patti was just the opposite. She wore her emotions on her sleeve and churned and burned her busy way through a revolving door of suitors.

Patti was also an excellent golfer. When springtime rolled around, she convinced Truck to be her partner in the company's nine-hole Thursday afternoon golf league. She usually spotted him three shots a side and won nearly every side bet they made.

On or off the course, Party Patti was outgoing and smiled easily. She enjoyed companionship and, after a few beers, often morphed from a quiet, polite midwesterner into a sexy, prowling tigress. But Truck and Patti refused to let intimacy ruin a perfectly good friendship. Their relationship remained comfortably platonic.

Truck adored Patti as his closest female pal and soon began to trust her with his feelings—something he did with no one else.

And so, Party Patti and Truck spent the next two years in adjoining classrooms, teaching basically the same stuff to hundreds of adults divvied up by computer into random classes of eight.

The goal was to assemble a culturally diverse eight-person learning group. Selling had no biases and typecasting or stereotyping people was as silly as a prospector cheering over fool's gold. Talent came in all shapes, sizes, skin colors, sexual persuasions, and preferences. You could either do it or you couldn't, and Truck believed being a professional marketeer was one of the purest ways for anyone to earn an excellent living.

Truck had zero selection input and each week merely played the human cards the computer chose to deal. His job each Monday was to find that talent and develop it.

It didn't take long to realize that this job involved a lot more than just teaching. Soon Truck was a bandleader of situational leadership, rotating through varying roles, including one as a consoling father figure. Over the next two years, three male students died of heart attacks—one playing volleyball in the gym, another shooting hoops. The third arrived from the airport, felt tired, checked in, and fell asleep in his room. He never woke up. Heart attack. Boom! Gonzo. Only 40, he left a wife and three little kids. No warning, no second chance. Checked in and checked out within minutes.

Truck sat with the personnel director when she phoned the fellow's home and broke the news. He heard the man's wife wailing through the earpiece of the telephone receiver. For Truck Roberts, such a simple thing as a phone call became a numbing dose of cram-it-down-your-throat reality. For the woman on the other end, one ringing telephone suddenly shattered her life into a thousands shards of pain.

As he walked slowly back toward his classroom, Truck could only imagine the devastating hurt of a young family so tragically destroyed.

But the job created more joy than sorrow and the part Truck liked best was the part he was hired to do—take some of the company's most experienced salespeople and sharpen their skills.

The company had 44 sales trainers on the global training staff, and within six months Truck was considered one of the best. He had earned his spurs the hard way—toting a bag out in the field, making sales calls, being told "no" a trillion times, and managing to get enough "yeses" to be successful by the various yardsticks the company used to measure its top performers.

Truck had battled in the trenches and was well respected. He was also smart enough to learn from his students, especially the skilled ones, so the longer he was in the job, the more effective he became.

He would also never find a more picturesque place to work. The campus sat centered like a 40-acre egg yoke in the geographic center of 2,400 acres of perfectly pristine woods that hadn't been hunted or disturbed in nearly 20 years. The relentless crush of Northern Virginia commercial and residential growth continually drove more and more animals into the safe sanctuary. With this development pushing in from every direction, each day seemed to stuff more wildlife onto every single acre.

Truck spent two hours a day in the woods. Some days he hiked, some days he ran, but often he just walked quietly through the woods with his camera. Truck shot thousands of photographs throughout all four seasons of the year, mostly of picturesque whitetail deer.

If his students liked wildlife and Truck liked the students, sometimes after class he'd take them along on his hikes. Truck was choosy which students he invited and rarely guided more than a handful in a month. He never went alone with a woman.

As he neared the end of his two-year rotational term, Truck had learned a lot more than he'd taught—all good instructors do. And, with just two more classes to go, he could finally see the finish line.

Truck robotically set up his next-to-last classroom late Friday afternoon for his Monday morning arrivals. As usual, the eight students were from all over and one fellow was due in from New Zealand. He didn't recognize the name.

It took an hour to half-moon into position the student desks and chairs, distribute materials, label each with a carefully hand-printed magic-markered nametag, and make sure the classroom looked orderly. First impressions mattered.

As usual, Truck played music as he set-up his classroom. He was a creature of habit and played certain albums on certain days. Friday afternoon set-ups belonged to Bonnie Raitt while Monday morning's welcome song before each new class began was Louis Armstrong singing "What a Wonderful World."

Truck always played Satchmo's signature song at eight o'clock straight up, let it finish, smiled broadly, and then punched the small OFF button. "The Welcome Hymn," he fondly called it.

Monday would be Satchmo's next-to-last performance and Truck held out little hope the computer would conjure up a student collection a whole lot less forgettable than their predecessors.

Sure, some spectacular things had happened over the year, but nearly all occurred outside the four whitewashed walls of his small classroom. And since it wasn't November (and breeding season for the deer), there was little chance that a buck and doe would leap into the saddle of love and "get it on" as a zealous, determined pair had done last fall. The deer stood in the flowerbed right outside Truck's classroom window and shared their love for all to see at one o'clock in the afternoon.

"Try competing with *that* when you've got a room full of middle-aged people just back from lunch," he told Patti that afternoon at the break station.

"I didn't bother trying," she replied. "We all watched it, too."

But this was February—cold, dark February—and there would be no voyeuristic animal show. Truck simply hoped the computer doled out a decent mix of low-maintenance personality types. Maybe he'd be lucky enough to catch tropical fish barehanded and get a room full of independents—cruise-control types of students who would allow him to work on autopilot.

Never, *ever*, would Truck have believed the surprise the computer spit out this time.

The Redhead Arrives

Cushla Wimsett arrived in Northern Virginia after 18 hours in coach on two United flights, Auckland to LAX and LAX to Washington Dulles.

Wired from the travel, crossing the International Dateline, and a 17-hour time difference, Cushla checked in, then braved the freezing winter cold and went straight over to the gym for a long workout. She ran for an hour on a StarTrac treadmill, then did a complete weight circuit on all the machines.

Afterward, Cush jogged the 500 yards back to her room and took a long, hot, steaming shower, emerging completely refreshed. She blow dried her shoulder-length reddish hair, fixed her eyes, checked her manicured red nails, accented her makeup, and tossed on a multi-colored Canterbury top. After tugging on a pair of size-4 dress jeans, Cushla slipped tied on her nearly new size-6 white Asics running shoes, trimmed in colors that matched her shirt and jeans.

Briefly, Cushla studied herself in her half-length mirror. What a difference a year made, she thought. She looked every bit the well-manicured professional woman. She had learned to like that look. It made her feel self-confident but also, well, pretty in a feminine way.

Cush walked downstairs and over to the cafeteria. She loaded up on frozen vanilla yogurt that snaked its endless coiling way out a big stainless steel lever-armed dispenser. Everything was free, as much as she could want, and Cush skipped over things she needed to chew in deference for sugary things that melted. She was excited to be in America. This was her first trip and any place that lets you eat free ice cream 'til your tummy hurts would be a fine base of operations, indeed.

Around nine o'clock, she decided to go to the bar in Building Two to drink a soda. Cushla was the lone Kiwi to fly over for sales school, and opted to stay busy writing postcards to the Posse and her boss.

At the crowded bar, about 80 percent of the circling coyotes were older men. Cush could tell if someone was in sales or service simply by looking. The salespeople were nicer looking, dressed better, and more physically fit. The service people looked like people who twisted screwdrivers, kicked stubborn machines, strung corotron wire, and cleared paper jams for a living.

Cush drank a Diet Coke from a tall glass of ice as she looked around to people-watch. "The washed and the unwashed," she thought to herself. "Wentworth and Regal Prep."

Like all pretty girls in the company pub, Cush never had to dip into her wallet to pay for drinks after the first.

"American men are well trained," she thought as a second soda was delivered without her asking. "Phoebe would love this— all these men and all this attention. Bird would, too.

"Just another day at the office for Mitzi," Cush decided. She was already looking forward to calling Mitzi and telling her all about the American men.

Much to her delight, Cushla looked around the bar and spied a dartboard hanging on the wall between a couple of pinball machines and a large neon-decorated jukebox playing hits that were ten or twenty years old. Bored, she walked over and flipped some darts at the board. They were cheap, badly mangled things that flew like vampire bats.

The floor wasn't taped for dart playing so she measured it off and marked it herself. A couple of older men, copier repairmen with big beer guts, came over to play rotation and Cush threw haphazardly on purpose to let the games stay close. She'd feasted on pigeon before and closed out each game whenever she got bored, pretending to get lucky four or five shots in a row.

Two Cokes was her limit, so after the second one, she said good night and turned in for the evening. Cush wanted to be well rested for her first day of class in America.

Monday Morning

For a smart company, the building quadrangle had a dumb numbering system—or so Cushla thought as she anxiously wandered around looking for her classroom. The big campus had several buildings, each with six floors, plus underground passageways. Each floor had several dead end hallways with odd-shaped rooms. The alphanumeric combinations used to label everything made no sense to anyone with a modicum of logic.

"Numbered by a Regal Prep valedictorian, no doubt," Cush fumed as she hurried along. She hated being late to anything and repeatedly checked her watch. Finally, just a few minutes before eight o'clock, she found a woman who knew where she was going and politely steered her the rest of the way. Cush opened the door to her small classroom and slid into her seat—the only one vacant—just as the door self-closed and latched behind her.

Louis Armstong music played on the stereo. She noticed her desk's white cardboard nametag read *JEFFREY WIMSETT, New Zealand.*

When Cush glanced up at the instructor's empty facing desk and read the nametag, her eyes bugged out. The tag said *TRUCK ROBERTS.*

Just then, the door behind her opened and in walked the instructor, a tall good-looking man wearing a suit. She recognized him instantly. A year ago, green-haired and braless, she'd fleeced this guy out of beers at the Trap. "I wonder if he'll remember me," she thought as she slid down and slouched in her seat.

The class took turns introducing each other. When Cush's turn came, Truck looked at her intently. Finally a glimmering light bulb of recognition illuminated, all 15 watts, and he smiled.

"I remember *you*," he said slowly. "What the heck are you doing here? Last I saw you was in Auckland. I thought Jeffrey was a guy. Now I remember . . . Jeffrey *Franklin* Wimsett. Your father wanted a son. The dart thrower with her girlfriends."

Truck briefly told the class how they met and how Cush beat him tossing darts in a pub for a couple beers. He never mentioned her green hair, which she silently appreciated.

"You still throw those things?" Truck asked.

"A wee bit," Cush admitted sheepishly.

"There's a dartboard in the pub," Truck answered.

"Oh really?" she replied innocently. "Thank you."

During the class introductions, Truck did his personality typing and decided the computer had doled out four compliants, one attention-seeker, one hero, and one independent. Could be better, could be worse. About an average mix, actually. He wasn't sure yet about Cush.

Class continued uneventfully according to the choreographed schedule of the sequenced subject modules. Truck pulled the plug at five o'clock sharp, dismissing the students with a stern reminder about drinking and driving.

The students dutifully filed out, several deciding to go to the gym and others opting to check in with their home offices.

Cush did neither. She went back to her room, changed, and went outside in the freezing cold for a four-mile run.

Thursday Night

Near the end of the program, Truck made good on a Tuesday promise made at the morning break station that if Cush had a good week in class, the two would go to a quiet and private early dinner. It was her idea, not his.

They went to the Serbian Crown, about five miles east and just off Route 7. It was a short drive, just 15 minutes by car. Truck didn't go there often—only on special occasions—but considered this to be one. He didn't share that with Cush, however.

The Crown was famous for its impeccable service and waitstaff, excellent food, and, most notably, frozen test tubes of various flavored vodkas. The icy vodkas were quite popular with hard-drinking businessmen and political power brokers. Cush and Truck passed on the opportunity to try one, but watched the suits surrounding them bomb the shooters down the hatch one right after another. It seemed like Moscow at happy hour.

Dinner was both comfortable and uncomfortable for Truck. On one hand, he avoided socializing with students whenever possible and yet he was comfortable around Cush—even though she always asked very blunt questions he hated to answer. Cush wasn't shy about asking deeply personal things that drilled between his ears, and south toward his heart.

Both those areas were dangerous geographies to a man who prided himself on never letting anyone behind his own well-bunkered emotional firewall.

At this stage of life, Truck was introspective and never chose to "communicate," as Party Patti called it. Communication required four things: a sender, receiver, channel and message. And he harbored no interest in being a sender.

Sharing feelings ranked right down there on the enjoyability scale with spending a wheelbarrow full of take-home pay on unexpected auto repairs.

Happily dissecting her glazed pheasant, Cushla suddenly paused, looked up, and asked, "What are you running from?"

She was very matter-of-fact about asking and patiently waited for an answer.

Truck laughed a nervous, uneasy laugh and leaned way back, recoiling at the unexpectedly blunt verbal body blow. Cush asked the question so easily, then backed off and smiled with the innocence of a happy young child, that, despite feeling emotionally naked, Truck somehow felt compelled to answer.

He figured if he could evade Cush's question with one of his own, he could redirect the conversation. "I'm not running from anything," he finally replied. "What makes you ask such a thing?"

"It's *so* obvious," she said with a sigh. "Don't you like your life?"

"Of course I do," he replied, again defensively, hoping she'd mercifully choose not to probe further. "Why do you ask?"

"Because," she said quietly after a sip of ice water and lifting a small piece of thigh meat with her fork, "I don't think you do."

Truck planted his left index finger in the center of a cocktail napkin and nervously spun it in a clockwise circle. The napkin spun six complete times before the silence was broken.

Cush asked another simple question. "If you like your life, then tell me this. What *is* life?" she asked. "What is it to you?"

"Life? What's life? I know all about life," Truck stammered. He stalled, searching for the correct, carefully selected words. He wasn't exactly sure which ones he'd pick but he was damn certain "pinkie" would not be among them.

"OK," Cush cooed. "If you know all about life, Mr. Teacher, and since you like yours so wonderfully much, would you please explain to me *exactly* what it is?

"I'm waiting," she added, her words framed by the radiant smile of a pearl-toothed Cheshire cat with a mouth full of helplessly trapped canary.

Unfortunately for Truck, he heard his own words before he thought them carefully through. "Life. Uh, life. Life's what you do between shaves," he replied confidently. "That's it. *That's* what life is."

Truck knew it was a stupid answer as soon as he heard it. He grimaced at Cush's predictable reaction.

Cush laughed. *Loudly.* Very, very loudly. So loudly, a half-dozen people paused from chugging their vodka shooters to turn their heads to see what was so funny. What they saw was a large man fidgeting in a chair because a woman half his size was toying with him between the ears.

"How *lame!*" exclaimed Cush after she finally stopped laughing. "How bloody *lame!* Is that what you *really* want out of life? Smooth shaves? My God, my God, my *God!*"

Truck fumbled for response, then spit out another beauty. "All I want out of life is to have at least six guys to carry me when my turn comes," he said unconvincingly. "That's all I ever wanted."

Truck knew *that* answer was even more stupid than the first. Even the vodka-chuggers eavesdropping at the next table thought so and leaned over with a test tube vodka for Truck to try. "Here pal," the fellow urged. "You need this more than I do."

Truck demurred. But once Truck said what he did—however stupid—he had to try and sell it, so Truck shut up and wondered if he looked as dumb as he felt. He guessed not. He guessed he looked a lot dumber.

"Why are you so defensive?" Cush persisted.

"Whaddya mean 'Why am I so defensive?' I'd rather not remember things I can't forget. That's why I'm so defensive."

Again Cush laughed. "What kind of lame, introspective, clichéd possum swill is *that?* You are *pathetic*, Mr. Roberts."

"Twice burnt, twice learnt, Cush," Truck said with a wry half smile, ignoring the bait yet still trapped in the purgatory of bad cliché answers. "Tried that communication stuff before. All it got me was a pair of broken hearts that got more scars than Evel Knievel."

"The motorcycle daredevil who did all the stunts," Truck added quickly, intercepting Cush's quizzical expression.

Cushla had no idea what was so evil about a Knievel in the first place, especially since she didn't even know what a Knievel was. She assumed a knievel was a fierce American forest animal. An evil knievel must be extra mean, with sharp claws and fangs.

Cush said nothing. She didn't press the issue and dropped the subject. But she never broke eye contact with Truck as she reached over, picked up her water glass, and took another small sip. Cush decided to let Truck off the hook. She stopped asking personal questions. He was, after all, buying an expensive dinner that she asked him to go on, and paying dearly for this interrogation.

He was also obviously stonewalling. "Typical gutless male," she thought as she smiled faintly. "What is it with men?" she thought. "Why are they so bloody terrified of their own feelings? Kiwi men are the same bloody way."

Cush remained silent. She simply sat there gently swishing the last of the water in her glass. And smiling.

Truck sat across from her, saying nothing but trying to figure out what it was about this odd girl that enabled her to see right through him. He felt like his skin was totally clear and transparent. It served to hide no emotion if Cush chose not to let him.

In one way, it felt religiously good. In another, it was quite alarming. Whenever Cush looked right at him, demanding eye contact, Truck felt like he was dropping his boxers for an intrusive exam. It was an eery and uncomfortable feeling. No one had ever made him feel this way—not even Dominique the first time she talked dirty in French.

Truck felt like he was being magnetically lured into the age-old "Intimacy vs. Intimacy Avoidance" clash of the sexes and wasn't quite sure what to make of, or how to handle, the personal questions she asked. Like it or not, he realized the Alamo walls guarding his soul were being easily and gracefully polevaulted by a pixie-sized Kiwi who cleared them all with plenty of room to spare.

Worst of all, Truck feared this was just the beginning. He wondered if a bull's-eye was painted where his heart was supposed to be. If so, this woman was going places he really didn't want her going.

Mercifully, Cush decided to let him off the hook when it came time to order dessert. She changed the subject and asked instead about fishing.

But as Truck looked between the half-melted glowing yellow candles and across at the ice cream-spooning redhead, the good part of all this discomfort was that Cush was, after all, just being Cush. She was blunt and direct when she spoke with everyone, not just him. She wasn't mean—she simply didn't mince words or beat around the bush whenever she thought of something she wanted to say. Cush spoke directly; she spoke to be understood.

Even in class, her accent and looks put a soft-hearted spin on things—like ripping apart a classmate's logic or dismissing an American tradition like baseball. Baseball was a silly waste of time, she said, like dreadful cricket where one player must dress like a lobster in order to play.

Truck, who loved the sport, couldn't help but laugh at the seriousness of her words. She had opinions, Cush did, and was never shy to share them. If Cush thought Truck was running from something, then she was confidently matter-of-fact about saying so.

After dessert and fresh-brewed coffee, the pair adjourned the Serbian Crown and drove a few miles down Route 7 to a big amusement complex in Reston. The Family Fun Center had everything, it seemed—everything except darts.

"Thank God," thought Truck as they entered the giant high-ceilinged game room. "Maybe I can reestablish my dignity."

Fat chance.

Cushla proceeded to whip Truck at every game they played. She beat him at air hockey by scores of 7-2, 7-1, and 7-0. Then she beat him at foosball—the table soccer game where you twist the handles to make the men spin around and kick the rolling ball—by scores of 8-4, 8-1, and 8-2. Truck took a short-lived 1-0 lead in game two and then got blitzed with an eight-goal barrage so furious in its action that it seemed like Cush had 25 miniature soccer balls rocketing around simultaneously. Cush had one four-goal run where Truck never could twist the right handle quick enough to swing his man around and kick the ball.

After foosball, Cush won three straight games of 8-ball. Pool was never Truck's strongest sport and he failed to sink more than two balls in any one game. This proved not too surprising since Cush twice ran the table.

Finally, Truck decided to try his luck at skee-ball. Skee-ball was a game parents often played with their children because they could easily defeat the children while telling the kids how great they played. It was so easy, any moron could compete.

Skee-ball was simple: You rolled a hard little wooden ball the size of a shot put down an alleyway with a ramped lip at the end. The lip caused the rolled ball to pop up in the air. The ball then typically landed inside one of five decreasingly smaller circles. The circles awarded points based on the size of the oval. The littlest circle—the smallest and farthest away from the lip—earned 50 points. The next four ovals decreased in points from 40, 30, 20, to 10. If you were a really lousy aim and somehow managed to miss the giant sized ten-point circle for a gutter ball, well, you got what you deserved, which was zero.

There were nine balls in skee-ball, with total points plainly displayed on a lighted scoreboard odometer atop the back of the skee-ball machine.

Truck lasted exactly one game. Cush and Truck played side by side with, at his insistence, Cush going first. "Ladies before gentlemen," he said. "Forever and always." So, Cush rolled first and they alternated from there.

After one ball, it was 50 to 10. After two balls, it was 100 to 30. After three balls it was 150 to 40.

After nine balls, the final score was 450 to 130. Cushla Wimsett rolled the first perfect game in the history of the Family Fun Center.

When her last "50" dropped in the hole and the score registered on the overhead scoreboard, bells rang, yellow emergency lights whirled around, and Cush jumped up and down, clapping and screaming with joy.

Packed in all around her was a boisterous crowd of 50 or 60 other customers who milled around, cheering and hollering like they'd just seen Don Larsen's 97-pitch perfect game in the fifth game of the 1956 World Series.

Truck buried his chin in his chest and slumped his shoulders like Willie Loman near the end of "Death of a Salesman." He wasn't just getting beaten at things; he was getting pulverized.

Cushla was awarded her pick of any stuffed animal in the house and selected a giant pink bunny rabbit. It was a mutant thing, nearly six feet tall with long floppy ears and black eyes. She immediately handed it to Truck so he could carry it around and pretend he'd won it.

The rest of the evening consisted of driving go-karts, then hitting plastic yellow baseballs in the batting cage. The go-karts were predictable enough—Cushla passed Truck and waved with her right hand in the air, tweedling her fingers as she zoomed by. Truck could also see the damn bunny ears flying in the wind, since Cush had taken the rabbit with her when she loaded into her cart.

As humbled as Truck was, his dignity was slightly restored in the batting cage. Cush couldn't hit fastballs and he could, so he took her into the fastest of the three speeds the cages offered. The ball came in around 80 miles an hour and Cush never touched one. Truck got a piece of every pitch, popping up a couple, hitting a few grounders, and smacking a few solid line drives.

"How do you do that?" asked Cush. "Show me. Teach me. Please?"

No harm in that, thought Truck. So he bought a few more tokens, had Cush step back inside the cage, and called in instructions. "Remember: You need to do four things. First, keep your head still. Second, keep your hands back. Third, keep your front shoulder closed."

"Head still. Hands back. Shoulder closed," she parroted. "What's the fourth?"

"Watch the ball hit the bat."

"Watch the ball hit the bat," she repeated. "Got it."

With that, Truck slid two tokens into the machine, the lights turned on, the hard-dimpled yellow plastic baseballs slid down a chute into the pitching machine and gunned another fastball. Cush missed again. Then she missed again, again and again.

"Will you help me, please?" she called out to Truck as the fifth pitch whizzed by her bat and thudded against the green mat hanging behind the plate where the umpire would be.

"OK," said Truck. He stepped inside the cage, placed the rabbit against the backstop fence, stood behind Cushla, wrapped his arms and body around hers, and gripped the bat with both big hands overlapping hers. She backed her butt flush against

Truck's front, then wiggled. He assumed that was her way of digging into the plate and he really liked it.

Truck pulled the bat up and back, waited for the ball to be pitched, and made a wood-chopping hack down and through the strike zone. They hit the ball solidly and whistled a line drive right back at the pitching machine. Cush squealed with delight. She had hit a ball from that silly game of baseball.

The two were missed the next pitch and it smashed the stuffed rabbit right in the face. Truck and Cush hit grounders on the last couple of pitches and when the indicator light shut off to signify the round was over, he quickly stepped back and away. Standing together seemed awkward—like dancing after the music stopped playing. He didn't want her confusing batting practice with intimacy.

Truck was partly relieved and partly disappointed when Cush didn't make a big deal out of his standoffishness. "C'mon," she said nonchalantly. "I'm thirsty. Let's get a soda and head back. I have a busy school day tomorrow. Mean teacher, you know."

"Monster," Truck said. "Ogre, is what I hear from the buzz at the break station."

"They're saying it there, too?" asked Cush innocently. "I thought it was just in the cafeteria.

"Don't forget my bunny," she said. "Poor bunny," she cooed, smothering the bunny with kisses. The rabbit had a dirt bruise under his right eye. It looked just like a shiner. Either the ball gave it to him or Truck did.

Friday was a school day and Truck had a rule never to show up unprepared. As Cush bought the lemonades, a glance at his watch told him it was time to go.

She handed him both drinks and flipped a quarter high in the air. "Call it," Cush said as it tumbled end over end back down toward her open right palm. "If I win," Cush said as the coin was in the air, "you have to take me to the airport tomorrow. If you win, I'll take the bus."

"Uh-oh," Truck thought. "Here we go again." Competitively speaking, he wanted to win. But losing wouldn't be so bad either.

"Tails," he called as Cush slapped the hidden coin flat on the back of her hand.

Without looking, Cush confidently pulled her hand away. "Heads," she said to Truck. "I never throw tails. Twelve full revolutions. Easy to do if you practice. Take a look."

He bent over and looked. When he squinted closely at the quarter, he swore he saw George Washington wink. Heads it was. Truck just shook his head and took a sip of lemonade. He'd battled this girl for two hours and couldn't even win a coin flip. But, deep down, he was glad the Truck Roberts Airport Shuttle Company would be in business Friday afternoon.

Fifteen minutes later, as Truck drove slowly along the winding campus road, the headlights of his car washed across the distant images of several deer feeding undisturbed in the open grassy meadow.

He pulled up and parked outside Cush's residence building in the central plaza's circular drop-off area. Truck didn't know what to do or say. Cush spared him the stuttering uncertainty of spitting out something lame or stupid. He was grateful she chose not to begin another emotional track meet in his head. It was crowded enough already.

Smiling ear to ear, Cush simply held up her right hand and waved in a "toodle-oo" farewell finger roll. "Lovely," she chirped. "A lovely evening.

"See you tomorrow, Man on the Run," she added cheerfully as she hopped out of the car. The mutant bunny was clutched in a headlock under her right arm. Cush was four strides gone before Truck could even protest his new nickname.

Suddenly she stopped, pivoted, returned to the car, and stuck her head back inside the still-rolled-down passenger window. "Man on the Run," she asked sweetly, "can we go for a run around the property tomorrow after class? After all, we'll have plenty of time since you'll be driving me to the airport anyway."

"Sure," Truck said. "After class." He smiled weakly and "toodle-ooed" her back. Truck then watched Cush walk the 40 yards to the residence hall door, silent with his thoughts. When she was out of sight, he started up the car again and drove the 15 minutes home. He went straight to bed, emotionally exhausted.

Truck was sound asleep by eleven-thirty. He dreamed of Cush—especially the way she kept digging her firm, wiggling self deeper and deeper into the batter's box.

$\mathcal{N}$ever Run After Work

Friday's final day of class was typically uneventful. With no major projects remaining, the morning session was a review of the week's earlier work that ate up the clock from eight until a coffee break at 10 o'clock. Then, from break until the lunch hour, Truck reviewed how the material they'd covered during the week fit into the specific strategic directions the company was planning to take.

He also reminded the students that what they took away from the week and applied in their territories was really up to them— that the class was designed to help them win the deals they were supposed to win, and some of the ones they were supposed to lose. That, he said, was the hallmark of a professional salesperson.

And with that message, just as the second hand on the big black Hamilton wall clock joined the hour and minute hands at "12," Truck Roberts pulled the plug on this class. Just one more to go, he thought.

The students scattered and Truck was free either to decompress or turn the room around and prepare for his final week of teaching.

The set-up could wait. He chose to read the paper and relax.

Cush arrived back at the classroom for their afternoon run promptly at one o'clock. Truck had already changed and was poring over the sports section of the *Washington Post*, spread wide across his desk, when she unlatched the classroom door and stepped inside.

"Whoa!!" he thought as he gave her a subtle up-and-down visual once-over, "She looks *good*."

Cush studied him quickly, too. "He looks good," she decided. "Nice powerful thighs and well-defined, muscular calves. Better than I'd expected."

As they left the classroom, Truck flipped out the lights. He couldn't help but look at Cush's posterior, which featured a muscular roundness—an athletic roundness—nicely accentuated by a pair of form-fitting black running tights. He winced and mindlessly bit the bent knuckle of his right index finger in mock hunger. Cush looked good from all angles, he decided. A very beautiful woman. He remembered thinking that even back in Auckland when she was hidden under all her green hair and pierced ornaments.

Truck was in pretty good shape, but Cush ran like an Ellerslie steeplechase champion. The two didn't talk much as they found a comfortable running rhythm.

Truck decided to take her on his secret tour. In the two years he had run the property, he'd come to know every hillock, stream, and honeysuckle patch tucked inside the kaleidoscopic corners of the flowering acreage.

When he wanted to, Truck could run the property for over an hour without seeing anyone or being seen himself. This seemed like a good day to prove it, and off they went, downhill toward the Potomac. The pair looped down a terraced slope behind the cafeteria and cut over to a walking trail that headed a half-mile down to Goose Creek. Goose Creek was a 30-yard-wide stream whose mouth exhaled into the Potomac.

There pair followed the trail as it gently arced to the right and meandered southeast along the mighty Potomac River. The Potomac flowed past the length of the property, then menadered ten miles farther down before tumbling down a scenic spillover called Great Falls.

Rich people lived there on million-dollar estates.

From there, the famous river curled another 15 miles or so to and through Washington, D.C. and past the famed cherry blossom trees lining its banks. It eventually mixed into the brackish water of the gaping Chesapeake Bay.

Truck wished the Potomac was cleaner, and more clear, but said nothing as he huffed to keep up with Cushla's fast, effortless, and easy-breathing strides. His footsteps were heavy. Hers barely crinkled the fallen leaves.

They wove along the banks of the Potomac for nearly two miles before veering onto a faint trail Cush didn't see. Truck knew it was there because he'd cut the trail with his own big feet during the two years he'd run the place. Looping through hundreds of dogwoods and other flowering trees that he didn't know by name, they emerged near a small pond, three acres in size, tucked inside a well-hidden clearing. Truck guessed several types of ducks and geese would be sitting on the pond waiting to greet them.

Truck was right. Cushla loved the colorful birds. Wildlife in America differed from wildlife in New Zealand and she saw exciting discoveries in seemingly the most simple of American things.

Cushla had never seen a squirrel close up, for example, or a fox. She saw both of them seconds later as the trail merged into an old, abandoned logging road. There before them, in the center of the overgrown logging road, stood a red fox—frozen motionless with a freshly killed gray squirrel clenched between its teeth.

Cushla shuddered and let out a gasp, stopping nearly in place. Truck stopped also, but gently said, "Out here, all of the animals live together. It's part of the natural order."

"Tell that to the poor little thing's mother!" exclaimed Cushla, still alarmed at the sight of the fox and squirrel.

The fox had dinner plans and scooted off into a thicket. The pair resumed running along the old logging road, hopping from time to time over fallen trees and dodging mud puddles where possible. Truck loved cross-country running—far more than pounding the pavement—and Cushla felt the same. There was something extraordinarily peaceful about the muted silence of their footfalls, the rhythmic sounds of inhaling and exhaling, and the childlike joy of hopping over trees or skirting puddles—or choosing to splash down into one if they simply felt like it.

A few minutes later, the pair came to a paved road, the main entry drive bisecting the school property, and they had to cross it. With luck, no one would see them. Truck sometimes even hid in the tree line, waiting for cars to pass so others wouldn't learn about the faintly marked trail he was running. Sometimes a man simply wanted to be left alone—alone with his problems and worries, his thoughts and ideas.

No cars were in sight, so both quickly hopped across, accelerating like eager young drivers punching the gas at a stale yellow light. Ten strides on the other side put them behind a honeysuckle thicket and invisible again. The two slowed down and rhythmically ran on, heading toward one of Truck's favorite spots.

He had found the wild turkeys center on one of his very first exploratory runs during a misting rain a month or two after arriving at the center. Truck typically left the wary birds alone because he didn't want to scare them away from this safe, secluded locale that provided food and shelter.

Truck said nothing to Cushla, thinking that if the turkeys were there, she'd be thrilled to discover them herself. And if they weren't there, he wouldn't look like a loutish know-nothing for saying they would.

But, the turkeys *were* there, six in all—four hens and a pair of 20-pound toms with six-inch beards. Cush and Truck stayed 100 yards wide of the wary birds and Cush's eyes stayed glued to them with every stride.

She said nothing but etched the memory of each one deep in her mind. Cush also spied a lone skunk trundling along about 30 yards on the far side of the biggest tom. Cush recognized the skunk from pictures and reputation, and silently pointed to it as they ran by. Later, Truck told her it was probably a female searching for food since the approaching springtime soon would mean a litter of baby skunks.

Truck just smiled and kept running. They had about 15 minutes to go and just ahead was a meadow field. Another surprise awaited there.

The Meadow

The hardwood trees that protected the turkeys near the lowland soon gave way to a gentle terrain rise and a ring of mature pines that encircled a large open field of wind-waving meadow grass. The grass, between knee and hip high, swayed back and forth like a Kansas wheat field.

Deer came here for two reasons—to graze and to sleep. At any given time, this 80-acre meadow might host anywhere between ten and 50 deer. When spooked, the deer bounded away, white-tailed flags raised, bobbing away from danger through the high thick grass before choosing a spot and quickly lying down to hide out of sight.

The only meadow trail was around its perimeter. Truck didn't like the perimeter trail nearly as much as simply running several hundred yards right through the middle of the high grasses toward the distant tree line on the opposite side. That route normally spooked the deer resting in the grasses ahead, and Truck chose that route on this excursion.

Halfway through the meadow, Cushla suddenly hollered, went down hard, grabbed her right ankle, and rolled around in tremendous pain. She had a sprain, a bad one, and worse—maybe a broken ankle.

Truck stopped immediately and rushed over, trying to comfort Cush as she thrashed from side to side in the waist-high grass. He had sprained his ankle dozens of times during his basketball days and knew how much it hurt. One time he even got hurt during a called time-out, and, as far as Truck knew, he was *still* the only player in basketball history to actually break an ankle while the coach was drawing a play on a clipboard. He didn't plan to share this small bit of personal history.

Well versed with bum ankles, Truck gently grabbed her smooth fibula and looked at her ankle. It looked fine. No swelling, no puffiness. He'd never seen a sprain or break where nothing swelled before and saw no sign of skin discoloration.

Cush leaned back in the meadow grass and looked at Truck expectantly. There, before Truck's eyes, was the fantasy and dream of every man's life. Softly, Cush looked at him—and *through* him—with her penetrating green eyes. She looked through his eyes, past that hanging little boxing bag uvula in his throat, past his trachea, around the horn at his spleen, and directly down into his shorts, which were suddenly getting very crowded.

Slowly, expectantly, Cush licked her lips and pouted them open just a fraction. She held both arms out to him.

Truck then did what every noble, gentlemanly, red-blooded American male *should* do. He leaned down, let her wrap both her arms around his neck, drew her close, and picked her up sideways in a powerful cradle lift. He then set her gently down onto her good foot and helped her hobble the final mile back to the dorm.

Truck knew Cush wasn't hurt. And he also knew she'd never give him the satisfaction of admitting it. So, Cush pretended she really *did* have a sprain and fake-limped all the way back to her residence hall. He helped her every step of the way, letting her lean on his shoulder and hop along, one step at a time. It takes a long time to hop a mile, especially when you're faking it.

Back at the dorm, Truck waited in the common sitting area while Cush showered and changed for the ride to the airport. It was a 20-minute drive to Dulles and they still had plenty of time. He brought the car around so she wouldn't have far to fake-limp.

Cush didn't say much on the drive to the airport, opting instead to stare out of the window and pretend to see the scenery. Inside, she was embarrassed beyond belief. Humiliated. Had her ploy worked and she'd seduced him as intended, it would've been the sex that fantasies and carved-in-stone lifetime memories are made of. Instead, she felt hurt and insulted that Truck ignored and rejected her advances.

Meanwhile, Truck's own cerebral tug-of-war raged between his uneven sideburns. His conscience and penis-motor were having a full-grunt, heels-dug-in, muscles-strained skirmish. No, it actually wasn't a skirmish. It was closer to a World War of disagreement.

The noble half of his brain congratulated him on being such a gentleman.

The horny (regular male) half of his brain screamed how in hell he could *ever* be so stupid not to plug into that girl like a runaway jackhammer when she obviously wanted him to.

Cush hadn't just delivered herself on a silver platter. Hell, it seemed like a diamond-encrusted *platinum* platter. And what did he do? He looked at her like she was 105 pounds of heroin and the cops were knockin' at the door, that's what. He had panicked.

Truck's noble rational chalked it off as another student trying to "do" the teacher—an impersonal physical act, rather than a personal, emotional act. In doing so, he chose to typecast a girl who was uniquely singular at everything she did, though Jeffrey Franklin Cushla Wimsett would never live long enough to deserve to be typecast as anything.

This girl was one of a kind and Truck's heart knew that.

His head said otherwise. Hence the battle.

"You did the right thing," said his Noble Brain. "She's just a tease—a student tease. She doesn't care about you. She just wanted a notch on her belt to cap off her American vacation."

Macho Brain, meanwhile, had other thoughts. *"YOU INSIPID MORON!"* it shouted. "What the *hell* were you thinkin'?

"Every man on the planet would kill for a shot at this and here you had it—room service, baby, room *service!*

"And you *blew it!* You are *HOPELESS!* You are *pa-thetic!* You are a *Loser* with a capital letter L twice the size of one in the HOLLYWOOD sign overlooking Beverly Hills!"

So, as the war raged on between Noble Brain and Macho Brain, Truck Roberts drove to Dulles Airport, carefully following the speed limit. He, too, pretended to look at the scenery. Yet, through the silence, two separate three-ring circuses were running helter-skelter under the Big Tops of a man and a woman's crowded craniums. Each hosted a sell-out crowd of emotional confusion.

Once Truck looped off the main highway onto the Dulles Access Road and toward the departure terminal, he decided it was best for both to do a quick curbside check-in and make a hasty farewell. Truck wanted a quick getaway—much like a deer flagging its tail into the hopping invisibility of waving meadow grass.

As if trying to minimize his stupidity—or add to it—when Truck got out and Cush was getting her things together, he popped his Louis Armstrong album out of the car stereo and shoved it into its plastic case. He dropped in a business card, too. And on the back of the card he hurriedly scrawled nine capital letters: "MWYADAETM." This time he wrote "XO" and signed his name.

When Cush was fake-hobbling like a flamingo at the curbside check-in counter showing her tickets to the baggage clerk, he unzipped her travel bag's side pocket and slid the plastic album case inside. Just after Truck rezipped her bag, Cush turned with a look of clinical fatigue and said, "International flight. I can't check my bags here. I must go inside." Truck peeled off three bucks for the porter to carry her bags since he couldn't leave the car unattended.

They awkwardly shook hands goodbye and Cush fake-limped her way inside the automatic doors, waving off the porter's offer to get her a wheelchair.

"Gotta give her credit," Truck smiled admiringly. "She's keeping up the con right to the end."

With that, Truck climbed into his car and drove back to school. He wanted to set up for his next class—his final class—before heading home. He'd go do it to stay busy.

Deep down, he was unhappy to see Cush leave.

And while Truck drove back to work for a couple more hours, out on the Dulles tarmac a jumbo 747 headed for Los Angeles waited patiently in the takeoff queue. The attractive redhead in 28A stared out the window and saw nothing. Tears welled up in her eyes, but she held them back.

Cush stared out that window during the entire one-hour runway delay, then finally dozed off, mouth half-open, shortly after the jumbo jet finally rumbled through takeoff and pointed its black-coned nose west.

Truck, meanwhile, found Party Patti setting up her room when he return to his classroom. He went over and told her all about what soon became known as "The Meadow Incident."

"You did *what?*" Patti cried incredulously. "Are you *nuts?* You've gone mad!

"No man turns it down! Oh my God, Truck. You've got to get out of this place! It's gotten to you! It's finally happened—this fruitcake factory has driven you *totally* insane."

Thus reassured he'd done the right thing, the noble thing, Truck Roberts staggered next door and robotically resumed setting up his classroom.

Cush was so upset and so confused, she called Mitzi from the airport in Auckland and told her what happened.

"He's obviously gay," said Mitzi. "No man turns it down. *Ever.* It's not you, honey," she said, intently. "It's him. Gay boy. Gotta be. Got to *be.*"

"That's what I wondered about," said Cush. "But I don't think he's gay. He tried too hard at all the games I beat him in. He even gave my stuffed bunny a black eye."

"Well," said Mitzi. "Even if he's not gay, he's certainly not normal. And trust me—there are a million more men out there, and at least four dozen are normal.

"Forget the screwy American. We need to find you a normal one."

And, as things turned out on both sides of the wide, wide Pacific, The Meadow Incident would haunt both of their lives for a long, *long* time.

*T*idal Wave in Daytona

Truck danced through his final class, waved goodbye to the training center, and moved back to South Florida. His reentry into town marked a do-over as far as women were concerned. He settled into a familiar corporate role as a sole contributor—a salesman—and enjoyed the peace of mind that controlling his own destiny provided.

But outside of the office, Truck's ineptitude with women seemed to prove that while he was in D.C. all he really learned about the opposite sex was a whole lot of nothing. And every passing month, he seemed to understand less about women than the month before. Women weren't like car engines, or keeping an aquarium, or cooking perfect ribs on the barbecue grill. There wasn't a flow chart, schematic diagram, or documented procedure to understand them.

Nope. At times, understanding a woman seemed harder than taking med school exams while on psychedelic mushrooms. Truck never understood what they thought and rarely what they meant. They spoke in Girlese—a foreign tongue to modern man.

For example, when a woman spoke, Truck thought she meant her words literally. He learned the hard way that literal translation only applied to one specific phrase in the English language—the most dreaded combination of six terrifying one-syllable words a man could possibly hear—the heinous and dastardly "I like you as a friend."

Those nine vowels and eight consonants marked the death knell of more romances than Americans who've made toilet stops at McDonald's. In each case, the numbers were like the sign at the Golden Arches: Billions and Billions Served. And when it came to relationships, men everywhere would rather take a booming round of double-barreled salt pellets in the each butt cheek than hear the words "I like you as a friend."

When uttered by a woman, that damning phrase was nothing more than a shorthand way of saying "I can do better than you. Now beat it. Get lost. Get out of my face."

And Truck Roberts, it seemed, led the entire heterosexual planet in women friends. He had platoons of them. Squadrons. Entire high-heeled, well-perfumed armies. Rows and rows like the legions of Terra Cotta Warriors in Xi An, China.

Nearly every woman Truck ever dated segued into friendship during or after the first date and one day he just got flat-out fed up with it and phoned his pal Ben for advice. Ben loved women every single hour of every single day. He thought Truck recently hit the mother lode of golden goodness at the bank and should keep mining it. After all, just because four tellers in a row dumped him, at least they agreed to go out.

Ben said guys needed a key vertical industry for dating. He chased waitresses; another buddy ran wild through hairdressers; Mountain did well with convenience store clerks. Shoot, thought Truck, maybe Ben was right. Maybe bank tellers really *were* his destiny.

He called Party Patti and asked for her view.

She thought the banking thing was nonsense, that Truck's biggest problem focused on his admitted inability to "communicate."

There it was again. The dreaded c-word. Most men would choose a colonoscopy by a blind med student before voluntarily spilling their guts to a girl and "communicating."

Next to the annoying phenomenon that women never, *ever*, forget *anything* said to them, the dreaded c-word was man's second greatest enemy. Becoming "a friend" was a close third.

"You have to learn to *com-mu-ni-cate*," Patti explained slowly, as if Truck were a remedial student hearing the word for the first time. "If you can't learn to *com-mu-ni-cate*, you'll *always* be a slug."

"Communicate. Right. Gotcha. Will do," he replied with a touch of mock and lot of frustration. "How the hell do I communicate? What I say they don't hear and what they say they don't mean. What's a guy supposed to do?"

"Give me an example," said Patti. "Give me an example of what you're talking about."

"No problem, no problem. How much time you got? A few days?" Truck jabbed piggishly. "Here's a few. I get these all of the time. 'How do I look?' is one. And another favorite is 'Oh, I'm not really that hungry.' Or 'You're a really nice guy.'"

Patti cut him off there. She already had plenty to work with. "Truck," she said, "a woman communicates *between* the words, between the lines. When a woman asks you how she looks, there is only one answer and that answer is 'great, terrific, beautiful.'

"The question is intended to validate something she already knows. If she didn't already know the answer, she'd never bother asking about herself in the first place.

"And, oh! If a girl asks you how she looks, "*Thin*" is always an acceptable answer, too.

"Oh. One other thing. If a woman says she's not hungry and you know she really *is* hungry, obviously she'd like to go somewhere nice for dinner. Somewhere special."

"Special is girlese for *expensive*, right?" clarified Truck. "Somewhere the waiter's dressed better than me, right?"

"Certainly," said Patti. "Who doesn't enjoy going to a nice restaurant? Don't be such a tightwad.

"The nicer the restaurant, the smaller the portions. The smaller the portions, the more apt your date is to feel content at the end of dinner.

"I know this will come as a big surprise, Truck, but most women don't like that big, distended, triple-bacon-cheeseburger and chili cheese fries bloated-stomach feeling that men so valiantly worship and love to wash down with beer.

"And who knows? If you take her somewhere nice, well, maybe she won't end the evening by just shaking hands and telling you what a nice guy you are."

"Yeah, what's up with that?" asked Truck. "What's up with the 'nice guy' thing?"

"Would you rather be called a nerd? Or a loser? Or a flatliner? Or a flawed human being?

"Women are different than men. When we say something designed to get rid of you, we always say it nicely first. Subtly.

"If you're too slow or thick-headed to get the message, then we have to resort to more male-like terms. And if you still don't get it, then we tell you we like you as a friend. That one usually does the trick."

"What about the three little words?" Truck asked.

"Oh, women love to hear the three little words," Patti said. "All the time. Especially if, by some freak of nature, you're not drunk and naked at the time."

"Not *those* three little words," Truck said. "Not the three they want to *hear*. . . the three they always *say*."

"And they are?"

"'Maybe another time.' Or 'Let's be friends.' Or 'I'm seeing someone.' Even worse, the dreaded 'I have plans.'"

"Bitter little toad today, aren't we?" replied Patti.

"How would *you* feel if you called a women and her reason for not going was that her library book was due in a few days?"

"Ooh. That *is* a bad one. When did that happen?"

"Nine minutes ago, give or take. Right before I called you."

"Call her back," advised Patti.

"Call her back?" asked Truck. "Why should I call her back?"

"Cause. I wanna read that book. Find out what it is."

"You're a big help," said Truck. "Thanks a ton."

"Any time, sweetie. You know the number. Good luck. And remember: *Com-mu-ni-cate!* Care. Share. Whisper. The more fun you are to talk to, the more likely she'll keep you around to listen to, since all women *love* hearing about themselves."

A week later, Truck took Patti's advice about communicating. He called up Ben again and told him to meet at the Lauderdale Hooters so they could crunch some delicious charred-beyond-recognition chicken wings—wings as tender and chewy as bituminous coal and served by buxom dumplings stuffed in happy little orange nylon shorts.

Truck also wanted to discuss potential female communication strategies like Patti suggested.

It was there, only three wings into a strategy session at table four, that the duo hatched their grand plan. They would hold a contest—their very own contest—to help meet girls.

They called it "The Perfect 10."

The Perfect 10 would be a selfishly designed competition targeting girls whose combined shoe size and school grade point average added up to, well, a perfect 10.

Since Ben and Truck were attracted to polar extremes when it came to girls, the fellows figured The Perfect 10 strategy would enable them both to meet the kind of girls they liked. Truck, for example, preferred really smart girls—the smarter the better. Small was good, too. So he figured a high GPA and small feet were a good combo.

Ben was the opposite. He loved legs, the longer the better, and always believed the prettiest girls were the ones generally found on the left half of the educational bell curve. So a tall goddess on academic probation suited him just fine.

The guys spent over $500—most of it Truck's—on a dozen radio spots and one small newspaper ad. They spent another $1,000, again most of it Truck's, on prizes.

The "Perfect 10 Citywide Search," as they called it, was held in North Miami Beach at Aventura Mall late on a Saturday afternoon. A radio station even came down to do a remote, since the event had caught on with its listeners. Some people loved the contest, others wanted to protest, saying it was chauvinistic and demeaning to women, to which Ben replied on air, "If it's bad for women, then why are we giving them prizes just so we can meet them?"

Truck winced. But Ben's answer stumped the protester who immediately agreed that if men around the world did the same thing—gave gifts to strange women for no logical reason at all—then the world would, indeed, be a much better place. Especially when such kindness took place at the mall.

Well, thanks to the radio hype, when the appointed Saturday rolled around, the guys ended up with 42 entrants. The oldest was 57. The youngest was nine. Neither made the finals.

From this smiling prison lineup, they whittled the group first to ten semifinalists, then five finalists. Then the guys made a tactical blunder. Since the audience for this event was raucous and large, numbering upward of 300, the guys decided to let the audience vote for the winner and runner-up. They would choose the winner on noise, cheers, and applause from the masses.

"That was a bad move," said Ben later.

"We have no one to blame but ourselves," said Truck. "We didn't do enough homework on the front end."

The Perfect 10, as voted by the crowd, was a big-footed pygmy who flunked out of school. She even brought papers to prove it. The runner-up was a goddess, a leggy blonde model on academic probation named Kitten.

Ironically, The Perfect 10 Citywide Search was one of the few contests held in malls anywhere across the great United States in which the grand prize was a $25 gift certificate to Dillard's department store while the runner-up received an all-expense-paid trip to the Bahamas.

Unfortunately for the fellows, Kitten's boyfriend took time off from work and joined her for the relaxing fruits of the leggy blonde's second-place finish. The happy couple even sent a thank you postcard from their three-day, two-night holiday sexathon at the Atlantis resort on Paradise Island.

Both Ben and Truck ended up briefly dating a couple of girls from the contest, but the relationships fizzled like sparklers in the rain.

Truck felt more discouraged than Ben. He liked brains. Smarts were the ultimate aphrodisiac, which seemed odd since they'd used *his* money and none of Ben's to fund the entire promotion.

Handing over the championship trophy to a fat-footed midget who'd placed her hand on Truck's butt when the newspaper photographer clicked a picture didn't help, either.

To Ben, on the other hand, brains meant nothing. A demonstrated ability to inhale and exhale was his sole requirement. So even though the contest didn't work out the way they drew it up, its disappointing result was no big deal to him. After all, he got on the radio and in the newspaper. And it wasn't even his money.

A month later the two guys said the hell with finesse and decided to drive north to the famed yellow-brick-road of least resistance: Daytona at Spring Break. The place would be flooded with college girls from every state in the nation.

"If we can't find somebody here," Truck said as he wheeled to a halt in front of their oceanfront hotel, "we're pathetic."

Ben said nothing. There was nothing to add. The Father of the Meadow Incident had just uttered the Mantra of Ultimate Truth. For in Daytona, even the hopeless had hope.

The boys proceeded to go on a weekend bender and ended up in a loud beer joint late at night with two deaf girls, both seniors from Gallaudet College in Washington, D.C. To the fellows, it was loud. To the girls it was, well, just normal. A nice place to sit around and sign.

After they crudely drew some artwork on cheap paper napkins, the guys learned the girls were camping in a tent outside of town. Gallantly, they offered them eighth-floor oceanfront accommodations at no charge.

The party adjourned to the hotel. From there, Ben and his girl went for a romantic stroll along drunk-strewn Daytona Beach. Truck, meanwhile, sat outside on the eighth-floor balcony next to his date. They said nothing. They simply sat there and watched the distant waves roll in, slither back out, then roll back in again.

Truck decided to make his move. He faked a yawn and put his arm around her shoulder. She didn't resist, so he leaned over, kissed her, and slid his hand inside her shirt.

She still didn't resist. "I love Daytona," Truck thought as he gently caressed her soft skin. It was a long drive here but, dammit, it was worth it.

Suddenly, a massive tidal wave thundered down from above. Truck thought it was a tsunami. So did the girl, but she didn't know how to sign "tsunami."

The floodwaters quickly receded and careful investigation proved it was not a tidal wave but was the official end of a ninth-floor keg party. The frat guys above had lugged their tub of melted ice over to the railing and tipped it over—showering Truck and the deaf girl before the pair had even a clue what was going on.

The sudden wall of frigid water crashing on her terrified the girl. Her loud, wailing guttural deaf yell terrified *everybody*, especially Truck and the guys upstairs.

All the guys upstairs heard was a loud, mournful, bloodcurdling wail and, from the sound of it, figured some girl downstairs was being strangled by a psycho who could come up and finish them off next. So, they called hotel security and security called the cops. Two minutes later, just as Ben and his girl returned from their kissy-faced beach stroll, two policemen and three hotel people piled into the same very same elevator and everybody pushed button eight.

When the elevator doors slid open at the eighth floor, everybody tried to pile back out through the doors at the same time, too.

Something was obviously wrong, but Ben and his girl didn't have a clue what. Ironically, everybody thundered down the long hallway together. They all plowed to a halt at the end of the hall in front of Room 824.

Ben gaped at his date with untrusting suspicion while his date looked at him and put up her dukes. The cops pounded furiously on Truck's door, yelling, "This is the police! Open up!" They had drawn their guns and were waving them high in the air.

The agitated arrival of the local constabulary clearly put a romantic damper on the rest of the evening. The deaf girls got the hell out as soon as they could.

Ben's even made the crazy loco sign with a loopy finger next to her brain as the two frantically signed their way down the long hallway toward the elevator.

The soaked one with cold breasts pushed the "L" button about 100 times trying to make the doors close faster. And as the metal curtains of the elevator doors drew shut, the wet girl also gave Truck a defiant farewell salute. He stood in the hall, mouth open and speechless, and wondered where the girl had learned to sign in Italian.

So much for Daytona.

Well, things got worse for Truck before they got better. A few months after Daytona, he spied a pretty woman shopping in the grocery store and, on the spur of the moment, decided to take Party Patti's advice and communicate.

He chased the girl criss-cross down several aisles. The woman had a wobbly wheel on her cart, so Truck could listen for her when she accidentally lost him several different times in a row. He finally used a reverse-the-cart-backtrack maneuver and cornered her in Frozen Foods.

Remembering what Party Patti had said, Truck boldly told the girl how pretty she was, how he'd like to get to know her, and the entire rest of his pathetic life story and past relationships before he even asked her name.

He missed nothing that might terrorize a woman who'd rather not be trapped by a live turkey next to a frozen one and it certainly didn't help a whole lot that Truck pinned her against an open-top console freezer where pointy clusters of king crab legs jabbed her repeatedly in the derriere as he moved closer and closer.

Truck communicated that he wanted her phone number. "Glad to meet you, Trixie," he said, sticking out his right hand to shake hers while holding her scribbled phone number in his left. "I'm Truck. Truck Roberts. I'll call ya. We'll have a great time! I just know it!"

Unfortunately, the sheer excitement of the moment caused Trixie to write down the wrong phone number on the little scrap of paper. Truck tried it four different times and got the "this call cannot be completed as dialed" recording every time. He thought Trixie might be dyslexic so he dialed the last four digits in various combinations. There were 24 combinations and he irritated 24 different people. Finally, Truck called Party Patti for suggestions.

Patti told him the girl gave him a bum number to get rid of him and he was lucky she didn't spray him with mace. And poke him in the eye with a crab leg.

Truck volunteered that maybe he could just hang out at the store for hours on end waiting for her to return.

"She won't go back," Patti predicted. "You polluted the store. Now it's haunted. *HONK! Thanks for playing our game!* The best you can hope for is that she hasn't dyed her hair, sold her house, and moved out of the United States."

But Truck kept plowing forward, one grindstone-nosed day after the next. Patti wondered if Truck ever would find someone for the long haul. She also wasn't convinced that he'd learned a whole lot from the Titanic-sized wreckage of his previous relationship failures. For a smart guy, Patti thought, he sure seemed dumb and a very slow learner.

Patti told Truck several times he seemed to be searching for something without being sure of what he was really looking for. And if *he* wasn't sure what he was looking for, how would he ever know when he found it?

"I'll know," Truck insisted in one of their conversations. "I'll know. It's like art. Ever go into an art gallery looking for something in particular? No. You never do. You go in, look around, and when you see something that's right—you know it. That's what I mean. It's like art."

"It's not like art at all," argued Patti. "Love isn't like buying art. Love is stomachaches and sleepless nights and listening to the words of songs on the radio. It's days apart that last forever and nights together that fly by like jets.

"Love is *not* a signed limited-edition print. And for your sake, you'd better hope for the stomachache because I've seen your taste in art. The only thing your place is missing is a glow-in-the-dark velvet of dogs playing poker."

Patti went on, telling Truck his approach to women—staring them down to make eye contact with every one he saw—reminded her of a "Will Work For Food" guy bumming change on a city street corner. For the umpteenth time, she reminded him to do some deep-down soul searching and decide what he really *was* looking for. If he did, at least then he'd have a snowball's chance of finding it. Right now, she opined loudly, he didn't.

Truck thought carefully about this last piece of advice. Maybe he *did* need to get a better grip on what he hoped to find. In the meantime, though, he stubbornly believed the right one would some day look back.

So Truck kept searching every face he ever passed—the female ones, anyway. He ended up doing laps around the world, never seeing what it was he was looking for. As he continued to struggle, he occasionally thought back to the day in the meadow with Cush. He wondered how she was doing—whether or not she was married. He guessed she was and that she had a baby girl.

Indeed, Truck decided it would be a lot easier to go through life as a girl. Being pursued had to be a hell of a lot better than being the pursuer. Clearly it couldn't be worse.

Three weeks after his latest conversation with Party Patti and fortified by a cranium of fresh advice, Truck Roberts would cross trails with destiny. There, he would have to choose which of those two unmarked trails to travel—the well-worn one or the one less traveled.

It would prove to be a very tough decision.

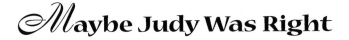
Maybe Judy Was Right

While Bonefish was as happy as a clam at high tide in his role as a Bahamian celebrity, the humans weren't aging nearly so smoothly.

Truck was hardly alone in his dating adventures. Half a world away, there were days, many days when Cushla Wimsett wondered that perhaps American comedienne Judy Tenuta was right: The only reason people date is they're too lazy to commit suicide.

After Cush had returned from her trip to America, she had chalked Truck Roberts off her list of potential suitors and continued her on-again, off-again search for the rarest of all species: A Decent Normal Guy.

Cush normally needed ten minutes or so after meeting someone to decide whether to date him. If she went out with him, within an hour she knew if she'd ever bother seeing him again. Some decisions took less time, but few took longer. Far more missed the cut than made it.

After each failed dating adventure, Cush was more convinced than ever that dating was a lot more trouble than it was worth since every man had one of two redundant flaws—either very bad habits or a warehouse full of emotional baggage. Lots of them hit the "exacta" and had both.

Even Mitzi got her share of misfits. Once she got so exasperated, she called her date "Samsonite." To his *face*. Mitzi told the guy he had more baggage than the whole bloody company. Within five minutes, Samsonite was summarily packed away for good.

Gradually Cush began spending more time in the horse business. Instead of a job or a hobby, it became a life. And for most folks in the industry, it can be no other way.

Within six months of returning to New Zealand, Cush quit her high-paying job with Truck's company. Fed up being chased around the desk by male morons with situational ethics and gin-fueled libidos—men whom refused to acknowledge that a skilled businesswoman could outperform a male counterpart—Cush traded her corporate job for a low-paying one at Takanini, the training track where she helped out back in her school days.

After Cushla's first exposure to horseracing at Ellerslie, the nation's finest racetrack, she quickly fell in love again with the intrinsically unique sights, sounds, and smells of an industry built on two-minute jousting matches of high-wire rider acrobatics. As amazing as the horses were, so were the men and women who rode them. Guiding the thundering hearts and hooves and souls of the determined four-legged athletes required shock absorbers for thighs, calculators for minds, and boundless courage to persevere when a single mis-step could cause paralysis—or worse.

What Cush learned at Ellerslie on race day, and again at Takanini's training facility, was that all great horse people had acquired a well-developed sense of touch with the animals and an eagle eye for detail. The mighty animals never spoke but always left clues—and skilled, ever-vigilant horse people could read them like a newspaper. At least they made it seem that way.

Cush poured a lot of physical and emotional energy into the horses she helped train. She quickly became regarded as a top-flight exercise rider with an astute feel for the individual needs of every horse she worked.

Twice she rode the brilliant filly Sunline, an experience she later told a newspaperman was like riding in a Ferrari. Sunline, like all great racehorses, glided effortlessly. Riding her, Cush couldn't even feel the great champion's hooves touch the ground beneath her as they flew along the backstretch like a sailing yacht with a tailing breeze.

Sunline was a cantankerous thing, but those two sun-streaked dawn workouts provided Cushla with an inner assurance that working in this industry was, in fact, what she was supposed to be doing with her life. Though she was making half as much money, she felt twice as happy. It was a price she cheerfully paid.

All she needed now, she thought, was someone else to share it with.

Unexpectedly, the horses led her directly to him.

A Trip to Karaka

At some point in its life, just about every New Zealand racehorse worth owning walks its way around the tight circle of Karaka's sales ring. Selling bloodstock, especially Thoroughbreds, is a very big industry in little New Zealand.

Being a small country, New Zealand cannot sustain the enormous racing wealth created on some of the planet's most perfect soils. With just three million citizens, New Zealand was a breeding nation first and racing nation a far distant second.

Each late January and early February, New Zealand Bloodstock's Karaka Sales Complex in South Auckland became the center of the Southern Hemisphere racing universe. The nation's top 1,500 Thoroughbred yearlings were vanned in and run through the single ring for inspection before being sold to buyers from all around the world. The vast majority found new owners and left the country.

Most of the horses stayed in the Southern Hemisphere and ended up racing in Australia. Others were shipped to Singapore, Japan, and Hong Kong. A few went even farther—across the globe to Dubai, South Africa, and the United States.

New Zealand was steeped in horseracing tradition and excellence—and had been ever since the brilliant and legendary racehorse Phar Lap was sold under the gavel of New Zealand

Bloodstock's founding company. Since 1927, the industry had continually delivered top-performing racehorses into an increasingly competitive global industry.

Since New Zealand Bloodstock held several auctions each year at Karaka, Cush quickly became immersed in preparing many of the horses for sale. This work took several forms, from riding and fitness preparation of the animal to grooming its showy appearance for the sale ring.

As Cush's connections in the family circle of the industry broadened, she was soon involved with just about every aspect of the business except the buying and selling. To her it was stressful—and one of the biggest reasons she decided to leave the corporate jungle. If she had the money, she'd own every horse and never sell any—not even the slow ones. Cush wanted them all to live happily ever after, whether they could run fast or not.

Since the National Yearling Sales had so many millions of dollars at stake, she routinely put in 16-hour days for months on end helping several breeders prepare their animals. And at her very first premium select sale, Cushla Wimsett made a dramatic entrance to the mesmerizing world of million-dollar horses.

A yearling colt that she prepared and paraded, a grandson of the legendary New Zealand stallion Sir Tristram, brought a cool $1 million at auction. So intent on showing the jet-black beauty, she had no idea what numbers kept flashing and changing high on the big board behind her. But when the gavel fell, Cush looked up at the tote board high on the wall and saw a seven-digit number. Her lips moved as she counted the zeros. When she mouthed the sixth zero and processed the total number—one million dollars—something Karaka had never seen before suddenly took place.

She fainted on the spot. Crumpled to the ground. Out cold. The young colt just stood there, looking down at her like the Tin Man did in "The Wizard of Oz" when Dorothy fell asleep in the big field of poppies just outside of town.

Attendants rushed in, quickly led the colt out of the ring, and tended to Cush. While she was curled motionless in the wood chips, several foreign men began a lighthearted but boisterous bidding war. Her sale price was up to $700,000 when her eyes fluttered back open. As soon as the auctioneer saw she was okay, he good-naturedly pounded down his mallet, and hollered "*Sold! To Bidder 99!*"

Cush looked around and saw no horses. Then she heard everyone laughing and applauding. Making the best of an embarrassing situation, she got a standing ovation as she stood up, dusted herself off, bowed slightly, and politely waved goodbye.

Seeking sanctuary back in the barns, Cush prepped her fillies and colts but opted not to accompany any more back into the ring.

It was during one of the many inspections that prospective bidders often make that Cush met a smartly dressed, good-looking man named Timothy Holden. Timothy was a pinhooker—he speculatively bought and later resold horses to turn a profit. He was also a bloodstock agent, buying for several overseas buyers who trusted him to make their selections and spend their money as if it were his. For a young man of 28, Timothy had become skilled at what he did and earned a sizable living doing it.

After Timothy finished studying the tall bay filly from all angles and reviewing her medical charts and X-rays, he turned to Cush and smiled. "Hello," he said, introducing himself while sticking out his hand. "You won't faint if I buy her, will you?"

"Hello," Cush smiled back sheepishly, shaking his hand firmly. "For a million bucks I might. Please tell me you're not Bidder 99."

Timothy laughed. "No," he said. "I'm not Bidder 99. But I wish I were."

That brief exchange was how Cushla Wimsett met Timothy Holden. Before the end of the day, Timothy had stopped back several more times and the two made plans for dinner that Saturday evening.

Timothy took Cush to Antoine's, considered by many to be Auckland's finest restaurant. She wasn't sure what the final bill totaled, but knew the wine alone cost more than everything Gavin had ever bought her added together, including her rollerblades.

So from that day forward, Cush's life disappeared inside a tightly insulated circle of fast horses and the hustling young horseman, Timothy Holden.

Timothy purchased six horses during that fateful January premier yearling sale. Two were from New Zealand's top breeder, Sir Patrick Hogan. Few could, or would, argue that Sir Patrick Hogan was one of the best in the world at what he did. And what Hogan did was breed champion racehorses, the greatest in the Southern Hemisphere. He did so within the hedge-bordered paddocks of his 500-acre farm on the corner of Hautapu and Discombe Roads, just off Route 1 about 90 minutes south of Auckland.

The region was New Zealand's best for raising horses and the location, in the heart of the Waikato Basin, provided a near-perfect combination of climate and magically rich, dark soil. The grasses in Waikato sprouted luscious thick green blades jammed full of bountiful nutrients. Sir Patrick's immaculately manicured horse farm was smack dab in the middle of it all—midway between Cambridge and Hamilton.

Most of Hogan's early fame and success came as the result of five things: the four hooves connected to the great stallion Sir Tristram, plus the very thing that made the stallion a stallion. And it was that horse, Sir Tristram, who springboarded Hogan from just another small-town farmer with big dreams and a highly leveraged bank account into a respected global figure with an impeccable track record in the sport of kings.

When he first started out, Hogan, having been raised a farmer, decided to breed Thoroughbreds. He set out on a long and frustrating search for a stallion—a search that led him to his destiny.

Hogan borrowed the money to buy the Irish-bred Sir Tristram out of a sale barn in France because he believed the son of Sir Ivor was the best-bred stallion prospect he could afford. Sir Tristram was beautifully bred, but not physically impressive. His racing career record was good, but not great.

Hogan bought the horse over the telephone without ever having seen him. In fact, his bloodstock agent advised against it. The agent was in France, on the other end of the line, standing next to Sir T and describing the horse to Hogan from the tip of his muzzled nose to last strand of his swishing tail. Because the horse was not a great physical specimen, the agent urged him to pass.

Hogan bought him anyway. Despite the objections of many of Hogan's early partners, young Patrick the visionary stuck by his horse. Sir T's story went on to become the stuff of legend.

Once purchased, Sir Tristram had to be quarantined in England before export to New Zealand. That night, his holding barn caught fire and all but Sir T and one other horse perished in the blaze. Sir Tristram bolted out of the barn, which horses rarely do, and jumped a fence to escape the flames. There, Sir T happily discovered he'd hopped directly into a field *full* of mares.

Eager to show the girls his prowess, Sir Tristram shook off the momentary stresses of the fire and began practicing his craft immediately.

One mare, however, was apparently unimpressed that Sir Tristram neighed with an acquired French accent and kicked him right dead square in his, um, retractable breeding device.

The next day the phone rang in New Zealand. After hearing the whole story, Hogan pulled the receiver away from his ear and looked at it in disbelief. Then and there, for better or worse—and this episode clearly fell into the "worse" category—Sir Patrick Hogan decided Sir Tristram was his "guy." Patrick had hocked his future on this incorrect-looking grandson of Round Table and, for richer or poorer, the connection would be 'til death do they part.

As history relates, Sir Tristram proceeded to make Hogan a millionaire many times over. Sir T proved to be the greatest stallion ever to stand in the Southern Hemisphere, fathering 45 different Group I champions—the very best racehorses in the world.

Sir Tristram also taught Patrick that a strong enough sense of belief and conviction—spiced with a touch of good old-fashioned Irish luck—could make miracles and dreams out of hope, hard work, and ambition.

But the famous horse, far from an angel, caused a lot of dramatic worry on Hogan's farm the morning the Queen of England accepted Hogan's invitation to stop by for a tour.

"Paddy," as Hogan nicknamed Sir T, wasn't the kindest of horses. Sir Tristram once grabbed Sir Patrick's brother by the shoulder—chomping down to get a good grip with his teeth—then picked him up and tossed him, on the fly, over a three-railed wooden fence and completely out of his paddock. Fortunately, Paddy liked the Queen well enough. He was a model four-legged subject on the sunny afternoon she came by to see him.

Just over an hour north of Cambridge Stud was Karaka, the auction site where Hogan's breeding skills were validated each January at the national select Thoroughbred yearling sales. Hogan's young horses took the top five places in the Karaka sale, each bringing in over one million dollars.

Staggeringly, nearly one dollar of every four that flowed through the entire 1,500-horse premier sale accounting department ended up in the coffers of Sir Patrick Hogan and Cambridge Stud. He was earning one-fourth of the money from less than one-tenth of the horses sold. Timothy Holden's purchases certainly helped.

Sir Patrick had 120 mares and sold every yearling they produced. He kept none. The horses Hogan chose to race were ones he went out and bought, just like everyone else.

Despite his enormous financial success, the game to Sir Patrick wasn't the money; it was the competition—the winning. Hogan wanted to breed the best horses in the hemisphere by figuring out which stallion should go to which mare to produce the soundest, fastest offspring. He also wanted to win races on-track by buying horses other men chose not to, then have those horses do his talking for him. Hogan's runners spoke loudly since he'd purchased several Group I champions at public auction for what many considered bargain prices.

On the farm, Sir Patrick made almost every decision worth making. In addition to deciding which racehorses to buy, he kept total control over all broodmares, stallions, and breeding matchups. He was, by nature, an autocrat. One touched by good fortune, certainly, but an autocrat nonetheless. When it came to anything concerning Cambridge Stud, "I have every vote," he was fond of saying.

Hogan's people worked six 12-hour days a week, but no one on the farm worked by a clock. Everyone stayed until the work was completed. And dawn brought plenty more.

But Hogan led by example. Everything he asked his people to do, he'd do himself. He mucked stalls—although not as often as the others—and he'd be out there planting flowers side by side with his newest of hires. Sir Patrick spent countless sleepless nights delivering foals during each four-month birthing season. He was a hands-on guy with the relentless energy of ten men, thoroughly immersed in every aspect of his operation.

Indeed, Sir Patrick had the success skills all great men do: drive, ambition, vision, talent, and a passionate love for his vocation. Horsebreeding wasn't a business to Hogan. It was what he was born to do—his life—and he thrived on every tiny fragment of the millions of details that success demanded. "I have an absolute romance with horses...," he'd say, "... entwined with humans."

And how Sir Patrick Hogan entered the life of Cushla Wimsett directly resulted from his omnipotent attention to details others often couldn't see.

He had first noticed Cushla's work at Karaka a year before when she prepped auction horses for Murphy Reed, a friend of Sir Patrick's. Reed ran a small breeding operation, just a dozen mares, but he bred quality Thoroughbreds. His animals were meticulously cared for and typically brought top dollar.

Cushla met Mr. Reed while grooming some racing stock at Auckland's Takanini training stable. When time came to auction eight of his yearlings at Karaka, Mr. Reed hired her to help make them look and show their best.

It was that eye for detail—Cush's ability to make each animal look its absolute best—that Sir Patrick noticed. Regarded as the nation's greatest equine marketer, Hogan could tell at a glance whether a horse had been prepared by love, skill, and knowledge, or simply by a hired hand.

Sir Patrick was also extraordinarily superstitious. "I'm as superstitious as a buggery," he said at one auction. Hogan would not walk under a staircase, not even Karaka's, despite the fact that during a typical yearling sale he'd have to make hundreds of repetitive detours simply to avoid it.

It was during one of these circumventions that Sir Patrick Hogan and Cushla Wimsett accidentally bumped into each other.

"Sir Patrick!" she blurted apologetically. "I am *so* sorry!" Everyone in the industry knew, or knew of, Sir Patrick Hogan. Cush was embarrassed at cutting a tight corner and nearly running down the nation's most famous horseman.

"No," replied Sir Patrick, "I owe *you* the apology, my dear girl. I should look up from these silly auction books and watch where I'm going more carefully.

"You work for Murphy Reed, do you not?" he asked without waiting for a reply, since he already knew the answer. "I like your work. You have a good eye for your animals. You see the details. You know your horses and I've noticed the quality of your work. Your animals are always beautifully prepared."

Cush flushed with embarrassment and could think of nothing to say except, "Thank you, Sir."

"Well, I must be going," Sir Patrick said, "but if you ever choose to come to Cambridge, please call my office, Miss …"

"Wimsett," she replied with a blushing smile. "Cushla Wimsett. Thank you, Sir. And good luck with the rest of your horses. They are all beautiful," she said.

"Thank you, Miss Wimsett," said Sir Patrick with a smile. "Best to you as well."

They shook hands quickly but firmly. Hogan headed to the barns while Cushla continued back inside the auction oval. A half-hour later, Hogan had been watching from the upper concourse when Cush fainted. He had clapped and cheered along with everyone else when she bowed and made her embarrassed exit.

Sir Patrick had no idea if Cushla would ever show up looking for work, but if she did, he'd hire her. He knew she would meet the high standards of Cambridge Stud.

When Cush first watched Sir Patrick in action at Karaka, she saw the same skills many others who'd come to know him already had. Hogan's mind was always churning, always processing, always thinking. That was the way she wanted *her* life to be, too. She wanted everything to fit together. But to do that, she needed to learn more and make some changes. She was in a rut, knew it, and wanted to change.

And that was why, a year after she first bumped into Sir Patrick near the stairwell at Karaka, Cushla decided to pick up the telephone and call Cambridge Stud.

Hogan was in, took her call, and invited Cush to join his team at a salary that was even higher than what Cushla hoped for.

Her timing was good; she'd be familiar with everything she needed to know before foaling season began.

Timothy balanced the geographic inconvenience of Cush moving 60 miles away with the benefit of gaining valuable access to a lot of inside information. Timothy told her he thought the move would do her good, she'd learn a lot, and the greater distance between them wouldn't change their relationship one little bit.

That was the problem, she thought as she packed to move. To Timothy, *everything* was business. Everything and everybody in his life was only as important as the information it provided him to buy and sell horses for profit. It was the *dollars* that consumed Timothy, never the people and certainly not the animals. Horses to him were hollow four-legged robots with hip numbers in an auction guide. Cush wondered if he even realized that horses were warm-blooded personalities with hearts and souls of their own.

Hogan normally employed 25 full-timers on his farm; 45 during the foaling season. Many applied, few were selected. People came to him for work—he never had to recruit—and Sir Patrick was selective about the people on his staff. He employed skilled, loyal, hard-working people. Several full-timers even traveled all the way from his native Ireland for long learning apprenticeships before eventually returning home to run their own operations.

Anyone who had earned the right to better himself or herself had no bigger promoter behind them than Sir Patrick Hogan. He knew everyone, and his succinct opinion often carried more weight than 10,000 pounds of promises.

"When you come to work for me," Sir Patrick told Cush the morning she arrived, "I tell you all the same thing: The boss will always do what's best for him. I have every vote. And if you want to better yourself, come to the boss.

"I expect hard work, hustle, and extreme attention to detail. And if you make a mistake—a preventable mistake—I'll come down hard on you. I believe that 90 percent of failure and 90 percent of excellence come from individuals.

"The rest...," he added with a sigh as he leaned back in his deep leather chair, "...you can blame on bad luck." Coming from Sir Patrick, bad luck seemed to a grudging acknowledgment rather than an admission of uncontrollable circumstance.

"I'll feed you well, house you well, and pay you well," Hogan continued. "In exchange, I expect you to work hard, harder than elsewhere perhaps, because I strive for excellence.

"My property is tidy. The grounds of Cambridge Stud, especially those around the office and stallion barn, are immaculately kept, yet we have no gardener. Everyone chips in when there is work to be done. So, in that regard, everyone is a gardener.

"I have a standard of excellence for the farm and my horses. Over the years, we've generated a huge respect."

"Yes, Sir," Cush replied with a smile. "And I'd like to help protect that."

"Don't protect it!" Hogan replied with mock indignation. "Don't protect it, young lady! *Enhance it!*"

Cush laughed. "Yes, *Sir!*" she replied. "But I can't do that from here. Let me leave you to your work and I'll locate some of my own."

Hogan smiled as he rose from behind his large desk and shook her small, strong hand. "If you have any trouble locating some," he added with an arched eyebrow, "give me a call."

Cushla moved into a small ground-floor apartment overlooking one end of six foaling paddocks. Quickly she disappeared inside the daily demands of the never-ending cycle of totality that life at Cambridge Stud demanded. The work kept her busy and thoughts of Truck Roberts soon faded into the past like shrinking objects in a rear-view mirror. She saw Timothy less frequently and thoughts of him began shrinking, too.

Cush quickly immersed herself in farm life and, like everyone else, she did whatever had to be done. Her work ethic was matched by some, but exceeded by none.

One night, after an exhausting 12-hour day wrestling with headstrong yearlings, Cush went for a long run. Sir Patrick, working late in his office, looked at his watch as she ran down the tree-lined driveway. He looked again when she returned 75 minutes later in the darkness of a half-moon night. The following morning, Cush was the second of 25 employees to arrive for breakfast and had a cheery "good morning" for everyone as each arrived. That impressed him.

Sir Patrick smiled at the fabric of this young woman but never mentioned it to her. It was, he would say later, one of those "little things" by which he measured people. "I don't care what people do while I'm around," he said, "nearly as much as what they do when I'm *not* around."

When Cushla's first foaling season arrived, it seemed as though she went three months without sleep. She simply wanted to stay up for every foal whose little hooves were coaxed out of Momma by Sir Patrick and the team out in the foaling paddocks. All told, 250 yearlings—nearly half of them Hogan's—would hit the ground in the foaling paddocks at Cambridge.

Everyone's energy seemed inexhaustible when the foals arrived. It had to be. Each toothpick set of spindly legs could be worth millions. Everyone on the farm knew they were welcoming to Earth one wonderfully warm-blooded treasure after another—regardless of its eventual sale value.

At Cambridge Stud, Cush witnessed daily miracles. She worked hard with the rest of the team to safely deliver each precious wobbly-legged foal. Just as feverishly, they diligently assisted and protected each exhausted mare. Sir Patrick and the others, including broodmare manager Swampy McCallum and longtime yearling manager Marcus Corbin, learned they could rely on her to make good decisions quickly.

The pregnant broodmares spent their final days waiting to deliver in one of the grassy two-acre holding paddocks. A crow's nest white-roof observation tower, staffed around the clock, was located center stage like the bull's-eye on a big grassy dartboard. Alerts were broadcast immediately whenever a mare went into labor. Cush, who volunteered for the worst time slots, was ever vigilant. She had the eyes of a Leupold telescope. Even if a black mare hid in the shadowed grass of the far distant corner, she would spot her.

The only times Cush voluntarily came out of the observation tower was when one of the foals was in trouble and had to go to the infirmary. Sir Patrick had constructed a small foaling hospital, complete with a waterbed for the baby. An adjacent low-walled stall for the mare, feathered with clean shredded paper, was next to the waterbed.

Here, the endangered foals were hooked up with IVs, given medication, and tended to during emergencies. Cush spent countless days and nights there—one of a select few Sir Patrick fully trusted with these fragile animals.

Each season, only five or six of the foals needed to go to the infirmary, but Cush treated each one with the soft-spoken love the nearby mares understood and trusted. She cried every time she prepared one of these special fillies or colts for later sale at Karaka. Having watched them survive after such early struggles and grow to become strong healthy racing prospects, these yearlings became part of her life—not dollars and cents or anonymous hip numbers at a sale. That was always the worst moment of the year for Cush—when it was time for these extra special yearlings to head to Karaka and leave the farm for good. Timothy felt otherwise; he never bid on any of them.

One special preemie, a colt bought by Australian furniture dealer William Beck, was named Steamboat Springs and sold for nearly $700,000. Steamboat Springs went on to become a champion Group I winner three times over. Steamboat was a son of Zabeel, Sir Patrick's marquis stallion following the passing of Sir Tristram. He raced with the grit and fierce determination of an ultra-competitive world-class athlete.

Cush kept a photo taken by Jeff Roan, the farm's perfectly named stallion manager, the day the tiny colt who would become a champion finally wobble-stepped his way out of the infirmary. In the photo, the colt was flanked by his mother on one side and Cushla on the other. The jet-black colt with the white-starred forehead had spent nearly three weeks on the waterbed, taking in fluids and antibiotics intravenously while trying to stave off an infection that nearly killed him. It was a maddening struggle to help the little guy grow strong enough to stand and feed from his mother.

Cush prayed a thousand prayers—and changed nearly that many diapers—as the gritty preemie colt battled his way back from near-death to full recovery. She never left his side in that shed and would have stayed there for three more weeks if necessary. She knew that, Sir Patrick knew that, and all the others knew it, too.

After the fragile colt survived, Marcus even let Cush keep a special eye on him, right up to preparing Steamboat for sale at Karaka. Cush had previously met Mr. Beck, the man who bought him. He had purchased some of Sir Patrick's horses before and flew over from Melbourne to visit the farm during Sir Patrick's annual auction preview.

That sunny afternoon, Sir Patrick asked Cushla to present the colt to the 50 invited guests. Most were wealthy Australian horsemen like Mr. Beck. So she dressed in her best and wore a stylish emerald green Armani pants suit with a double-breasted blazer. Her fitted slacks sat perfectly on her hips and billowed down over her best Italian leather high-heeled boots—boots she rarely had the chance to wear.

She also wore her late mother's favorite jewelry—pearl earrings and a matching necklace.

Cush had the colt alertly on his toes. He was an athletic-looking animal and Sir Patrick knew she could present him even better than he. She told the visitors the entire life history of the colt, sharing all she knew.

Mr. Beck asked only one question and it was a short one. These pre-auction yearling showcases were always poker games—no one wanted to tip his or her hand on which horse or horses interested them the most and Mr. Beck was no exception. "Miss Wimsett," he asked, "in a word . . . how would you summarize this colt?"

"One word?" Cush clarified respectfully.

"Yes," he said. "One word. Or two if you need it." Several others laughed when Beck doubled Cush's latitude for response.

She paused politely for a moment as she searched for the right word, then smiled when she found it. "Astute," she replied confidently. "He's a very astute horse."

Sir Patrick, standing to the side, smiled. It was a good answer, a very good answer.

When sale day finally came, Cush had Steamboat perfectly prepped and rode with the horse when he was vanned north to Karaka. Sir Patrick gave her the option of showing the colt in the ring or having him do it. She let her boss show him, opting instead to stand near the ring entrance doorway, tears streaming as she kissed the gritty yearling on the forehead moments before Sir Patrick stepped him through the sliding wood doorway and into the auction ring.

Sir Patrick was a great showman, peacocking around with his horses, trying to ignite the competitive spirit among the bidders. Dueling egos could make the numbers fly and Sir Patrick was a master of creating spontaneous combustion.

But as she watched, Cush thought about what Sir Patrick told her in his office the day he hired her. He was right: It wasn't about the money. Even as the dollars, then digits, clicked ever-higher on the big white-lightbulbed scoreboard—just as the auctioneer lifted his gavel to pound down a hammer-down sale price of $680,000—Cush softly spoke her feelings to herself. "The money doesn't matter," she whispered. "It just doesn't matter. It's the love and all the emotions that matter."

Two years later, Jeffrey Franklin Cushla Wimsett would remember standing on that precise spot—the auction floor doorway—crying and remembering exactly what she was thinking at the time the hammer fell on Steamboat.

Yes, two years later, that same set of feelings would once again tidal wave over her like cold spring water tumbling down a mountain waterfall. She'd be feeling the same way, but for a totally different reason.

No, the money wouldn't matter. What mattered would be inside: a restless, fluttering flock of butterflies that steadfastly refused to fly in formation. For Cush, it too would be the love—and definitely *not* the money—that really mattered.

And, at this precise moment, half a world away on a small Bahamian island, a small, proud family was struggling to face a worsening situation in which the money really *did* matter.

Soon enough, a simple twist of fate would tap all of these folks on the shoulder.

$\mathcal{S}$addling Up in South Beach

Right after Cush had quit her corporate job, Mitzi decided it was time to start her own business. She had a flair for fashion and design, and began marketing her own line of customized sunglasses coupled with matching bikinis. Mitzi called her line "Kiwinis."

Mitzi's idea was brilliantly simple: She developed a vast array of different sunglass styles, then imprinted the image of each specific style onto the fabric of matching bikinis and swimsuits. By having a rainbow variety of colors available for each style, Mitzi quickly and easily had a full product line of fashion combinations. And Mitzi being Mitzi, she insisted both the sunglasses and bikinis be made of top quality materials.

Another part of her marketing scheme turned out to be shrewdly unique. You couldn't buy one—either the glasses or bathing suit—without the other. The sunglasses and swimsuits were packaged, distributed, marketed, and sold only as matched sets. And all were contained inside clear little tubes adorned with her picture, modeling each product in its own color and style.

With more than four dozen different styles of sunglasses to imprint on the swimsuit fabrics and nearly as many swimsuit cuts and styles, Mitzi instantly owned a huge product line with more than enough sizes, styles, and colors to fit every woman who wanted to ride the hot new tidal wave of Kiwini fashions.

Her product line and its advertising slogan, "Wear Kiwinis or nothing!" became extremely popular and Mitzi targeted aggressive ad campaigns in many major hot-weather cities. They were even popular in Sydney and Melbourne—a surprise in view of the natural rivalry between New Zealanders and Aussies. But fashion knew no borders and, judging by exploding sales in Australia, Mitzi soon was clutching a large fashion kangaroo firmly by the tail. Judging by the Australian sales figures, that kangaroo's pouch seemed stuffed to the brim with profit dollars.

Mitzi was thrilled by her Australian success, but viewed the U.S. market as the motherlode. She decided to move to Miami and set up camp in South Beach. Almost overnight, Kiwinis became a roaringly huge success—a must-have product—and just two months after arriving in South Beach, Mitzi's photo was splashed on the cover of *Ocean Drive* magazine. Mitzi was a star—and her fashion business was raining money faster than she could count it. Soon it took an entire accounting department to keep track of it all.

Within months, Mitzi's swimsuit line grew wildly popular in South America, especially Brazil. Fashionable Rio, in particular, went Kiwini Krazy. Mitzi was treated like a rock star during her first publicity visit there. More than 100 dozen roses were waiting in her hotel room. They were from Brazilian men who'd only seen her on the cover of swimsuit tubes.

Obviously, life had changed more quickly for Mitzi in Miami than for Cush and the girls back in Auckland, and Mitzi wanted to share the fun with her friends. Firmly entrenched in the South Beach social scene—a definite "A-lister" invited to all the parties that mattered—Mitzi wanted the Posse to come over for a vacation and meet the hunky men of Miami. Mitzi repeatedly phoned the girls and urged each of them to come knead the hedonistic sands of South Beach with their own little toes.

When Mitzi first started calling, the timing was bad for Cush. She had just met Timothy, things were going well, and she was helping several owners prepare valuable horses for upcoming sales.

"Maybe in a few months," she told Mitzi in late November.

Mitzi was disappointed. "Promise?" she coaxed as she spun around her office chair and watched the early-morning rollerbladers glide down Ocean Drive.

"Sure," said Cush from half a world away. "When I can. Bad timing now. After the sales, OK?"

Even Bird and Phoebe sensed that Cush needed some time to settle into what she was doing. From the looks of it, Timothy had potential. Both told Mitzi they'd also rather wait until all three could come to the States together.

Mitzi then extracted a promise: Within 100 days, the Posse would, in fact, be riding together toward an unforgettable life-changing trip to Florida.

Mitzi kept calling—dangling a Florida vacation in front of the Posse's bored and saucer-sized eyes—but those 100 days soon turned into 200, then 300, and even 400.

Fifteen months had passed when the phone rang in Mitzi's office one day. She picked it up and heard Cush's voice on the other end of the line. Sir Patrick had sold a pair of broodmares to a Californian and Cush was flying them over. Timothy was too busy to join her, but encouraged Cush to go. Phoebe and Bird quickly volunteered to accompany her.

Mitzi was thrilled at the news and squealed delightedly. "Bloody 'ell, woman!" she cried. "It's about time! I thought I was going to have to send over a submarine and steal you off that North Island!"

"Is week-after-next OK?" Cush asked. "I can drop off the horses for quarantine in Los Angeles, then come down to Florida. Phoebe and Bird will meet me in L.A. and we'll all fly in together."

"Together again!" cried Mitzi excitedly. "The Posse rides to-gether again! I can't wait to see you! Just let us know your schedule and I'll be waiting at the gate.

"Love you, Cush," Mitzi added before hanging up.

"Love you too," Cush replied. "See you soon."

And so the Posse was soon destined for the glamour, excitement, and handsome hunky men of beautiful South Beach.

Two Weeks Later

Mitzi was waiting at Miami International, three men in tow and each holding flowers, when the other three-fourths of the Posse straggled off their red-eye connector from Los Angeles.

There were hugs and squeals and hip-hops up and down when the girls ran up to each other in a bit of what a rugby player would call a "love scrum." Phoebe cast an appreciative shoe-to-hair glance at a muscular Brazilian named Raul who handed her a huge bouquet of tropical flowers and kissed her on both cheeks.

"Señorita Phoebe?" he asked.

"Oui. Si. Yes. Uh-huh," she said, accepting the bouquet like a prom queen.

"Buenos días, Señorita Phoebe. Welcome to Miami. I am Raul."

"Yes, you certainly *are*, aren't you?" cooed Phoebe with an extra touch of sugar. She loved this town and hadn't even claimed her luggage yet.

Bird, meanwhile, shuffle-stepped sideways to meet Roberto. Roberto handed over his flowers to her and guessed she was Señorita Pajara.

"Pajara? I'm Señorita Bird. There's no Señorita Pajara here," Bird said sweetly.

"Pajara is Bird, a female bird, in Spanish," offered Roberto.

"I knew that," Bird said with a blush. "Pleased to meet you. I am, in fact, Señorita Pajara."

"And I am Roberto."

Cush watched all this quietly. Leave it to Mitzi to show up with escorts. Cush wondered if they were paid or volunteed.

Cush's flower-bearer was a short muscular weightlifting type guy with zero body fat. Sort of like the anti-Gavin. His name was

Eduardo. Eduardo bowed sweepingly at the waist and offered her a huge bouquet of beautiful flowers she'd never before seen. Cush half-jokingly curtsied in response, mumbling only, "Gracias."

True to form, a big limo waited outside. The girls had their noses pressed against the glass the entire 22-minute drive over to Mitzi's place on the beach, marveling at the incredible mansions ringing the small islands dotting the causeway across Biscayne Bay.

Mitzi had a lovely apartment right on Ocean Drive, the epi-center of South Beach. Big money, the girls soon learned. Business was booming for Mitzi and here she was, a Kiwi stuck smack dab in the vortex of South Beach's fashion and modeling industry, not to mention the relentless nightlife that went along with it.

The girls settled in, changed into their suits—personalized one-of-a-kind Kiwinis, of course—and headed across the street for a fry at the beach. Four hours later, they returned stop-sign red, walking gingerly stiff-legged like zombies risen from the dead.

"You must've sounded like *bacon* laying out there," laughed Mitzi when she saw them.

"I should be so lucky," moaned Bird. "I feel like all my, *ow*, skin, *ow*, shrunk, *ow!*" she painfully said as she slowly winced and sat down on the deep tan leather sofa. Climbing back out would hurt worse than appendicitis.

A couple of hours later, Mitzi had some errands to attend to and asked Cush to tag along. Something was bothering her friend and Mitzi could clearly tell.

The two girls got in Mitzi's champagne-colored Lexus and pointed it north up Collins Avenue. The cold-blasting A/C felt like a death row reprieve to Cush, whose light skin looked like the bloody inside of a cooked-rare T-bone steak.

"What's buggin,' kiddo?" asked Mitzi as she pulled the car out of the garage and glided onto Collins Avenue.

"Oh, I don't know," said Cush. "Maybe it's me. Sometimes I think I just don't understand men at all," as they slowly passed the famed Fountainbleu Hilton. Cush was a movie fanatic and remembered the hotel from the third James Bond movie, "Goldfinger." Sean Connery was such a great Bond, she thought, that all the others since have looked like little boys.

Cush turned away from looking at the hotel and said with a wry smile, "It just seems that sometimes men just don't say what they really mean."

"Of course they don't," laughed Mitzi. "What do you expect? They're only men. You're not exactly dealing with a superior intellect, you know.

"OK, look. I'll give you some examples," Mitzi continued. "When a guy says, 'I'm really not that big into foreign films,' what do you think he really means?"

"That he likes other kinds of movies better," guessed Cush.

"Wrong. What he really means is 'Reading captions is a bore. Let's just go to a sports bar and watch hockey—or rugby or whatever—on TV.'

"And when a guy says, 'I want a trusting relationship,' what do you think that means?"

"Um, uh, it means that both people trust each other. He trusts me and I trust him."

"Ah-*ha!*" Mitzi said emphatically. "*Wrong!* When a guy says he wants a trusting relationship, what he really means is: 'Service my needs but never check up on what I say or do. Believe every word out of my mouth and never remember any of it, no matter how preposterous my excuses or logic may seem.'

"*That* is what a 'trusting relationship' is to a man," Mitzi summarized dramatically.

"Timothy said bringing the horses over would be a good break for us both," Cush replied. "He encouraged me to come. He said I could see my friends on holiday and that he 'needed a little space.' What's this space thing all about? The last time a bloke told me that, I tossed his dinner plate out the window and told him to go find his meat loaf out in his precious *space*," said Cush. "What the bloody 'ell does a man need *space* for?"

Mitzi swiveled her head sharply sideways at Cush the moment she heard the s-word. She was wide-eyed. "Space?" she asked. "Space? One year together and he told you he needed *space*?

"Good for you, Cush! You gave him half the bloody planet! When a guy says he needs space, either he's got another woman on the side and he needs some room, or he's just working so much he doesn't know whether to wind his watch or play Twister naked by himself. If *that's* the case, he might just need some quiet. Everyone does, from time to time. You know—personal think time."

"Where are we going?" asked Cush, as they entered Bal Harbour. Mitzi had the left turn signal on and turned the car off North Collins Avenue.

"Beauty parlor, darling," smiled Mitzi as she shoved the car into PARK and turned off the ignition. "You, sweetie, are getting a makeover. My thank-you present for coming over. One of several, if you don't mind."

Cush was thrilled. Her last makeover was years ago—the day before she interviewed with Truck's company.

Cush, whose red hair, lime green sleeveless blouse, and sunburned skin made her look like a small-breasted Christmas ornament, slowly emerged from the passenger's side of the parked Lexus and baby-stepped her sunburned way toward the beauty salon. *"Roberto's"* was written in large script on the window.

Inside were the three guys she'd met at the airport. All were working. And all three, she learned, were gay. And, she also learned, they were magicians with their craft.

Three hours later, Cush emerged with perfectly tinted auburn hair, nails to die for, and an even better understanding of men than when she first arrived in Miami. For example, when men give girls flowers at the airport, maybe it really *doesn't* mean they want to sleep with you. With each other, maybe, but not with you.

Cush rarely took much pride in her mirror image, but she paused for a long look, with Mitzi smiling beside her, just before they left Roberto's salon. Cush couldn't remember the last time she looked this good. Or felt this good. She turned and hugged Mitzi tight around the neck, whispering, "I love you. Thank you!"

"Me too, Cutie," Mitzi replied. "C'mon, Nieman's is having a sale. Gotta get you dolled up now. I have a funny feeling you'll have a busy week while you're here." Cush said nothing, thought a moment about Timothy, then erased the thought.

The girls stepped across the street to the luxurious Bal Harbour shops and melted some serious plastic. They shopped 'til they dropped, which didn't take as long as usual since Cush was exhausted from a blended mix of travel and sun.

Not long after, an hour after dinner, a bleary-eyed Cush lost her battle to fatigue and decided to turn in early. As usual, she counted foals rather than sheep and had barely reached a dozen before she drifted off. Like it or not, the hunky, handsome men of South Beach would have to wait another day.

The Prodigal Son Returns

Meanwhile, a scant 50 miles across the Atlantic, a difficult time for Anvil and Alma was coming to sad conclusion. Both were getting older and money was suddenly squeezing the family tighter than a boa constrictor fixing lunch. Eight months before, Anvil fell and severely hurt his knee, which kept him from doing his guide work. It also meant the searing pain of standing hour after hour to hand-craft a wooden boat would limit him to just one or two hours of work at a time. Working full days was out of the question.

The injury meant Anvil managed to build just one boat that season, rather than two, and the steady money his guiding usually delivered had dried up. No matter how Anvil looked at things, he kept arriving at the same conclusion: The horse would have to go.

Bonefish was now nine years old. In Anvil's view, it was time to call Truck and return Bonefish to the mainland since he was bull-headedly against giving the horse to someone on the island. Alma chose not to argue. She loved Bonefish as much as her husband, but Alma knew that if the horse stayed on Bimini, Anvil's pride would make him feel like a failure every time the old gray gelding stepped across his path.

Carving out an island living was always a struggle, even in the best of times. Now, in the worst of times, every discussion ended with the same conclusion—however painful the day would be, it was time to send Bonefish back to the States.

Anvil stared at his black kitchen telephone for a long time before finally picking it up and dialing Truck's number one slow digit at a time. The call lasted less than a minute. When Anvil re-cradled the receiver, his eyes welled-up with tears. He pressed the side of each, rubbing away the teardrops just before they fell.

Truck called back a couple days later and told Anvil that if they could get Bonefish back to Miami within a week or so, he'd help find someone to buy him. He couldn't guarantee anything, but he'd call all the riding stables scattered around South Florida and hope for a yes from somebody. If so, he'd give Anvil the money, which Anvil needed but said he didn't want.

Truck also promised to poke around the track and mentioned a claiming race in ten days or so for old horses. Maybe someone running in it might buy Bonefish cheap since that person would have an obvious affinity for older animals.

What Truck didn't mention was that he thought their chances of selling the horse for anything more than nickels and dimes was about the same as pole-vaulting the Washington Monument.

Anvil made arrangements with Sully Davis to borrow the Bimini Water Taxi, which usually shuffled people back and forth across the channel between North and South Bimini. Anvil let Sully use his bonefish skiff and gave him two tanks of gas to use while they were gone.

Whenever the seas died down, they'd cross. During March, the winds were rarely still and northeast winter gusts often made the Atlantic a bouncingly miserable and dangerous place to be. But almost miraculously, Anvil caught a break. According to the marine weather report, there would be four to five days of perfect, unseasonably nice weather starting in 72 hours or so. Upon learning that, he planned to leave on the second day of calm seas.

Sure enough, the warm front arrived like it was mid-July instead of March. Even better, there wasn't enough wind to launch a kite. If you were looking to ferry a horse across 50 miles of ocean in a flat-bottomed water taxi, you'd drop to your knees and thank God for such a lucky break.

Crossing the Gulf Stream and its perpetual currents was always tricky since the Atlantic Ocean and Gulf Stream were mighty fickle dancing partners. Some days, they waltzed; some days they tangoed. And some days they slam-danced. Whenever weather systems collided, the ocean quickly became dramatically roiled, rough, and dangerous. No experienced seaman ever shoved off to cross without first carefully checking the local marine forecast.

But Anvil, Bonefish, and the gang got perfect conditions and, unless something unforeseen happened, the weather posed no danger on the crossing from Bimini Harbour to Biscayne Bay. In fact, the trickiest part of the journey might come when the group reached Miami.

Customs was down by Port of Miami—a massive deep-water canal dredged to accommodate the giant cruise ships that sailed from Miami throughout the Caribbean to glamorous spots like St. Thomas, St. Martin, Barbados, and Aruba. The deep narrow channel usually meant swift currents. Anvil and his son would wait until they were near Miami Beach before worrying about which of the three coastal entryways into the protective harbor of Biscayne Bay was safest. For simplicity's sake, they hoped to enter at the Port of Miami. For safety's sake, they'd take the least dramatic.

The night before leaving Bimini, the horse, father, son, and nearly 100 friends and family had walked up to the Wesley Anglican Church on Queen Street's highest ridge and prayed for a safe crossing. Church-goers had been encouraging miracles since 1858—the year it was built—and everybody there that evening prayed their hearts out. They asked for one more slice of divine intervention from within its green-trimmed white walls.

After church, there was a good-luck party down by the water at Bimini Bay Front Park and half of the people on the island came out to see Bonefish, pet him, and hug him goodbye. Anvil even had to borrow a metal cash box from Weech's hardware store to hold the nickels, dimes, quarters, and dollars the people brought to bet on their behalf—just in case they were allowed to enter Bonefish into that race for old horses Truck talked about.

Anvil urged them all to reconsider. He intended to sell the horse, not run it. The *last thing* he needed was half of the island mad at him for losing money none of them could afford to lose on a race they probably couldn't even enter, much less deserve to be in.

Despite his relentless debate, when he finally packed the gray tin cash box inside the boat's console under the steering wheel, Anvil had $212 in small bills and change from 62 different island residents. Alma had written a list of who gave what and Anvil winced when he saw $10 next to her name. He had no intention of betting so much as one thin dime. He'd return all the money when they returned back to Bimini.

After church, Anvil and T-man packed the water taxi under the dock lights so all they had to do in the morning was load Bonefish aboard and shove off on the long, slow chug to the mainland.

Anvil didn't sleep a wink. This horse, clearly, had become much more a part of him and this island than he ever realized. But he also knew it was best for everybody—especially Bonefish—to get him back to the States.

Time to Go

The meteoric red-balled sun lifted out of the ocean and over the bonefish flats to the east. Anvil rode his golf cart down to Captain Bob's Restaurant for one of Miss Bonnie's tummy-filling fresh-cooked breakfasts. It was just after six o'clock and the coffee was still brewing. The morning's first customer, Anvil sat and talked to Miss Bonnie about how all he wanted was for things to be OK and for no one to get hurt.

He also told her he hated being in a position of losing so much money the townspeople had scraped together. He hated to see it "pissed away like that," in his terms.

"Have faith, Anvil," Miss Bonnie told him. "If you do right by others, others will do right by you." Then she handed over a large waterproof sack of sandwiches, chicken, and cookies to take on the boat.

"Besides," she added with a smile, "the people aren't betting that money on *you*. The people are betting that money on Bonefish." And with that, Miss Bonnie also handed over a clear plastic sandwich-sized baggie full of peppermint candy and red licorice for the horse.

Anvil rode his golf cart up the dusty street to his house, parked, went inside, and collected T-man. He let T walk Bonefish from the paddock and sheltered lean-to that Anvil and Truck skipped an entire day of fishing to build, all the way down the full length of King Street toward town. It took 20 minutes to reach the wharf. There, crowded around the Customs dock at seven-thirty, at least 200 people were waiting to say goodbye, pet the horse one last time, and wish them safe crossing.

It was a tough time for Anvil. But he never doubted the correctness of what he was doing and completed the boarding process with mechanical efficiency, never missing a step. Bonefish obediently stepped aboard and stood center-deck, facing the bow.

It was only a matter of minutes before they would cast off the lines, wave goodbye, and chug out into the harbor. As Anvil untied the rope from the port stern cleat, Weevil Stuart came up holding aloft a brace of fine, freshly gutted wahoo. "Here Anvil," said Weevil. "Sell dese fish and put dee money on Bonefish."

Anvil just looked at Weevil, shook his head disbelievingly, then grabbed the two wahoo, and grunted them aboard and into the 151-quart ice chest. He said nothing.

He could hear all the kids hollering "Bye, Bonefish! *We love you!*" Anvil had tears in his eyes as he pointed the nose of the taxi out of the inlet and turned right, to the west, toward the seemingly endless sea before him.

And so they chugged away from home, a land of 1,300 friends, and toward a metropolitan area of three million strangers—a man, a boy, and a horse floating across the Atlantic Ocean in a slow-moving, shallow-sided, blue Bahamian water taxi.

Anvil got seasick an hour into the trip. The waves were negligible, but once offshore and out of the sight of land, Anvil always got seasick. He always fished the flats, in shallow water, and never went in deep water. Here he was, a fifth-generation boat builder who got sick from some kind of aquatic phobia. When he was younger it bothered him, but now he just accepted it.

T-man was the exact opposite. The bonefish flats bored T to tears. He loved the call of the deep blue water and giant powerful fish like tuna and wahoo. T-man, whose real name was Arthur, picked up his nickname when he stubbornly wrestled a 40-pound yellowfin tuna into submission on his eighth birthday. That tuna fight lasted an hour and a half, and T-man angrily refused all help from his uncle Thaddeus and teenaged cousin Marcel. Thaddeus called him Tuna Man after that and the nickname stuck.

At the time, T-man himself weighed but 49 pounds. At the end of the day, both the victor and the vanquished were hoisted upside down and weighed on the Bimini Big Game Club's dockside scale. Years later, the photo still hangs directly across King Street on the stairway wall at the Compleat Angler Hotel.

And so, since the Gulf Stream curled tightly near the Bimini western shoreline, T-man couldn't resist dropping a fishing line to troll as he chugged across the ocean with his dad and horse. T trolled a small cero mackerel, about 16 inches long, skipping it perfectly 40 yards behind the boat atop the crest of their ever-widening, gently rolling wake.

Two hours into the trip, about 16 miles from Bimini, the father and son spied a Cuban raft no more than 200 yards away. Anvil put his small binoculars to his eyes and looked at the raft. It was empty. "Thank God," he muttered softly to himself. "They were saved."

Anvil remembered a recent story in the *Miami Herald* about a raft not so fortunate. The refugees swung way too wide in the fickle currents between Cuba and Florida, and vectored too far from shore to paddle out of the powerful Gulf Stream. Eight Cubans perished. The men who found the raft chose to fish under it rather than tow it in and caught 64 mahi-mahi dolphinfish out from under its shade. When the fish quit biting, the fishermen set the raft ablaze, creating a funeral pyre 35 miles off the Boca Raton coast.

Two minutes later, Anvil abruptly stowed his binoculars and ran to the side railing. He bent over and began dry heaving. Seasickness was his deepwater curse and it was there—with his nose a foot from the sea—that he first saw the shadow. Seconds later, he saw the giant fish just before it struck.

Bonefish saw it too and neighed loudly.

The marlin spied the surface-skipping baitfish, excitedly turned purple, spun to the right, and powerfully tail-pumped its way directly toward T's trolled mackerel. T-man had never caught a marlin before, but there was little doubt he was about to get the opportunity.

Anvil was too stunned to say a word. He simply turned from the rail and looked at his son, his eyes wide and jaw open. Spittle remained on the left of his chin. He simply pointed behind the boat.

The giant fish smacked the mackerel with a right-to-left slash of its broom-handled bill. T-man grabbed the rod, flipped the reel into free spool, thumbed out line to create slack, and let the cero drop back. The bait, looking injured by the swipe of the marlin's broad bill, fluttered slowly down from the surface.

The marlin circled back tightly, swallowed the mackerel, and quickly headed south—toward Key West—with two powerful swipes of its massive tail.

T-man waited, let the fish run, then slammed the reel into gear, cranked in the slack line and yanked back on the rod three times in powerful succession as quickly as he could. The huge marlin exploded out of the water, shaking her enormous head from side to side twice before crashing back into the sea. She ran, jumped like a bounding greyhound, and ran some more. In a flash, she was 100, then 200 yards away.

T-man knew the boat wasn't fast enough to chase the fish down if she got too far away and tried to keep as much pressure as he could on the 50-pound test line without having it snap. His arms burned like molten steel bands. He gritted his teeth and held on.

The marlin turned back toward the boat, took two powerful tail strokes, and leaped out of the water barely 30 feet from where they all stood with mouths drop-jawed open in awe—and that included the horse. Bonefish's eyes looked like a giant Atlantic squid —20 white-eyeballed-inches in diameter and wide, wide open.

The marlin fell back into the sea again, flopping sideways a mighty splash that sent a wall of salty water crashing into the boat's open cockpit. Bonefish neighed again, even louder than before, but he was too scared to rear up on his hind legs. He just stood there bug-eyed like Anvil and T-man while T-man hollered at his dad about what to do and Anvil hollered at T-man for hooking the damn thing in the first place.

Bonefish then pooped, which was certainly understandable.

Well, the long and short of it is that T-man grittily muscled that big blue marlin for as long as he could. After 55 minutes, he managed to work the fish again near the boat. This time, as it poked its big head out of the water, T-man heard a loud *"Ker-POW!"*

Anvil had stood on the side railing, leaned out, and fired a perfect shot with the flare gun. He killed the fish instantly at a range of six feet. He knew the noise, the blood, and the fish would attract sharks almost immediately, so he lassoed its tail and T-man, and he wrestled in a tug-of-war to slide the fat marlin out of the sea. They found out on marina scales six hours later the massive fish weighed 408 pounds.

With the big dead marlin prone on the deck, Anvil and T-man just looked at it, looked at each other, and hugged. Bonefish skipped the hugging. He just kept looking at the fish. Bonefish was not a big fan of large marlin, especially this one.

Matter of fact, Bonefish wasn't even a fan of small marlin. He much preferred peppermints and licorice, which T-man gave him a handful of for not going wild at the sound of the flare gun or sight of the marlin. Bonefish ate his candy slowly, but never took his eye off the fish. He didn't like that marlin—dead *or* alive—and couldn't understand why it was invited aboard in the first place.

Anvil covered the marlin with a heavy blue plastic sheet to protect the meat from the sun. After all, they were only a third of the way to Miami. He also looked at T-man, who was rooting around in the big cooler for either an orange soda or another trolling bait.

"Don't even think about it," Anvil said.

"No problem, Pop," smiled T-man, emerging with a soda. "Thirsty?"

Five hours later, they caught the tide change just as Anvil had hoped and, with the dangerous currents of Government Cut negated by a slack tide, Anvil was able to chug through an annoying parade of curious criss-crossing jet skiers and head toward U.S. Customs at the Port of Miami.

Once they cleared customs, the water taxi plowed another hour north up Biscayne Bay. They were safe now, in calm, shallow, and protected waters. Anvil used the radio to call Mountain, and both Truck and Mountain were waiting with a horse trailer when the water taxi arrived at Keystone Point Marina in North Miami.

Under normal circumstances, the marina was only about a ten-minute drive up Biscayne Boulevard past Aventura Mall and across the county line to the track. But the arrival of a Bahamian water taxi loaded down with a 1200-pound horse and a 400-pound blue marlin hardly qualified as normal.

The marina people wanted to call the paper to get a photo and free publicity, but Anvil didn't want to wait. Bonefish didn't care; he seemed content to hang out in the shade of a leafy palm by the dock, staring directly into Minnow Thomas' overflowing fish box to see the fish Minnow had caught that day. Minnow was a local legend around town—one of the top guides in South Florida. He'd fished for more than 300 days this year and had never caught a marlin that big. The skilled captain admired the huge blue and laughed at the story behind it as he emptied his fish box. He tossed 16 mahi-mahi and wahoo up on the dock for cleaning.

T-man helped Minnow fillet the mahi-mahi and steak the wahoo, then hose and scrub down his boat. Minnow had an evening tarpon charter beginning at sundown. On a good night, Minnow would jump three big tarpon using palm-sized live palm-sized mullet or giant live shrimp for bait. The biggest tarpon parked in the deep water of the cruise ship channel, Government Cut, right where T and his dad had puttered into customs a couple of hours before.

When they finished cleaning the boat, Minnow peeled off a $10 bill and handed it to T-man to thank him for his help. T-man beamed and pocketed the cash. For T-man, that $10 came in very handy later in the week.

Anvil, meanwhile, was itching to leave, but he had cut a deal with the marina. They would all wait for the press if the marina would ice down the giant fish and help him encase the gutted marlin in a billfish carrier, which was a specially designed zip-up body bag the marina had on-premise.

Once the newspaper photographers came and left, which didn't take long, the guys loaded the horse and the iced-down, body-bagged marlin into the horse trailer and drove 15 minutes north up Biscayne Boulevard to Gulfstream Park.

The older three men rode in the pickup truck's cab while T-man rode inside the trailer with the horse and fish. So far, this was already the greatest adventure of his life and they'd only been gone for eight hours.

Up front, the men squeezed together tightly, three across, on the truck's bench seat. At the first red light, Truck couldn't resist reaching over and leaning on Mountain's car horn while ducking down and out of sight behind the passenger door. That left Anvil and Mountain sitting there snugly next to each other looking like black and white gay lovers. Everybody in the cars around them looked over and stared in disgust.

Both of his buddies took turns f-bombing Truck all the rest of the way to Gulfstream. He laughed like hell. He'd sat by the door on purpose, just to pull off that little trick.

Every Restaurant
Needs a Good Horse

It was late Sunday afternoon when the guys pulled into Gulfstream's Receiving Area and unloaded Bonefish into the Receiving Barn. T-man stayed with the horse while Anvil and Truck ran off to figure out what to do next. They'd been given tentative permission to keep Bonefish there for two nights, pending approval from the vets and an assumption that coming from only 50 miles away waived the need for Bonefish to be quarantined.

Quarantining was done down at the airport, Miami International, and that was one thing Truck and Anvil wanted to avoid.

Bonefish's blood tested fine. Test results from his Coggins screening for infectious equine anemia revealed traces of little more than peppermint candy and red Twizzlers licorice. Miraculously, after a couple of meetings and several phone calls, Bonefish was allowed to stay. Since he had left Gulfstream, and now returned and never lived anywhere else but Bimini, the USDA cut them a big break and waived the need for quarantine. Bonefish practically lived his whole life about as far from Gulfstream as Palm Beach to the north or Key Largo to the south, so the Feds decided quarantining was unnecessary.

Monday

Monday morning, the guys met for breakfast at six o'clock and returned to Gulfstream to try and sell the horse. Bonefish had run the white sandy Bahamian beaches his whole life and looked quite fit. Anvil didn't realize how fit until he looked at the other horses around the barns. Bonefish's breeding and daily workouts with T-man bouncing along on his back gave him a defined musculature much like a real racehorse. Anvil walked around and examined the other older horses on the backside. They all appeared much the same except for one. That horse, two barns over, was named Bushrod. Bushrod was all muscled up in the shoulders like heavyweight boxer Mike Tyson.

If somebody had purchased all of these other horses—and Gulfstream housed 1,300 of them—then, shoot, somebody just might buy Bonefish, too. Surely someone had to know *somebody* who'd like to own the son of a Kentucky Derby winner—cheap.

Truck and Anvil decided it might help if they could get Bonefish out on the track for a morning run. To do that, they needed a trainer. One of the Receiving Barn grooms suggested an old black fellow named Luther. Though he was a groom now, Luther still held a trainer's license. He'd had a small string but lost it a year before because of a lost battle with the booze. Luther didn't know anything *except* horses, so he stayed on as a groom, determined that some day he'd earn the chance to prove he'd learned his lesson. It was a bitter experience for him to dig up the $100 necessary to renew his trainer's license, even though he had no horses. But Luther paid it as a personally imposed "stupid" tax to remind himself what he needed to fix in his life.

Truck vaguely recalled Luther's name around the backside, but had never met him. When Truck and Anvil sought him out, they found Luther sitting on a bale of hay and polishing leather, explaining to a skinny guy wearing a paper Snack Shack hat and white restaurant coat why show business gave great value to society. Truck thought the skinny guy looked vaguely familiar, but couldn't place him.

"The circus *is* important," Luther insisted to his companion as Truck and Anvil approached. They stepped around another groom hosing off a jet-black colt, an expensive son of Kingmambo.

"It keeps the midgets off the streets," he said. With that, Luther looked up and greeted his visitors.

After introductions, they all walked back to the Receiving Barn and Luther looked Bonefish over. "You know," he said slowly, rubbing his chin reflectively, "he looks a lot like a horse we had here years ago that never left the gate. Damnedest thing you ever saw."

Truck and Anvil just looked at each other.

"Um . . . it *is* him," Truck finally admitted. "We're sort of hoping he's outgrown that."

What Truck didn't realize was that the *Miami Herald* had run a feature story in the morning paper about a gray Bahamian horse that had just crossed the Gulf Stream in a water taxi. Bonefish's picture was in the *Herald*, too. This horse would be a lot harder to sell today than yesterday—especially to horsemen.

Unfazed, Luther who'd read the story over morning coffee, decided that training *any* horse was better than training none at all. He opted not to mention the story and chose to cut a quick business deal: For 30 bucks a day, he'd work the horse and help find a buyer. If Luther found one, he got one-fourth of the cash.

The others agreed and they all shook hands. "Let's see what he's got. I'll get Piso to breeze him three furlongs," Luther said. "If we time it right, we can make him look a lot faster than he is. I'll get Piso to run him hard right past a couple of them other Gozzleheads," he added with a wink. "And if we can't beat 'em, we'll arrange to have them beaten." Luther laughed loudly. He was *killin'* himself.

Truck and Anvil just turned their heads sideways and looked at each other. Words were unnecessary. Truck shrugged. If this guy could help sell the horse, then God bless him. They didn't care how he went about doing it, either.

The prospect of entering a race at Gulfstream Park with a horse that spent more time on the beach than a Baywatch lifeguard seemed as feasible as running for president, naked. And that thought had never occurred to Truck. But the moment Truck and Anvil shook hands with Luther, the idea took on a life of its own for the trainer. Luther figured if he treated Bonefish like a real racehorse—and pretended he really *was* one—then maybe he could convince someone to buy him. If he played his cards right, he'd have his cash in hand and Anvil could skeedaddle out of town before the seas even kicked up again.

Silently, Truck wondered if Bonefish could outrun *any* of the thousand-plus horses surrounding him. "Surely he must be able to," Truck mused silently. "Then again, probably not."

The small group discussed Bonefish's typical routine back home, including his long morning runs with T-man on the beach. Luther perked up when he heard how often Bonefish worked. "Maybe he's got a foundation," he said, shrugging his shoulders. "Piso will give him a breeze. If nothing else, it'll make the horse feel better. We'll take it easy and shop him if we can. See you Gozzleheads later."

Apparently, Luther called everybody "Gozzlehead," which, if nothing else, served to make this fellow fit right in with the rest of Team Bonefish.

Truck and Anvil again shook hands with Luther and left. They had a long walk to make around to the front side of the track. That's where, much to Anvil's surprise, he learned that he was, in fact, already a registered and legal-to-race Thoroughbred owner. The papers and thumbprint Truck made him sign years ago when he delivered Bonefish to the island were owner's papers. Ever since that fateful day, Truck sent off Anvil's annual renewal dues each year, more out of romance than practicality. Truck never thought the horse would leave the island, but now that they were here contemplating this implausible pipe dream, they might as well roll destiny's dice if the croupiers allowed.

Anvil and Truck reached the front side of the track about the same time Bonefish stepped out on the track to work. Anvil recognized the familiar galloping stride of his four-legged son and proudly enjoyed watching him stretch out and go. His rider was low in a crouch as they flew past the empty clubhouse. Bonefish eased up entering the turn and jogged his way around to the backside barn.

Luther was waiting as Bonefish stepped off of the racing surface. He was surprised how easily the horse was breathing. "Horse OK," said the rider in broken English. "No problemo."

To Luther, the impossible—entering this old gray gelding in a race—suddenly was now merely improbable. They'd breeze the horse again in a couple days. In the meantime, Luther decided to try sell him for $7,000.

Later that afternoon, Bonefish started getting restless inside his stall. Anvil and T-man weren't surprised. A morning gallop couldn't offset living in a box for a horse used to Caribbean trade winds and the hypnotic tranquility of the ocean's tidal changes. After his morning cool-down and bath, Bonefish stubbornly dug in and refused to go back in his stall. Six hours later, he still wouldn't—and remained tied to a nearby shade tree.

Barn life made Bonefish uncomfortable. Too much to worry about. Too much going on. Too many places for rats to hide. Bonefish was too used to staring at the sea and waiting for a swaying palm to drop an occasional coconut to adjust to all the hustle and commotion of the backside of a major track like Gulfstream.

He remembered this place and didn't like it.

At T-man's urging, Anvil and Luther decided Bonefish would be better off staying on the water taxi so he could see, hear, and feel the rocking of the water and watch the boats go by—just like home. It took a few hours of looking, but they finally found the perfect place.

Anvil, T-man, and Luther walked 20 minutes east of the track and toward the ocean. There, right on the Intracoastal Waterway in the shadow of the Hallandale Beach drawbridge, they spied a 120-foot-long wooden dock at the back of the Manero's Restaurant parking lot. Together, they decided to investigate.

Manero's, the famed horseman's hangout, was parked right on the corner of 26th Avenue and Hallandale Beach Boulevard. It was perfect. The restaurant was less than a mile from the track. An easy walk.

Anvil and Luther stepped inside, met with the owners, and explained what they wanted to do. Once convinced they weren't on "Candid Camera," the owners agreed to let Anvil park the water taxi at the dock. For the horse's safety, they said Bonefish would be better off arriving around sundown. By then, most of the narrow canal's daily boat traffic would have subsided. It was much calmer in the evening than during the daytime—much less commotion and far fewer ricocheting backwash waves.

And so, at dusk, T-man dutifully walked Bonefish from the Receiving Barn to the rear of the Gulfstream stable area, took a left at Mark Hennig's stable, and stepped through the narrow chain-link fence gate bordering the track and the Hallandale electric substation. Following T-man's lead, Bonefish stepped around a 12-foot drainage ditch and crossed over onto the Golden Isles Tennis Center and Bocce Ball Courts.

Patiently walking five feet behind Bonefish was a black-and-white barn goat named Elvis. He took a liking to Bonefish the moment they met. And when Bonefish left the Receiving Barn, Elvis decided to go with him.

The poor man's circus parade walked past the tennis courts, past the bocce ball players, then turned left down Egret Drive before turning left again a block later. An immediate right clopped them across an unnamed 100-foot finger canal walkover. A quick jog to the left on Golden Isles Drive and an immediate right down

Diana Drive looped them right around to SE 26th Avenue and Manero's Restaurant. It was simple, safe, and easy. Back streets all the way.

The horse, goat, and T-man all walked out on Manero's dock at the back of the parking lot. One by one, they walked down the boarding ramp onto the water taxi and settled in for the evening. In a matter of minutes, Bonefish was snoring, rocking gently in the vigilant company of his new guard-goat Elvis, contentedly dreaming of pink conch shells, white sandy beaches, and swaying palm trees under a setting sun.

Soon, the trio had unexpected company. Several neighborhood alley cats took a liking to the iced-down marlin zipped inside the billfish body bag on the back deck of the boat. The strays milled around, scheming and dreaming of ways to drag the giant feast off the deck and into the darkness of night. They were also meowing what sounded like a furball-choked sonata from the musical soundtrack of "Cats."

It became chaotic guarding everything and trying to sleep at the same time. Surrounded and outnumbered, T-man felt like a lone security guard at the Miss World Pageant.

In the morning, the folks at Manero's came to the rescue and let T-man put the marlin inside their walk-in cooler until it was time to head back home. That made T a lot happier but angered all of the cats.

All told, it was a quiet three-quarter-mile walk from the track to Manero's and the tiny unnamed canal walkover soon became known around the neighborhood as Bonefish Boulevard. In the morning, when T-man reversed this path, dozens of neighbors came out to see the horse they had read about in the paper and seen on the evening news. The kids scurried along to pet Bonefish. More of them petted Elvis, since he was smaller and easier to keep up with. Elvis didn't care. He just kept walking.

They stayed at Manero's the rest of the week, arriving each afternoon at dusk. They left each morning between five-thirty and six o'clock to head back to the track. Each night they returned, the folks at Manero's had added more creature comforts to the water taxi. They even hired a guard to keep an eye on everything.

Tuesday

The week's already improbable course of events took on a whole new dimension Tuesday afternoon when Truck and Anvil showed up at Gulfstream's Horse Identifier's office. As they turned over Bonefish's papers, they learned that a message was waiting for Truck. Apparently someone had anticipated his arrival and called down looking for him.

Puzzled, Truck scrutinized the green writing on the pink "While You Were Out" message sheet. "Is there a dart board around here somewhere? I'm thirsty. Love, Cush. P.S. We'll be in the Turf Club—1 p.m." Truck was bewildered when he saw the name.

Still holding the note, he slowly lowered his right arm, wrinkled his face, and blinked twice. What in the world was *she* doing here? This whole thing was getting more surreal by the moment.

An hour later, Truck stepped off the Turf Club elevator and walked over to announce himself at the registration table. "Oh yes, Mr. Roberts, we've been expecting you. This way, please."

Truck hadn't seen the Posse in years, but spied the girls from 100 feet away. He saw them whisper to each other and look in his direction as he approached.

Cushla had her back to him, then turned to look when Mitzi asked if that was him. Cush beamed a radiant smile and ignored her sunburn to jump out of her chair and rush over to meet him. Truck reached out to hug her. "God, it's good to see you," he thought as he closed his eyes and tightly squeezed her in his arms.

"Dammitall!" Cush wailed. "Oh my friggin' sunburn!"

The others all laughed as Truck recoiled and let go like she was a baked potato he'd just barehanded out of a hot oven.

For the next hour and a half, the Posse peppered Truck with dozens of questions about the horse they had read about in the morning paper. The girls had seen the story and photos of the water taxi in the *Herald* and came to the track hoping to find Truck, meet his friends, and see Bonefish. Apparently, the story was buzzing all over South Beach—especially since it had a dotted-line connection to Mitzi the A-Lister.

When Truck left the Turf Club just after the fourth race to walk back and meet the others, he had four pretty girls on his arms. He was the envy of every dirty old man in the place.

That night, when T-man and Bonefish returned to Manero's, they saw a big new tent and sleeping bag already set up in the center of the wide dock. T also had a power cord, television, and stereo. He was now officially roughing it in style.

Two TV crews stopped by for a look-see, as did four different newspaper reporters. And, like any good fisherman, every time a reporter asked about it, T-man's marlin grew 20 pounds heavier than in the interview before. By Thursday, it'd be up to 500 pounds, easy.

T-man liked the publicity. He was starting to like the horse business very, very much.

Wednesday

Wednesday was another early morning because Luther wanted to turn Bonefish loose again for a short work. Again, Luther had Piso Mojado, his little buddy from the Snack Shack, work the horse. Piso zipped Bonefish a fast, short sprint—just two furlongs—to see if the gelding had any acceleration. Bonefish had some speed—he ran the quarter-mile comfortably in just under 25 seconds flat—but he certainly wasn't a flier. The horse ran the second furlong faster than the first, even though he had to swerve around a horse that drifted slightly off the rail.

Truck, Anvil, T-man, and Luther were all leaning over the outside guardrail, side by side, when Piso cantered up on the horse after the workout. He gave Luther a thumbs-up sign and said, "Ees OK."

"Well then," Luther said slowly as he stared out at the other horses still circling the track, "it seems we have a decision to make."

"What's that?" asked Anvil. He hoped someone had offered to buy Bonefish. Maybe Luther had received an offer.

"We won't be able to sell him here unless you run him," said Luther. "So the decision you have to make is whether you want to run him."

"In a race?" T-man chimed in excitedly.

"In a race, Gozzlehead Junior," replied Luther. "I don't know if you Gozzleheads can get in it, but there's a race on Saturday for older horses—geldings nine years old and up. One mile. A long way for a horse with no experience. But one way or the other, you'd better decide soon. Entries close today."

"How good are the other horses in it?" asked Truck.

"Some good, some not so good. That's why they run the race—to find out," Luther replied. "Give it some thought. Let me know what you Gozzleheads decide."

After a brief discussion, the guys decided to give it a try.

Truck borrowed a barn phone, called the track president's office, and asked for a minute of his time. Truck and Anvil still had a whole lot of talking to do and knew it. Truck also asked the president's assistant, Tina Van Doran, if Gulfstream's Racing Secretary Moe Bennett could take a moment and sit in.

"Five minutes," Tina replied after she made a call. "That's about all we've got. I'll call Moe for you, too. But hurry. Mr. Douglass has a conference call scheduled that will tie him up for a couple of hours."

"C'mon," Truck urged Anvil. "Now the real selling starts."

So, around they went to the Executive Offices. Both men paused and inhaled deeply before stepping inside the one marked *"Donny Ray Douglass—President."* Reality had arrived. Now they had to talk their way into a race they shouldn't be in.

"No. Hell no. Absolutely no. Absolutely, positively, hell no!" cried the Racing Secretary, once he heard about Bonefish. "This isn't a *circus*. It's a business—a regulated business—with strict rules and regulations. Your horse does not meet the criteria required to run at Gulfstream Park."

"We aren't asking to break any laws. We just want permission to run the horse on Saturday against a bunch of horses his own age," explained Truck. "What's wrong with that?"

"No maidens over four years old," recited the Racing Secretary without even looking. "Page 3 in the Condition Book."

Truck took his argument to a bigger-picture level. "You could get an exception approval for this race. The horse is fit. Go look at him. See for yourself. The whole purpose behind this race is public relations and marketing. God knows, the business needs it. For Pete's sake, it's the walkout race on the last day of the meet.

"Let this horse run and people will come see him. You know it, and I know it. The novelty factor alone puts fannies in the chairs—especially if you market it right."

"Why do you want to do this?" asked the president bluntly. "Why now? Who in their right mind would pick a world-class venue and decide to start a horse's racing career at the age of nine? It just doesn't make sense.

"Moe's right," he continued. "This is not a dude ranch and it's not a circus. It's Gulfstream Park—where the nation's finest professional *racehorses* race.

"Especially so with *this* particular horse," the president continued evenly. "From what I remember, when this horse was here six or seven years ago, he refused to even leave the gate. What makes you think he'd do so now?"

President Douglass leaned forward in his chair, then asked the hardest question of all. "How would I look," he said slowly, "if I let this horse in the race, people actually bet on it, and the damn thing sat there and did nothing? I'd be the laughingstock of the industry," he said, answering his own question. "And I don't like it."

With that, he stopped talking, sat back in his deep-cushioned chair, and waited for an answer.

Truck was stuck. Logic was often a formidable foe—especially now. But not for Anvil.

"I agree with you, sir," Anvil said quietly with his deep, Bahamian-accented drawl. "I agree with everything you said and you could've said a lot more and I'd still agree with you, sir. If you let Bonefish race and Bonefish don't race, then everyone is sad.

"I have a cash box on the water taxi," continued Anvil. "In it are $212 in nickels, dimes, quarters, and crumpled dollar bills from 62 people in Bimini who believe in their Bonefish.

"For *their* sake, sir, please let Bonefish prove whether they are right or wrong.

"To you, this is just another race with old horses. To us, Bonefish *is* Bimini. He is not just another horse in a barn. He is one of us.

"Bonefish is the hopes and dreams of the children on our island. And Bonefish is the hopes and dreams of the old people on the island.

"Island people *need* dreams, Mr. Douglass, sir. Dreams are the only way to make our island bigger. And make our lives bigger.

"I will bring you the cash box, sir, and let you see it. And when you open that cash box, you will hear the voices of all the people of Bimini cheering for their horse.

"Bonefish will not win your race, sir. But he will try his very best. Of that, I am certain. Of that, the people of Bimini are certain."

Anvil then stopped talking. He sat back stiffly and looked the track president right dead square in the eye. Douglass twirled his black Montblanc pen in circles many times around while he thought about what he'd just heard.

Without this horse, the meet's final race was just a bunch of old horses running in a circle. With this horse, this race—an otherwise forgettable and innocuous two minutes—suddenly had a personality. So, without expression, he slowly turned to Moe and said simply, "Find a way. Figure out a way to get the horse in the race—but make damn sure everybody on the planet knows its history. The last thing we need is anybody betting on it."

Racing Secretary Bennett shrugged his shoulders, gritted his teeth, and obediently nodded. He wasn't happy. He was a professional and took his work seriously. To Moe Bennett, this was a step toward merging horseracing with pro wrestling.

The four men stood and shook hands all around. "Good luck," said the president with a smile. "You're going to need it. We're *all* going to need it."

"Yessir," said Anvil. "Thank you sir."

Once safely down the hall and out of earshot, Truck turned to Anvil and said, "That was a hell of a speech. How'd you do that?"

"I dunno," said Anvil. "I just hope the son-of-a-bitch runs."

Anvil then left to go back and tell T and Luther they had a race on Saturday. Truck also told Anvil to have Luther figure out which jockey should, or would, ride Bonefish. They'd meet back at the stall in one hour to figure out what else they still had to do.

With the race three days away, the legal owner and trainer now in place, Team Bonefish turned its attention to finding a jockey. All of the track old-timers remembered Bonefish back from his days as Whodathunkit. Naturally, no jockey wanted to be humiliated—or hurt—by sitting atop a horse that sat down and rolled over when the starting gates flashed opened. The meager riding fee—the "jock mount"—just wasn't worth the risk.

With no seasoned jockey wanting the ride, the ones who wanted it were not the kind of guys who got along with Luther. So Luther lobbied for Plan B. Plan B was Piso Mojado.

The Little Man with the Great Big Dream

Piso had worked at the track for eight years at the backside Snack Shack eatery and before Luther lost his string, he'd exercised many of Luther's horses. That all stopped a year ago when Luther lost his horses. Piso was only a substitute now—an afterthought substitute exercise rider—and didn't get to ride very often. Mostly, he threw away paper plates, cups, and plastic forks, and washed cooking pots.

Piso had never ridden a horse in a live race. But he'd twice ridden Bonefish in workouts and hadn't fallen off, so in his mind that was proof enough of his ability.

In fact, Piso was the same thin Cuban guy who looked familiar to Truck when they first approached Luther early Monday morning. And years ago, Piso was the one who gave Truck phone change the morning he arrived from the Swap Shop with the horse in tow. Now it seemed that fate had brought them all full circle.

The trainer always promised Piso a ride—a real ride—if he ever got his string back. Luther's dream was to have another horse; Piso's was to ride one. Destiny and opportunity were about to shake hands.

Piso Mojado got a license to ride by the State Racing Steward, but it wasn't easy. Florida's state racing rules said a jockey must be qualified to ride. There wasn't a written test; it was more a subjective decision. All riders were supposed to have starting-gate experience. Piso didn't have much, but then again neither did the horse. They seemed a perfect pair. But it took a hell of a lot of arguing and convincing for the steward to finally relent.

Luther helped Piso fill out the license application, which was in English. Cush filled one out, too, just in case. On it were questions like where you've exercised horses and if you were a felon. It was the steward's job to guard against a dangerous situation for the horses and the other riders. When lives and money were at stake, bullshit had to pass through a fine-meshed net.

When the steward balked at approving Piso's application, Cushla volunteered to ride the horse instead. "I worked at Ellerslie and rode at Takanini for seven years," she told the steward firmly. "You haven't a bloody horse in the place I can't ride sidesaddle."

The steward had never had such a crowd in his office before: eight people, including four sunburned New Zealand girls, all trying to find a jockey for a horse no professional wanted to ride.

"Pick your poison," said Truck. "Him or her. They can both ride, but we only need one."

Two other apprentice riders were in the race, which ended up helping the argument that finally got Piso a license to ride. The clincher came when Luther asked for a minute alone with the steward. He explained the truth about how Piso had arrived in the U.S. in the first place—by bailing a small, barely floating, homemade leaky boat drifting north in the Gulf Stream for four days. Piso risked his life by hoping to float away from Castro's oppression and toward somewhere he might one day get a chance to do something with himself and his life. Eight years of dutifully washing dishes six days a week at the Snack Shack for minimum wage hardly qualified as living the American dream. Piso never missed a day of work and never caused a single bit of trouble. All the man wanted was a chance.

To further work the guilt angle, Luther also explained the story behind Piso's name. Piso spoke no English at all when he was rescued off the Fowey Light reef stanchion in South Biscayne Bay. When taken ashore by the fisherman who found him and turned over to Immigration, Piso was terrified at the thought of being returned to Cuba. So when the Immigration officials asked him his name, he was too scared to use his Cuban name. He looked over the official's shoulder, saw a yellow "Wet Floor" sign clapboarded open to protect a mopped area of tile floor, and recited its Spanish translation.

"Me llamo Piso Mojado," he said. The officer wrote it down on the form and from that moment forward, Piso's new life in America began under the Spanish moniker for Wet Floor.

"Besides," Luther shrugged to the steward. "He'll probably lose by 40 lengths anyway, even if the horse *does* decide to leave the gate. And you know this horse. History says there ain't a whole helluva lot of chance of that happenin.'"

"Look," urged Truck, chiming in. "This is a PR race and it's a PR jackpot. The horse is a public relations story, the people behind the horse are a PR story, the trainer is a PR story, and the jockey is a PR story. Nobody will get hurt. Promise," he said, crossing his heart with his right index finger while two fingers of his left hand were crossed and hidden behind his back.

The steward relented. He wasn't thrilled about it, but he relented. He remembered back when Piso first showed up looking for work at the track and ended up at the Snack Shack. He admired the guy for sticking around so long in such a mundane job despite all the belittling abuse he took from some of the more well-to-do jocks like Taco Perez. "Well," he finally said, "I'll give a shot to the guy who's been here. The last thing I need is a pretty New Zealand girl getting splattered all over the national news."

Cush didn't like that remark and wished the steward's butt were a dartboard. But for the good of the cause, she kept her thoughts to herself.

Piso was fingerprinted, affirmed he wasn't a convicted felon, and had another photo taken since they wouldn't let his backside Snack Shack ID card be used for jockey room access.

Piso Mojado was now licensed to ride horses in the state of Florida. But benevolence only went so far and the steward made it crystal clear that one single screw-up meant he'd yank the license and it'd be another million clean dishes at the Snack Shack before Piso ever got another one.

With that, he signed Piso's license, shook hands, and said, "Hasta luego."

In his own version of self-created broken Spanish, Luther looked at Piso and said something to the effect of, "No screw-ups, Gozzlehead Mojado. Don't play leapfrog with a unicorn." Luther had no clue what "unicorn" was in Spanish, so he called it "unicorno."

Piso solemnly looked back at Luther, crossed his heart, and, in his most sincere fractured English, replied, "Piso no up-screw."

Thus reassured, the group happily conga'd single file triumphantly out the steward's doorway and back into the hall. Deeply and audibly exhaling, Luther turned to Anvil and whispered, "Never underestimate the power of Gozzleheads in large groups. Was that a smoke bomb of logic or what?"

And so, with an ear-to-ear lightbulb smile, Piso clutched his papers and nearly floated back to the Snack Shack to do the dishes. He had a horse. And he had a race. Piso Mojado would get to ride. His name would be in the newspaper, *El Nuevo Herald*, the Spanish edition of the *Miami Herald*, so other Cubans would see. It would be in the *Daily Racing Form*, too.

After 28 years of living, Piso Mojado had tears in his eyes. He was finally a somebody. There were many days over the last eight years when he wondered if his float to freedom was worth it. Those doubts were officially over. For one day in his life—this Saturday—28 years of crawling uphill would be worth every agonizing moment.

That is, of course, if the horse decided to leave the gate.

Thursday

Now that he had a horse, a jockey, and a race, Luther needed a strategy. He realized his only chance to interest anyone in buying the horse would be if Bonefish somehow managed to run on the lead—however briefly that would be. The plan, then, was to have Bonefish run to the front and hold on as long as he could. Leaving the gate would certainly help.

Luther also made arrangements for Piso to watch videotapes of the other horses in the race and study their running styles. The pair mapped out who would run to the front and who would lay back. The muscled Bushrod seemed far and away the best horse in the race and he would stalk the leaders, then close with a rush to the finish.

"Whatever you do, Piso," Luther said, "don't lay back in the pack. That and two dead cats'll get you a stinky livin' room. You need to get him to the front and hang on."

Luther never told Piso that when the race started and the gates opened, his mount quite possibly would sit down, lay down, roll over on top of the jockey, and scratch his back in the dirt while kicking at the air. He also knew strategy was little more than practical noise to Piso, but hoped Bonefish could run fast enough, long enough to get a piece of the purse. "Piso," Luther said slowly, "your strategy is simple. Hold on. Hold on like you'll be deported by some Gozzlehead if you fall off."

Piso's eyes got big. He didn't understand much English, but he understood "deported." And he damn sure didn't want that to happen. Piso gave serious consideration to SuperGlue'ing his buttocks to the little racing saddle as extra insurance. At home, with no one around, he experimented with Velcro, but it wasn't strong enough to hold and he kept falling out of his chair.

Piso was determined not only to stay upright and on his horse, but also to try his darnedest to show he could ride and win a piece of the action. He didn't know enough to realize they were chasing extremely large butterflies with extremely small aquarium fishnets.

The purse money for the race would be doled out 60 perfect to the winner, 19 percent for second, 12 percent for third, 5 percent for fourth, and 4 percent for fifth. Both Piso and Luther would get 10 percent of the winner's share if Bonefish won. They'd get half of that for second or third.

Piso was getting $55 to ride the horse, no matter what happened, and he was happy about that. The $55 represented a full day's pay all by itself. But the chance to make more was there and he would do his best to hang on. And no matter what happened, Piso knew one thing for sure: He was the first man in Snack Shack history to saddle up and ride the son of a Kentucky Derby winner. No one could *ever* take that away from him.

More importantly from Anvil's perspective, if Bonefish beat somebody—anybody—then maybe some horseman might actually buy him.

But if Bonefish wouldn't leave the gate, or embarrassed them all with a last-place sightseeing scenic tour, then it was probably time to wave goodbye, grab whatever pony money they could get from a kids' camp, and head back to the Bahamas. The taxi would be weighed down with $212 worth of "dead wood"—losing betting slips—to prove to the islanders that Anvil had been right all along.

Thursday Evening at Manero's

Thursday night, 200 feet from the water taxi—inside the restaurant bar adorned with horseracing photos of past great champions—no one knew what to make of the odd parade that came and went each evening and morning. The family-owned restaurant had been serving steaks and seafood since 1953, two years after Gulfstream opened, and no one could recall *ever* having a racehorse and a goat camp out in the parking lot before. In fact, none of the 300 wood-framed photos lining the restaurant walls showed the horses standing on anything but dirt or grass.

Even Jacob Burns, the fabled horseracing writer, wasn't quite sure what to make of the animal tied up at the dock. Sitting in the booth beneath the 1978 Florida Derby April Fool's Day winner's circle photo of Jorge Velasquez and #6 Alydar, Burns mulled over what to write in his next column for the *Daily Racing Form.*

In his 61 years of covering racing around the world, Jacob Burns had seen it all and heard it all. But an old gray gelding that arrived in town with a giant dead marlin as a Caribbean pontoon boat refugee, then prepped for its racing debut at Gulfstream Park in the parking lot of an Italian restaurant was a new one to him.

"God I love this sport," Burns thought. He sketched out a lead in the dog-eared leather notepad he'd gotten 40 years before at the Hippodrome in Buenos Aires. "A lifetime of dreams answered and prayers ignored. And now this."

Every instinct told him this was nothing but a carnival stunt. But then again—maybe not. Stoop-shouldered and shuffle-stepped as many 90 year olds are, Burns rose slowly from his table, signaled to the bartender to hold his booth, and slowly moved toward the dimly lit parking lot in an inch-by-inch procession of determination.

Outside, Burns shuffled all the way to the dock where he stood in the darkness for nearly two minutes. Camp Bonefish was quiet, the only sounds the lapping of the late-night waves against the boat and the light alternating snores of the horse and goat. Two minutes was enough. He'd seen what he needed to see. Jacob had the lead for his column.

Burns turned, then shuffled back inside the bar and over to his booth. He dropped heavily into the red-padded seat and took a long sip of delicious scotch.

Jacob Burns firmly wrote three words in his notepad, then wrote the same three words again—in capital letters—and underlined each. "When pigs fly," he scrawled, his pen pushing down hard against the unlined white paper. *"WHEN PIGS FLY."*

The Golden Geezer Gallop

When Saturday finally rolled around, Team Bonefish knew nothing, other than this day would be unlike any other—regardless of what happened. Bonefish slept in, snoring as usual, until a six o'clock foghorn signaled the drawbridge to open. It was time to get up and go. He hated that damn foghorn.

Saturday's tenth race was, basically, a heavily conditioned goodwill stunt to help the horsemen on the backside, plus generate some positive play in the press. The fans seemed to love the idea of it, too. The race was a mile, for geldings only, nine years old and up.

Holding this event was a smart racing move, typical of the astute win-win management style of Gulfstream President Donny Ray Douglass. He was a widely respected marketer among horsemen across the American racing scene. Gulfstream Park had hosted the Breeders' Cup World Thoroughbred Championships several times, and put on a great show each time.

The media—especially the television and newspapers—had picked up the story and given it a lot of local promotion. The romantic notion of an old horse—a Derby winner's wayward son—crossing the ocean at the age of nine to run in a race made for tantalizing copy.

Bonefish's entry ended up dramatically helping the track turn a nice profit from the race. Thanks to the media blitz, an extra 2,000 fans showed up that day to watch the gray horse that had crossed the Atlantic.

Bonefish's race was the walk-out race—the last race on the day's card—and the greater-than-normal interest would help keep the fans around to bet a couple more races than they normally would. Instead of leaving after the seventh or eight race, the fans would stick around to watch the curious gelding and see what happened.

By coming out and betting Saturday's entire race card, those 2,000 fans meant an extra $400,000 worth of wagers to Gulfstream Park. And since Gulfstream kept roughly 20 percent of those extra wagering dollars, Donny Ray's decision to let Bonefish run proved financially astute. Even with half that extra amount—$40,000—peeled off for the horseman's purse account, the remaining balance would be an unexpected windfall to Gulfstream's bottom line.

Both major area newspapers, the *Fort Lauderdale Sun-Sentinel* and the *Miami Herald,* ran Saturday photos of Bonefish in the sports pages after mentioning the upcoming race in both Thursday and Friday's racing news. And any "pub" is great in the horseracing business—as long as it's not a photo of an injured animal or stubborn gelding sitting on his can in the starting gate. Judging by Saturday's larger-than-usual crowd, the publicity worked extremely well.

So far, at least, Bonefish was good for business.

Douglass dreamed up and decided to sponsor this particular race as much for advertising and good will as anything else. He had seven old veteran geldings regularly running at Gulfstream—all professional racehorses on the downside of good-to-mediocre careers—and Donny Ray figured he'd reward their owners and trainers with a thank-you race that posted a decent purse plus a bonus for the winner. The track's horsemen recognized and appreciated this clever race concept as a creative marketing gesture.

Donny Ray was a popular track president, thanks to his persistent efforts to make Gulfstream races fan-friendly fun for its customers while assisting the horsemen whenever possible. The size of this race's purse—$32,000—was good but about average.

Gulfstream generally awarded about a third of a million dollars a day in prize money. The track's younger and faster horses deserved the bigger purses and got them.

Yet Donny Ray Douglass understood that any connection he could create between the fans and the athletes of the sport—be they two-legged jockeys or four-legged horses—couldn't be anything *but* good for business.

His idea behind this particular race was to promote the racing of the older horses by creating personalities. Since geldings weren't retired to stud as were so many of the sport's brightest young stars, the fans could get familiar with their names and recognize them in the programs. The older horses, when sound, also helped fill out racing cards. The more horses in a race, the bigger the payoffs could be for the bettors. Short fields were bad for business so every starter helped.

Geldings raced frequently, since their sole purpose was to turn a profit for their connections. They'd run races and make money. A non-revenue-producing gelding was about as useful as a fishing rod on the Space Shuttle. If a horse didn't pay for itself, it wasn't long for staying on track, eating hay, and running up rent, vet, and training bills.

So, Donny Ray decided to help his geldings. The tenth was set up as a claiming race with an unusual twist. In addition to the purse money of $32,000, Gulfstream put up a $24,000 training bonus payable to the winning owner on behalf of the victorious horse. The bonus money would cover future-year training expenses for the horse to stay housed in South Florida and run at the two primary tracks—Gulfstream Park and Calder Race Course. Whoever won this race would, in essence, be on scholarship to race the whole next year well rested. He'd be placed in the best-possible spots for success without having the pounding pressure to run all the time, simply to earn his keep.

Donny Ray even envisioned this race becoming an annual event. He also figured that with a touch of luck and continued good health, the winning gelding would be back the following year to defend his title and Gulfstream could market *that*, too. His vision coupled name recognition for these geldings with the dawn of a new end-of-the-meet tradition. Donny Ray even had a big trophy made up, engraved with a giant **G** on the front, with all of the words emerging from the one giant **G**. The front of the cup was beautifully crafted and looked gorgeous.

Gulfstream
olden
eezer
elding
allop

The Gulfstream Golden Geezer Gelding Gallop was a good gimmick, a nice promotion. Considering its true position on the radar screen of racing, the race got *tons* of media play. After all, it was just a bunch of mediocre old horses running in a circle to fill out a season-ending race card for not a whole lot of cash.

The fact that these horses were claimers kept someone from shipping in a better horse just to grab the cash. In a claiming race, all the entrants were up for sale. And, in this case, the price was $25,000 for any of the eight entries in the field, except for Bushrod at $30,000 and Bonefish at $20,000—a remarkable show of asking-price bravado for the connections of a horse whose racing debut would come as a senior citizen. And Bonefish's past was no secret to anyone—potential bettor or potential buyer. The press had made dead, solid certain of that. So had Moe Bennett and Donny Ray.

Claiming races were common at every racetrack in America. Anyone who wanted to claim one of these horses—buy it—had to fill out some paperwork ahead of time and submit it to the claims clerk. Buyers also had to have enough money in a horseman's account to cover the cost. The horseman's account covered various expenses like entry fees, jockey fees, and horse-claiming funds. Owners received periodic statements that listed winnings and revenues along with various expenses and deductions.

Claims could be made right up to 15 minutes before race time. If more than one horseman put in a claim for a specific horse, then a track official shook some pills and pulled one by random chance to determine who got the official claim.

Generally, maybe one horse every other claiming race was claimed. Every once in a while, two might get picked in a race, but not very often. The most claims put in on a single horse at Gulfstream was 20, at which time the owner realized he made a big mistake, undervalued his horse, and probably shouldn't have entered him. When 20 guys in a shrewd business see something you don't, chances are good *you* are the blind mouse surrounded by a circle of whisker-licking cats.

Three pills would rattle following the tenth race for the race's heavy favorite—the muscular jet-black veteran Bushrod. Bushrod's owner intended to sell and planned to use the sale proceeds to fund a promising two-year-old's upcoming racing season. He also thought it was a good time to dump the risk of hanging on too long to an old horse capable of a breakdown with every stride. He'd owned Bushrod for two years and made enough to buy the two year old. Now he'd sell Bushrod to cover the cost of racing the younger horse.

Grabbing a claimer—any claimer—was a big risk. Buyers had to figure out why the horses were being made available in the first place. Was there something wrong with the horse? Was it injured? Were the connections placing it to compete against less-talented racehorses and improve the horse's confidence with a win? Or was the trainer simply down on the horse?

Sometimes the owner simply needed the money. Many a horse has been sold to dodge, spite, or outmaneuver a divorce attorney. The aftershocks of some naked human intertwinings have caused a few remarkable changes in ownership throughout the history of the equine industry.

It is *caveat emptor*—buyer beware—whenever a horse is claimed, young or old. Several years ago in Kentucky, a fellow borrowed a large sum of money from a bank to buy his first Thoroughbred at Churchill Downs. The fellow claimed a five year old that finished a promising third in the claiming race.

The horse promptly died of a heart attack during the 45-minute van ride back to the man's small nearby farm. Ouch. The fellow owed the bank the entire loan amount.

Since a claimed horse was a bought horse, a lot of owners remain suspect of the soundness of claimers and steer clear of them. Every horse entered in a claiming race is for sale for a reason, but no rule exists that says the current owner must reveal why.

Normally, the claiming price for all of the horses in a race would be close to the same. But this was shaping up as anything *but* a normal race.

Anvil tried to remain poker-faced when Truck told him about Bonefish's price tag. Hell, Anvil would take $300 for the horse—no questions asked. For 20 grand, he would not only give up the horse, but at low tide he'd also be willing to dog-paddle all the way back to Bimini.

Now that T-man had the big marlin safely on ice back at Manero's cooler and it would be sold for two bucks a pound when they got back home, anything Anvil managed to get for Bonefish would be found money. And if Anvil couldn't sell the horse to somebody here, he'd go to the Swap Shop, sit in a busted lawn chair, and wait—if *that's* where the money was.

— ◆ —

And so, Bonefish was officially entered in a claiming race with seven veteran horses that had raced a total of 574 times—an average of 82 starts per horse. Altogether, Bonefish was running against horses that had won 70 races and had earned more than $2.4 million in prize money. Bushrod had won 14 of those races and well over $600,000 all by himself. Trackside, there was no mystery why Bushrod was the favorite—he was clearly the best horse in the field.

The Daily Racing Form's succinct comment about Bonefish's chances—"When pigs fly"—found little argument when Truck and Anvil shared a glance at the folded paper and Anvil read it aloud. Both just shrugged. "Well," said Anvil quietly, "they may have a point."

Thanks to Jacob Burns, that three-word aerial-porcine reference seemed to be the magic buzz-phrase of the week. And as the Bible sheet of racing, *The Daily Racing Form*, sayeth, so goeth the money at the windows. Bettors do what *The Form* says. And *The Form*'s follow-on phrase after "When pigs fly" was slightly less encouraging. "Better luck with a three-legged yak," the reporter wrote.

The Racing Form tabbed Bushrod, an odds-on 4-to-5 favorite, as the day's best bet on the entire Gulfstream card. In the pre-race summary, it said simply, "Class of field. His near-best plenty good enough."

Saturday's post-position draw was held Thursday afternoon. Bushrod, the heavy favorite, drew the seventh spot. Team Bonefish got lucky and was assigned the eight-hole, the farthest outside spot.

That was good. On one hand, if Bonefish decided to compete, he could get out and run without being boxed or throttled. Then again, Bonefish would start farthest from the inside rail and closest to the grandstand. All of the fans would easily see him if he just stood there or sat down when the starting gates opened.

Bonefish's morning line odds were 99-1. When the board first flashed the odds 25 minutes before post time, 99-1 was still there—only because the tote board couldn't illuminate three-digit numbers.

Race Time

When late afternoon and the tenth race finally came around, Team Bonefish waited patiently in the saddling paddock with the horse. Piso was the last of the eight riders to emerge from the jockey's dressing room.

Piso wore borrowed racing silks personally selected by Victor Sanchez, the color man responsible for all 4,600 shirts in the anteroom inside the jockeys' quarters. These were Victor's own colors, purple and gold, his parents' favorite colors. Victor designed the shirt himself several years before. It had never been worn.

Piso was nervous. He'd reported to the jockey quarters two hours before the race, just as the rules required. Basically, he sat on the padded sofa by the pool table, staring at the TV but seeing nothing. He was glad the big boys were not riding his race since he was nervous enough already.

Pat Day had already showered, put on his suit, and left for the day. He had stakes horses to ride in California on Sunday. But before leaving, Day stopped by the sofa where Piso was nervously drumming his fingers to wish him luck and shake his hand. Stunned but grateful, Piso leaped to his feet and pumped the Hall of Fame rider's hand vigorously.

"Gracias, gracias, gracias," Piso repeated a dozen or more times. He held the right-handed clasps of the superstar with both of his own hands and kept shaking repeatedly.

Just before it was time to go, Jerry Bailey came over, too. Bailey had just won the ninth race and was finished for the day. "The four-path, kid," Bailey told him. "Follow the four-path. It's grabbing the best." Victor translated the tip into Spanish just to make sure Piso understood.

Now the young jockey was more nervous than ever. It got even worse when Victor walked over and smiled. "It's time, Piso," Victor said softly. "Time for you to go win your first race and time for my colors to be in their first photo."

Piso stood, hugged Victor, then suddenly broke away and ran into the bathroom to throw up. Victor just shook his head. For 29 years, he'd doled out racing silks to the greatest talents in the history of the game and watched them ride billions and billions of dollars worth of world-class animals. And in all those 29 years, he couldn't recall a nicer kid ever being this nervous about getting legged-up on a worse horse.

Victor was Puerto Rican, and understood what it meant to be young and Latin and clutching a straw in a dream of American hope. As Piso ducked hurriedly around the bathroom corner, Victor quickly blessed himself and said a silent prayer that this kid would have a safe ride. No matter what happened in the next half-hour, this day would positively change Piso's life—that much Victor knew for sure. For now, at least, this lifelong nobody was finally a somebody.

But even Victor Sanchez, who'd watched thousands and thousands of races spanning three decades at Gulfstream Park, Calder and Hialeah, never imagined the quixotic journey his special silks were about to take.

Gulfstream Golden Geezer Gelding Gallop
10ᵗʰ Race, 1 mile. Purse: $32,000
Claiming, 9-year-olds and up

Horse	Age	Starts	1st	2nd	3rd	Earnings	Odds
Manifesto	10	114	16	11	12	$ 287,463	10:1
Mister Invisible	9	83	5	5	7	$ 199,405	15:1
Aqualung	9	60	7	7	9	$ 191,607	6:1
Nuclear Warhead	9	71	8	12	9	$ 315,221	9:2
The Rambler	10	99	11	15	13	$ 262,458	8:1
Benny New Shoes	10	90	9	16	18	$ 488,909	4:1
Bushrod	9	57	14	11	9	$ 677,507	2:1
Bonefish	9	0	0	0	0	$ 0	99:1
Field Totals		*574*	*70*	*77*	*77*	*$ 2,422,570*	

Racing Connections, 10ᵗʰ Race

Horse	Owner	Trainer	Jockey
Manifesto	Richmond Stables	Peter Coen	Thomas Andrews
Mister Invisible	George W. Simmons	M. DeB. White, Jr.	Marvin Fisher
Aqualung	David M. French	Mark W. Andregg	Juan Gallegos
Nuclear Warhead	Grayson Matthews	Paul South	Bruce Hall
The Rambler	Sardano Racing	Tony Coleman	Raul Reyes
Benny New Shoes	Charles M. Reed	Katie S. Reed	Bryan M. Reed
Bushrod	Okataina Racing	Brett Olson	Taco Perez
Bonefish	Anvil Sanders	Luther O'Neil, Sr.	Piso Mojado

Gulfstream Golden Geezer Gelding Gallop
10th Race, 1 mile. Purse: $32,000
Claiming, 9-year-olds and up.

Entries	Odds	Pre-Race Comments
Manifesto	10:1	Veteran campaigner with 16 wins. Should close but might be too far behind leaders.
Mister Invisible	15:1	Training sharply after long layoff. Crafty connections. Should menace if slow pace. Prefers shorter route.
Aqualung	6:1	2nd to Bushrod last outing. Better at six furlongs. Worth a shot at a price.
Nuclear Warhead	9:2	Legitimate threat with a good trip. Crafty connections with a hot jock.
The Rambler	8:1	100th career start for solid pro and Gulfstream fave. 3 wins in last 10 starts. Could menace.
Benny New Shoes	4:1	Running well coming in. Capable. Figure in exotics. In money nearly half his careers starts (43 of 90).
Bushrod	2:1	Class of field. Twice average earnings per race of all others. His near best plenty good enough.
Bonefish	99:1	When pigs fly. Better luck with saddled yak.

"*C*uando Los Cerdos Vuelan!"

When Victor hollered into the bathroom that it was time to go, Piso quit heaving, spit twice in the toilet, rinsed, and spit again in the sink. Then he stiffly walked outside the jocks' room and into the fading sun 30 seconds behind the seven other riders. Piso slowly walked to paddock and the #8 saddling stall where Truck, Anvil, T-man, Luther, and the horse were waiting.

The girls, Mountain, and Ben were behind the spectator railing, cheering and waving. Piso, smiling weakly, turned, and waved back. Several in the crowd took pictures of Piso. Except for his riding license, they were the first ones taken of him since the Snack Shack made his ID badge eight years before. Piso wondered how he might be able to get one of the photos to keep as a souvenir.

To get Bonefish to break from the gate, T-man suggested a strategy that usually worked back home when he needed to get Bonefish's stubborn butt in gear. T-man tied together a pair of red Twizzlers licorice sticks to the end of Piso's whip.

Luther looked at Anvil skeptically. "It can't hurt," shrugged Anvil. "He loves licorice."

When riders-up time finally arrived, Piso hopped aboard Bonefish and twice circled the walking ring before beginning the long, dutiful walk through Gulfstream's tunnel out onto the racetrack. Piso looked all around for Isa Mercado, his loving girlfriend. They had prayed for health and happiness this morning, like every morning, at His Place Ministries, the little white chapel on the backside of the track—a tennis-ball toss from the Snack Shack. A million prayers had been made there. Some answered, some not. The chaplain gave Piso his first change of clothes the day he arrived at Gulfstream and Piso had not missed a day of thanks since.

Moe Bennett had been in the chapel too, praying real hard about something of his own. For some reason, Moe kept looking at Piso the whole time he was kneeling.

After prayers, Piso asked the chaplain for a special blessing. The chaplain placed his hand on Piso's shoulder and gently said, in Spanish, "You have to believe in yourself and trust the Lord, Piso. *That* is the secret."

Piso was thinking of the chaplain's early-morning blessing when he finally spied Isa by the grandstand side of the crossover turnstile. She was waving wildly and blowing kisses furiously. Piso blew one back. Then he blessed himself with a sign of the cross and sat tall in the saddle as the horse left the paddock area and stepped inside the tunnel. They began the long walk toward the starting gate.

When they emerged out the tunnel's far side and stepped onto the main track, Piso was no longer a dishwasher. He was someone all these people had come to see. Many, he could hear, were calling his name.

Ready or not, it was time to race.

Bonefish was the last of the eight horses to load into the starting gate. And he was in no hurry to do so. Finally, the gate hands shoved his fat butt in there and closed the gate behind him.

Following Luther's only instructions, just after Bonefish loaded and the gate hands climbed free, Piso leaned way forward and dangled the licorice-tied end of his whip down in front of Bonefish's nose. In replays after the race, the video monitor clearly showed Bonefish staring transfixed at the licorice, intently cross-eyed, as the bell rang, the gates slid open, and all the other horses exploded out in a ball of flying dirt and thunder. At the sound of the bell, Piso did as instructed and gently touched the inside of Bonefish's right ear.

Bonefish stood there for just a moment, saw the other horses bolt together, then instinctively decided to go. He broke cleanly, determinedly chasing the Twizzlers on Piso's dangling whip.

The Gulfstream Golden Geezer Gelding Gallop was underway and the hoof-thundering octet dug into the soft, loamy soil for the first of eight furlongs in the mile-long race.

Once Bonefish broke cleanly and ran after the others, Piso pulled back his licorice-tipped whip, crouched down low, and held on. Against all odds, this was a real horse race, and Bonefish and Piso were in it.

When Bonefish left the gate and took off after the rest of the horses, Luther, Anvil, and Truck just looked at each other blankly. It had dawned on none of them that the horse might actually decide to compete. Now they wondered if Piso could ride him for a mile without falling off.

Up in the President's Box, Donny Ray Douglass audibly exhaled. Moe Bennett held his face in his hands, choosing not to watch. Judging from the roar of the crowd, it sounded to Moe like his time in morning chapel was well invested. Now that the horse had decided to run, Moe's only hope was that Bonefish galloped in the right direction.

The gods continued to smile through the first turn and Bonefish was running exactly as Luther hoped he would—a push-button horse that ran on his own.

Bonefish's sudden candy-propelled decision to run pogosticked him out the gate like a scared cat with a pack of dinner-sniffing Dobermans in hot pursuit. He ran smoothly, just like any one of his 2,000 powerful gallops toting T-man along the Bimini shore. Years of long, early-morning beach runs had muscled Bonefish well, and Piso settled him into a nice rhythm on the perfectly tilled and compacted racing soil.

Three horses—Nuclear Warhead, Manifesto, and Mister Invisible—bobbed head to head for the lead. Bonefish was last but just four lengths behind as Nuclear Warhead led by a nose and flashed past the first quarter mile in 24 seconds flat. With six furlongs to go, the pace was slow enough that it was still anyone's race.

They churned toward the race's midway point. The horses, still bunched tightly together, pounded toward the half-mile mark. Nuclear Warhead passed it first, clocking in at just over 48 seconds. Tightly bunched, the horses headed for the far turn.

The race was setting up for a strong closing rush, which suited Bushrod perfectly. So far, Bushrod was on cruise control, drafting just behind the leaders, biding his time and waiting for the signal to shove it into overdrive.

Suddenly, from a shrub on the inside rail, a wayward squirrel spooked onto the track, then changed its mind and scurried back off. The movement startled Nuclear Warhead, who wasn't wearing blinkers. The horse jumped to the right. Warhead bumped hard against Mister Invisible and both horses lost stride, briefly stumbling but neither going down. Piso held on for dear life as Bonefish looked to his left, swerved to his right, and kept running.

Both Nuclear Warhead and Mister Invisible had lost momentum, fallen back, and would not be able to catch up. They were out of it.

With three-eights of a mile remaining, Bonefish took advantage of the sudden traffic jam to his left and moved up on the outside. Piso carefully kept him clear of the others.

As Nuclear Warhead and Mister Invisible drifted right and began dropping back, veteran jockey Raul Reyes began an early move and ducked The Rambler down to an opening along the rail.

Benny New Shoes swerved right, and wide, around the faltering Mister Invisible while Manifesto did the same to the left of Nuclear Warhead. With The Rambler on the rail, Benny New

Shoes on his right hip, and Manifesto in the middle, Bonefish gained a half a length. The horses were four across on the lead.

Bushrod was lurking, gliding along as Bonefish's shadow, waiting patiently for veteran jockey Taco Perez to turn him loose for a strong closing run to the wire. Perez had Bushrod exactly where he wanted him and confidently marked time with a hand ride, waiting for the right moment to turn the race favorite loose. One well-timed burst of late speed and this race was in the bag.

Up in the stands, everybody in the place was screaming and hollering like it was Cigar and Holy Bull going eyeball to eyeball in the Donn Handicap years before.

Suddenly, Aqualung dropped back a half-length, then another. He was tired and the parachute was out. Normally a six-furlong sprinter, Aqualung couldn't keep up for this race's extra quarter-mile. He would fade and finish last.

It was now a five-horse race with a quarter-mile remaining. Remembering what Bailey told him before the race, Piso tried to steer Bonefish to stay in the solid footing of the fourth lane from the rail.

Bushrod continued to stalk Bonefish as the horses flashed past the eighth pole. In a galloping flash, the horses had less than 220 yards remaining in a wide-eyed, ear-pinned-back, straight-on sprint to the finish.

The crowd was roaring louder now than ever before, drowning out the echoing call of the track announcer over the grandstand loudspeakers. Victor Sanchez, standing down on the rail watching his silks loom larger and larger as they got closer, suddenly started jumping up and hollering like he was ringside in Manila when Ali fought Frazier.

With just 180 yards remaining and the crowd cheering louder and louder, Bonefish ignored his searing lungs and fought his way a nose ahead. The Rambler moved up on the rail and stayed eye to eye and three across with Benny New Shoes and Manifesto. All of the jockeys except Piso were repeatedly smacking their whips on thundering hips.

Out of the corner of his darting eyes, Piso saw what the other jockeys were doing and tried to whip Bonefish once to spur him on—but instead he hit him with the licorice and briefly lost balance. Piso quickly re-centered over the saddle, reached up, and patted Bonefish quickly twice on the neck.

That was the move Taco Perez had waited for—a riding mistake by Piso—and Perez shoved Bushrod into overdrive, urgently smacking him twice on the right rump, then once on the left. That was Bushrod's cue and the horse reeled up into a narrow opening between Manifesto and Bonefish that Taco expected to widen as the fatigued horses began to separate.

But as Piso determinedly steered Bonefish to stay in the four path, just as suddenly the running lane Taco thought would be there wasn't. It had closed in and Bushrod had no room to pass.

With 100 yards to go and no time to go wide, Taco Perez decided to save ground, brushing up to and bumping past Bonefish, making himself enough space to blast his way between Bonefish and Manifesto. Taco shifted his whip back again from his left hand to his right and deftly smacked first Piso, then Bonefish, in the charge to the wire. Angrily he shouted above the thunder, *"Cuando los cerdos vuelan!"*

Piso reached out to take a swing at Taco and missed, just as the horses flashed across the finish line to a photo finish. The crowd was on its feet and roared at the furious finish, not knowing for sure who had won. By a head-bob at the wire, Bushrod finished first.

Crossing the finish line, Piso was furious at Taco Perez and didn't know what to do. But Bonefish had a plan of his own, running right through the finish line and chasing full speed after

Bushrod and his jockey as the "INQUIRY" light lit on the infield tote board.

Bonefish's eye was burning from the whip shot he'd taken and he was plenty mad about it. Perez stood in his irons to pose and shake his whip defiantly in the sky, then immediately sat back down as Bonefish and Piso came chasing after him. The two tired horses chased each other 'round and 'round the track. Even the outrider ponies struggled to intercept and separate them.

The post-race chase actually made it on ESPN-TV later that evening. The race didn't, but the chase did. It was the first time a member of Bonefish's family had been on ESPN since his brother tried to do the outrider pony during the post parade of his final race at Churchill.

Finally, Taco ducked an exhausted Bushrod back toward the grandstand rail, hopped off, side-saddled his way over the rail, and ran full-speed into the steward's cabin at the finish line to grab the phone. He needed to quickly explain his side of the mess to the stewards. Meanwhile, Piso and Bonefish were about 100 yards away and gaining.

The closer Piso got, the faster Taco talked to the stewards. Basically, he blamed everything on careless riding by Piso, but told the stewards he did not think the jockey deserved to be suspended.

As Piso and an exhausted Bonefish reached the nearby railing, Taco said *adios* to the stewards, hung up the phone, hopped onto the scale to check weight, got cleared by the clerk of scales, and hopped back off just as Piso climbed over the guardrail and headed toward the hut. The clerk of scales waved him in to talk to the stewards, too.

Taco stood 50 feet away in the winner's circle, waiting for the race to become official. He was watching Piso's every move. Piso was obviously angry and agitated, but Taco couldn't hear what he was telling the stewards.

Piso suddenly tossed down the phone, jumped on the scale, and locked his furious dark eyes on Taco. When he saw how angry Piso was, Taco decided that perhaps the photo could wait. Fistfights in the winner's circle were bad for business, so Taco bolted out of it and clumsily ran toward the grandstand tunnel while Piso waited impatiently on the scale. Obviously, Taco was headed for safety of the jockey's quarters as fast as his shiny black riding boots could possibly travel.

When Piso jumped onto the scale, he caused the needle to quiver wildly, costing him several precious seconds before it finally settled back down.

While impatiently waiting for clearance from the clerk, Piso clearly saw Taco bolt the winner's circle and run down the tunnel. Taco had a 30-yard head start when Piso was finally waved off the scale. Determined, he jumped off and chased Taco all of the way through the tunnel, narrowing the gap with every stride. Taco reached the dressing room first and flung the door open just seconds ahead of Piso. Piso then flung it open again before it had even fully closed.

There, Piso trapped Taco inside the laundry room. Furious, he wrestled Taco to the ground, then picked him up and angrily stuffed him upside-down into the big open trashcan next to the scale in the center of the dressing room. The entire time, Piso kept shouting over and over the same phrase Taco screamed at him during the race: *"Cuando los cerdos vuelan!"* which was Spanish for *"When pigs fly!"*

Both men kept hollering like hell, none of the words being quoted from Mother Teresa although the word *Madre* could clearly be heard repeatedly in a non-secular context.

Taco had too much pride to ever be outridden by a dishwasher. And Piso decided that the appropriate place for a trash talker was *in* the trash, *among* the trash. So he stuffed him there.

Taco decided to stay put in the trashcan until Piso carefully took off and returned his borrowed silk shirt to Victor Sanchez, put on his Snack Shack uniform top, ID badge, and paper hat, flung the door open, and stormed outside into the setting afternoon sun.

Victor just stood there, smiling. He'd been at Gulfstream 29 years and seen a few guys go at it from time to time, but he'd never seen anything quite like this. Piso had heart. Win, lose, or draw, Victor's silks had been well represented. He couldn't have picked a better man to wear his colors.

Just as Piso blasted angrily out of the jock's room, a spontaneous roar went up from the crowd. The steward's inquiry was completed. After watching tapes of the last furlong and witnessing the track meet of ensuing hysteria, the stewards agreed 3-0 to adjust the order of finish. Bushrod was taken down for jockey interference and dropped from first place to third. The Rambler was moved up from third to second. Bonefish was moved up from second to first.

Down on the track, T-man was holding on to Bonefish, feeding him leftover licorice one stick at a time to calm him down. The horse was breathing so hard, it took him twice as long as usual to chew each piece.

Upstairs, Donny Ray Douglass and Moe Bennett looked at each other like they'd just seen Secretariat in the men's room. Neither believed what they'd just witnessed. Beneath them, every fan in the place was on their feet, cheering.

And over in the press box, all of the other writers turned to Jacob Burns, pushed their noses up with their forefingers, and started oinking. Ever the distinguished professional, Jake responded by pushing up his nose and oinking back.

Piso, however, was nowhere to be found. He was stomping his determined way all the way back to the Snack Shack. Some Cuban fans intercepted him and explained in Spanish what happened.

Piso ran around in a sideways panic like a duckling chased by a bass, then zoomed wide-eyed to the winner's circle with his right hand atop his head to keep his paper Snack Shack hat from flying off.

Donny Ray Douglass was already there, smiling broadly in the winner's circle with the big engraved trophy, a bunch of grasshopper-happy first-time horsemen, and an angry horse with one eyelid swollen shut contemptuously chewing red Twizzlers licorice. Finally the winning jockey showed up and leaped aboard his mount when the trainer got down on all sixes and let himself be used as a running footstool. Mountain intercepted Piso on the fly, caught him in mid-air, and simply placed him carefully astride Bonefish's back like he was storing groceries on the top cupboard shelf.

And that's how the winner's circle photo was taken: a smiling jockey wearing a Snack Shack shirt and paper hat atop a squinting horse chewing half a stick of red licorice, flanked by a groom-turned-trainer-for-a-day, surrounded by four pretty sunburned girls from New Zealand, next to a smiling Bahamian boy holding a rope tethered to a goat named Elvis, while the boy's dad stood smiling proudly. And next to the dad stood Truck Roberts, his right hand in his pant pocket tightly holding a $200 win ticket on #8.

Bonefish paid $206.60 to win and Truck had it 100 times. Mountain, who got cut off in the photo, stood on the periphery. He, too, was eating red Twizzlers when the shutter was snapped. He, too, had his hand in his pocket, although it's unclear what exactly it was doing in there.

When the official photo was taken and the commotion finally died down, the track vet hustled over to look at Bonefish's right eye. Bonefish had a severe laceration to the eyeball that resulted in blurred vision and shadow blindness. From the looks of it and given his age, the vet doubted Bonefish would ever race again.

Since Bonefish was hurt because of a foul, Donny Ray Douglass had little choice but to award the training bonus, in toto, to the owner, Anvil Sanders, and make a magnanimous show of doing so. Anvil, who 20 minutes before was planning on selling or trading Bonefish at the Swap Shop on Sunday, had now grossed over $43,000 watching his pet horse run once in a circle and retire undefeated. Anvil got 60 percent of the $32,000 purse, plus the $24,000 that Donny Ray had committed to training fees.

It was more money than Anvil had ever earned in any of the 53 years he'd been on the planet.

The wagering payoffs were enormous. Team Bonefish all had money on him, but not much. Thanks to the *When Pigs Fly* assessment by *The Daily Racing Form*, Bonefish paid a whopping $206.60 to win, $88.40 to place, and $26.20 to show. The exacta paid $1,601.00.

The short but happy conga line to the cash window was gyrating like Charo in a nightclub. As the girls waited their turns, they were jumping up and down and "screaming in New Zealandese," as Mountain described it.

Truck stood in a fog at the window while Mountain waited right behind him. He'd won more than $20,600. Together, those two guys funded nearly half the entire Gulfstream win pool bet on Bonefish.

Luther, who'd put the $156 balance of his savings account on the line, walked off with over $16,000 in winnings plus another $4,300 more from Anvil after Donny Ray paid out the whole training bonus in a lump sum.

Anvil was last in the cashier's line. He held just a lone $2-to-show ticket worth a little over $26. He bet nothing—zero, nada, *zipska*—on his own horse to win.

T-man razzed his dad mercilessly about that, and asked his father to cash T's own $10 win ticket while Anvil was at the window. T-man was too young to legally bet but smart enough to use a middleman. He had Truck lay down the entire $10 Minnow Thomas paid him for cleaning fish earlier in the week. "Put it on his nose," T told Truck solemnly before the race. "Every penny." T-man parlayed Minnow's boat-cleaning money into $1,000.

Anvil would go back to Bimini with nearly $22,000 in cash for his friends, including $1,200 for Weevil's two wahoo that Anvil sold for $6 apiece to Minnow when they first reached Miami and landed at Keystone Point Marina.

Altogether, the money the islanders won wouldn't fit inside Anvil's tin cash box. Donny Ray ended up giving him a cloth money sack stuffed full of bundled winnings for the people back home.

Piso made out, too. He had taken $30 of his $33 life savings and bet it on himself and the horse. He won $3,100 there, plus another $4,300 from the purse money and bonus, plus another $2,000 in public appearance money that Anvil let him keep when the Swap Shop paid for Piso and Bonefish to stop by for a two-hour promotional appearance on Sunday.

All told, Piso scooped up a quick $9,400 in two minutes—a lifetime of wages in Cuba where workers earn $20 a month—and more money than Piso had ever seen in his life, much less at one time. Since more horses and more races would follow, for him, there would be even more money to come.

Piso got a quick piece of advice from Luther before speaking with the media. "Take the high road," Luther told him concerning his dispute with Taco. "The low road's too crowded with Gozzleheads. Talk about your horse and your ride and winning, and not about Taco Perez."

Piso did as instructed and, as a result, he picked up rides at Calder on nearly 40 more horses over the next two weeks while Taco Perez served a suspension for reckless riding.

A reporter from the *Sun-Sentinel* even compared the race and Bushrod's disqualification to that of the great stallion Nureyev, who was disqualified in the English 2000 Guineas in 1980 when his jockey got boxed, laid back, then plowed his own way through.

Nureyev's disqualification was the first in that storied race's nearly 200-year history—dating all the way back to 1809 when Abraham Lincoln's father was still trying to get to second base on dates with Abe's mom. The reporter also pointed out that Nureyev won only $42,018 on track in three races while Bonefish earned $43,200 in one. So, according to the writer's logic, Bonefish was in good company.

Phoebe was the only one who didn't bet on the race and her lip quivered in disappointment as everyone around her celebrated. She was visibly upset, especially since the other girls—Cush, Mitzi, and Bird—each bet $2 on Bonefish to win and won a couple of hundred bucks each.

Mountain looked over at Phoebe, saw her, and smiled. He waved an upraised ticket between his right index and middle fingers and asked sweetly, "Wanna buy a ticket? On sale. Just $2 for pretty girls." Phoebe leaped up and hugged Mountain around his neck. Phoebe happily took her place in the cash line. That $2 win ticket sacrifice would later prove, after the sun went down, to be one of the more astute financial decisions Mountain ever made.

Afterward, the happy gang was ready to celebrate. The men had an errand to run and told the girls to head down for a victory party at Manero's while T-man walked Bonefish over to visit the Spit Box for his post-race urinalysis and cooling down. The fellows would meet back at the track and usher the champ down to the restaurant as soon as they returned from shopping.

The men got one of Donny Ray Douglass's courtesy van drivers to haul them south down U.S. 1, then east across the Broad

Causeway to the same Bal Harbour shops Mitzi and Cush had visited earlier in the week.

Before leaving, Truck scribbled a note and stuffed it and ten $100-bills in an addressed envelope, then handed it to Mark Mercer, one of Mr. Douglass's top assistants. He gave Merc a $20 tip to deliver the sealed envelope to its Miami Beach address right away.

Merc took off like a rocket out of the parking lot, easily beating the delirious Keystone Kops trying to gang-pile their tumbling asses inside the courtesy van. Once the guys arrived at the ritzy shopping center, they all marched directly into the ultra-chic Hermes store. There they stood, shoulder to shoulder, looking like marauding Huns arriving to ransack a small innocent European village.

The clerk, a beautiful willowy Brazilian model-type named Maria de los Santos, was taken aback when all five—Truck, Mountain, Anvil, Luther, and Piso—each purchased a different Hermes scarf after asking her to model it. As the beautiful Maria wrapped the first gently around her shoulders, the boys all wagged their fingers side to side.

"No, Maria," said Mountain friskily, shaking his head sadly.

"You're doin' it all wrong," chimed in Luther. He looked over to Truck. "Help her, Gozzlehead."

Maria was perplexed. She'd worked at the store nearly three years and was a top salesperson. She'd modeled hundreds of scarves before and no one had ever complained.

"Here, let me show you," offered Truck. He folded the scarf five times, then stepped forward and gently blindfolded Maria, carefully covering her eyes before gently knotting it behind her head. Once she was blindfolded, Truck softly caressed both her shoulders while softly whispering something the others could not hear that made Maria smile.

"Ooooh," cooed Maria. *Bad* boys!"

"Good boys!" said Mountain. "Bad *girls!* I'll take five. My girl's got wrists and ankles!"

Laden with silk for the ladies, the fellows piled back in the van and returned to Gulfstream. The girls were waiting. They wanted everyone to make the victory march together. Having collected T-man, Bonefish, and Elvis, the swelling entourage paraded back to Manero's.

Hundreds of fans patiently waited along the procession route and dozens of them clicked their cameras. Even the bocce ball players stopped playing and clapped their hands while hollering congratulations as the old gray horse walked slowly by.

By the time they snaked across Bonefish Boulevard and the rest of the way to the restaurant, Manero's had turned the dock and half the parking lot into Celebration Central. The staff had chipped in and gave T-man a brand new deep-sea fishing rod and reel as a gift. A big wicker basket full of Twizzlers and candy was waiting for all the little kids who came by to visit the famous horse with the bandage on his eye. Elvis even got a leather collar with ELVIS engraved on a brass nameplate.

Elvis also got a large pizza with the works, which he ate in about 10 minutes. He had gas—very bad gas—all through Saturday night and well into Sunday morning.

The party raged well into the night, moving inside the restaurant when the guest of honor and his guard goat got sleepy. At midnight, the men presented the girls with their Hermes scarves, souvenirs of one of the most improbable wins in the history of American racing. Mountain gave Phoebe just one and never mentioned the other four. They would come in handy later in the week.

Since no one put a claim in on Bonefish, well, Anvil still owned him. And since Anvil won more than a year's pay in two minutes, he was taking Bonefish back home, for good, as soon as the seas and swelling of his horse's blood-stained eye subsided.

By the time they were ready to return to the Bahamas, the bunch of them had bought so much stuff for the kids on the island, they had to load it all onto the Hatteras and let Mountain bring it across. The stockbroker who owned it, Tightslax, was in New York, so the coast was clear to borrow the yacht again.

With the horse, the goat, the body-bagged billfish, the big bag of cash, and the championship trophy keeping Anvil and T-Man company, the water taxi would be crowded enough—especially since T-man now had an extra line to troll for marlin.

Smoke-Alarm Chops

Because of the chaos at the track on Saturday, Donny Ray Douglass gave his people strict orders to red carpet Anvil, T-man, and Bonefish until things sorted themselves out. Since the horse was injured and probably would never race again, Donny Ray needed to keep a positive spin on the PR for the ever-watchful media—something he was happy to do and would've done anyway.

Anvil stayed over on the beach at the Sheraton Bal Harbour, compliments of Gulfstream Park. Donny Ray also put a car at Anvil's disposal, a black Lincoln, which he took full advantage of. T-man refused to leave the horse's side and slept on Manero's dock every night. They remained neighborhood celebrities.

The weekend hullaballoo subsided by Tuesday. By then, it appeared the return trip to the Bahamas could come as early as Friday or Saturday, weather and ocean permitting.

The Thursday marine forecast called for calm seas on Friday. The vet decided there wouldn't be much of a risk for the sea spray to burn Bonefish's injured eye, but he promised to stop by early Friday morning to patch it up before the floating menagerie shoved off for the long chug home.

So, according to plan, Anvil and T-man would cross back over Friday morning with Bonefish, Elvis the goat, the still body-bagged and iced-down marlin, and the trophy. The stray cats still milling around were free to make their own decisions.

For safety's sake, Mountain would transport all of the gifts they purchased over to Bimini on the big Hatteras. Phoebe announced she'd go with Mountain to keep him company. Much to

Phoebe's annoyance, Bird and Mitzi decided they'd tag along on the Hatteras, too.

And where Bird and Mitzi went, Ben was sure to follow. The way the cruiser was filling up, there'd be room for Truck and Cush only if they water-skied the whole way across.

The pair opted instead to fly over Friday afternoon on the seaplane and rendezvous with the others late in the day at the big island celebration scheduled for Bay Front Park in Bailey Towne.

Thursday afternoon, before packing up to head home, Anvil drove Gulfstream's courtesy car to Aventura Mall and splurged one last time on more gifts for Alma. She had, from day one, been the greatest wife in the history of history and never asked for more of Anvil than to call home if he was going to be late for supper. She had gone so long without so much that since Anvil now had a big fat bag slam jam *full* of printed dead presidents, it was fun for him to buy her a lot of nice things, all long overdue.

Anvil got Alma a brand new, beautiful big screen TV and satellite dish for watching her beloved soaps and game shows. Anvil and T-man also, after a loud and demonstrative fashion argument, compromised on two new Sunday dresses, matching shoes, and a matching black leather Coach purse.

Anvil then went to the jewelry department and bought her a set of tooth-sized pearl earrings and matching necklace. The pearls would get more *oohhs* and *aahhs* from the other women on the island than all the other items added together.

After shopping, Anvil and T-man drove to Manero's for a farewell feast. They stuffed themselves on steaks and fresh vegetables, then waddled outside. It would be an early night since Friday would be a long and exhausting day for both.

Anvil walked T-man back to the dock and hugged his son goodnight before heading back to the Sheraton, where he quickly fell asleep face down in the pillow. He dreamed of push-poling his way around the flats in the company of Tyra Banks. In the dream, Tyra had absolutely no interest whatsoever in fishing.

As Anvil drifted off to sleep, five miles away his only son stayed up until midnight, listening to his music CDs, and practicing new solo dance moves on the dock in the shadows of the Hallandale Beach drawbridge. This had been fun, but T was looking forward to going home. He also planned to fish the entire way back.

Mountain's Apartment

While Anvil and T made their preparations to go home, the fellows had other things to worry about. On Tuesday, Ben and Mountain invited Bird and Phoebe over for a home-cooked dinner on Thursday, hoping for a little romance to follow.

They planned on entertaining at Ben's place. Never in six million years would they *ever* plan to host anybody but a decontamination squad at Mountain's. His place was such a mess, the cockroaches kept rearranging the furniture.

Ben, unfortunately, arrived home Tuesday evening to a notice stuffed in his mailbox that on Thursday morning his apartment building would be insect-bombed. He never really understood the logic behind the bug-bomb theory. Sure, they'd kill a ton of bugs—everybody in Florida had them, even the rich people—but generally the bugs simply ran or crawled next door until the coast was clear, then ran or crawled home.

It seemed like a lot of money and inconvenience just to make bugs get some fresh air and exercise.

Regardless, since bug-bombing by law meant two days to air the place out and bulldoze away the complex's dead bugs, Ben and Mountain didn't have much choice. Ben's place was out. They had to switch venues and entertain at Mountain's.

Ben had heard Truck's stories about the legend of Mountain Trombley. About how, as a kid, Mountain used to win money from the other neighborhood kids who bet Mountain he couldn't kill spiders just by breathing on them.

Truck said he saw him do it twice, both times to daddy long-legs. "They just curled up and died," said Truck admiringly. "Just like *that*," he said with a snap of the fingers. "Mountain leaned over and breathed on them real hard from about four inches away. They just froze—laid down—and those spindly little legs curled right on up, just like the Wicked Witch of the West's toes in 'The Wizard of Oz' when the house squished her."

Ben should've realized something was up when Mountain told him they needed to meet at seven in the morning—a full 12 hours before their scheduled dinner date. Expecting a long day, Ben went for a brisk four-mile run at six and was wide awake and ready to go by the time he met Mountain for breakfast.

When he finally stepped inside Mountain's apartment, Ben Bentley stood in the doorway and panned the living room from side to side, saying not a word, just taking it all in. He stood frozen, mouth agape, slowly moving his field of vision 180 degrees from one wall, through the battle zone, and across to the other.

Carefully, Ben took three steps forward, skirting what was either Godzilla's training diaper or Swamp Thing's boxers. Landmines of emanating odiferous toxin were strewn and hidden everywhere. Ben uttered not a sound for several long moments. "Sheesh," he muttered softly, "the Daytona deaf girls would dislocate their fingers tryin' to describe this."

Mountain lived, basically, like Sasquatch with no cleansing implements.

Ben had been a lot of places and seen a lot of things. But he'd *never* seen a place like this. "The Den of Sin," he whispered half-aloud and unbelievingly. "Behold the Den of Sin. Either that," he mused, "or I just entered the Twilight Zone during Sweeps Week.

"Jesus, Mountain," Ben finally muttered, "munch at the dump. That's what we invited them to—a munch at the dump." Just to make certain, Ben then turned to Mountain and asked, disbelievingly, "You *do* live alone, don't you?"

Mountain nodded. This was self-created. "A little messy, huh?"

"No, Mountain," Ben replied. "This isn't messy. We're looking at five hours of balls-to-the-wall cleanin' before we'll even get it to *messy*. We'll need a daisy chain detonation of well-placed explosives just to reach Base Camp."

The men's brilliant romantic dinner plan suddenly presented an entirely different set of challenges—especially since the guys had offered it to the girls as "a quiet little evening at home, with the guys doing all the work."

Clearly they'd oversold it. Overcommitted. A nice restaurant wasn't even an option. The girls were expecting a home-cooked meal and—like it or not—the fellows had to deliver. They were too deeply gaffed to get off the hook and—the worst part—it was self-inflicted.

Without another word, Ben retreated out the front door and disappeared for about ten minutes. When he returned, he looked unhappy.

"Where'd ja go?" asked Mountain. "Not that it's important. I'm just glad you came back. I thought maybe you were takin' off for good."

"I tried to rent another apartment," Ben replied, "offered a month's rent for one night of use, but the manager said no."

"Where do we start?" asked Mountain earnestly.

Ben just shook his head. A quick tour of Mountain's closets yielded none of the required ammo. This would be man-against-microbe, a high-energy, all-out war. No prisoners left.

"C'mon, Fart Blossom," Ben said to Mountain, using his pet name for his gigantic friend. "We got some shoppin' to do."

"Right behind you, Buttface," said Mountain, responding in kind. "Let's git it."

Well, there's nothing quite like team apartment cleaning to bond two men in pursuit of an evening of romance with vixens of desire. The pair piled into Ben's car, drove to the nearby Publix grocery store, and spent nearly $80 on cleaning stuff. When they went through the checkout line, a 20-something girl with *Marianne* on her name tag looked at the combination of cleansers and suds and said, "Let me guess: Mother coming for a visit?"

Mountain looked at his shoes and sadly shook his head no.

"Girlfriends?"

Both Ben and Mountain looked at their shoes and nodded. Mountain handed Marianne four 20s to pay the bill and back they drove, now suitably outfitted for battle.

So, while the girls spent a relaxing day on the sands of South Beach gawking at the Speedo-clad men and Kiwini-clad fashion models, Ben and Mountain were knee-deep, waist-deep, shoulder-deep, and eyeball-deep in suds and crud.

Stonehenge was easier to build than this place was to clean. Changing America's cruddiest apartment into a romantic sweet-smelling lair of seductive opportunity took the bold guts and fearless courage of polar explorers.

They tornado-scrubbed all day long. Ben lost the coin toss and had to clean the bathroom, which took three hours. He finally emerged just before noon, lightheaded from ammonia fumes but victorious. He raised both arms in triumph—his left hand holding aloft a bent, bristled toilet bowl brush while the knuckles of his right hand were bleeding. In it, he clutched the frayed and shredded remains of a gray scouring pad. Mountain thought Ben looked a lot like Ali moments after the ref stopped the Thrilla in Manila: He was victorious, but out on his feet.

After a five-minute standing lunch, the men returned to the scene of the grime and battled on. Ben headed for the living room and Mountain pushed open the swinging door into the kitchen and courageously stepped inside.

Readjusting his safety goggles, Mountain began powersanding the oven. The charred remains of uneaten culinary residue from hundreds of random and unexpected explosions were black-caked to the oven's walls, base, burners, and grill bars. Forensic scientists couldn't identify half of the stalactite crud Mountain prepared to do battle with.

Mountain pressed down the start button of his whirling sander, squeezed in his shoulders, sucked in his gut, and wedged awkwardly inside his oven. With fervor and purpose, he blasted the black coal into a dust storm of swirling volcanic dust. Midway through, he paused and wiped the sweat off his forehead with the sleeve of his right biceps. His brow blackened. Coal mining was easier work.

Coincidentally, Thursday was a full moon. A full moon was the only time of the month Bird was vulnerable to the allure of romantic entanglement. It was something chemical or biological, but once the full moon came around, she turned from an igloo in high heels into a wolverine of lust and desire.

Bird was well aware of the full moon and talked about it with Phoebe that day at the beach. Both girls anticipated a romantic dinner over candlelight, and hoped to cap off their American holiday with a nice dessert of handsome foreigner if the opportunity presented itself.

Dinner Time: Come and Get It

Mountain sent a limo to fetch the girls and bring them over promptly at seven o'clock. Doing so served three purposes: First, the extra time gave him the chance to toss nine giant stuffed-full trash bags over the apartment's second-story railing and down to Ben, who would drag them over to the dumpster. By the third bag, Ben had learned not to catch them on the fly.

Second, both men needed extra time to shower and change clothes. Cleaning the apartment took a lot longer than anticipated.

And third, girls *like* limousine rides. The limo would greatly increase the odds of them staying over. Or so it all seemed, using man-logic instead of common sense.

When Mountain looked out the window and saw the limo pull up, he hollered, "Oh God! Red alert! Red alert! Incoming! Incoming!"

Ben looked quickly around, took all of the remaining cleaning stuff, and tossed, jammed, and crammed it inside the hall closet. He power-whipped the door closed just as everything started tumbling out in an avalanche of spilling confusion. The door shut, however, and latched. Spring-loaded or not, at least the last of the cleaning crap was safely out of sight. As far as Ben was concerned, he never wanted to see it again.

The work paid off. The apartment looked livable. More importantly, it smelled girly. Clean-girly, which both Ben and Mountain assumed was good. Men's apartments often had the odiferous zoological barnlike allure of a primate exhibit and, earlier in the day, this one certainly had. Now it smelled more like a department store gauntlet where saleswomen lined up to spray customers with competing perfumes. The two cases of pine-scented aerosol deodorizers certainly helped.

Through the window, Mountain looked down into the street and watched the girls step out of the limo. They looked good. *Really good.*

"Hot, Ben," Mountain reported excitedly from his corner-curtain viewpoint. "They look hot!"

"Mountain," Ben said slowly, "anybody with enough guts to show up here with us is automatically hot, regardless of what they look like."

"Phoebe looks hot," Mountain said, still peeking as the girls walked upstairs toward the apartment. "Bird looks hot, too. Not as hot as Phoebe, but pretty hot."

Mountain swung the door wide to meet the girls.

"You're really hot," Ben said to Bird as he walked over for a hug.

"I know," she said. "I am. The A/C was out in the limo."

"We're both hot," Phoebe said to Mountain.

"I *told* you," mouthed Mountain smugly to Ben.

"You have the A/C on?" asked Phoebe, finishing her earlier statement. "It's miserable out there."

"Sure thing," Mountain called back.

With pleasantries dispatched and the girls nibbling on cheese and crackers, Ben and Mountain left the living room and hid in the kitchen. It was time to cook dinner.

Behind the sanctity of the swinging kitchen door began a flurry of pan-banging activity. The girls could hear the refrigerator and pantry doors open and close repeatedly, so they figured the guys were hard at work creating a masterpiece.

Actually, they were getting a couple of beers out of the refrigerator and tossing a couple of empties in the pantry recycle bin—but details are details when it comes to culinary creation and masculine artists forging edible artworks.

For their main course, the men selected pork chops. Chops were good for several reasons: They were small, easily identifiable, fit in a pan, and most importantly, they were almost impossible to mess up. Any idiot could cook a pork chop.

Plus, pork chops were more romantic than macaroni and cheese, and lent themselves to both red and white wine. The guys congratulated themselves on the brilliance of such a strategic menu selection. Pork chops would be perfect.

Rather than pan-fry them, the guys opted to drown the chops in barbecue sauce and cook them in the oven. However, three minutes before the timer went off, the smoke detector did, triggering a heated debate between Ben and Mountain about whether the chops were truly finished.

As smoke billowed out of the oven and the kitchen's ceiling sprinklers rained on them, Ben insisted the chops were done. Mountain insisted they weren't, since the timer hadn't buzzed.

Mountain anxiously punched the oven light to look inside— not to see if the chops were done, which was impossible since they were engulfed in black diesel-like clouds of smoke-shrouding immolation—but rather to check whether his proudly sandblasted oven was all crudded up again.

When the timer finally *did* go off, the argument ceased. The chops were officially done. Neither Ben nor Mountain knew how to turn off the timer buzzer since they'd never used it before, so they simply ignored it and kept cooking while it kept loudly buzzing.

The kitchen was now smoky, wet, and noisy. The girls called in through the swinging door, asking if the guys needed any help.

"No, we're fine!" called back Mountain. "Everything's under control!"

Ben looked over at Mountain like he'd just thrown the life preservers back to their rescuers and told them they'd prefer to *swim* from the iceberg to the Jersey shore. "Lookit this, man!" worried Mountain. "They look like chunks of asphalt.

"Hell, man!" he added with grave concern. "What're we gonna do now? We gotta do *somethin'*."

"No problem," said Ben. "Gimme those. I can fix that."

Ben took the charred pig chunks, scraped off as much of the black as he could with a knife, rinsed them under the kitchen faucet, and scrubbed the meat with a scouring brush. With persistence, he scraped off enough burnt stuff to make the chops look like, well, like chops that had been in a street brawl after escaping a five-alarm tenement fire. "Gangland Pork" they could call it.

While the two men wrestled the chops, another battle—vegetables versus technology—was dramatically escalating only six feet away.

The baked potatoes in the microwave provided the next clue that the men were just a touch overzealous in their haste to trust flames to provide flavor. Ben told Mountain that baked potatoes took 45 minutes to cook. He was referring to potatoes in the oven, not the microwave.

Mountain misunderstood. While Ben was preoccupied and busily sculpting the chops, Mountain's giant paw had palmed all four baking potatoes and tossed them into the white radiation box, punched 45 minutes onto the timer, and wiped his sweat-beaded brow on his right shoulder sleeve.

"Nothin' to it," he thought as he paused for a swig of beer. "We'll get there yet. Potatoes are filling."

Midway into their fiery 45-minute nuclear condemnation, the potatoes began taking a route rarely seen to a dinner plate. First they smoldered, then they inflated like smoking grapefruits.

The men suddenly heard the microwave rattling an Argentinean tango on its four rubber feet. Eyebrows arched, the pair bent over, side by side, and leered down for a peek.

The men's faces were touching cheek to cheek as they looked inside the little microwave window. Something had to be wrong. Gurgling little explosion noises were coming from inside the small white appliance. An acrid smell, not unlike hair on fire, seeped from the frame of the microwave doorjamb. So did smoke.

"Think they're OK?" asked Mountain.

"Open it and see," said Ben. "We only need two. If we can save theirs, we can skip ours. We can tell them we don't *like* potatoes."

"*You* open it," retorted Mountain. "You know more about cooking than me. Besides, the timer hasn't gone off yet."

Ben leaned down and pressed his nose near the rumbling box as the countdown clock decreased from seven to six to five to four and closer toward the ding.

With Ben's snout against the glass, at the count of two the lava blew, blasting the door wide open and smashing into his nose, bloodying it with a straight right piston-shot, just like the picture-perfect punch Rocky Marciano sent Jersey Joe Walcott into Never, Neverland during their heavyweight championship fight.

Ben staggered backward and went down on his butt. He just sat there, dazed, as the angry potato lava roared down the countertop. Vesuvius had erupted and was spewing the gooey vengeance of a thousand angry ancestors.

It was headed his way.

All four potatoes burst into bubbling smoky lava, fueled by what seemed to be an underground supply chamber of piped-in molten tater. Ben blinked twice, shook his head to regain his senses, and quickly crab-scrambled backward to escape the river of raging spuds. Blood trickling out his right nostril, Ben wiped it with the back of his right hand, looked at the fresh red trail of liquid pain, and said with seriousness, "The potatoes are *out*.

"Figuratively *and* literally," Ben reported matter-of-factly, "the potatoes are *out*."

Meanwhile, out in the living room, the girls heard the big potato boom, looked at each other, laughed, and clinked their wineglasses. There was a war raging in the kitchen. Of that they were certain.

The men were immersed in the midst of a valuable life lesson: When culinarily overmatched, there's a majestic nobility in simply ordering Chinese food. And power in home delivery. Safety, too.

But, undaunted, the men refused to surrender. Onward the battle raged.

Ben decided to call their creation "blackened pork cutlets" since he knew "blackened" was a type of dish commonly served in expensive restaurants. He'd been to New Orleans and half of the stuff on Brennan's menu was blackened something-or-other. Blackened was good. It was trendy. And it was, well, apt. By every measurement standard, this dish certainly qualified.

Surprisingly, the blackened pork cutlets proved just a touch chewy. Each bite took 20 minutes to get down. "Wow!" said Ben after finally wind piping the lumpy first bite. "This musta been one strong pig. You can't even chew him."

"It's delicious," lied Phoebe, smiling directly at Mountain. "How's yours?" she asked sweetly.

Mountain's jaws were chewing up-and-down and in-and-out, moving five miles a minute from side-to-side. Mountain's strategy was power chewing. He finally made an aggressive commitment and did a dramatic python-swallowing-a-rabbit body-bend gulp, shook his head, and twice blinked his eyes. Finally, he smiled back at Phoebe and said, "Good."

Silently Mountain thought to himself, "A gator would spit this back up onto the riverbank and go back to huntin.'"

He then chugged a whole glass of water and exhaled like a pro wrestler. "God," Mountain thought. "We cleaned all damn day for *this?*"

Privately, Phoebe wondered how the hell Mountain ever got so bloody big trying to eat charred carpet. The plane left for New Zealand in three more days and, at the rate everyone was chewing, they'd have to skip dessert just to make the flight.

Bird, meanwhile, was having little success sawing through her pork chop. She simply wasn't strong enough to overpower it. Mountain saw Bird struggling and hopped up from the dinner table, yelling "'scuse me!" over his shoulder when he was halfway to the hall closet. Mountain had a portable jigsaw in the closet and, although he'd never plugged it in and tried it on meat before, this certainly seemed as good a time as any.

"Don't open that!" cried Ben as Mountain twisted and pulled wide the unlocked doorknob.

Too late.

The closet exploded, just like the microwave. A landslide of brooms, brushes, buckets, soapsuds, cleansers, rags, and mops came tumbling out in a clattering blast and surrounded Mountain. He stood there calmly holding his ground. The knee-high avalanche had him completely encircled.

"Damn," Mountain muttered as he looked up on the shelf. "No jigsaw. I musta lent it out." Impassively, he ignored the mess, returned to the dinner table, and sat down.

Ben then gallantly took it upon himself to saw Bird's dinner. Soon she, too, was chewing the unchewable. Midway through the meal, she wondered if she'd finish while the moon was still full.

After dinner, Phoebe and Mountain excused themselves as Mountain hoisted her over his shoulder and headed toward Mountain's room, ostensibly to look at his "coin collection." The coin collection was, in fact, a penny jar on top of his dresser that held about four dollars worth of copper leftovers.

Mountain used to have one of the biggest penny collections Ben ever saw, but he cashed it in during a pal's autumn bachelor party in Las Vegas. Yet ever since that Vegas trip, Mountain had begun rebuilding his penny collection. Apparently Phoebe really liked it because the pair stayed locked up in his room for a quite some time looking it over. And by the sound of Phoebe's happy squeals, some of the coins she really liked.

Ben focused his attention on Bird. Carrying her wine into the living room, he said with a smile, "Perhaps *we* should adjourn to the sofa and learn a little bit more about each other.

"I, for example, am a Cancer," he continued as he ushered Bird to the couch.

"Oh, don't be so hard on yourself," Bird said cheerfully.

"I meant my sign," said Ben. "I'm a Cancer."

"A horny little Cancer, aren't you?" asked Bird as Ben rubbed her arm and prepared to launch his first attack.

"Oh, don't say horny," Ben protested. "Let's just agree on the positive merits of repetitive horizontal contact."

"Oh my," said Bird. "The little chef uses big words. I am *impressed!*"

To help stutter-step Ben's advances, Bird quickly began a nervous discussion about chastity and its virtues. According to her, becoming "pure again" was less about having people accept you the way you are, and more about learning to love yourself. It helped her be centered, she said. Bird almost mentioned her full-moon fetish but decided not to. She wanted Ben to pursue her. The chase—ah, yes, the chase—would make the capture that much more exhilarating.

"It enhances my awareness," Bird said of her rekindled virtuosity. "And it enhances my creativity. And it enhances my inner self."

"Have more wine," urged Ben as he hurried to refill her glass, sloshing it on Mountain's already rainbow-stained coffee table. "It'll enhance my chances with your inner self, too.

"You're not a tease, are you, Bird?" Ben asked as he handed her the glass.

"I hate teases," she replied. "And if you don't say or do anything really stupid, I'll probably continue to feel that way. But, in answer to your question, no, I am not a tease and I'm not a flirt," she said as she took a sip of wine.

Much relieved, Ben broke out in a big smile.

Finishing her sip, Bird continued her thought with a smile, adding, "I simply prefer non-contact stimulation."

That one stopped Ben in his tracks. His expectant smile wilted as fast as his expectant masculinity, which was stuffed and standing by on-call inside his brand-new, just-out-of-the-package boxers. Ben scratched his head twice. He had no logical reply.

So, he leaned over and kissed her.

She kissed back.

In a wild frenzy, Ben and Bird wrestled each other like dancing circus bears and began hugging and kissing and rolling around in a love scrum reminscent of a two-out-of-three-falls Texas steel cage match. They even rolled off the sofa. They climbed back up, kissed some more, and rolled off again.

Ben was excited, Bird was excited. The full moon was shining and tonight Bird decided that men were good for more than just lawn maintenance, auto repair, carrying luggage, taking out the trash, and ruining good pork.

But Bird wasn't in a hurry and had an answer for Ben's every move. When she struggled to make his efforts at releasing her bra clasp four times harder than it had to be, Ben finally pulled his kissing face back, looked at her through tired eyes, and said, "Dangitall, Bird! Tryin' to git in your britches is harder than cookin' dinner!"

Bird wasn't sure whether that was good or bad. She decided on good. "Why, thank you," she said. Then she squeezed Ben's re-inflated baby Ben through his pants, laughed and let go, and they went right back to Greco-Roman wrestling.

Meanwhile, by the sound of it, Phoebe was still really enjoying Mountain's coin collection.

But, sadly enough, the early-morning run, on the heels of five hours of sleep, followed by the chemical fumes of a ten-hour cleaning mission, topped with a few glasses of New Zealand's magical Brancott Reserve Chardonnay, all conspired against Ben Bentley.

Stretched out on the sofa, holding Bird in a tight, relaxing horizontal embrace, he closed his weary eyes to rest for just a peaceful moment.

Then he fell asleep, exhausted, with his mouth half-open. Out like a light and gone for the night. Zonkerville.

And Bird—who tried shaking him, talking dirty, licking his ear, and unbuttoning his shirt to wake him—finally just gave up. Moon or no moon, her night was over.

With Phoebe and Mountain's help, Bird decided to bury Ben under a carefully stacked ceiling-high pile of furniture from which it was impossible to crawl out. When he woke up Friday morning, Ben Bentley was hopelessly and helplessly trapped.

Even worse, the full moon had now passed.

While Ben and Mountain were chasing the girls around Mountain's furniture, ten miles away Cush and Truck were guests of Donny Ray Douglass at a small after-hours farewell dinner party in the Gulfstream Park Turf Club.

The guests were enthralled with Cush's stories about New Zealand and peppered her with questions. Cush and Truck had a great evening and finally left around ten o'clock. Not in a hurry to go home, they ducked inside Chef Allen's gourmet restaurant for a sinful late-night dessert.

As they talked about everyone but themselves, the laughs came easily. She talked a lot about Timothy and their horses. To Truck, Cushla seemed content. She had her life very much in order, very much in balance, and he was happy for her. In a selfish way, Truck envied her happiness.

He seemed relaxed around Cush and she wondered why this nice man still insisted on living his life with a barbed-wire fence around his feelings. He hadn't changed a bit in that regard since the last time they were together; she could see it clear as day whenever she looked into his eyes. But this was not the time or place to pursue the discussion. She doubted they'd play Skee-Ball tonight, either.

After dessert, Truck drove to the beach and dropped Cush off at Mitzi's. When they arrived, he said goodnight and made no effort to extend the evening. Truck wondered if she would lean over and kiss him good night. The move would have to be hers. He wouldn't make it.

Neither did she. Cush just stuck out her hand, like the first time they played darts. She shook his firmly with a soft smile, saying only, "Thank you, Mr. Roberts, for a lovely evening. Shall I see you tomorrow?"

Truck felt awkward and foolish, but this was a question with a right and wrong answer and he wanted to get it right. He was unsure what to say. Cush expectantly waited for an answer.

Finally he mumbled, "Good night, Miss Wimsett. Eight o'clock for breakfast, then sightseeing?"

"Eight-thirty," Cush corrected. "I simply *must* get my beauty rest."

Cush laughed, and stepped out of the car, gently closed the door, and walked toward Mitzi's front gate. Then she turned the key, walked under the wrought-iron archway, and stepped inside.

She never paused to look back.

Back Across the Pond

Friday morning, Piso and his girlfriend Isa came down to Manero's dock to say goodbye. Luther was already there. The fortunes of all three had changed in the flash of good luck that this peculiar horse had brought into their lives. As much as they wanted to, they couldn't go to Bimini with the others to celebrate.

Piso was now an apprentice jockey and earning money. Isa, who'd always loved Piso—Snack Shack paper hat and all—now dreamed of a wedding ring, their own home, and a living room full of screaming little Pisos.

Luther even picked up a small string of horses, eight in all, from an owner who wanted to cut him a break and thought he'd earned a second chance.

Two cats that refused to leave the marlin stayed aboard the water taxi when it was time to shove off. Anvil named the cats, a male and a female, Marlin and Brando, vetoing T-man's choice of Mulder and Scully. Both would get seasick right alongside Anvil once they reached the open ocean waters.

Luther hopped aboard and duct-taped the Gulfstream's big championship loving cup to the overhead salon roof of the water taxi. In the piercing Florida sunshine, it glinted like a glistening golden beacon. Once they arrived home, Anvil knew exactly where that cup was going—right to the church so everyone could see it.

Anvil and T-man ate a sunrise breakfast, fueling up on bacon, eggs, and fresh orange juice, then prepped the boat for the long chug home. When it was time to go—just past eight o'clock— they hugged and waved goodbye to everybody, then pushed off from Manero's dock. They chugged south through the Intracoastal Waterway toward Bal Harbour and North Miami where they'd purchased all the Hermes scarves. At Haulover Inlet, Anvil steered the taxi left and headed east under the high-spanned bridge. The tide was just turning from slack to outgoing. With the current gently helping, the water taxi nudged its way through the parallel rock jetties and out into the open Atlantic.

Several kids raced from the beach out to the end of the jetty, pointing at the horse and waving their arms high. Half a dozen fishermen also recognized them. T-man and Anvil returned their waves of greeting. Even Bonefish and Elvis looked over as if to acknowledge their fans.

The horse and goat watched the people carefully until the water taxi nosed its way beyond the tip of the jetty and into full open water, leaving the friendly people behind. Bonefish then turned back to face the bow and stared forward at the endless ocean before him. He seemed content. He seemed to know he was headed home.

At the Apartment

About the time Anvil and T-man were ready to shove off from Manero's, a tapping on the Mountain's living room window glass awoke Ben from a peaceful sleep on the sofa.

Bladder pressing, it took a few moments to realize he was hopelessly trapped under a carefully engineered, ceiling-high stack of piled-up furniture.

Bird had called Mitzi late Thursday night, told her about Ben's romantic flameout, and Friday morning Mitzi met the others for breakfast and followed them over to Mountain's to see the trapped human wreckage. They wanted to take photos.

The girls arrived and looked through the living room window, tapping loudly to get Ben's attention. He heard them and looked over. As he got his bearings, he knew three things for sure: Nature called, he looked like a fool, and he was hopelessly pinned beneath a towering Eiffel of two coffee tables, six chairs, a big dining room table, a kitchen table, an end table and—crowning the summit of Mount Furniture—a three-foot-tall Stieffel lamp, plugged in and shining like a beacon. A well-used toilet bowl scrub brush was tied to a chair leg and the bristles dangled three inches from his nose.

When Mountain saw Ben looking distressed, he did the appropriate thing. The manly thing. He mooned him, dropping his pants and pressing his prodigious gluteus flush up against the glass to the maximus. Then he wiggled it from side-to-side with enough gusto to cause a whimpering rubbing-glass kind of sound. Sort of like Windex, only a lot pinker and a lot louder.

Everybody laughed and went inside, insisting on talking to Ben for the longest time before beginning the slow, tedious process of dismantling Mt. Furniture. Ben finally wriggled an escape and made it to the bathroom on the dead run, cussing loudly as his belt and pants raced for morning emancipation in the porcelain sanctuary.

"Friends," he sighed as he stood over the toilet and looked cross-eyed in the bathroom mirror. "What would I do without them?"

An hour later, they trekked down to the marina. Mountain had loaded up the various gifts for the islanders inside the salon of the cruiser Wednesday evening, so the boat was ready to go when the gang arrived.

As Mountain fired up the twin engines, Phoebe asked if they weren't overloaded with the weight of all the others staying aboard. Wouldn't it be safer if only she and Mountain went over with all this stuff? After all, it looked so *heavy*.

"Nah," said Mountain. "The weight's not a problem." He explained several fine features of the yacht to Phoebe, including the fact that it was outfitted with radar, a global positioning system, and, if necessary, an autopilot.

"Autopilot? You mean the bloody boat can go where it's supposed to automatically? It steers its bloody self?" Phoebe asked wondrously. "You don't have to stand here the whole time and drive? My, what a wonderful bloomin' concept! Perhaps you can show me later?"

"Sure," Mountain said. "Once we get clear of the harbor and out to sea, I'll show you how it works."

"*Promise?*" she cooed.

"Promise," said Mountain. He was impressed with her interest in boats, marine electronics, and automatic directional devices.

Truthfully, Phoebe didn't give a damn about boats. Or electronics. Her only nautical concern was the readiness of Mountain's torpedo. His pink one. Last night Phoebe learned the real reason he should be called Mountain. And it had nothing to do with his prodigious girth.

Before shoving off from Keystone Point Marina, Mountain called Anvil on the radio to see if he wanted to be escorted across. The racetrack and water taxi were just a few miles up the Intracoastal Waterway and a rendezvous would be easy.

"No, go ahead," squawked back Anvil's scratchy radio voice. "We'll use the radio. We'll check in every 30 minutes. If we have a problem, we'll call right away. The seas are flat calm. We'll be fine. A long slow chug will do it."

"OK," said Mountain. "But don't do anything risky. Holler if you need anything. We'll take our time and fish along the way so the girls can have some fun. We'll never be too far from ya."

"Ten-four," acknowledged Anvil.

"Ten-four and out," said Mountain, hanging up the mouthpiece.

With that, Mountain untied the dock ropes and idled his powerful twin diesels out of the narrow canal, first to Biscayne Bay, then up to and under the high-arching Haulover Bridge. In 20 minutes, they were clear of shore, past the jetty, and into the green waters of the ever-deepening Atlantic.

Ben, meanwhile, was trying to convince Bird and Mitzi to make the crossing topless.

"OK," Mitzi agreed, "we'll do it, provided you go bottomless."

Ben thought about that offer, disappeared downstairs, and re-emerged a minute later *au natural.* Upstairs on the flying bridge, Mountain winced and shook his head while Phoebe looked on intently. Compared to Mountain, Ben was a minnow.

"OK," Ben said happily as he stood before Bird and Mitzi. "Your turn now."

"Oh, we changed our minds," said Bird. "But it's OK with us if you want to do that."

"You have to rub on your own lotion, too," cooed Mitzi. "That is a rather cute little thing, isn't it, Bird?"

Phoebe called down her opinion from upstairs on the flying bridge. "Much like a penis only smaller," she voted.

All three girls laughed and Ben disappeared downstairs to put his swimsuit back on. He reappeared a few minutes later as if nothing had happened.

As they neared the unmistakable blue color line marking currents of the Gulf Stream, Mountain mentioned how good the fishing usually was.

"Oh, can we catch a fish?" squealed Bird. "I'd love to catch a real fish."

"As opposed to a fake fish?" teased Ben.

"Ben's got a baby worm for bait. I bet they'd like to bite *that,*" teased Mitzi. Bathed in tanning oil, hidden behind sunglasses, and clad in a thong Kiwini, she looked like a 3-D Jessica Rabbit.

"I prefer to consider it a powerful, wriggling, writhing *eel,*" shot back Ben.

The girls all laughed. "It wasn't last night," reported Bird.

Mountain saved his friend by calling for Ben to take the wheel while he climbed down and readied some trolling rods. Once they were seven miles offshore and Mountain saw the pronounced color change clearly defining the edge of the Gulf Stream, he free-spooled the lines back into the wake of the big cruiser and stuck each rod in a side-mounted rodholder. They trolled four rods, two off the stern and two others spread wide from outriggers on each side of the boat. Back and forth they trolled, parallel to the beach and right along the edge of the Stream.

Luck was with them. In a matter of minutes, the line laundry-clipped to the right outrigger snapped out of its pin, the reel sang like a songbird, and a colorful, bait-crashing male mahi-mahi dolphinfish greyhounded across the stern 60 yards behind them. He was a big bull, a fish Mountain guessed would weigh in at 30 pounds.

The Kiwi girls were mesmerized. All three pushed each other toward the fighting chair. It never dawned on any of them they might catch something so big and acrobatic.

Sure enough, Mountain trolled right along the edge of a long weed line smack dab into a big school of the colorful, highflying dolphinfish. Mountain told the girls if they left the big one they hooked swimming in the water by the side of the boat, all the others in the school would stay nearby. They could then catch plenty, since the school would remain next to the big bull at boatside.

Mountain was right. They caught plenty of fish. In all, they hoisted 19 of the pastel-splashed beauties out of the water and onto the deck. The fish ranged from 13 to 34 pounds and nearly filled both below-deck coolers built in under the floorboards.

None of the girls ever touched a fish. They just yanked them out of the sea and slung them around at Ben. They took a special delight in fish-slapping him whenever his back was turned. At the end of the hour, slimed and bloodied, Ben looked and smelled like Mountain's bathroom right before he had cleaned it.

These fish would go a long way toward fueling the island party awaiting them in Bimini. Few things in the sea tasted as mouth-watering delicious as the light, flaky meat of a freshly caught mahi-mahi. And nobody knew how to fix them better than the Bahamians.

After the bite was over and the action stopped, Mountain cranked in the lines and stowed all the gear. He called Anvil on the radio and gave him a full report. The two boats were only a couple of miles apart. From the flying bridge, Phoebe could clearly see them through the binoculars.

While Ben scrubbed down the deck from splattered blood and fish slime, the girls retreated inside the air-conditioned cabin salon for quick showers and cold drinks. Mountain finally climbed back up to the cockpit and gently slid the throttles of the droning twin diesels back to a slow cruising speed. When Phoebe reappeared, freshly showered and bubbly happy, she told Mountain she wanted to see how the autopilot worked. He flipped a switch and winked at Phoebe, who immediately disappeared down the ladder and scrambled below deck like a rabbit diving into a dirt hole with a hungry fox in pursuit.

Ben was left to straighten up and fillet the fish, most of which had smacked him, whacked him, and attacked him while still alive.

He could hardly wait.

So, while Ben was jabbing a piercing fillet knife into gooey pods of fish guts again and again, Mountain was below deck sticking something else into something else again and again. Judging by the sounds emanating from the locked stateroom, Bird assumed Phoebe had found Mountain's coin collection again. Bird and Mitzi high-fived Phoebe's good fortune and, thus inspired, began playing another game of "Who Would You Rather Be With?"

Unknown to Ben, he advanced twice during their game, but lost out in the third round to the old wrinkled American actor Gene Hackman.

The River of Grass

Since Truck and Cush were flying in the seaplane over to Bimini in late afternoon, they spent most of their day touristing around Miami and its suburbs. After an outdoor breakfast at the News Café, he drove her around Coral Gables, slowing down along the mansion-lined lower Biscayne Bay waterfront to near-stops in front of both Madonna and Stallone's former homes. Cush gawked at the sight of both beautiful estates.

They briefly stopped in Coconut Grove and shopped at CocoWalk, with Truck buying a Dan Marino football jersey from the souvenir counter inside Marino's second-floor restaurant. Cush disappeared into the ladies room and emerged wearing the jersey, happily modeling it for Truck with a full-turn spin. "What do you think?" she asked. Cush had no clue who Marino was, but loved the jersey's aqua color.

"I think Marino never looked so good," said Truck. The girl at the counter laughed.

The two then piled back in the car and, convertible top down, headed out Tamiami Trail through Little Havana toward the Everglades. They drove a dozen miles past the Florida Turnpike before pulling into the gravel parking lot at Gator Park.

There, Truck and Cush hopped into a big airboat along with five other passengers and a portly, bearded guide hidden behind a pair of Oakley flare-style sunglasses. The guide's nametag read "Willie the Wonder."

Willie fired up the airboat's giant caged fan blade and zoomed them out the trails through the grass flats. They spun around and through the Everglades for the next hour, stopping every ten minutes or so as Willie cut the juice to the big propeller and glided near expectant alligators.

Cush and a small girl from Boston took turns tossing marshmallows to the gators from Willie's plastic bag. The gators seemed to love them, gliding over and popping the marshmallows off the surface with a quick snap of their jaws. Most of the gators were small—seven feet or less—but several 12-footers sunned themselves on matted dry weed beds scattered throughout the famed slow-flowing waterway. "The River of Grass," the Everglades are called. It was easy to see why.

On the ride back in, Willie decided to spice up the morning and troll for tips by performing several scream-inducing high-speed 360s. Cush screamed the loudest.

After the boat ride, Truck drove back toward Miami, driving east through Little Havana. He pulled in front of "Havanarama," a well-known local Cuban cafeteria, and parked next to a giant red-barked and peeling gumbo limbo tree. "A tourist tree," Truck smiled to Cush as they climbed out of the car.

They ordered a traditional lunch: a Cuban sandwich and Cuban coffee. Ever the tour guide, Truck wanted to jam in as much South Florida color and culture as possible into what little time remained in Cush's holiday. They sat at a picnic table in the shade of the gumbo limbo. Four beautiful orchids grew 20 feet away.

Cush liked the warm crusty bread and the sandwich but eyed the tiny plastic cup of brown liquid suspiciously. She had never tried Cuban coffee before and didn't know why it wasn't served in a larger cup like other coffees. She wasn't really much of a coffee drinker anyhow.

Shrugging her shoulders, she hoisted the little cup and fired the thick hot goo down the hatch. She blanched at the bitterly strong taste. In less than ten minutes, the caffeine jolt hit and she started chattering like a gossiping chipmunk. Truck laughed. He never bothered to tell Cush that one stiff shot of the stuff could keep you awake for the rest of your life. Two shots can make the dead get up and polka in the morgue.

Cush's verbal motor kept running the whole half-hour drive back through Miami, up I-95, and east on the MacArthur Causeway to Watson Island and the seaplane. It was three o'clock when they arrived for their four-fifteen flight. People treated them like Bahamian heroes when they checked in. Here, Truck and Cush were mini-celebrities, and even the two guys handling baggage in the back came out to shake their hands. Everyone knew the story of Bonefish.

The seaplane was nowhere around so Cush stepped outside and walked down to the water's edge. She stared at the monstrous cruise ship tied to the dock on the far side of the half-mile-wide channel. It was an enormous vessel, far larger than anything she'd ever seen. The ropes that held it were as thick as branches of the mighty lunchtime gumbo limbo tree. The name on the cruise ship's stern read "Majesty of the Seas."

She was awestruck by its sheer enormity. Each individual letter spelling out its name on the transom seemed a mile high. "My God," she said in awe. "Lookit the bloody thing. It's *twice* the size of the island hoppers we get from Australia."

"More people *work* on that ship than live on the island where we're going," Truck said as he walked up and stood next to her.

A couple of minutes later, at five before four, Cush heard a low-pitched growl high in the white cotton clouds. She looked up and to her right, just above downtown Miami and high in the east, she saw a bug-sized, then gull-sized, then pterodactyl-sized and, finally, plane-sized craft buzzing its noisy way toward the open water. It was headed toward a skittering splashdown in Government Cut as its water lapped against her black sandals. She had never seen a seaplane land before and was fascinated to realize an airborne plane could become a seaworthy boat so quickly.

The small, white, twin-propped floating Mallard commuter plane splashed down a few hundred yards away, turned into a modified-v-hulled winged boat, and propeller-chugged its noisy way toward the shore where they stood. Cush and Truck scampered out of the seaplane's way and watched as it turned onto the cement ramp and rumbled loudly up and out of the sea.

The seaplane slowly rolled 50 yards to a parking area where the motors were cut, the props stopped spinning, and wheel chocks were manually wedged under the two wing tires. A six-step ladder unfolded from its tail section.

Cush was transfixed, seeing and retaining everything. Truck got a kick out of simply watching her. She exuded a child's love of living, Truck decided. A rare and admirable trait.

Fifteen minutes later, it was time to board and Truck and Cush hiked up those six ladder steps, ducked inside, and picked a pair of seats on the right side of the plane. They were two rows from the open cockpit where the pilots sat. The complicated display panel of gidgets and widgets and gadgets and gizmos were in plain sight.

All the seats were filled in this 16-passenger plane. Truck and Cush were two of only three white people on the flight, besides the pilot and co-pilot. The rest, she guessed, were Bahamians heading home.

The pilot cautiously wheeled the plane down the white cement emergence ramp and back into the sea. Cush looked out the window as the plane rolled into deeper water, the hull providing boat-like buoyancy once the water was too deep for the wheels to touch bottom.

Cush could feel the hydraulic lifting of the wheels into the breast of the ship. Once the wheels were safely up and locked out of the way, the pilot throttled more speed and the two big propellers thundered the seaplane's acceleration. Bouncing and splashing, it taxied parallel to the entire length of the massive cruise ship nearby at ever-increasing speeds.

Zooming along like a speeding ski boat, it finally got lift. Cush watched out the window as the sea returned its prize to the sky. The plane climbed slowly and steadily, passing a battery of tall condos guarding the ocean door.

"That's Fisher Island," Truck said, seeing where Cush was looking. "Million-dollar condos for rich celebrities like Oprah, Whitney Houston, Boris Becker, and people like that."

As Fisher Island passed from view, so did the white sandy shores of South Beach. The plane pointed dead east. Far to the south, Cush could see a light tower on a pile of rocks, surrounded by a bunch of boats, fishing boats, she guessed. Truck told her that tower was Fowey Light and people in the boats were fishing for sportfish, probably livebaiting for the great tailwalking sailfish and hard-fighting yard-long cobia.

Truck also told Cush that Fowey Light was where Piso was rescued from his four-day escape on his homemade barrel raft. Looking down in awed silence, she couldn't imagine the courage it took for Cubans like Piso to shove off from their homeland and bob like a cork in a desparate hope for freedom.

As the ocean deepened, it changed colors. Light green turned to dark green. It washed into light blue, then dark blue, and finally, a magical sapphire blue that trademarked the magnificent Gulf Stream. Truck pointed out the distinct color change to Cush, which she saw immediately. From the sky, she traced the edge of the Gulf Stream on the airplane window with her finger.

"The Gulf Stream is like a river in the ocean," Truck explained. "Its water currents are warmer than the ocean's, plus it flows steadily, south to north, at about five miles an hour. It travels from the Caribbean, past the Florida Coast, then all the way up off New England. It passes closest to shore right here. Right now, it might be only five miles from shore. The more north we go, the farther from shore it gets. Off the northern U.S. coast, for example, the Stream is hundreds of miles from shore.

"The giant ocean fish travel the Stream," Truck continued. "They migrate up and then back down, and the fishermen know it. This natural wonder is always alive with fish. All kinds, all sizes. And the law out there is infinitely simple."

"What's the law?" asked Cush as she stayed riveted to the scenes outside of her window.

"Eat or be eaten," he answered. "Everything out there has a choice: Either eat or be eaten. Teeth don't sleep."

Cush shuddered. What an awful way to die.

Truck pointed south. "Cuba's *that* way," he said. "The northern flow of the current is what encourages the Cuban rafters to try and float to safety. That's why they risk their lives for a chance at freedom. Key West is 90 miles from Havana, a two-day float in a strong current, but Key West is farther away from the Gulf Stream than here. So, often the rafters will float for three or four days to try and get off this coast. Then they can paddle out of the Gulf Stream current, into the slower ocean water on the beach side, and coordinate a hard paddle ashore with an incoming tide."

Cush turned away from the window to ask an important question. "Do they usually make it?"

"Now they do. During the two major Cuban exoduses—when Castro pulled the plug and said that anyone who chose to leave could—well, that was bad. Many died. Rafts and bits of rafts were found all over the sea. Pieces of hundreds washed up on the beach day after day for several months. It was terrible."

Cushla said nothing, but absorbed everything Truck told her. She looked for tiny bobbing rafts but saw none. They were also seated on the wrong side of the plane to search for Bonefish and the powder-blue water taxi.

Too quickly, the best 25 minutes in North American avionics neared an end. Out of the distant deep blue sea rose tiny spits of sand. The more the plane droned downward, the larger the sand grew. They could see trees pop out of the sand, then piers and pastel-colored cottages.

The seaplane banked to the right, glided south a bit, then banked back left to the north, lining itself up with the narrow channel opening separating North from South Bimini. The channel was no more than 200 yards across. The water was glass clear and Cush could see the underwater coral way down deep, just like on the travel brochures.

The seaplane dropped ever so slowly, an inch at a time it seemed, as it neared the harbor and touched, pulled up, and goose-splashed back down in a 500-yard wake-spraying slide. The seaplane noisily bounced halfway up the length of the island before the pilot made a tight J-turn. Now a winged boat, they loudly roared back down the calm harbor.

The seaplane slowly turned toward shore, then noisily groaned its way out of the water and onto the paved ramp near a small green hut at the southern tip of North Bimini.

"We're here," said Truck with a grin as he unbuckled his seat belt. "Who'd ever think a place this special could be half an hour away from three million people? Hope you like it."

"I love it already," said Cush. "As long as they've got a loo, I'm sure it'll be perfect." With that, she stooped and crab-walked her way out of the little plane and down the six-step portable ladder into the radiant Bahamian sunshine in search of a toilet.

By nightfall the rhythm, music, and hypnotic magic of this tiny little island would nudge them both one more unexpected step toward emotional confusion.

Hail the Victors

The island was buzzing with the excitement of a hero's arrival. At least three dozen Bahamians impatiently waited for the plane to unload, most just wanting to see Truck and Cush. Everyone, it seemed, wanted to hear about the miracle of Bonefish at Gulfstream Park.

Customs was a five-minute check-in and walk-through. From there, the pair walked for three minutes to the bayside customs boat dock for a progress report on Anvil. They were much relieved to hear the floating circus was only about eight miles away. The water taxi, in regular radio contact, should arrive in just over an hour.

Mountain's cabin cruiser was already in and tied up dockside at the Bimini Big Game Club. He had cleared customs half an hour before and Truck spied the big Hatteras when the seaplane made its J-turn in the harbor. Anvil had waved Mountain on ahead so he didn't have to worry about the cabin cruiser's giant wake rocking the water taxi's flat modified v-hull.

Cush and Truck walked five minutes up narrow dusty King Street, then veered into the sportfishing club's marina where Mountain's cabin cruiser was docked. The big man was sipping a Snapple Kiwi-Strawberry drink in the fighting chair when they walked up. The marine radio was on in the background.

"Hi, Mountain!" Cush called out with a wave. "Where is everyone?"

"Well, Mitzi's over there," Mountain pointed, toward the biggest yacht at the end of the dock. It was 60 feet if it was an inch. "The feller who owns it came over and introduced himself.

He told Mitzi it was Happy Hour on his yacht and I reckon she thought it'd be rude not to accept."

"No doubt," agreed Truck. "Where's Ben?"

"He's sleepin'."

"Where's Bird?" asked Cush.

"She's sleepin' too."

Truck looked at Cush and Cush looked back at Truck, both saucer-eyed at that information and the thought behind it.

"Separate staterooms," said Mountain, interpreting the glance.

"Romeo and Juliet, eh, Cush?" kidded Truck.

"Speaking of Romeo and Juliet . . ." Cush turned to Mountain and teased, "Hey Romeo! Where's Juliet?"

He hoisted his water-beaded half-empty bottle of Snapple and took a long, right-handed gulp. Then he belched. "Ah, she's sleepin' too," he smiled proudly. "*My* stateroom."

With that, he finished his drink, winked, got up, and climbed below deck to check on his Sleeping Beauty. He re-emerged a minute later, heard on the crackling marine radio that Anvil was close, and decided to organize a welcoming committee. He received customs clearance to chug a boatload of family and friends back out to escort them in the rest of the way. Fifteen people helped Mountain unload all the gifts onto the weathered gray dock, then piled aboard the Hatteras to head out and greet the heroes.

Anvil and T-man had just radioed customs that they'd be dockside in less than an hour, somewhere around five-thirty, and reported fish on ice that needed immediate attention. Anvil didn't mention what type of fish, and Truck wondered if T-man latched onto another bus-sized marlin.

Word of their impending arrival spread around the island and by the time the escorted water taxi finally turned the protective corner of the channel, 400 people, maybe even 500, were waiting.

Truck and Cush stood on the edge of the customs dock and waved at the boatload of happy folks leaving on the Hatteras to go meet the gang. They waved until Mountain rounded the southern point and curved out of sight, gunning his yacht back into the Atlantic.

Truck decided to take Cush up to meet a few other folks before the mayhem of the floating circus arrived. The two walked up to the Compleat Angler Hotel and stepped inside the squeaky screen door for a quick hello.

Once inside, they were greeted with a bunch of happy hollers and waves and a sky full of hoisted Kalik beers to clink the arrival of the architect of an island dream. Humphrey, the hotel manager, offered free drinks to both, shook their hands, and welcomed them to Bimini.

Just as at customs, a dozen folks at the Angler bar crowded around Truck, shook his hand, shook Cush's hand, and told her how nice it was to meet her. Cush got a starlet's welcome and seemed puzzled by all the fuss. Truck was a nice guy, sure. But why the red carpet? "Why do they like me so much?" she asked him as Humphrey spilled their Cokes over the mounds of ice in both of their glasses. "What did I do? I didn't do a bloody thing."

"They've never seen me with a girl before," Truck said, trying to look as serious as possible. "Maybe they're just relieved to find out I'm not gay."

"You're not?" asked Cush, eyes wide with surprise. "That day in the meadow I wasn't so sure. Mitzi said you were. She said you had to be."

Truck looked at Cush, tweaked her nose with his thumb and index finger, and said, "You know, I got home that night and wasn't so sure myself. That was a very odd day."

With that, the pair clinked glasses and hoisted a toast.

"To Bonefish," Cush added.

"To Bonefish," echoed Truck.

"To Bonefish!" chorused the others.

Truck and Cush finished their soda at the Angler, walked over to Captain Pat's golf cart rental, and rented cart #21. As usual, it was the last cart Pat had to rent and, as usual, it still featured a wicked out-of-alignment pull to the left. And it had no brakes.

"Sorry," shrugged Captain Pat.

"I'll adapt," laughed Truck. "C'mon," he said to Cush. "Let's go for a ride. I'll show you a bit of the island. We can ride up to the top of Queen Street and watch for Anvil's boat. By now he might be visible. If not, he will be soon."

With that, Cush linked her right arm in Truck's left and they walked from Captain Pat's office back down the dock, past the weigh station and ice machine, and beyond the blooming olean-ders toward the wayward golf cart.

Truck was conscious of Cush grabbing his arm and felt OK with it. It seemed more natural than awkward, which was a surprise to him. She replied by punching Truck in the right shoulder with a clenched right fist. She smacked him pretty hard. And laughed while doing so.

Home at Last

It was quite the arrival scene at the customs dock, especially when the crowd saw T-man's giant marlin plus the two yellowfin tuna and three big mahi-mahi dolphinfish he caught on his new rod. Between what T and the girls unloaded, there would be plenty of fresh fish tonight for the island party.

T-man said that once he caught his biggest mahi-mahi out from under the shade of a big sheet of floating plywood in the middle a weed line, he had visions of another marlin. Anvil worried about that, too, and made T-man stop fishing. T-man quit until Anvil dozed off for a nap. Then T-man slipped his lines back out and caught the two tuna, the second of which frantically flopped all over the deck and finally tail-slapped the fool out of his old man and woke him back up.

Anvil immediately got seasick again and both cats crouched next to him at the railing. All three hung over side, queasily talking to the sea.

As soon as the last rope secured the water taxi to the dock, Anvil triumphantly hoisted aloft a big canvas sack for everyone to admire.

In it was all the money. Donny Ray's people helped Anvil by carefully figuring out exactly who got what. Each person's winnings were inside zip-lock bags with name labels. Anvil told the cheering crowd that he'd dole out the winnings at the party in the park to everyone who contributed.

The happy caravan then snaked its way down the two dusty miles from the dock to the bayside park next to Anvil's house and the baseball field. T-man held the big Gulfstream trophy high overhead, like the Stanley Cup, while he perched atop the roof of his dad's golf cart. Alma slowly drove it accompanied by the tuna, the mahi-mahi, and two cats.

Dozens of kids ran alongside the cart. Anvil walked beside it, holding on to Bonefish's lead while Elvis walked on his own next to Bonefish.

The marlin, however, would miss the party. She went straight to the fish house for processing and, one hour later, a thin ribbon of whispy black smoke threading above the island smokehouse signaled the marlin's official welcome to Bimini.

Once the victorious procession arrived at the park, Anvil had all the money-winners sit in the baseball stands. He read down his list and every name brought an enthusiastic cheer from the stands. All told, Anvil doled out more cash than anybody on the island could ever recall legally seeing. He paid Weevil, the fisherman who gave him the two wahoo to sell, last of all, dramatically counting out a total of $1,240 cash—all in twenties.

"*Wa-hooooo!*" bellowed Weevil. Then he paused for a second and scrunched up his face. "Wait a minute!" he continued. "The horse paid $200 to win! Six dollars?! Six dollars? You sold *two* wahoo for $12? *What's wrong, witchoo man?*" he swatted at Anvil good-naturedly. "Those wahoo were worth $20, *not* $12!" protested Weevil.

"Those wahoo were worth $600 apiece, Mon," replied Anvil.

"Good point, Mon," cackled Weevil, breaking out into a self-created boogie-stepping dance jig. "They be *solid GOLD wahoo*, brother!"

Anvil laughed and shook hands with Weevil. Weevil sure looked a lot smarter today than when he showed up at the dock holding those two toothy fish aloft by their tails.

"How much you have on him, Anvil?" Weevil asked with a grin. "You musta had a ton o' money—a *ton o'money!*"

Anvil suddenly blanched at the thought of the money he just forked over to Weevil, compared with the $26.20 he collected from his lone $2 show ticket. But he didn't stay melancholy for long. After all, he made more than a year's pay in two minutes watching his horse run once around a dirt circle. "I did OK, Weevil," he finally replied with a soft smile. "I did OK."

The party raged well into the night. Calypso music was already booming loudly when they arrived and it stayed that way. If anything, it got louder as the native Kalik beers disappeared and fueled the celebration. The Calypsonians, the house band at the Compleat Angler, played for four straight hours before wearing out and caving in to boom-boxed CDs.

Bonefish was lying down in his paddock under his lean-to, listening to all the noise and feeling happy to be home. His eye hurt but he was back where he belonged and that was all that mattered. Tomorrow he could run on his beach, walk around town, and see all of his friends. If he got lucky, some might even have candy.

Elvis was curled up, as usual, against Bonefish's back. He was going to like it here, he thought. And he really liked the island music. It had a lot catchier beat than the country music they played back at the track.

Casa Grande

Around ten o'clock that night, Truck and his pals adjourned up the road to the Bimini Bay Club at Casa Grande for a quiet unwinding. A small private party was set up and waiting. Sixteen trudging steps up from the driveway delivered them to Bimini's most beautiful view.

Casa Grande was an old mansion built on the island's north end—its best location. It was 50 years old, built by an inventor who devised a lot of gadgets and gizmos for automobiles. The building had three floors with guest rooms on the upper two. A slab stone deck was all around the ground floor surrounding a large curvy kidney-shaped pool. The place had been designed and built for entertaining.

Ninety yards from the house, a romantic stone gazebo had been built on the end of a small walkway jetty that extended about 100 feet into the sea. The jetty faced west, toward the spectacular sun that gently melted each day into the sea. Heaven knows how many women through the years had been held and kissed there.

More would be tonight.

Alma had arranged a surprise, too. Once the guests were comfortably situated around the pool deck relaxing in the light evening breeze, a melodic sound suddenly wafted from the rocks. It was a lone, soulful saxophone.

These were, in fact, the beautiful floating notes of Miami sax star Joe Shashaty baring his soul to the heavens. Alma had flown him over from the mainland to play for the dozen or so invitees that evening. Joe stood on the sea wall, closed his eyes, and, softly spotlighted by a nearly full moon, wailed his magic to the sea and stars.

Cush recognized the musician from the flight over. Shashaty was the third white guy on the seaplane and his music was hypnotically romantic.

After two songs, Cushla asked Truck to walk out to the gazebo. She linked his arm and held on tightly as they slowly stepped out above the breaking waves of the sea. There, inside the gazebo, Cush asked Truck to point out the Big Dipper. "Up there," he said, pointing to its outline in the heavens. "The Dipper is the group of stars that outline the sax."

Cush recognized where he pointed and rested her head on his shoulder. Truck held her close, his right arm around her back. They stayed that way for a minute or two, then turned back to rejoin the others. It was Truck's idea to leave.

At midnight, Alma took the girls upstairs for a quick tour of their rooms. On each bed, they found a pair of roller skates. The upstairs deck at Casa Grande made a complete loop around the beautiful old mansion—a design trait built specifically for the first owner's wife who loved to skate. The girls giggled as they laced up their skates and rolled around and around under the stars, listening to Shashaty's beautifully baleful sounds massage the scattered, slow-moving clouds before heading up toward the heavens.

Alma got great joy watching the girls—and the guys, too, for that matter. Truck was like a son to her and she wanted to see him happy. For some reason or another, when it came to women, this wonderful man seemed to live life like he was falling backward out of a chair. Alma wasn't sure why. Maybe, she thought, like many young men, he simply didn't know what it was he was looking for.

Truck talked once or twice about some day settling down, but then just as quickly dismissed it. And as he and Alma watched the girls happily skate laps around the deck, the topic came up again. This time, however, Truck was the one who raised it.

"Richard Jeni was right, Alma," Truck said.

"Who's Richard Jeni?" asked Alma, not recognizing the name.

"White guy," Truck answered. "A comedian."

"What'd he say?" asked Alma.

"He said, "Ahhh, *divorce*. I know it well. From the Latin word meaning to rip a man's genitals out of his wallet."

"Oh, Truck!" she started. "Whatchoo talkin' 'bout a divorce for? You need to get a *date* before you need to worry 'bout a divorce!"

Alma chided such foolish talk. "For a smart man, Truck, you are pretty dumb," she said scornfully. "There is no life without love. You are old enough to know better. And anyone who loves children the way you do needs some children of his own to love him back."

"Does Anvil feel the same way?" Truck asked.

"Oh, he wouldn't admit it. Anvil will tell you he was born, went to elementary school, and got married.

"Then he'll show you his Diaper Diary. He kept track of every single one of T's diapers he ever changed and marked them down on a paper on the refrigerator door. Reminds him all the damn time, too. When Anvil gets mad at T, he'll go into the closet, rummage around, and pull out that old scrap of paper."

Truck told Alma kids were the last thing—the very last thing—he had to worry about. To have kids, he needed a partner and his right hand didn't count. And, for that matter, neither did his left. His track record in conjugal relationships was not good. He had, he said, a particularly difficult time dealing with how different levels of intimacy constantly changed a relationship.

"Dangitall, Alma," he said as the girls screamed and rolled past again, "it seems like if a guy gets intimate with a girl, she automatically wants to get closer. Guys don't want that," Truck said. "Guys just want things to stay the same."

"Truck, honey, things *can't* stay the same," Alma replied. "And I don't think you're right that men want things to stay the same, either. I think sometimes men get even more distant *after* foolin' around than they do before. And *that,* Truck Roberts, is wrong. Dead wrong, if you ask me."

Alma was nothing if not opinionated. She spoke to be understood. She was like a big black Cush when you came right down to it.

Truck looked at her, almost helplessly. "Look Alma," he said, "For whatever reason, women have a much wider range of emotions than men. They care more. More often and deeper."

"And what's wrong with *that?*" Alma fired back as the girls zoomed by again. "Why don't you try it sometime? Why don't you share your inner feelings?

"Share what's inside that heart you insist on keeping locked up 24 hours of every single day, will you? It wouldn't kill you.

"And you know something else, Truck? You might even like it.

"How many days you got, Truck? Not on this island, but in your *whole* life? Maybe 30,000? How many you got left? Half that, if you're lucky? And how many of *those* are you just gonna mail in and waste because you don't want to risk gettin' close to somebody?

"How many special days you had, Truck? Days chiseled deep inside your heart and soul? Special days, Truck—wonderful, magic days you never forget?

"This day could've been one of those special days if you simply decided to let it. But you didn't. And so could tomorrow. If you let it.

"If you've got feelings for this girl, look at her and tell her. It won't kill you and she don't bite. An' it don't cost *nuthin!'*

"Look, Truck," Alma continued, "before you got involved with a couple of bad women. The wrong ones for you. So what? They is both over with, baby. They gone. And I'm glad. You be glad, too, OK? Do youssef a lifelong favor and let it go.

"Just once, Truck, try livin' your life between your belt and your shoulders," Alma said, pointing first at his heart, then his waist. "Live it between there.

"Not here," she chided, pointing a scolding reminder at his groin. "This," she said, still pointing south, "ain't nuthin' but the divining rod of trouble.

"Save *that* thing for *special* occasions, not *every* occasion!

"Remember, Truck," Alma said softly, "live it *here*." As she said it, her forefinger again gently tapped his heart. "Live your life from *here*, Truck," Alma repeated, now placing her right hand directly over his heart. "Happiness hides here. You got it in you, Truck. We all do. You just need to know where to go to find it.

"An' I got three last things to say to you, Truck Roberts," Alma concluded.

"What's that?" he replied with a faint smile.

"One is that I love you like a son of my own.

"Two is that if you let this one go, there'll be a foot of snow on this island before you find another one like her."

"We're just friends, Alma," Truck protested. "She's got a boyfriend back home in New Zealand—a rich guy with lots of horses."

"Don't interrupt me!" she scolded. "And three, you go get a good night's sleep. You gettin' up early tomorrow. Me 'n Anvil got the two of you booked on the early plane out. The others are all going back in the afternoon, after you're gone. You two need a day together.

"And," she stood on tiptoes to whisper in his ear, "what that boyfriend don't know won't hurt him.

"Remember, Truck," Alma concluded with a warm, loving smile. "It's here," she reminded him, patting his heart. "It's here. Tomorrow you live your life from here, OK? Don't you dare waste that sunrise, sunset, or any moment in between with that girl. You live that whole day tomorrow from deep down inside. Live it the best you can from the time you wake up in the mornin' 'til the time you fall asleep at night."

"OK, OK," said Truck, arms upraised in a surrender sign. "I give up!"

"Promise?" asked Alma as she stepped up and loomed within four inches of his nose.

"Promise! Promise! I surrender!"

"One last thing, Truck Roberts. You like baseball so remember what they always say in baseball, OK?"

"What's that, Alma?"

"You can't go through life with the bat on your shoulder."

"You can when a girl's pitchin', " Truck said with a grin.

They laughed together and shared a long hug. Truck went off to his room and, within ten minutes, the open-aired sound of the crashing waves onto the old rock jetty cradled him into a deep, contented sleep.

He dreamed of being out on the rock jetty, under the gazebo with Cush, much too preoccupied to point out the whereabouts of the Big Dipper.

$\mathscr{A}$ Day in the Keys

Rousted early and hustled down to the seaplane, Cushla and Truck flew back to Miami on the Saturday morning flight. Cush couldn't get over the difference between where they'd left and where they soon arrived. The seaplane hummed over Miami Beach, looped over the wide part of Biscayne Bay up around the 79th Street Causeway and banked west-to-east for a gliding splashdown at the Port of Miami.

As she did on the flight over, Cush pressed her nose against the window the entire way. Approaching the mainland, they could see giant condos lined Miami Beach like pumpkin teeth on a toothy Halloween carving. Truck watched Cush intently studying the famed waterfront strip and leaned over. "It was all a big sand bar 'til a bridge was built in 1913," he said. "Then millionaires lined up from here to New York to throw money at it. They all stopped throwing when the stock market crashed in 1929."

Another of RCCL's massive cruise ships, *Grandeur of the Seas,* was in port, taking on supplies for a late afternoon departure and six-island cruise. "A hundred years ago, only 1,000 people lived in all of South Florida," Truck said. "Less than Bimini has now. But when that ship pulls out, four times more people will be piled onto its decks than live on the island you just left.

"But," Truck added, "the island has one more horse."

Ten minutes later their seaplane splashed and slid into Biscayne Bay, then rumbled up the concrete ramp next to the little green Pan Am office. Quickly they cleared customs and were free to go.

Truck and Cush climbed into the metallic teal Mustang and lowered the convertible top. It was a beautiful blue sky and white-feather-cloud morning—perfect for a 90-minute cruise to the Keys.

They drove south along Route 1, through Coral Gables, past the exit to Key Biscayne, then through the quiet farming town of Homestead and its still-scarred reminders of Hurricane Andrew. Truck told Cush all about the powerful storm. He had evacuated, as he and his neighbors had been told to do by the police. Andrew was a hurricane of furious force, with winds upward of 200 miles an hour. Gas pumps, he said, were twisted around like corkscrews. Giant boats were thrown a mile inland. Truck pointed out Burger King's corporate headquarters.

"They found fish and shrimp in the third floor," he told her. "All of the windows were blown out."

"In fact," he added seriously, "after the storm the place looked just like Mountain's apartment."

They both laughed loudly.

Truck suddenly slowed, flipped on his turn signal, and pulled into a drive marked "Knauss Berry Farm." He looked at Cush and smiled. "Hungry?' he asked.

"A wee bit," she replied. She really wasn't but Truck stopped here for a reason so Cush thought the proper thing was to find out why.

"C'mon," he urged. "You're in for a treat."

And what a treat it was. The unmistakably wafting lure of delicious hot cinnamon pulled them both inside by their nostrils. Cush quickly thought how remarkably hungry she could get when her nose decided to cast a morning vote.

Five minutes later, Cush emerged from the store, snout-first and fangs buried into the biggest, hottest, and most delicious fresh-cooked cinnamon bun on the entire planet. She didn't know whether to attack and devour it quickly because it was so warm and delicious, or nibble and make it last longer. She opted for a shark attack, taking big bites, as wide as her hinged mandibles could chomp.

Truck emerged a moment later with a bun of his own and a pair of mango shakes. They piled back in the convertible and resumed the drive south. A couple of minutes later, Cush saw a sign on her side of the road. "KEY LARGO 22 MILES" it said.

Truck cruised carefully down one of the nation's most dangerous roads, the two-lane stretch of Route 1 connecting Florida City and Key Largo, pointing out the massive osprey nests built high atop several of the power poles rising from the tangled mangrove marshes lining the road. The nests were made of sticks, weighed hundreds of pounds, and lasted for years. The osprey were fishermen and, from these high vantage points, the big birds could glide west to Florida Bay or east to the Florida Straits that fed the Atlantic. This thin vein of a road that ribboned its way through the mangroves was all that separated the two bodies of water.

The pair pulled into John Pennekamp Coral Reef State Park just as Cush's straw struck the bottom of her wax paper cup and started delivering more noisy air bubbles than mango shake. She looked at Truck and smiled. "Perfect timing," she said. Pennekamp is America's only underwater marine park and its protected reefs teemed with tropical, warm-water fishes. Truck hoped they'd be able to snorkel.

They reached the visitor's desk just in time to get the last two seats on a mid-morning glass-bottomed tourist boat. They chugged a few miles offshore to a reef and snorkeled among thousands of fish of all sizes—including several big barracuda. One of them eyed Cush's shiny golden cross necklace like a thug casing a convenience store. She gurgled seawater when, in the blink of an eye, the 'cuda darted within a foot of her mask.

Cushla loved the colorful fish and the spectacular coral reef. The water was warmer and clearer than back home and the reefs teemed with endless varieties of small fish. To Cush, the reef fish seemed to be wearing colorful little uniforms.

But the highlight of the two-hour face-down float came when a fat guy from Ohio lost track of his splashy surface cruising and accidentally snorkeled his way up right up Cush's butt, solidly plowing snorkel first into the business end of her bright orange Kiwini bikini.

That made her choke on seawater, too. Cush thought the Ohio fat guy was a Kiwi-eating shark and panicked. She thrashed, splashed, and wildly screamed for help. Truck was 20-feet away and swam over to calm her down. Wisely, he stopped laughing before he arrived.

By one o'clock, the pair was back in the Mustang, cruising deeper into the shimmering matchless natural beauty of the Florida Keys. They caught a break with the traffic, which moved smoothly past Tavernier and farther south past Plantation Key.

Cush asked where they were headed. Truck looked over, hidden behind his sunglasses, and smiled. "To the next stop on the tour," he teased.

The Keys are mile-markered, with distance indicator stakes stuck alongside the length of Route 1 labeling proximity from Key West north to the mainland. At Mile Marker 85, the Mustang slowed in Islamorada and turned left into the parking lot for Theatre of the Sea. Here, Truck taught Cush how to feed stingrays by hand. She also got to tail-toss a barking sea lion a few six-inch herrings.

Cush had never done anything like this at home and was mesmerized. Truck got a big kick out of watching her unabashed and energized happiness. He felt like a conductor nailing a Mozart symphony. Everything was going right.

He saved the best for last, having made special arrangements for Cush to swim with the porpoises. Actually, Truck didn't plan it—Alma did, from Bimini. She told him on the way to the seaplane. "God bless her," he thought, for such a wonderful idea.

As much as she enjoyed everything else, Cush loved the porpoises best of all. Holding onto the rubbery gray dorsal fin of an aptly named male called Grasshopper, Cush went on a power-tailed full lap tow around his huge enclosed home. Then suddenly Grasshopper dove, losing Cushla. Seconds later, he skyrocketed back out of the water and into a zooming series of four quick high and powerful horizontal leaps. The dolphin again lapped the perimeter of his pen, this time just for show and without the tow-along freeloader.

Grasshopper finished with a flourish, leaping sky high on his fourth jump, then crashing back down into the water flat on his right side like a belly flop. The huge splash nailed Cush, who was peacefully bobbing in the water six feet away from where Grasshopper made his thunderous water-walled re-entry.

Truck laughed out loud so hard and so long that his ribs hurt. He wished he had it on video like some of the other tourists did. The frozen look of wide-eyed shock on Cush's face just as she realized what Grasshopper was doing—moments before impact—was a freeze-framed instant of everything Alma said it would be.

After the dolphin escapade, Truck called for a lunch break and the pair barely pulled out on U.S. 1 before pulling back off again, hard and fast, this time at Holiday Isle at the northern end of the Mile Marker 84 bridge.

They pulled up stools at the Holiday Isle Tiki Bar hut, famous for legendary parties and the birthplace of a famous tropical drink: the rumrunner. The two tried one over lunch.

Cush wasn't much of a drinker and started babbling on about everything. Truck just watched and listened. Everything she said he carefully listened to and that, in itself, sure was odd for a fellow who earned his living filtering out 90 percent of what he heard and earning 100 percent of his money from the 10 percent he chose to remember.

Cush's voice differed from others—he simply loved the sound of it. Her vocal pitch and cadence were as comfortable as the sound of bubbling aquarium water. Somewhere during her divulgence of the kindness and wonders of the island people in Bimini, she looked right at him.

Truck looked back. He looked through her eyes, like she always looked through his. Hers shot lasers of emotion right into the pit of his stomach. He felt the shuddering jolt of impact. It was every bit as big and real as Grasshopper's crash landing. He had the funny feeling this was what Alma was talking about.

Quickly, Truck shifted into emotional defense, sensing there was no future doing or saying anything he'd regret. No, not today. Not here. Not now. The day was only half over. No need to ruin it now.

"Of course the islanders are wonderful people," Truck said softly. "Remember what Mark Twain said: 'We're all alike, on the inside.' The world is full of wonderful people—including you."

Cush's eyes welled up when Truck quoted Twain, her favorite American author. She had read Twain all through Wentworth. Back home, Timothy never quoted anybody but rugby players or horse auctioneers. No question about it—the rumrunner had wobbled the little dart thrower.

Lunch finished, Truck excused himself for a moment, disappeared, and returned a few minutes later with a pair of life jackets.

"Now what?" quizzed Cush, with a happy smile and slightly flushing cheeks.

"No more rumrunners for you, young lady," Truck said. "One's enough. Now we go for a ride. C'mon," he prodded. "We won't be long, but we've got an appointment. Some friends are waiting to meet you."

"My God, Truck Roberts," protested Cushla. "More friends? Do you have friends everywhere?"

"You'll like them," Truck replied. "Promise! C'mon now, hustle up, little Kiwi. Your taxi awaits."

With that, the two walked over by the sandy shore where a two-person SkiDoo jet ski was beached. Truck muscled it backward into the sea, hopped aboard, and gunned the engine to life. Cush climbed on rather artistically, since her mount routine resembled a creative pommel horse exercise in the Olympics. Tiki Hut rumrunners were quite famous for choreographing many such spontaneous maneuvers.

Truck puttered the jet ski slowly out of the dock area, pointed his way though the piling posted channel markers, and took Cush for a quick circular zip in the sparkling Atlantic Ocean. He zoomed back past Holiday Isle and skimmed south, about 200 yards parallel to the beach and full throttle across the shallow, colorful flats.

They rode for several miles before Truck veered to the right, cut underneath the Lignumvitae Bridge, and headed toward the sheltered water of a protected cove.

He slowed from open throttle back down to a slow puttering chug, steered his way slowly left, and headed toward a half-covered dock with a half-dozen small outboards for rent. He pulled alongside a ladder at the end of the dock and made sure Cush climbed up safely. Then he throttled gently to his left and beached the jet ski.

"C'mon," he waved to Cush. "C'mon. My friends are over here."

She walked the length of the dock into shore and quizzically looked at Truck. She didn't see anyone around, but figured Truck knew where he was going so she dutifully walked alongside.

Truck turned left into an old office shack at the base of a second nearby dock. He pulled a $20 bill out of the right front pocket of his swim trunks and forked it over to the 50-ish fellow behind the old wood counter.

"Two of us," Truck said. "Twenty bucks worth, please."

"Take six buckets," the fellow replied.

And with that, Truck linked arms with Cush and steered her toward the open doorway leading onto the wide dock flanked on both sides by bobbing rental boats. The pair stopped in front of a big white floor console refrigerator full of bait.

A white egret stood nearby, perched motionless on a big blue aerated drum. It patiently waited to try and spear with its beak one of the hundreds of live shrimp paddling their way around the bubble-creating oxygenator.

From the adjacent outdoor refrigerator, Truck pulled out six small blue plastic buckets of thawed, palm-sized baitfish. Four of the six buckets he handed to Cush. Each contained about 15 fish. The egret stood quietly, watching carefully, but didn't fly away.

"C'mon," Truck said after closing the refrigerator door with a push of his right elbow. "My friends are out here. They'll be happy to see you."

When Cush walked 50 feet to the end of the dock, she almost dropped her blue buckets. The water boiled with huge fish, dozens of them, maybe even 100 or more, all tightly circling back and forth waiting impatiently for an afternoon snack.

"My God!" she screamed. "Sharks!"

Truck laughed. "They're not sharks," he chuckled. "They're tarpon. Giant tarpon. They don't have a tooth in their head. People have fed them here for 20 years."

Just then, a huge tarpon rolled by, popping the surface with a quick opening and closing of its huge bony mouth. The fish weighed more than 200 pounds—nearly twice Cushla's size.

She panicked and tossed a whole bucket of fish—plastic pail and all—into the water, setting off a feeding melee reminiscent of a rock star tossing a souvenir into the front-stage scrum of a rowdy crowd.

Moss the Boss, a black and white border collie whose job it was to chase away the pelicans, ran back and forth along the end of the pier, barking three times at the sudden commotion.

Giant fish flew, climbed, swirled, and thrashed everywhere. Bullets of blur jacks, Truck called them, zoomed in from the fringes of the frenzy. They used their superior speed to steal away some of the food from the slower tarpon 20 times their size.

"Um, Cush," Truck suggested as he leaned down and stretched to retrieve the empty, half-submerged blue plastic pail. "That was good, but the general idea is to feed them one fish at a time and hold on to the bucket. Tarpon don't eat plastic buckets.

"C'mon, sit down here next to me," he urged as he patted the wood on the end of the pier next to him. His feet dangled just above the roiling water and hungry fish.

"No way!" she protested. "I'm not being eaten alive by some monster shark!"

"They're not sharks," Truck repeated. "They're tarpon. No teeth. C'mon. Calm down and have a seat. Be polite. They want to meet you. Plus, they're hungry."

Cush finally calmed down, sat down, and started tossing the food to the fish one piece at a time. Soon she recognized some of the tarpon by identifying marks Truck pointed out. She noticed how different the fish were from one another, not cookie-cuttered. The tarpon, she decided, were like horses—each had its own distinguishing markings. And, like horses, each had its own personality, too.

One female tarpon in particular caught Cush's eye. The fish was obviously old and quite scarred but, more noticeably, it was huge. She appeared to be longer, thicker, and 30 or 40 pounds heavier than any other.

"The Mother of All Fish!" Cushla cried. "That's you! The Mother of All Fish!"

They spent the next hour sitting shoulder to shoulder on the end of the pier, dangling their legs just above the surface and tossing in a baitfish to their new-found friends every minute or so. Eventually, only a butterfish remained in the bucket.

Cush aimed for The Mother of All Fish, whose head rose completely out of water and caught the butterfish in mid-air, popping her massive mouth closed just in time to beat a bold younger tarpon to the morsel and preventing the swirling jacks from stealing it away.

The two stood up stiffly, washed their hands at the dock's soapy freshwater washbasin, and climbed aboard the jet ski for the 20-minute skim back to Holiday Isle. As they puttered away, Cush turned half-around and waved toward the dock. She hollered out, "Bye, Mother of All Fish!" and grabbed Truck tightly around the waist.

Cush held on tightly as they zoomed under the bridge and back toward civilization. Robbie's little dock, tucked away and hidden at Mile Marker 77.5 off the southwestern corner of the bridge, was the secret elixir that capped off a perfect day. Once back at Holiday Isle, it was time to head back to Miami. And as the orange sunset disappeared into Florida Bay, ending their day in the Keys, Cush couldn't have been happier. Every moment had been sheer magic.

The return drive to Miami along U.S. 1 would take a couple of hours, so Truck stopped for stone crabs to snack on during the trip. Since the claws were already cracked, Cush peeled off the broken bits of shell, swabbed the heavenly chunks of crabmeat with mustard sauce, and stuffed them into Truck's mouth as he drove. Once she realized how hot the mustard sauce was, she loaded one up and burnt Truck's nostrils, bringing tears to his eyes. She thought it was really funny. He didn't, but pretended he did.

The two rolled back into South Beach around eight o'clock. Truck parked in a pay lot a block from the News Café. From there they could walk to drinks and dinner, and still be close enough to get the car when it was time to take Cush to the airport.

Truck opted for the beautiful and mystical Delano for cocktails. He loved the interior design of the Delano—the flourishingly artistic talent of the gay influence, he told Cush.

They ordered glasses of wine at the inside bar, then walked back by the pool to sit and relax. The pool area was special, too. A dozen padded double-sized lounge chairs picket-fenced the length of the pool's south side. Each had a closeable curtain for privacy.

When Truck looked at the lounges, he saw an open meadow of wavy grass and opted not to risk ruining the day. Silently, Cush wanted him to. Instead, they simply sat a glass table, faced the ocean, and talked of nothing worth talking about.

Wine glasses finally empty, they left the Delano and, arm in arm, walked slowly south along Ocean Drive past the late Gianni Versace's mansion. Truck pointed out the front steps where the famous fashion designer had been standing when he was shot and killed. It was terribly sad but typical of what could, and did, go on from time to time in Miami. Bad people spent a lot of time there, basking in the sunshine of the international crossroads and gateway to South America. And bad people tend to do bad things.

Cushla squeezed Truck's arm a little tighter and slowly walked several blocks farther south, down to Lario's for dinner. The great singer Gloria Estefan, "the Popette of Miami" Truck called her, had opened the eatery several years before. It was a wonderful and stylishly popular place.

There, at Lario's, Truck introduced himself to Carlotta San Juan, the hostess. Carlotta recognized his name, smiled, and said a small package was waiting for Truck, delivered earlier in the day by courier along with a message that Mr. Roberts would be arriving around nine o'clock for dinner.

Truck smiled. Carlotta disappeared for a minute and reappeared with a small padded envelope. He didn't bother opening it, choosing instead to stuff it in his pocket. He gave Carlotta $10 for her trouble, which she gratefully appreciated. She air-kissed her thanks and Cush feigned jealousy.

The package piqued Cush's interest so she asked about it. "Oh," Truck replied, "it's nothing. I promised to pick up something for a friend, that's all. I wish it was something more dramatic than that."

Later that evening, at the airport, Truck would lose his nerve. Instead of presenting the gift box inside that small padded envelope to Cush as originally planned, he stuffed it inside the empty side pocket of Cushla's smallest travel bag. She would be busily preparing the rest of her luggage for check-in and never notice. Unfortunately, she wouldn't find that keepsake for many, many months.

Dinner, as always at Lario's, was wonderful. The events of the day began to catch up with both of them and even the half-bottle split of Merlot proved a formidable foe. Both were exhausted.

Soon, too soon actually, it was time to pay the check and head to the airport. In a surprising sendoff, Gloria Estefan herself arrived at the restaurant and stopped by each of the tables to say hello and thank the customers.

Cush was stargazed and hypnotized. When Truck mentioned Cush was from New Zealand and about to head home, Gloria shook her hand and sent the waiter upstairs. He reemerged a minute later with a CD and blue Sharpie pen. Gloria personalized and signed the CD to Cush and, smiling warmly, said, "Thank you *so much* for coming this evening. It means so much to us that you would choose our restaurant for such a special dinner."

Gloria then gave her a quick goodbye hug and moved on to the next table. Cush floated down the steps, out of the restaurant, and onto the crowded sidewalk. Truck just shook his head. If being from New Zealand got you a hug from Gloria Estefan, well, he was tempted to go back in and tell Gloria that *he* was from Antarctica.

Cushla was supposed to meet the others at Miami International at 11 p.m. by the United check-in counter. Truck glanced at his watch as he stood in the doorway of Lario's, waiting for her to re-emerge from running back inside to wave at Gloria again and powder her nose.

As he waited, Truck wrestled with his emotions and thought about what Alma said. This had been one of those special days Alma told him about. And, like she predicted, it had been that way from start to finish. Truck wished they could do all this again tomorrow.

He'd need to call Party Patti after this one. That much he knew for sure.

*C*ropduster in the Exit Row

It was 11 miles and 19 minutes out Fifth Street onto Route 836 West from Lario's to the airport. Neither Truck nor Cush said much along the way.

He parked in the short-term lot near Concourse F and went off to find a luggage cart, hoping for a free one. He returned three minutes later, mission accomplished. Truck had no clue what he'd say when it came time to say goodbye. It had been fun, but now it was over. Truck looked at his watch. It was 11 o'clock. Time to find the others.

The rest of the gang was waiting when Truck arrived at United, pushing Cush's stuff. She walked alongside acting like Leona Helmsley checking for dust when she saw her friends.

Ben, Bird, and Mitzi had left Bimini on the late afternoon seaplane. Sunburnt beyond recognition, Ben looked like a red salmon in full spawning colors because Anvil had taken him bone-fishing and Ben hadn't worn any sunscreen. On the flight back to the mainland, Bird told him he smelled like cooked turkey sausage.

The girls had spent the day with Alma and took a tour of both islands. Everywhere they stopped, people wanted to hear about Bonefish's great victory. They all felt like celebrities.

Mountain and Phoebe took the yacht back, leaving at lunch-time and powering their way across in three hours. They could've made it in two, but throttled back midway and used the autopi-lot. Phoebe wanted to see Mountain's coin collection again, luring him below by stripping naked and completely covering herself in glistening oil. From the time she stood posing and shimmering in the salon doorway calling, "Ohhh, *Mountain* . . ." until the Hatteras was on autopilot, it was, oh, 11 seconds.

Mountain couldn't have scrambled any faster if his pants were on fire, which, in a way, they were. He emerged 45 minutes later, a beaten warrior but a better man. His was a slow, contented climb back up to the flying bridge control center.

Cush filled in the details of their day to the others, especially mentioning Grasshopper and The Mother of All Fish. From the sound of it, everyone had a great time, but had run out of gas, which was just as well considering the length of the flight the three girls faced.

As the trio took turns checking in their luggage for Auckland, Mountain sidled up to Truck. It was obvious something was on the big man's mind.

"Um, Truck," Mountain said seriously, "I don't want her to go."

"Didja tell her that?" Truck asked.

"We talked," Mountain replied. "But she said she's gotta go. She lives there, you know."

"No shit, Buttwhistle," smiled Truck. "She lives there and you live here. What are you gonna do about it?"

"I was thinkin' 'bout going back over with her."

"Now?" asked Truck incredulously.

"Now, Truck." Mountain replied seriously. "My whole life women have looked at me like I'm a taxi meter. Dammit, Truck— *hermaphrodites* get more action than me!"

"They should," Truck replied dryly. "They've got more options."

Mountain ignored the remark and kept on talking. "I finally found me the one I want, Truck. She is the one for me. And I don't wanna lose her."

"Time zones and telephones," Truck said to his pal. "That's what you're lookin' at if you stay. That, plus one hell of a lot of mental masturbation. And assuming that mental masturbation part doesn't sound like a whole lot of fun, well, you need a passport. You don't need a visa, but you do need a passport."

Mountain patted the left side of his ample butt. "I got it here in my pocket. Still got it from the Bahamas.

"*I can go, Truck!* I won enough money on the race. I can go if I've got the balls. You can too! Let's both go! Me and you, man, me 'n you. Let's both go. We've got the money! Come with me, man."

"Mountain," Truck said with a smile as he put his left hand on his giant friend's right shoulder. "I've got no reason to go. But if you think you do, then I reckon there's only one other decision you need to make."

"What's that, Truck?" Mountain asked.

"You buyin' a one-way or round-trip ticket? The answer to that question might very well change your life, my friend," said Truck, now gently squeezing his friend's powerful shoulder muscles. "And that's *your* decision to make."

Mountain thought long and hard about that one. He hadn't considered that. Finally, Mountain looked over at Phoebe, engrossed in gossip with Bird and Cush, then looked back at Truck with a big smile.

"One way, Truck," he said. "One way."

"Then go, my son. When you gotta go, you gotta go. But don't forget to write," he added as he looked up at his big buddy and smiled.

Mountain reached down and bear-hugged the best friend he'd ever had. Well, the best friend he'd ever had up until he met Phoebe.

Mountain let go before Truck could black out, then confidently approached the United ticket counter. When the clerk asked if the trip was one-way or round-trip, Mountain looked over nervously at Truck for reassurance.

"Don't look at me, Mountain," Truck said. "*You're* the mental masturbator."

"I AIN'T MASTURBATIN'!" Mountain hollered loud, enough for all 60 waiting travelers within a 75-yard radius to notice. And, fortunately for them, he was right. He *wasn't*.

"One way!" Mountain said loudly to the lady behind the counter. "One way!" He checked no luggage, but had his passport in hand, which surprised the ticket agent. Generally, people traveling halfway around the world travel with more than the dirty underwear they already have on.

"I can buy a toothbrush around here somewhere, can't I?" Mountain asked the clerk.

The clerk laughed. "They'll give you one on the plane," she said.

"Then that's all I need."

Ticket in hand, Mountain walked away from Truck and toward the girls. "I'm 'a comin' with ya'all!" he boomed, waving his ticket in the air. Mountain then looked down at Phoebe and whispered softly, "An' I'm 'a sittin' next to *you*." He stood there laughing as she grabbed him around the neck and joyously hopped up and down like a runaway pogo stick.

Mountain couldn't say another word when Phoebe hopped up into his outstretched arms and hugged him like a coat of paint. Then she kissed him like they were trying to win a car in a radio station kissing contest.

Ever since the pair met, Mountain and Phoebe had been inseparable, like Bogey and Bacall during the good times. Truck had never seen Mountain like this. And Mountain had never seen Mountain like this either. He felt good about being like this, too. And he damn sure wasn't going to be the one to blow the whistle on it.

"That's the end of him," Truck thought with maybe a tiny twinge of jealousy. "Mountain did well," Truck mused. "He'd be hard-pressed to find a better woman than Phoebe. She'll take good care of him."

The girls and Mountain collected their carry-ons and slowly made their way toward the security screening checkpoint. Only ticketed passengers could go beyond it so Ben and Mitzi and Truck said their goodbyes here. Mountain handed Truck his entire key ring.

"Sell my stuff for what you can," Mountain said. "Don't worry 'bout none of it. Just get what you can get and bring the money over when you come visit."

"No problem, big man. Gotcha covered. I'll get Ben to help me," smiled Truck. He looked his buddy squarely in the eye and firmly shook his hand, which led to another of Mountain's air-escaping bear hugs.

"The place is clean," enthused Mountain. "Hell, man, you might even get some of the deposit money back."

Truck then turned to Cush and gave her a long hug goodbye. He finally pulled his head back and kissed her gently on the cheek, then whispered softly in her ear, "Goodbye, Jeffrey Franklin Wimsett. Best of luck. Take care of yourself, OK?"

She squeezed him a little tighter when she felt his words caress her ear. "Goodbye, Truck Roberts," she replied softly. "And don't you dare shoot darts for beers without me, OK?"

With that, the two separated and hugged the others goodbye. Mountain wanted to hug Truck again, but Truck waved his arms "no" and stepped back, saying twice was plenty.

Hugs finished, the girls and Mountain passed through security and stepped on an escalator. Thirty seconds later, they were gone.

Their flight left on time, banked west over the Everglades, and climbed quickly into the star-filled sky aiming for the Big Dipper. Cushla stared out the window, biting her trembling lip. This had been the greatest week of her life, and it was now ending with her being rocketed ten-miles-a-minute away from where she thought she ought to stay. In her heart, she wasn't sure she wanted to leave. This would be a very, very long flight home.

— ◆ —

Downstairs and outside of the airport, Truck flipped Mountain's keys to Ben since Ben had caught a lift to the airport with Mitzi. Ben drove the truck and dropped it back at Mountain's apartment, then picked up his own car and went home.

Truck, meanwhile, climbed into the Mustang and punched the button of his CD player hoping Louis Armstrong would distract his jumbled thoughts. Five million tourists a year came to Miami and, tonight, one of the smallest ones gave him a bigger stomachache than all of the other five million combined.

He'd once heard that getting butterflies was OK as long as you could get them all to fly in formation. To this point, Truck apparently hadn't read that memo. These butterflies were fluttering and ricocheting just about *everywhere.*

"Black gold," he mused as Armstrong's singular voice broke the silence. "Through the ears and to the soul like oil through a pipeline." Louie did his best to help salve the moment, but managed to tame none of Truck's fluttering friends. The butterflies ignored him.

Meanwhile, on the plane, Mountain had quickly and contentedly fallen asleep holding Phoebe's hand with her head resting on his shoulder. But his dietary intake over the past few days was percolating in some unusual ways. His fellow passengers bore the brunt of his flatulent expulsions, though Mountain was soundly snoring and totally oblivious.

The people a row behind Mountain pushed the overhead CALL button to summon the flight attendant with their complaints. They wanted to move but there were no open seats.

"Cropduster in the exit row," said the flight attendant, returning to report to her co-workers. Thus warned, the other flight attendants knew to steer clear of Mountain's row. They did nothing to assuage the pain of the distressed neighbors.

Mountain and the girls switched planes in Chicago, flew to Los Angeles, and arrived at LAX in early morning. They had a six-hour layover in L.A., so Mountain rented a car and drove the girls to Malibu. There, they kept moving up and down the beach with their beach towels, trying to attract a movie star. He later reported that the best they came up with was a shriveled old man who wanted them all naked in his jacuzzi—including *him*.

The following morning, Truck made Piso Mojado an offer he couldn't refuse. And that evening, Piso moved into Mountain's fully furnished apartment with his lovely bride-to-be, Isa. Truck pre-paid the rent for six months, telling Piso that if he was half the rider he appeared to be, six months would be all Piso would want of Mountain's place before moving out and buying a nicer place of his very own.

Piso and Isa were ecstatic; they finally had a private apartment. Shortly after Truck drove away, the two began to practice making little Pisos.

Truck also cut Piso a deal for Mountain's pickup truck, payable from ten percent of his weekly winnings from the Calder meet. Two days later, he won a race and, two days after that, he won another. Piso had the truck paid off before the Calder meet even ended.

That evening, Truck phoned Party Patti and told her all about the week. They talked for more than two hours.

"Did you do it?" she asked eagerly. "Didja get it?"

"I had the opportunity," Truck said. "But no. Wrong set of circumstances, wrong time. She's got a boyfriend. I'm sure she wanted to go home and see him."

"Sometimes you're just downright pathetic, Truck," Patti replied. "I love you with all my heart, but I just don't understand you when it comes to women. You are scared to death of a woman you're as happy as a kid on a playground to be with. Is there anything in that head of yours besides a Frequent Flyer odometer? Anything at all? Am I missing something?

"What the hell are you waiting for?" a thoroughly perplexed Party Patti asked. "To have the woman of your dreams club you on the head and drag you off by the hair? I wish Cushla had turned around and fired a dart in your ass when you walked away.

"You deserved it."

"Well, I still think I did the right thing," Truck protested. "Mountain did the right thing by leaving. I did the right thing by not doing anything."

"Keep telling yourself that," Patti said. "Keep telling yourself that and maybe you'll believe it. Tell it to yourself next time you're staring at a whole lot of nothing out an airplane window, heading for some city where your only pal is the bartender. Tell *him* you did the right thing.

"You did the *wrong* thing, numb-nuts," Patti concluded. "The right thing was to tell the girl how you feel when you're with her. How much you care. *That* was the right thing. Being a gutless chickenshit was the *wrong* thing!

"Think about it. Call me in a week, OK? We'll talk more."

"OK," he echoed. "I'll call in a week."

"Dammit," thought Truck after he hung up the phone. "Why does finding and fitting the right woman into your life have to be harder than a friggin' Rubik's cube?

"This shit is drivin' me nuts."

25 Possums

When the phone rang at four in the morning on the ninth of July, Truck rolled over, eyes still closed, and fumbled with the receiver. "Mufflebump," he mumbled into the mouthpiece. "The tango is not on my side."

"Dammitall, Truck!" boomed the voice on the other end. *"Me 'n Phoebe's gittin' married!"*

"Thank you, but I don't *want* any magazines," Truck replied groggily as he twisted half-around and squinted at the nightstand alarm. When he saw the time, Truck wondered who had died and why this rude man wanted him to buy ad-riddled periodicals—until he recognized the voice.

"Mountain?" Truck asked. "Mountain, is that you?"

"Yeh, baby! Me 'n Phoebe's gittin' married! We're doin' it, baby! She said yes! Can you believe it? I got me a wife! And she can cook pork chops and everything!"

"That's great," Truck said slowly warming up a smile. "I'm happy for you. When and where is this compelling need for ill-fitting rental clothes taking place?"

"Fourth Saturday in March. We're gonna get married here in New Zealand, in Phoebe's home town down on the South Island," Mountain gushed. "The Ork. Glencorchy. Little place, up north of Queenstown. You'll love it!

"And Truck," Mountain continued excitedly, "I want you to be my best man!"

"Best man?" Truck replied. "Dammit, Mountain, that means I have to rent a tux and dance with old ladies."

"Ah, don't worry," replied Mountain. "I'm makin' Ben dance with the old ladies. He'll strut around like a little James Bond, ordering them stirred-not-shaken martinis. He tries orderin' that shit down here and they'll pour him a cup of possum piss."

Truck laughed out loud. After a few more minutes of banter, the two friends hung down their phones half a world apart. Truck was now wide awake and stayed up. He showered, then fixed some wheat toast and hazelnut coffee. Nothing about the call surprised him. He had been expecting it ever since his large friend disappeared up the escalator at Miami International. He was happy for Mountain. Phoebe, too. Mountain would be a good and de-voted husband and she would make him a great wife.

March was a good time for a wedding. Late winter in the States, late summer in New Zealand. Any reason to visit was a good one, and this one clearly qualified.

March rolled around in the blink of an eye and Truck left the States the morning after St. Patrick's Day. He traveled alone be-cause Ben was stopping in Honolulu for a few days. He was a surfer and hoped for late-season waves off Oahu's North Shore.

After landing in Auckland, Truck spent a couple of days fish-ing with his old friend Lloyd. They drove the Range Rover past Cush's dart bar—the Horse & Trap. Truck said nothing as they did. Four hours later, they arrived in Turangi to flyfish Lake Otamangakau and their favorite river, the Tongariro. Their guide, famed Kiwi outdoorsman Ken Drummond, came through in fine fashion and Lloyd caught five monster trout that averaged seven pounds. Truck caught one, a relative midget, and spent most of his time taking photographs while pretending to be happy for Lloyd.

The North Island was a spectacular fishery and Truck loved it with the passion of the Colorado rivers of his youth. When he fished here, the days could last forever and they still wouldn't be long enough.

— ◆ —

On Thursday afternoon, the Air New Zealand flight to Queenstown took just over an hour. Truck was surprised to see Ben on the same plane. The waves were great in Hawaii, Ben said, ten feet or higher every day. And he had proof—eight stitches over his swollen right eyebrow—courtesy of a shallow-water wipeout and a coral reef head-butt.

Mountain was waiting when they landed. He was so happy to see his pals, he draped one massive arm around each guy's shoulder and squeezed. With his left arm, Mountain crushed Truck like a boa constrictor having a rabbit for lunch. With his right arm, he squished Ben's skinny thorax like a trash compactor.

Both recipients grunted simultaneously, like passing pigs in a sty saying hello. "*Damn* it's great to see you guys!" Mountain roared. "Is this *great* or what?"

Mountain then introduced the guys to a little sandy-haired fellow named Carl who worked for Phoebe's mother at the lodge in Glenorchy. It was his job to retrieve the guests and make sure the tuxedos were picked up from the rental shop.

The guys ignored the expected fitting and scooped up the tuxedos with the blind faith of men without style. As part of the traditional Queenstown welcoming ritual, Carl then drove out to the east end of town toward the old Kawarau Bridge. Spanning the river gorge was an old railroad trestle built in 1880. It was here, from this bridge 143-feet above the surface, that 120 people a day paid big money to jump off.

The Kawarau Bridge site was the world's first bungy site— the Yankee Stadium of *boing*. The sport was birthed here one year after Queenstown resident A. J. Hackett became famous by bungying off the Eiffel Tower—in a tuxedo. In the ensuing decade, Hackett and his partner, fellow speed skater Henry von Asch, made millions convincing people to jump off the bridge.

Henry and A.J. thought up the sport after watching video-tapes of African tribesmen ritualistically leap off high bamboo scaffolds with vines tied to their ankles. Some snapped short of the sand, some hit it with a thud. None of the tribesmen thought to use bungy cords.

Ben and Truck leaned on the spectator platform railing and watched, then debated the wisdom of paying to freefall 15 stories off an old wooden bridge. A recovery raft waited in the river, safely out of the current, to retrieve all of the jumpers eventually lowered to water level and untied.

From where the pair stood, the raft looked to be the size of a dime.

After watching three jumpers, Ben looked at Truck. Truck looked at Ben. Each knew what the other was thinking.

"No friggin' way!" they chorused. The pair laughed, high-fived, and turned back toward the van to find the others.

They didn't make it.

"Hey!" boomed a familiar voice. "Where you panty-waists goin'? You're in! Already paid for—both of you. Welcome to Queenstown. Go inside and sign your waivers. Hurry. We're up soon."

"Damn Mountain," muttered Ben.

"*Shee*-it," replied Truck. "I'm not so sure about this. If we die, we rented the tuxes for nothing."

Since special friends make for special memories, especially right before a wedding, all three signed up, weighed in, and slowly walked to the center of the old wooden bridge.

A young shirtless guy with long hair and two earrings in each ear stood in front of Ben. "How is it?" Ben asked him.

"Cool, dude," the fellow replied. "But once you stick your toes over the edge of the platform—whatever you do, dude—don't look down."

Mountain eagerly went first. At 6'7" and 361 pounds, Mountain was by far the largest jumper of the day and one of the biggest ever. He had more kilos than most folks had pounds and it was up to the jumpmaster to select the proper cord, calculate the amount of stretch the falling weight would create, and determine the appropriate length to let out for each jumper. Hackett's crew members were Rhodes scholars at these calculations as well as master psychologists. No one was to be pushed; everyone must voluntarily jump.

While Mountain's ankles were being tied, his jumpmaster, a black-haired Kiwi fellow named Chris Boddle, asked him what kind of jump he wanted. Did he want to reach the water or not?

"Well," Mountain replied. "I got a wedding rehearsal tomorrow afternoon, so I gotta be done bouncing by then."

"You wanna get wet?" Boddle asked.

"I don't need the wet," replied Mountain. "I just need to be done bouncin' by tomorrow."

Boddle made a few more rope adjustments, struggled to help a guy more than twice his size to his feet, and helped Mountain shuffle to the end of the wood platform. He looked down. The pea-sized raft looked ten miles away.

Mountain closed his eyes, inhaled deeply, and cannonballed straight down.

Truck looked over the railroad trestle boards to watch. Mountain was plummeting quickly. He looked like a safe in a cartoon, accelerating every ten feet. "Is he supposed to go that fast?" Truck asked Boddle as Mountain zoomed down past the halfway point.

"Well," Boddle replied slowly, "not really. But I guess we'll know soon enough. Most guys jump *out* a ways. They don't jump straight down."

All 33 people on the observation deck furiously clicked pictures as the big man zoomed by. Several smiling Japanese even posed in the foreground with the hurtling Godzilla falling behind them.

Mountain was going as fast as a dragster when the bungy cords stretched, then tightened. A foot from the river, he froze in mid-air for just a moment, then boinged back up. And never in his five years of tossing people off that bridge had Boddle seen what happened next.

Mountain zoomed all the way back up, all 143 feet, flying back up where he'd jumped off in the first place. All of the people on the observation deck, including the smiling Japanese in the foreground, took pictures of this, too.

Boddle's mouth gaped open. Mountain was smiling ear-to-ear as he bounced up eyeball-to-eyeball with Boddle and Truck. "This is *great!*" he enthused. "Make sure I'm done by tomorrow." With that, he zoomed back down and disappeared.

Well, Mountain bounced a good long time, nearly long enough for lunch, before the raft guys finally pulled him in and untied the cord from his ankles. Boddle, 15 stories up, was speechless. If this guy were a regular customer, A.J. and Henry would need an extra bridge just so other people could jump and they could still earn a living.

"That's unbelievable," Boddle mumbled to Truck as he shook his head and turned to tie Truck's ankles to the cord. "Nobody's *ever* bounced all the way back up before. I thought he was kidding when he said he needed to be done bouncing by tomorrow."

"That's Mountain," Truck smiled, "always a crowd favorite."

Ben and Truck's jumps were far less dramatic although Boddle dropped Truck into a perfect landing—perpendicular and half-in, half-out of the water. The cold Kawarau River water felt bracingly refreshing. Truck got wet to the belt, then slid right back up and out of the water like toast popping out of a toaster. "Magic," he said to the guys in the retrieval raft. "Greatest thing you can do with your clothes on."

The guys in the raft ignored him as they paddled him to shore. "Man, you see that giant guy with the beard? That bloke bounced all the back up to the bridge! A.J.'d love that guy! That chap was born for video."

Appropriately baptised into the adrenaline ways of Queens-town, the boys piled into Carl's old white cargo van and chugged out of town, twisting around two roundabouts and following the eastern shore of massive Lake Wakatipu north toward Glenorchy. The vast lake shone a sapphire blue.

"How far we goin'?" Truck asked Carl as they circled around.

"Twenty-five possums," he answered.

"What?" asked Truck, not understanding the answer.

"Twenty-five possums," Carl repeated, a cigarette dangling from his lips. "Count the dead possums. When you reach 25, we'll be in Glenorchy."

Sure enough, they rounded a lakeside bend in the two-lane road and *splat*—there in the road was a mangled and dead road-killed black possum. "That's one," grunted Carl. "Number two will be a wee bit up the road."

Sure enough, it was. With numbers three and four not too far beyond.

"Ninety million of the bastards," Carl bitched disgustedly. "Whoever introduced the bloody things to New Zealand should be shot at close range and fed a hand grenade for dessert. The damn bloody possums are eating up the whole friggin' country!

"And what they don't eat, the bloody weasels and stoats do," he added. "Leaves, treetops, bird eggs, you name it—they eat it."

"What's a stoat?" asked Ben. He'd never even heard of one before.

"Basically a brown weasel," answered Carl. "About a foot long with a black-tipped tail. Scavenging little buggers."

Ben and Truck got the distinct impression Carl didn't much care for possums and stoats.

Even New Zealand's treasured national symbol—the flight-less kiwi bird—was now in deep, deep trouble. For 70 million years the amazing nocturnal creature had survived in this country even though it had no tail, couldn't fly, and its nostrils were lo-cated on the tip of its long pointy bill.

The female kiwi—roughly the size and shape of an ostrich egg with feathers—laid her eggs on the ground, then turned over incubation chores to the male. This shared responsibility seemed quite appropriate in the nation that was the world's first to give women the right to vote.

But now, after 70 million years, New Zealand's lack of predators was endangering the kiwi, too. Its eggs were being gobbled up by the overpopulating millions of weasels and stoats relentlessly stalking the forest floor, while up in the treetops the possums chewed up acre after irreplaceable acre of foliage. Trees were dying everywhere.

The brushtail possums were not a native species, coming from Australia as a potential furbearer since their fur was nearly as soft as mink. But the possums in Australia had enemies while the ones in New Zealand didn't. Here, they enjoyed a fertile and slutty lifestyle. They died from just two things—old age and radial tires.

"Why don't they just get out of the way?" asked Ben as Carl intentionally thumped over yet another pancaked onto the asphalt.

"When they see headlights, they just freeze," he replied. "Don't move a bloody inch. It's harder to miss the bastards than it is to hit them."

Truck kept one eye on the road, possum counting, and the other on the magnificent lake 20 yards to the left. Wakatipu was an ancient lake carved out by a retreating glacier nearly 300 million years before and, except for the two-lane road, chugging old van, and occasional dead possum, there was nothing around but trees, scrub, the lake, and endless peaks of tall, craggy snow-capped mountains called the Remarkables.

Queenstown, basically, sat at the lake's midpoint while Glenorchy was 27 miles and 25 possums farther up—at the northern end where the Rees and Dart Rivers tumbled in. The powerful torrent of turquoise glacial run-off water from both rivers dumped into the lake very nearly side by side. Only propless jetboats and rubber rafts could navigate the swift currents and shallow rock-bottoms of the rivers.

About 20 possums into the trip, the men passed Blanket Bay, a new high-dollar resort built by a retired Levi Strauss executive. Rich people went there, comedian Robin Williams among the first. Williams brought his family just after it opened.

"Bad time of year," Carl said. "Bad weather, bad fishing. Seemed like a nice enough fellow. Quiet, actually."

Four possums later, Truck saw the small white wooden "WELCOME TO GLENORCHY" sign. Beneath the greeting, in smaller letters, it read: "POP. 130." Considering the town was 140 years old, it seemed to be growing rather slowly.

"Twenty-four," said Truck aloud. "Twenty-*four* possums, not twenty-five."

Carl flipped a dead match out the van's vent window and exhaled cigarette smoke as he slowed and tugged down his left blinker to turn from Oban Street onto Mull.

There, 20 feet ahead, was another dead possum.

"Twenty-five," said Carl quietly. "Twenty-five possums to Glenorchy."

A moment later, the van swerved into the parking row at the front of the Glen Roydon Lodge and graveled to a halt. "We're here," announced Carl. "We should celebrate. I'll have the lovely Janet pour us a Speight's." And with that, he hopped out and ran inside the bar.

While the others went inside, Truck paused for a moment and looked around. The visual splendor was startling. Glenorchy, all six tiny side roads of it, was prettier than Aspen. Prettier than the Monterrey Peninsula. He'd been around the world three times and this was the most beautiful place he'd ever seen.

"Lookit this," murmured Truck to himself as he stared at the emerald valley, sapphire lake, turquoise rivers, and bookending mountain ranges to his left and right—each a jagged majesty of coffee-brown rising above pine-painted treelines. The air was as pure as a baby's first kiss. He'd never seen such a perfect, natural, harmonic balance—anywhere.

"This," Truck said aloud, *"This* is where God went when He finished practicing."

Truck went inside the Glen Roydon Lodge, a clean, comfy, well-lit place—obviously well run. He'd barely sat down and raised a cold frothy beer mug toward his lips when he saw the girls come wheeling around the corner.

Phoebe, in the lead, joyfully ran over with her arms outstretched. Her mother was close behind. Cush, Bird, and Mitzi were five steps behind Mrs. Walker. Trailing them were two childhood girlfriends of Phoebe's who still lived in town.

They all looked terrific. With Mountain as ringleader, the girls crowded first around Ben, then swarmed over to Truck. He hugged them all, including Mrs. Walker.

It would be a fun weekend.

With Mountain's stag party later that evening, Truck didn't want to waste a beautiful late summer day sitting in a bar and "sloppin' up the piss," as Carl so eloquently called it. The Speight's could wait. Truck much preferred being outside to inside, especially on such a beautiful day in such a spectacular place.

Since Timothy wasn't arriving until morning, Cush volunteered to show Truck the valley the best way she knew how—by horse. "Dart Stables is just up the road," she said, tugging at his arm. "C'mon. Five-minute walk. If you're nice, you can ride Spartacus."

"Who's Spartacus?" Truck asked suspiciously. "A dart-throwing horse?"

"Harrrumph!" Cush mock-snorted. "I'll have you know Spartacus was a very valuable standardbred in his day. An excellent trotter. He sold for $40,000."

"My apologies to you and my apologies to Spartacus," bowed Truck. "In that case, it would be an honor and privilege."

Waving goodbye to the others, the pair walked over to the stables and saddled up for a two-hour ride. They rode through town, then past Glenorchy's modest 9-hole, par-33 golf course. Cush said the club had 15 dues-paying members and 14 of the 15 were 36-handicappers. The other, who had a 4 handicap, had won the club championship each of the past four years.

She also said that the first Saturday of every January—to celebrate New Year's—the course doubled as the Glenorchy horse track. Area farmers rode their horses into town from all over and raced them around the golf course. The Glenorchy Races were a big-time party. Thousands of people flooded into the tiny hamlet to celebrate New Year's and watch the races.

Truck smiled at hearing a town of 130 people had its own little golf course and racecourse, safely hidden in the cradle of heaven.

Their two horses stepped carefully through a small muddy creek, then splashed across the cold waters of the Rees River and on toward the Dart. The Dart was the river the Glenorchy jetboats raced up and down four times a day. Way off in the distance, Truck could hear a pair chasing each other upriver.

Spartacus knew the way—and with each plodding step along the faintly worn trail, the former racehorse wondered if he could still run fast enough to lose the outsized freeloader weighing down his back.

Everyone would find out soon enough.

But as they clip-clopped along, Cush pointed out the trees and birds and talked proudly of the surrounding countryside. Cush visited here often and she, too, loved this valley. Their stirrup-raised heels were splashed with cold water as the horses crossed the ancient river carved from the sweat of a melting glacier miles away and millions of years old.

Spartacus cared not for the poetry of the moment. He started trotting. Slowly at first, his pace quickened every ten yards. In a flash, he was going so fast that all of the nearby scrub-eating sheep and cattle looked up from their grazing just to watch Spartacus and Truck bounce on by.

"Oh God!" yelled Truck above Cush's laughter as she loped easily alongside on Stardust, her six-year-old mare.

To Truck, it was no laughing matter since he sported testicles. And just because Spartacus didn't, that was no reason for the gelding to remind Truck of such a distinct difference between the two with every bouncing step.

"Oomph! Ugh! Oh, *sheee-it!*" cursed Truck as he grimaced. His mind flashed back to Little League and the day Ricky Lee Fisher hit him dead square in the nuts with a fastball. That was the day Truck learned to wear a cup during baseball. He prayed for that cup now.

Well, Spartacus finally surrendered when Truck stood up in the stirrups and pulled the reins back so far the horse's gums were nearly in his ears.

Truck decided that, despite the surrounding grandeur of the scenery, maybe they should've walked. Life was too short for infomercials, soggy french fries, cheap wine, and bad-attitude horses.

"You OK?" Cush asked sweetly.

"Yeh, uh, fine. Just fine," he said through gritted teeth. Truck would yield no admittance of discomfort voluntarily.

During the rest of the ride, each thought went silently back to their run through the meadow that fateful day in Virginia. Today, like then, nothing would happen. Timothy had nothing to fear. Nature had issued an insurance policy on that.

Mountain's stag party was set for seven-thirty that evening, which was just enough time for Truck's extremities to stop gonging like a Chinese palace guard announcing the Emperor. The party was across the street from the Lodge at the Glenorchy Pub. There, the fellows couldn't trash the bride's mother's business, plus it was close enough for Phoebe and Mrs. Walker to keep an eye on Mountain and ward off any unforeseen naked female paratroopers who might fall from the sky in search of a wayward groom.

The party roared on until the 20 guys who showed up ran out of Speight's. The highlight came when Ben refused to drain a shot glass filled with a locally invented and super-secret formula and then was chased into the men's room. There, he crawled through a small, high window and slid to safety—inside a locked storage shed. He landed headfirst on a concrete floor. When released from his dungeon an hour later, a lump sticking a full two inches high rose directly out of the crown of his skull. It complemented his surfing bruise perfectly.

Friday's wedding rehearsal was set for one o'clock, with dinner at five. By seven-thirty, the guys would be free to head into Queenstown for Mountain's final night as a bachelor.

The wedding was taking place on a beautiful knoll alongside the Routeburn River at a scenic bend known as the Bride's Pool. The riverbank, about ten feet above the flowing Routeburn, overlooked as clear and beautiful a river as Truck had ever seen—a river National Geographic had sent photographers to photograph.

During rehearsal, Truck looked down into the deep pool and saw two large brown trout, five pounds or better, placidly finning their way back and forth along the edge of the facing current. As he watched, one or the other occasionally flared its gills to inhale a tumbling insect nymph bouncing down the river. It was a deep pool, 12 feet at least, but Truck could clearly see every rock and pebble on the bottom. And he knew that if he could see those trout, the trout could see him, too. A smart trout could live for years without leaving this pool.

It was easy to see why Phoebe picked the site. The nationally famous Routeburn hiking trail began just 100 yards away, on the far side of a swaying cabled swing bridge crossed one person at a time. About 23 miles long, the trail took two-to-three days to hike between the Routeburn and Hollyford Valleys. Each season, more than 10,000 hikers traveled to this remote area to walk all or part of the Routeburn Track.

During the Ice Age, glaciers covered this entire area. As the glaciers retreated over the past two million years, they cut and shaped the land behind them. That was how the giant lake was formed and how this magnificent valley came to sit between two mountain ranges. As the earth continues to heat, the Dart Glacier continues to recede and melt, feeding the rivers. Over the past 10,000 years, the glacier had steadily retreated to higher ground and withered in size.

At some future point, of course, the glacier will be gone.

The locals had noticed some obvious effects of a warmer world in other ways, too. "There are three types of beech trees in the forest," Carl told Truck as they prepped the wedding site. "Red, mountain, and silver beeches. Around the river are mostly reds, but all of the beeches have a five-year cycle. Every five years they seed. But the way the weather has been, the warm winters, all the beeches have seeded the last three years in a row."

"So what?" Truck asked, not understanding why it mattered.

"So," Carl continued, "more food and milder winters mean more rodents like possums, weasels, and stoats. More rodents mean fewer trees and fewer birds. It just makes every bloody thing that much worse."

Truck never thought of things like that.

But Glenorchy wasn't Las Vegas and once the sun went down, the boys decided to head to Queenstown for the rest of the evening. The girls stayed in, wagging their fingers and admonishing the men to behave themselves. Phoebe made Mountain promise not to drink and Bird told Ben to find a haberdashery and buy a stovepipe hat to cover his cranial lump. Cush gave Truck a hug and told him if he didn't behave like a gentleman, she'd make him ride Spartacus again.

Truck borrowed Carl's van and drove south along the eastern edge of the lake. They covered the 27-mile drive in 40 minutes. Ben counted 29 possums, up from 25 the day before. Must've been a tough night for them, too.

For a small town, Queenstown maximized its tourist dollar almost as well as Disneyland. A million tourists a year, two-thirds from overseas, stayed an average of two nights and three action-packed days. Two things fueled Queenstown's economy: a steady influx of tourist money and the relentless pursuit of adrenaline.

Wherever there was cash and adrenaline and a million tourists willing to trade one for the other, Ben figured there had to be women. He also figured the best way to find a lonely woman on holiday was to find a good martini.

Truck and Mountain weren't martini drinkers so they compromised. The Cigar Bar, on the lakefront promenade, sold imported Havanas. They could smoke big fat Esplandidos while Ben had his martinis and started an olive collection. He could also scout the tourists since the Queenstown casino was directly overhead and people continually streamed past.

Ben soon got restless. This was a bore. After the cigars finally exhausted their noble service, he asked a waiter where to go next.

"The casino's a waste of time unless you want to watch a bunch of old ladies play slot machines," the fellow said. "Go to the Bunker Bar. Visit Antonia. North on Beach, right on the side street alley. Little gray hut next to The Cow. Cheers, mate."

The Cow was a local landmark, a pizza and spaghetti house inside a stone 1860s farmhouse. Next door to The Cow was the little gray hut, unmarked except for press-on lettering stuck to the overhead doorjamb that simply said: "OPEN 5PM—5AM."

Well, the Bunker Bar was nondescript all right and from the outside, the place resembled a big tool shed. Truck looked at the others and shrugged. They shrugged back. He tried the old wooden door. It was open, so they stepped inside and when they did, Truck just smiled.

"Cha-*ching!*" cried Ben. *"Jackpot!"*

"Gawl," said Mountain, which in Mountainese meant, "I like this very much."

The Bunker Bar housed six candle-lit small brown tables, all occupied, a roaring black stove-pot fireplace stuffed with crackling hardwood, five barstools at the bar, and a large oval black wall clock permanently broken to read "2:10."

Ten feet from the bar, an open side door led out to a small courtyard where a dozen folks were mingling. All told, there were about 30 people in the place. At least half were pretty young women.

Luckily for the guys, three bar stools remained open. The other two were taken, occupied by a pair of attractive British girls. To Truck, each looked 28 or 30.

As the guys sat down, the manager came around the corner from the back. The Cigar Bar guy was right. This was, indeed, the lovely Antonia—small, naturally blonde, and unnaturally beautiful. Antonia had perfect pearly teeth, an hourglass figure with her sand perfectly distributed, and long straight silky hair—a deadly combination for a horny male tourist dressed in a Ben Bentley costume.

Spellbound, Ben looked at Antonia like a pit bull at a poodle. His teeth even showed. His heart started pounding, which painfully throbbed both the knot on his head and stitches in his brow. "Coca-Cola," volunteered Mountain. "On the rocks, ma'am, if that's OK."

Truck ordered a Perrier.

Ben tried impressing Antonia by launching into a rambling discourse on the life of the olive, from its birth on a rural Tuscan farm in Italy through its adolescent voyage around the world before its eventual arrival into the bottom of a Bunker Bar martini glass in Queenstown. In Ben's studied opinion, the true secret to olivian happiness was total immersion in a wonderful Antonia-made martini stirred, not shaken. Having finally explained all this as she glanced at her wristwatch, Ben finally ordered one.

When Antonia turned her back to reach for a martini glass, Ben looked at Truck and did the fluttering snake-tongue move male pigs often do. Truck just shook his head, a silent way of saying, "Don't even think about it. *Way* out of your league."

Ben sighed. He knew Truck was right. As Antonia mixed his drink, Ben mentally dumped her and refocused on the girls to his right. Both were from London, over on holiday. The prettier of the two, Lucinda, sat on the far stool. To talk to her, Ben had to talk through, or around, Stephanie, who sat directly next to him. Steph was, Mountain would say later, "a solid '6'. But Lucinda, well, she was an '8'."

To the surprise of many, this particular evening at the Bunker Bar ended abruptly. Ben asked Lucinda out to the courtyard for some fresh air. With a wink to Steph that he didn't see, Lucinda got up and followed Ben outside.

The invitation seemed like a good idea at the time, but Ben did not invite Stephanie along, which proved to be a bad idea. Another bad idea was using his patented "I got what you want and you got what I need" pickup line. Using the line was dumb enough; saying it in a loud voice so others could hear was gold-medal stupid. The courtyard walls had ears and apparently the walls did not like the sound of these 11 chauvinistic one-syllable words.

History will report that, while on the patio, Ben did not see Stephanie's approach. Nor did he see the overhand right she knuckled his left eye with. His martini glass, fortunately, was safely sitting on a small side table and escaped this incident unbroken. The olive remained unbruised, as well. Ben, however, did not.

To Ben's credit, he didn't go down. But he did sag against the courtyard fence as he covered up and protected both eyes. Stephanie then worked the body, drilling three straight right hooks into his unprotected ribcage. Lucinda winced with the sound of each repetitive thud. As Ben gasped for breath, he bent double and, just as he did, Steph let loose a flying left hook that nailed Ben right on top of the head—directly on his lumpy bruise from the stag party. The instant it landed he wailed like a mournful alley cat.

Satisfied, Steph stepped back just as Mountain and Truck ran up.

Lucinda never had a chance to tell Ben the girls had lived together for four years. She would have, but he never shut up and she couldn't get a word in edgewise. Nor did Lucinda have the opportunity to share that Stephanie's boxing nickname was "Piledriver," or that she was the reigning silver medalist in the women's welterweight division of Britain's Golden Gloves. Lucinda was sorry to see Ben get beaten to a pulp but, deep down, she liked it when Steph got jealous. It spiced up their relationship.

Anyhow, lovely Antonia was mortified. She ran over and booted them all out of the Bunker Bar immediately, with strict orders never to return. The Bunker Bar, she shouted, was for lovers—not fighters.

And so, that's how Ben Bentley got the shiner he awoke with on the morning one of his best friends was getting married. And it was also how the lump on top of his head grew another full inch while he slept. Between his surfing stitches, the lump on his noggin, and now the shiner, it had been a rough few days. At the rate this fourth week of March was going, he was praying he'd live long enough to see April.

But the best was yet to come.

Mountain Gets Married

Funny what can happen on a perfect Indian summer day in a country where furry things like possums, stoats, sheep, cattle, and deer outnumber people by 50-to-1.

Ben woke up in misery. His left eye was swollen purple and half-shut. The knot on his head was tall enough to play horseshoes on. The surfing bruise under his stitched right eyebrow had turned to a jaundiced shade of yellow. And to model this exciting new look, he'd paid a hundred bucks to rent a tuxedo.

Sunrise delivered wedding-day delirium to Phoebe and the girls. After breakfast, they all piled into the car and headed to Queenstown to get their hair done. Bird spent the entire drive trying to trade Ben for any other escort. She even offered cash. He would ruin her pictures and Bird was so mad, she wanted to clock him, too, but all the good spots were already taken.

The fellows, meanwhile, had work to do. After eating, they drove out to the banks of the Routeburn to set up for the wedding. If possible, it was even a more beautiful day than the day before.

It was a 17-mile drive from the Glen Roydon Lodge to the Bridal Pool and the final two-thirds were on an unpaved graded road. As a wedding gift to the family, Oly Olson, the local road works supervisor, had freshly scraped and graded the entire way from the paved road to the parking site on the Routeburn. This was a gesture of the highest kindness, as the road had last been smoothed five years before. Oly even sent the water truck behind the grader to water the gravel and keep the dust down.

At the turn-off for that graded road stood an eight-foot-high handmade wooden sign with arrows pointing four different directions. Each arrow named a town and distance in carefully painted black block letters three-inches high. As Carl's van turned onto the graded road, Truck stared out at the sign. The arrow pointing north read "PARADISE, 20 KM."

"Hmmm…" he thought. "Twenty kilometers. That's twelve miles. Twelve miles to Paradise. And here I thought I was already there."

Truck said nothing as they rumbled slowly along, simply opting to watch several pairs of rare paradise ducks feeding in bordering fields through the mottled brown dust of van's side window. The ducks mated for life, rarely strayed more than ten feet apart, and quacked incessantly every waking moment. Patti and Alma would say they "communicated."

Once at the wedding site, the guys unpiled all of the microphones, speakers, music, and cabling. Carl quickly scaled a nearby ridge-top and hid a small gas generator behind a big boulder so no one would see or hear it.

Mountain stood around and supervised. The others called it "doing nothing." One of Carl's pals from Queenstown, a tall thin guy named Chaz who looked like actor Donald Sutherland, owned a radio station and hooked up the audio equipment. Chaz set up two microphones, one for the bride and groom and the other for the minister. Ben and Truck sang off-key Sinatra duets to make sure the mikes worked.

Unfortunately, they did.

Mountain then sheepishly coughed up a cassette tape of native birds chirping and handed it over. Chaz looked at it, read the label, and nodded. "Good idea," he said. Chaz queued up and test-drove the tape. Two speakers on eight-foot stands filled the air with bird chirps. "Nice," Chaz said. "They'll add a lot. Good thinking."

"It was Phoebe's idea," Mountain said.

Chaz tested the wedding march music, and then the exit song. Satisfied that everything worked, the guys turned off the equipment, piled back in the van, popped open a final round of bachelor beers, and rumbled their way back to the lodge.

No one said much. Men rarely do as the matrimonial hour draws near. The groom is left alone with his thoughts, one of which is usually, "What the *hell* am I doing?" And his pals are left alone with their thoughts, one of which is usually, "What the *hell* is he doing?"

But by the time the van graveled to a halt in front of the lodge, all the men had but one common and dastardly thought: Ready or not, the enemy lays waiting. It was, in fact, tuxedo time.

As expected, none fit and everyone bitched. The guys had nobody to blame but themselves since not one of them bothered trying his tux on after scooping them up from the rental shop on Thursday.

"Dammittall," complained Ben as he posed before a full-length mirror. "What's the point? Lookit this. You rent the thing for half of what it costs to buy and *nothin'* friggin' fits!

"I can deal with a modest state of general untuckedness," he continued frustratingly, "but we're all gonna look like cartoon characters."

"What are you worried about your tux for?" Truck replied. "Nobody'll see your tux. Everybody's gonna stare at your face like you're the Elephant Man. You could wear a thong and bustier and nobody'd notice."

Ben ignored the dig and kept ranting. "Renting this stuff is a friendship tax," he said. "When I get married, I'll tell every guy I know they can either be in the wedding and rent a tux or give me half the cash and I'll leave them out. I'll make a fortune."

Mountain laughed as he looked at his pal. Ben's pant legs were five inches too long and the butt was saggy enough to smuggle a pumpkin.

"One size fits all," roared Mountain. "You look great, baby! James Bond the Second! The grandmothers will be linin' up for dances—and so will their mothers!"

"Oh yeah, wise ass? Take a look yourself," shot back Ben. "You look like a black and white body condom stuffed onto a rearing hippopotamus."

"I look *good*," posed Mountain, swivel-hipping half-sideways in each direction. "Buff magic, baby!" he crowed. "Ah *look* good, ah *smell* good, but tonight, baby, I'm a gonna *act baaad!*"

Mountain, of course, was about 40 percent bigger than any other primate in Queenstown and appeared nine sizes larger than his rental tux. Nothing buttoned. If Mountain sneezed, the whole thing was liable to explode right off his body and leave him totally naked. Except, maybe, for his brand new boxer shorts and the two differently colored socks he hoped no one noticed.

Eventually, the guys solved the groom's tux problems by scissoring up the back of his tuxedo shirt, creating two separate halves. Then they buttoned all of the buttons in the front and put it on him like a hospital gown, the back open. They closed the back with eight long horizontal straps of duct tape. Peeling them off would be Phoebe's problem.

Since Mountain's massive forearms and biceps couldn't bend inside his sleeves, they scissored the shirtsleeves off at the armpit, cut and duct-taped the shirt cuffs inside the cuffs of his jacket, and, as long as Mountain didn't ever remove his tuxedo jacket, he was home free. His tux jacket, miraculously, fit. Thinking ahead, Mrs. Walker had made sure of that. She had the local tux shop locate one in Auckland and send it down ahead of time. Everything else, they assured her, would fit perfectly.

And after the custom-tailoring, it sorta did.

Truck looked fine except for his purple face, which looked like Ben's swollen left eye only bigger. If his neck button didn't rupture an artery or choke him unconscious before the end of the ceremony, he could unbutton it at the reception.

Buttoned, the trapped blood made Truck's face glow like a pink neon sign on a desolate stretch of Mojave Desert highway.

Mountain had also asked Cleater Wimsett, Cush's dad, to be an usher. Cleater, Truck's buddy Lloyd, and Cushla's boyfriend Timothy Holden all flew down together late Friday evening from Auckland. Cleater was smart. His tux was perfectly fitted before he left. He could even walk down the wooden hallway in his shiny rental shoes without clopping.

Meanwhile, the girls were hammering and sawing their way to luminescent beauty and perfection. Each returned from the hairdresser wearing so much hair spray that any one of them could cut the wedding cake with a well-aimed head bob.

Soon enough, it was time to go. Two-thirds of Glenorchy's townspeople piled onto the Dart River Jetboat transport bus to go watch. Several of Phoebe's best childhood friends sat in the front of the bus. One in particular, Dereli Todd, started crying. She'd been married at the Bridal Pool in a beautiful springtime ceremony a couple of years before.

Phoebe's other best childhood friend, a girl nicknamed Lizard, anticipated Dereli's tears and handed her seatmate a handkerchief. Lizard had cried her very own Routeburn River of tears the day Phoebe left Glenorchy to attend school at Wentworth.

Lizard never married and probably never would, although half the men in town bayed outside her window after the pub closed down every Saturday night. Her principal companion these days was not a man but Miss Piggala, a 330-pound pet pig.

Lizard had long, straight brown hair and the thin willowy build of a TV star. She also now sported seven tattoos, only two of which—a lizard and dog—were usually visible. The rest were known only to more intimate friends.

Several neighborhood guys were also aboard the bus, among them Dangerous Dave. Growing up, Dave was Phoebe's next-door neighbor. The two sat together in every school class until Phoebe went away to Auckland.

Dave went from regular Dave to Dangerous Dave many years later, after his pack mule had a heart attack and died at the bottom of a steep ravine. It took Dave two days to hike out of the canyon and make his way back to town. There, Dave learned that by law he had to remove the dead mule from the canyon since the canyon was part of a national park and he couldn't leave it there to rot.

Like it or not, whatever was taken *into* the park had to come back *out* of the park.

Perturbed by this nonsensical regulation, Dave hiked a full two days all of the way back down into the canyon, confronted his still-dead and now bloated mule, and inserted a full stick of dynamite into its deceased posterior.

Dave then lit the fuse and ran like hell, diving behind a boulder just seconds before ignition. The mule, of course, exploded miles high—to Kingdom Come and all of the way back down. Mule bits rained down on the canyon for five full minutes. The echo reverberated for about an hour, too.

Dangerous Dave had beat the system.

Not surprising, no mules were included in today's wedding party. Dave sat near the front of the bus and would stand in the first row of streamside guests.

The bus arrived at the river half an hour before the ceremony. The guests were greeted by the birdcall recordings, which Chaz turned up loudly since the wedding music wouldn't start until the bride arrived. No one noticed the recorded chirps, despite the fact that the air was filled with a chorus of keas, South Island kakas, bush robins, and rare kakariki yellow-crowned parakeets— yet not a single bird perched nearby. In all, 80 happy guests were milling around when the bride's car arrived.

The Wedding

At precisely three-thirty, Phoebe stepped out. She looked radiant and glowed with happiness. The train of her long flowing scalloped-front wedding gown trailing behind, Phoebe safely inched her way the entire 100 yards to where her future husband proudly stood waiting atop the Bridal Pool knoll.

As Phoebe approached, Chaz punched the stereo's track two button. He dialed down the volume of the bird chirps to subtle background sounds. Then *The Wedding March* began to play.

Truck stood next to Mountain, his back to the flowing Routeburn. Ben stood next to Truck. Cleater was on the end. When Truck turned for a quick glance at the trout down in the pool, Ben leaned forward and huskily whispered, "I love weddings. Everybody's horny at weddings."

Truck turned back around, arched an eyebrow at Ben, and replied, "That'll change. Wait 'til *yours.*"

"That'll be a while," Ben answered. "Bad things happen when you're wearin' a tuxedo."

"Good song title," hissed Mountain. "Now shut up."

As Phoebe slowly drew closer, Truck thought about what Ben said. Everybody *did* get horny at weddings. Here they were all tuxed up, looking good albeit ill-fitted, and on their best behavior. But each one would scale the wall of a nunnery if a romantic liaison awaited on the other side.

Truck remained quiet. He glanced over to Cush, who happened to be looking at him. When she smiled, so did he. Truck then looked out in the crowd. He saw Timothy, standing ramrod straight in an expensive pinstriped suit. "Lucky bastard," he thought. "Lucky friggin' bastard."

Truck then looked sideways at Mountain and down at his duct-taped cuffs. Mountain still *did* look like a mutant Vienna sausage. But a happy one. Truck had a warm glow for his pal. Mountain had pulled off a minor miracle attracting a wife like Phoebe and appeared to know it. Truck's mom always said that in every relationship there's one overachiever and one underachiever. In this pairing, Mountain clearly overachieved in a very large way.

Phoebe looked gorgeous and Mountain's eyes widened as she stepped up by his side. Phoebe looked even better than he thought she would. All four girls, lined up in a row, looked absolutely sensational.

Chaz dialed down *The Wedding March* and increased the volume on the birds slightly. As everyone got in place for the ceremony to begin, Ben took a look at Phoebe in her flowing white gown and leaned over again toward Mountain. "Mountain!" he hissed, "She's wearin' white! Didn'tcha ever get that?"

Mountain pretended not to hear. He was in the love trance, miles above the surface of the moment, and totally hypnotized by the beauty of his bride. Spellbound, he couldn't take his eyes off her. Mountain was eyeing Phoebe like Tiger Woods looking at the Masters Trophy. Hell-fire if anything would get between them now.

So here, on the banks of the Routeburn under a sunny New Zealand late summer afternoon with the recorded songs of birds chirping, gentle breezes blowing, and brown trout blissfully feeding on drifting insect larvae in the pool below, the wedding ceremony officially began.

Based on the rehearsal, the ceremony would last 25 minutes. But things didn't go quite like they had in rehearsal.

Ten minutes into the ceremony, the bird chirp tape suddenly played a loud 20-second snippet of booming thunder, crackling lightning, and pouring rain—which caused all the guests to look to the heavens. Overhead, they saw nothing but blue sky. Almost on cue, all 80 guests looked sideways at each other and shrugged their shoulders. They refocused their attention forward to the minister reading the vows.

A few minutes later, a faint breeze in the treetops caused some seedpods in one of the old red beech trees to drop from the leafy canopy down to the forest floor. Two small mice feeding on pine nuts heard the seed pods land nearby and sniffed their mouse-crawling, tail-dragging way over to investigate.

A lone stoat, a foot-long brown weasel with a furry black-tipped tail, suddenly spotted the mice. The stoat was hungry and had been lured in from a nearby ridge by the recorded birdcalls. Birds, eggs, and nice fat mice were the stoat's lunchtime favorites.

So, just as the minister was approaching the "I Do" and "I Do, Too" part of the ceremony, the stoat spied the mice and made a run for them. The mice saw the stoat come running from the fallen log on the nearby hill and did what all doomed mice do to increase their odds: They split up. One beelined toward the wedding party and the other streaked toward the crowd of standing guests.

Several townspeople saw the mice, pointed, and screamed like stabbing victims. Wholesale panic broke out, not unlike the Titanic moments after the downstairs guests met the ocean water heading up the stairwell.

The minister kept reading. A little louder perhaps, but onward he plowed.

One mouse veered straight for the dark safety of Bird's long, lavender bridesmaid dress. Bird screamed, lost her balance backward, and disappeared from the riverbank. In a life-flashing-before-your-eyes sequence, she seemed to fall in slow motion— her arms waving, slip showing, legs spreading and, lastly, her ankles waving goodbye. Seconds later, she landed backward in the river with a thunderous splash.

On read the minister.

A few seconds after that came a second giant splash. Ben leaped in nobly to rescue Bird, which would've been a good plan had his straightjacket rental tux permitted him the freedom to move his arms.

On read the minister.

"Help!" Ben cried out. *"Help! I can't swim! I'm drowning!"*

Chaz turned to Cleater and asked the obvious question. "Then what the hell did he jump in for?" Cleater just shrugged. It was, after all, a very good question.

The minister ignored the thrashing and splashing behind him and just kept reading.

The stoat, meanwhile, ignored all the human fuss and just kept chasing the mice. The mice kept looking for dresses to hide under while Ben and Bird kept yelling for help from the river.

On read the minister.

"Oh, bloody 'ell!" yelled Lizard as she ran 20 feet toward the riverbank. "I'll save 'em!"

On the dead run, she hollered, "Don't stop Phoebe! Keep readin'—quickly as possible!" And with that, Lizard's long, lithe form jackknifed into the deep river pool like an Olympic springboarder. She grabbed Ben and Bird, one under each arm, and kick-splashed both over to the safety of the riverbank.

There, standing and gasping for air on the pebbled shoreline of the Routeburn River, all three soaked participants watched as the minister finally said, "I now pronounce you husband and wife."

The mice watched, too, since both ducked safely into a hidden hole at the base of a platter-shaped flat rock two feet behind Mountain. The frustrated stoat ran back up the hill.

The cameras held by the women in attendance were lovingly trained on the glowing bride and beaming groom.

The cameras held by the men in attendance were lovingly trained on the riverbank, as it became quickly obvious that Lizard's long clinging dress was unhampered by much in the way of undergarments. For the men in attendance, this was a free photo shoot for the *Sports Illustrated* swimsuit edition.

In quick succession, 12 guys got bonked on the head by wives and girlfriends, the repeating echoes sounding like a bongo solo by Ricky Ricardo at Club Babalu. Bird caught Ben gawking and windmilled him with a closed fist directly on top of his already lumpy skull. Her powerful cranium shot drove Ben straight to his knees in grimacing agony. He also wailed a guttural yell—not unlike a deaf girl doused by a tidal wave of unexpected ice water.

Ceremony complete, Mountain's first husbandly act was to scoop up his lovely bride gently in his powerful arms, take four steps left, and leap into the deep-water pool of the river below.

By now, the brown trout were thoroughly disgusted by all the uninvited intrusions into their domain and finned their way out into the Routeburn's swifter mainstream current. They turned around, caught the swift moving water, and coasted downstream 200 yards below the walking bridge to find a quieter place to live.

The stoat, frustrated at losing the mice in the well-dressed chaos, hid in a hollow log up on the hillside. Now that the mice escaped, he was determined to catch the flock of birds stuffed inside that peculiar black box. They couldn't stay inside forever—at some point they had to come out. And when they did, he was going to pounce.

The Reception

Mitzi, to no one's surprise, caught the bouquet. Bird didn't even bother trying for it. She'd tried once before, at an outdoor wedding in Auckland last summer, but she ricocheted off Phoebe and tumbled 100 yards down a steep embankment—tightly, like carpet rolling—before thudding to a dramatic halt six feet before rolling off a seawall and into the Hauraki Gulf.

As the men watched, Cleater offered a studied opinion. "That woman," he said dryly of Mitzi, "is an orchestrated medley of strategic refinement."

"She's hot, too," Ben added.

The guys, who feared such inanimate dangers as garters and bouquets, gallantly let a ten-year-old local boy named Evan Crawford catch Phoebe's garter. At the garter toss moment, all four of the guys—Ben, Truck, Lloyd, and Cleater—stood side by side, frozen like ice-carved figurines, arms chiseled to their sides.

Mountain carefully aimed the garter right at Ben, but it bounced off his chest and the little kid ran in and scooped it up.

To his credit, the little fellow knew just what to do. He marched right up to Mitzi and told her to grab a chair and cross her legs.

The garter danger safely past, the men gathered around the punch bowl and strategized. Sizing up the available women in the audience—and several seemed amiable to meeting the two American men—the guys debated the best approach to greet a lovely new friend.

"Face it," said Truck. "Everybody looks their best at a wedding. The men do and the women do. Especially the women. You could build a case for half of the women here."

"The secret is dancing the slow dances," chimed in Ben.

"The secret is dancing the slow dances with one of *these* in your pocket," said Cleater. The guys looked down where Cleater carefully palmed a medium-sized and half-ripe banana. He revealed it secretively, and four heads swiveled around to make sure none of the women saw it.

"Where'd you get the banana?" asked Ben, looking around quizzically. "I don't see any bananas."

"I brought it," said Cleater.

"You *brought* your own *banana* to a wedding reception?" asked Truck incredulously.

"You are *The Man!*" applauded Ben cheerfully. "Didja bring another one? I'll take one! I'll take one!"

Cleater smiled slowly and put his hand into his right tux pocket, slowly reemerging with yet another banana, which was an inch smaller than his own. Palming it carefully, he made the handoff to Ben. "Two bucks," he said.

"I've got a fiver," offered Lloyd. "Got a bigger one?"

Cush, meanwhile, stood nearby but out of earshot, talking with her fiancé, Timothy Holden. Truck couldn't help but study the pair. He mused over the concept of the overachiever versus the underachiever. Clearly in Truck's mind, Cush was a wonderful person. Timothy seemed a good man, too. Obviously, he made a good living in the horse business and that should make her very happy. He hoped things would work out, just like they'd work out for Phoebe and Mountain. Truck expected Cush to be the next of the Posse to march to the altar and thought she wouldn't last another year.

He watched them for several more minutes, hiding his eyes behind a raised cocktail glass. He sipped his drink slowly—absently—and wondered how the two met and what Cush liked about Timothy most. Knowing her, it probably wasn't the money. But then again, money never hurt.

Cush looked beautiful, he thought. Prettiest he'd ever seen, by far. He always thought she was attractive—even when he saw her with the green hair he knew she was a pretty girl—but he'd never seen her look so beautiful, so womanly, so sexy. It seemed like the older she got, the more beautiful she became.

Timothy, meanwhile, stood stiffly by her side and said very little. To Truck, he seemed restless even being here, glancing at his watch and waiting to escape from this stuffed-shirt purgatory.

Time was money and Timothy wanted to get back to Auckland. His mind was on distant horses, ringing telephones, and falling gavels. He'd parked a big money syndication deal to come here and didn't want to lose it.

Occasionally, Timothy left Cush's side to go bleed a scotch from the open bar. Cush and Timothy spoke little, Truck noticed. He couldn't hear what they said, but he'd been there, himself, before. He knew it was nothing that mattered to either of them.

The reception cruised along uneventfully, aside from the blushing excitement of the ten different women Mountain had Ben dance with. The youngest was 60 and seemed happily flattered as she waltzed against his banana. Afterward, she even brought Ben a double martini from the bar.

Truck also watched Cleater dance several times with Mitzi—clearly a surprising overachievement on his part. Clear, too, was the outline of the banana in his pants pocket. At least Truck *thought* it was his banana.

As the two danced, Cleater made small talk with his partner, but Mitzi interrupted and asked if he had a girlfriend.

"No," Cleater replied. "I was dating someone but got dumped."

"Why would any girl dump a handsome man like you?" cooed Mitzi.

"That's what I couldn't figure out," he replied. "I even told her, 'Hey, you're making a big mistake. You'll *never* find another guy like me.'"

"And what did she say?" asked Mitzi curiously.

"She said, 'I certainly hope not! If I were dropping your sorry arse, why would I *ever* want to go out with another one just like it? What sense would that make?'"

"Wow," replied Mitzi. "What'd you say to that?"

"What *could* I say?" replied Cleater. "I just shrugged my shoulders and said, 'Good point. Fair enough. Point well made.'

"I even told her I love her, love her to death," added Cleater. "I thought *all* women loved to hear that."

"Most do," Mitzi answered. "Such poetry even makes *my* knees shake a little. What'd she say when you told her that?"

"She said, 'If you love me to death, then how come you're not dead yet?'"

"Well *that's* certainly not good, is it?" laughed Mitzi. "I guess at that point you knew a BJ was probably out of the question, huh?"

That comment left Cleater speechless, so he just nodded and kept dancing.

Mitzi decided to change the subject. "What happened between you and Cush's mom?" she asked him bluntly. "Cush never talks about either one of you."

"Ah, it was me. My fault all the way, that one was. She was a good lady.

"I drank a lot. Way too much. Or so I thought. Then, *poof!* Suddenly she took ill and, *boom!* she was gone. And I was left to raise a little girl I knew nothing about. Thank God a neighbor friend looked after Cush and got her into Wentworth. Saved us both, actually.

"I was a terrible husband and worse father to two wonderful girls who deserved better than I gave. Nothing to be proud about. Thanks for askin.'

"But, if I had to do it over again, I would. Differently.

"That was the nut of it, plus the longer I was married, the more I missed sex. Near the end there I forgot what went where."

Mitzi cocked her head back, looked up at Cleater, and smiled. "Well," she cooed, "you're not married *now.*"

People blink, on average, 2,000 times a day. When Cleater heard that Mitzi's last statement, emanating from this particular set of ruby red lipstick-covered lips, he covered half a day's worth of blinks in the flash of a single fantasy moment. His heart raced like the Jumanji game board right before the rhino stampede. Cleater set aside the fact that Mitzi was one of his daughter's best friends. After all, he was by no means a cradle-robber. Cleater was simply willing to support the concept of "generationally differentiated relationships."

Mitzi put her head on his chest, said no more, and kept dancing. For some reason, she liked this guy.

Suddenly, the banana moved.

Truck enjoyed watching his pals, but didn't dance much on his own. As far as dancers went, Truck Roberts was overly Caucasian. He danced twice with Cush, first as members of the wedding party, and then again the last dance. That's when he saw her standing alone after Timothy preferred to respond to last call.

Cush and Truck danced slowly and comfortably together while the music played. Neither spoke. There was either nothing to say or way too much to cram into four-and-a-half minutes, so both remained silent.

When the song neared its conclusion, far too quickly in the unspoken feelings of both, Cush tugged on his shoulders and whispered in his ear. "Call me before you leave New Zealand, OK? I want to talk to you." Truck wasn't sure if she said it to be nice or because she meant it. She sounded sincere. But so had all the others.

Truck said nothing. He simply looked at Cush's emerald green eyes, smiled softly, and nodded okay.

"Promise?" tested Cush as she held out the little finger of her left hand to interlock with his. "Pinky swear?"

Truck studied her eyes again, paused for a moment, smiled imperceptibly, and nodded again. "Sure," he said, locking fingers. "Pinky swear. I'll call Friday when I get back from Great Barrier."

He then paused before deciding to say what he'd been thinking for the past four hours. For the first time since he'd known her, he simply spoke without worrying about the words. "You look lovely," he told her. "More beautiful than I ever imagined. The prettiest I've ever seen you. By far. Even prettier than the green-hair day you forgot your bra and fleeced me at darts."

He hadn't said much, but he sure felt better having said it. Maybe Alma and Patti were right after all. Maybe it was too much thinking that kept screwing him up.

Cush looked up and smiled. She said nothing. As the song ended, she stuffed a wedding napkin with her already-scribbled number at the farm into the breast pocket of his tuxedo jacket.

"Don't forget," she said as the music stopped. They shared a brief squeezing hug and stepped apart. "Call me."

The reception over, Cush left with Timothy and went straight to the airport to head back to Auckland. Truck sauntered off with the others to continue the party.

The Wheel to Nowhere

Visiting beautiful, desolate Great Barrier Island was one of the worst best times of Truck's entire life. Despite the spectacular scenery—bobbing blue penguins, hungry saltwater gamefish, massive centuries-old pohutukawa trees, and flowering hillsides of a hundred colors—Truck never felt so alone in his whole adult life. His thoughts stayed flooded with memories of absent friends.

Mountain's wedding had been an explosion of happiness totally absent in Truck's own individual life. Just that quickly, all the joy was gone like the morning dew. His friends scattered back to their lives, and he was left alone to shadowbox with his.

By his second day at Great Barrier, his loneliness was growing louder by the hour. Truck wanted to leave and go home. There, he could at least grab a necktie, climb back inside his personal human hamster cage, and resume furiously racing around his own wheel to nowhere. It wasn't much of a life, but it was his, it was safe, and at the moment it was all he had.

Two hours before Truck's commuter plane was finally due to leave Great Barrier for its half-hour hop back across the Hauraki Gulf to Auckland, he drove past the little seaside town of Port Fitzroy. A roadside yellow clapboard sign in front of the general store piqued his interest.

It read "GREAT BARRIER PIGEON-GRAM SERVICE." Below, in smaller letters, was printed *"The World's First Air-Mail Service."*

Here, in this tiny little seaside town, was a carrier pigeon service to the mainland. Whenever the need arose, the birds were banded with messages on Great Barrier, then released to fly 55 miles southwest to their roost in Auckland. The quickest made it in two days; the most leisurely took 20. Once the birds delivered the message to the mainland, it would then be forwarded anywhere you wanted it to go.

A hundred years before, this was the world's first such service. Now it was more ceremonial than practical since telephones and a half-a-dozen flights a day could shuttle the mail back and forth. Still, it was a novel idea that triggered an impulse.

Truck parked his car and stepped inside the general store. He exchanged pleasantries with an older woman who reminded him of his chatty Aunt Barb, then filled out the form she provided. She assigned Truck's mail to Aldo, a brown and white mottled four-year-old male pigeon. "Aldo's pretty reliable," she said. "He's better than most."

Later that afternoon, flying back to the mainland, Truck's plane accidentally struck a bird shortly after lift-off. It looked brown and white—and red. Truck hoped it wasn't Aldo, but never knew for sure.

Six days later, while Truck Roberts was back home in the United States and finally over the jet lag from his trip to New Zealand, the postman delivered to a horse farm midway between Cambridge and Hamilton an envelope addressed for Miss Cushla Wimsett. Inside the envelope was a tiny rolled-up carrier-pigeon message from Great Barrier Island that said simply: "MWYADAETM."

Aldo, apparently, had made it.

Before Truck left New Zealand, he had called Cush as promised. After 20 rings, she didn't answer the phone. Hearing the echoing, unanswered rings had hurt Truck deeply at the time. But emotional setbacks were nothing new to him. Not long after arriving home, that phone call, the wedding, reception, and all the rest of his vacation soon faded to black.

Since Cush wasn't there when he called, Truck dismissed her as being nothing more in his life than an emotional peculiarity of foreign travel. To her, he guessed, he was a puppet on a string and one who held no long-term interest.

As he flew back to the States, Truck decided the last thing, the *very* last thing, he needed was another downward-spiraling relationship, this one fueled by a disconsolate dart thrower from the other side of the planet. She had her life to live and he had his. They probably would never again intersect. In fact, they seemed to be those most dreaded of things—"just friends." Anything more, he thought, and she'd have answered the phone when he called. He never knew she was in the shower and never heard it.

After returning home, Truck called Party Patti and they talked for two hours. Patti still believed that Truck needed to stop being so insecure and negative—so *defeated*—and start trusting women closer to home with his inner self. As bad as Truck was with local in-person relationships, Patti surmised that long-distance ones were *way* beyond the scope of Truck's romantic capabilities.

She was not surprised that he had demonstrated the strength of soggy milquetoast while overseas. She'd learned several years back that, while she loved Truck like a brother, he was not a fellow you'd bet the mortgage on when it came to leaving himself vulnerable. Patti thought all of Truck's frustrations traced to the exact same thing—big, bad supermacho man Truck Roberts was simply too scared to let any woman scale the wall of inner privacy that guarded his heart.

However, she was surprised he never heard from Cush after the wedding, especially since she asked him to call. She expected Cush to have a bit more silk in her soul.

Day after day, Truck simply plowed on. Careerwise, he wrestled with the puzzling question of whether it was better to be a large trout in a small lake or a spit of plankton floating around in a corporate sea of confusion. Maybe the two brown trout submerged in the Routeburn had the right idea: Just find a safe deep pool and sit in it.

Truck spent the next year on the road but no matter how far he went, he could never seem to outfly the hollow feelings of loneliness that had checkmated him at Great Barrier.

The worst were the giant cities. He was never so alone as when surrounded by faceless millions. Through it all, he tried to be nice to the blur of meaningless strangers whose lives bisected his. But overall, Truck handled the endless business travel like most lonely men do—poorly and grumpily.

Life featured endless fog delays in San Francisco, bone-numbing December nights alone in wintry Montana, and late-night french fries for dinner in Boise. Truck never saw a town with as many french fries as potato-crazy Boise. Per capita, there had to be six or eight million fries for everybody there. At the airport, the stores sold big mesh bags of spuds-to-go. Even Piso, who knew a lot about fries, would be amazed.

Truck bottomed out emotionally during a wasted business trip to Puerto Rico. He ended up at the cockfights on Valentine's Day. For a lonely man, that was about as smart as paying strange women to go love their boyfriends in the Bahamas.

The cockfights were so miserably barbaric, the Hell's Angels would grimace. Few fights went the 15-minute maximum and judges stopped a bout only if one of the birds died or was unable to defend itself for a full minute, in which case the rooster was pretty much dead anyhow.

"This is like a really bad marriage," Truck thought as he watched. "The minutes are years. They just keep goin' at it 'til some judge finally decides one of 'em has suffered enough."

Truck left six matches into the card and caught a cab back to Condado Plaza. Despite the forbidding weather, he decided to go for a long late-night walk along the seawall toward Old San Juan.

That solitary walk produced the prettiest thing Truck ever saw in Puerto Rico: a fierce Caribbean storm.

Paradise rain, he later called it in a postcard home. The pounding power of the surf on the rocks, palms bending in the wind, empty hammocks in the rain, and turquoise turbulent seas.

Truck was neither Puerto Rican nor fluent in Spanish, so his business trips to San Juan were as effective as a pro wrestler leaping across the stage for the Bolshoi. Frustrated and sad, this savage night he simply splashed along, his hands shoved in his pockets, oblivious to the thunder, lightning, and pelting rain.

Cocooned inside his thoughts, the business rejection he could take. Far and away, much worse was the loneliness.

Truck's life was a windmill of cities and yet there was little glamour in what he was doing. Despite the money, Truck was beginning to believe there was more to living life than watching others live theirs. Only his vantage point—not his view—ever changed.

He certainly had none of those special days Alma had talked about. Alone in the rain, splashing back through the puddles from Old San Juan, tears welled up in his eyes as he recalled the unbridled joy of Mountain's wedding. Nothing remotely close touched his own life in a similar way. He started to cry when he realized the stark truth: Mountain was now far richer without money than he was with it. He hated the damn, awful, stinking truth.

Truck called Patti one Sunday night, paced in his kitchen, and whined about the sad monotony of it all. After listening for a long time, she finally got a word in edgewise. "Truck Roberts, you need to decide what's important in your life and what you really want to do. How the hell do you *ever* expect to meet a woman? No woman in her right mind is going to sit around waiting while you gallivant over God's four corners of the planet.

"If you want a real relationship, then you need to live a real life and have more to give than what you expect to get in return. One of these days—and you might be 100 years old when it finally dawns on you—it'll finally sink in to that fat, stubborn, traveling skull of yours that the joy is in the giving—not the taking. Get off the road, Einstein! Get off the road and get a real life.

"Toodles!" With that, she hung up and the line went dead. As always, Patti said a lot without using many words. She knew Truck like her own kitchen and minced few words when it was time to say what he needed to hear.

Truck decided Patti could be right, that as soon as he met someone worth getting off the road for, he would. But until then, he kept flying. It might be a bad life, but it was the only one he knew.

Finally, while filling out a police report after being pickpocketed at the Los Angeles airport, Truck gave some serious thought to getting off the road for good. Woman or no woman, maybe it was time to quit orbiting the planet in a necktie and re-enter earth's reality atmosphere.

The quick successive deaths of four friends fueled his thinking. One died of what used to be called natural causes. Another died by accident, cracking up his motorcycle. The third was the toughest of all. He died by his own hand, despondent over a business failure. Two months later, a fourth pal died after being swiftly overpowered by the horrible muscle-debilitating ALS—Lou Gehrig's disease. It's rare, but relentless. It caught Truck's pal and pulled him under the sod in less than 11 months.

Truck absorbed these losses alone. Each one hit harder than the last. His travels, the funerals, the endless knot-tying of logistics to coordinate planes, trains, and automobiles added up. Truck suddenly missed the simplest of things—playing golf and poker with pals, running familiar trails, and even having the humble sanctity of his own private bathroom. The fourth funeral finally triggered the decision to move back to Denver, where his roots and his parents were.

Once settled, another dilemma arose. Finding a girlfriend at work was out of the question. Corporate America was so schizophrenic, so paranoid, about sexual harassment that a simple compliment could be considered a "shade of gray" violation.

So, he treated the women at work like they were the girls of his youth—like they all had koodies.

Truck decided that what he was looking for—or at least what he told Patti on the telephone he was looking for—was someone like Cush. He wanted somebody with a little starch, a little panache, a touch of independent spirit. When Patti asked him why he didn't just go get the Cush that was already just like the Cush he was looking for, Truck dismissed the idea as impractical and nonsensical.

"I didn't say I'm looking *for* Cush," he said. "I said I'm looking for someone *like* Cush. There's a difference."

"What's the difference?" answered Patti. "Cup size?"

Truck ignored the caustic shot. "Cush and I would never work out," Truck said. "She's over there and belongs over there. I'm over here and I belong here. Plus, she's probably engaged or married by now. I even met the guy at Mountain's wedding. Nice guy. Good looking, successful, and loaded. All the girls liked him."

"You'd know if she was married," Patti said.

"What makes you say that?" he asked.

"She'd make sure you knew," she said. "She'd make sure you found out. Even if she didn't think you'd show up for the wedding, she'd invite you just to make sure you knew. At the very least, she'd tell Mountain and he'd tell you. That's just the way girls are."

Truck didn't argue. He just kept looking for someone sort of like Cush.

Once he quit traveling so much and settled into a Denver suburb, Truck dated a few girls but had a tough time figuring them out. Either they wanted sex or they didn't. Some said they wanted it but really didn't; others said they didn't want it and really did. It was all very confusing.

Truck continued to call Patti for counsel. She urged him to drop the mask he wore in public and persevere. Truck protested. "Everybody wears a mask," he told her. "Everybody has layers."

Patti didn't argue the point. "To a degree, you're right," she said. "Now drop yours and call Cush." She even offered to pay for the call.

Truck flatly refused. "What's the point of calling if I have no idea what to say?" he asked helplessly. "What do I ask her? *How's Tim?*"

"Sounding dumb never stopped you before," Patti countered. "You give awful phone. You always think before talking and that's half your problem."

"What's the other half?" he asked curiously.

"You don't have the guts to call in the first place."

Truck flinched. Calling Patti for advice always seemed like voluntarily reporting to detention.

She finally got Truck to agree to channel in on the good in people and ignore imperfections. She also told him to relax, pursue his interests, and be nice to everyone he met. And she made him promise to talk without thinking. The thinking always seemed to mess him up.

Unfortunately, things didn't get a whole lot better. Truck even cracked up his car watching a girl walking her dogs. He spied a leggy blonde—one with a figure like the reclining girl silhouetted in silver on trucker's mud flaps—being tugged along behind a pair of magnificent Irish Wolfhounds. She looked beautiful, even hidden, under a floppy hat and sunglasses. She also looked familiar. He thought she looked just like Trixie from Frozen Foods.

Truck's head swiveled as he drove toward, then past the woman and her dogs. The road, however, didn't swivel an inch. It turned left and Truck didn't. His car slammed into the facing curb head on, blowing out both front tires in two claps of booming thunder. The car's hubcaps flew off and rolled on edge, one peeling off to the left, the other to the right. They rolled 70 or 80 feet before spinning 'round and 'round and wobbling onto their sides. And Truck's front-end alignment was knocked more crookedly than a drunk's footsteps through a maze.

The woman hurried away, as her terrified dogs accelerated to escape the awful stalker. Truck never saw her again, despite driving the exact same road at the exact same time of day for 17 consecutive days.

It was then and there, sitting on the curb waiting for the tow truck to arrive, that Truck decided if he could do it all over again in the meadow that day, he would have acted normal, not noble. He should've done her in the field like she wanted.

Maybe then things would be different. Maybe *then* they'd have both lived happily ever after.

ack at the Farm

Far away, on the other side of the world, Cushla's car hopped a curb and smacked a light pole when she stared at a guy with a washboard stomach rollerblading his Great Dane along Auckland's Tamaki Drive. She wasn't hurt, but the smash crumpled the nose of her car. The guy skated over to make sure she was OK. As luck would have it, he was already married. Worse than that, the guy had no brothers. And her car cost $800 to fix. It was hardly the idyllic way to spend her only day of the week off.

After Phoebe's wedding, Cush stayed in a deep funk for several weeks. New feelings she hadn't dealt with popped up for the first time—and she didn't like them. Deep down, Cushla felt both restless and hollow. She was looking for something, but wasn't quite sure what it was. Cush wasn't convinced Timothy was the answer, but maybe he was and she was too afraid to accept it.

She also began to think seriously that people got married simply to get out of dating and put an end to all this awful tedium.

Cush certainly wasn't looking for another Truck—that much she knew for sure. Every time the day in the meadow flashed through her memory, she got embarrassed all over again. But just as quickly, she tossed the recollection aside. Her life was in front of her, not behind her. Of that, Cush was dead solid certain. Besides, if he'd cared about her, he would have at least phoned before he'd left.

Regardless, Cush didn't know whether these new feelings were normal or not. Maybe it was age. Or her cycle. Or the stark realization she wasn't a kid any more. Watching Phoebe get married was exciting, but maybe Cush's halfhearted attempt at catching the bouquet gave her a clue that her own marriage might create more questions than it would provide answers. She wasn't certain she wanted to be married and even less sure she was happy being single. Worst of all, she couldn't think of any other options.

Four months after Phoebe's wedding, Timothy proposed to her. Hardly romantic, the asking came while they watched TV. To Cush, it sounded more like a business than marriage proposal. But she accepted, ignoring the deep down pangs of doubt that screamed "No! No! *Hell, no!*" while her ears heard her voice meekly vote, "Yes."

But Cush shrugged off the negative feelings. She spent a lot of time tossing darts and thinking about a lot in general, nothing in particular. Something was missing. The glue. The glue was missing. Timothy and Cush had set no firm wedding date, talking vaguely of the fall, which left them both about eight months to change their minds

She decided the best thing to do was simply get married, quit her job at Sir Patrick's farm, and compete in professional dart competitions around the world. She was certainly good enough. Timothy could keep his job selling horses and pay for all the expensive things he thought were so damn important.

Cush would miss the farm. As hard as Sir Patrick worked them, it was an exhilarating industry when things went right. Everything she'd hated about the political crap in the corporate world evaporated the moment she drove through the beautiful wrought-iron gates of Cambridge Stud.

And where the corporate world was filled with stufflebums who set alarm clocks so they could wake up and make unimportant stuff seem important—well, in Sir Patrick's world, all that mattered most were the animals. Hell would freeze over too thick to ice fish before she'd ever go back to that corporate nonsense. Cush's customers now were pregnant mares, wobble-legged newborn fillies and colts, and scary little mice that spooked her from time to time by playing peekaboo in the feed shed.

Thank God there were no stoats.

Cush started playing her Louis Armstrong album in the evenings before bed. She thought of Truck whenever she opened the CD box and saw his name on the business card he'd placed between the inside plastic cover and the CD sleeve. She had never pulled out the card or seen the handwritten note on the back.

Occasionally she wondered what he was up to, often dreaming of that day in the meadow. But all of her dreams had a far different ending. She dreamed they made love for hours and days and weeks on end, pausing only for a beautiful wedding with horses and deer all around. And then, she dreamed that they lived happily ever after.

She wondered if Truck ever thought about that day. Probably not, she decided. In a way, the dreams disturbed Cush greatly. They were not the kind of thoughts that should occupy her mind if she was engaged to marry someone else.

Searching for something new and relaxing to try on her day off, Cush tried to talk Bird into going to flyfishing school so they could learn to trout fish. Bird passed, saying she was too busy, and in doing so was quite direct.

"You don't want to catch a *fish*," she told Cush on the phone. "You want to catch a *man*. A real man. You want to catch a real man so you can toss back that self-centered, buy-and-sell, money-hungry, tunnel-visioned simpleton you've got now. That's the one you need to go to: manfishing school. Go to that one, Cush. Skip the trout thing."

Despite the counsel from her closest friend, Cush decided to go anyway.

Ever the independent spirit, she went by herself and quickly picked up the rhythmic nuances of the sport. Flycasting wasn't dissimilar to darts. Good casting, like accurate dart throwing, required rhythm and repetition. Both were technique sports, not power sports. It didn't take long to figure out why Truck enjoyed it so much.

Cush was a fast learner. On her third lesson, the instructor took his four students—three men plus Cush—onto the Waipa River just south of Whatawhata to fish for real. Cush was the only one to catch more than one trout. In fact, she caught three, including two without help. They were small rainbows, about a foot long, that she released. Cush carefully tried to unhook each one without touching it by leaving the fish in her net while she fiddled with the tiny hook to push it out of the trout's soft-tissued mouth. She then flipped her net inside out and watched each little trout quickly zoom away.

At the end of the trip, she felt proud of herself—as did her instructor. "One fish, Miss Wimsett," he said with proud drama, "is an accident. Two fish, Miss Wimsett, is a coincidence. But three fish, Miss Wimsett, well, three fish is absolute *skill!* Congratulations! You are now an official flyfisherman!"

"*Woman*," she corrected. "Flyfisher*woman*."

Six months later, with the yearlings off the farm, it was the slow season and Cushla asked Sir Patrick for a long weekend to compete in Wellington for the New Zealand Open Dart Championship. She talked Bird into driving down with her.

Timothy and Cush had recently agreed they were still engaged but wouldn't yet pick a date, which seemed to be the desired preference of each. Both were self-contained—he with his horse-trading and she with the farm and her darts—and neither seemed enthralled with the realities of a permanent relationship. But both were too scared to toss off something so convenient in exchange for being alone. Doing nothing was much easier than doing something. Doing nothing was what they both seemed to do the best.

If nothing else, a trip to Wellington would be a fun getaway. Wellington was the nation's capital and New Zealand's third largest city, behind Auckland and Christchurch. The city sat on the southern tip of the North Island, the wind always blew, and the weather was usually nice. Cush hadn't been there in a long time and looked forward to the trip.

Bird left Auckland at noontime and drove to Cambridge to pick Cush up at the farm. It was a long drive down Highway 1 to Wellington, so the girls wanted to stop halfway and stay the night at the bottom of Lake Taupo. They decided to splurge and aimed for the Tongariro Lodge, the place Cush heard Truck talk so much about.

Since he'd been there and loved it, she was curious to see what it was like. Plus, the lodge was famous—lots of world figures and foreign dignitaries fished there. Even in fly school, the fellows had talked of the Tongariro, so Cush also thought it would be fun to peek at one of the world's most famous trout rivers.

With Cush taking a turn at the wheel, the girls drove along the eastern shores of Lake Taupo, magnificent in its shaded blue colors. They headed south and passed Waipahihi, Waitanhanui, Te Rangiita, and Motupapa.

At the Waitanhanui River mouth, Cush saw one of the famed picket lines of fishermen standing in the shallows of Lake Taupo. One of the men had hooked a big trout that leaped clear of the water at least three times as they approached. She watched the battle in the rear-view mirror of her car until a bend in the road took them out of sight.

Just north of Turangi, Cush saw the lodge's turn-off sign. She gravel-roaded Bird's little blue Toyota off the paved highway and onto Grace Road. The lodge was a couple of hundred yards on the left. They turned in and parked in front of the largest building.

The property had several tastefully maintained red-trimmed, tin-roofed cabins scattered around its lush campus. It was a beautiful setting—unlike typical fish camps that reeked of man-created smells.

It was five o'clock when the girls walked up the steps and into the beautiful foyer. The lodge had a rustic look and was tastefully decorated—homey and relaxing in a stylish, well-appointed way. The dark-stained wood walls held dozens of framed photographs of famous people smiling and holding huge rainbow trout. Several monster trout were stuffed and put on prominent display. All seemed as long as Cush's arm and had the girth of a rugby ball. To Cush, the giant fish seemed big enough to swallow her whole. Her fly school trout were one-*tenth* this size. At best.

"No wonder Truck liked it here," thought Cush as she looked around, wide-eyed. Bird had ventured off in search of the toilet and then checked them both in, using her Bank of New Zealand Visa card. After she ventured through the lodge's fashionable halls, Bird was smitten too.

The great room—a social room, really—looked out over the mighty Tongariro River. Looking at the pictures and the river gave Cushla the spurious urge to catch a trout, even a wee one. She asked to borrow some waders and equipment. Mrs. Haffield outfitted her from head-to-toe, then handed her a fly rod. She wished her luck as Cush waddled out the back porch door and down toward the famous stream.

Bird tagged along and watched from the rocky shore.

Mrs. Haffield also sent one of the guides, a handsome guy, about 30, to make sure Cush started off OK. A big fishy-looking pool of deep water swirled behind a boulder near the lodge and the guide, an Irish chap named Paul McMullen, thought they might start there.

With a couple of reminders about arm angles, Cush's casting quickly returned to form and she was soon able to advance the fly in the vicinity of where she wanted it to land. The Tongariro was

100 feet across and Cush could heave the fly halfway, which was good enough.

The guide first had Cush throw a Wooly Bugger, an olive-green fly pattern lassoed with sparkly thread that resembled a leech or small baitfish. She lofted the two-inch fly to mid-river and let the current run with it. Then she lifted her rod tip and swung the fly in wide arc. Cush pulled her line back in, using six-inch tugs to make the fly look as though it was swimming upstream and into the current.

No luck.

After several tries, Paul switched Cush's fly and tied on a pheasant-tailed nymph. The nymph imitated a bug hatching from the river bottom and swimming its way up toward the surface. He put a pinch of soft lead a foot above the fly and looped a small white floating wool strike indicator eight feet from the weight. The wool would act like a float to signify a take.

The guide flipped the rig out into the edge of the current—not in the fast water and not in the slow water but along the seam between the two—and handed Cush the rod. He told her to watch the floating white wool. If it went under or stopped drifting normally, she needed to quickly raise the rod tip since a trout might have taken the fly.

Paul also told Cush to make sure the fly drifted naturally. There couldn't be any resistance on her line or the water friction would make the fly look unnatural in the water and the trout would ignore it. The fly had to tumble along the river bottom as if it was free-falling downstream.

Well, sure enough, she got a take. On Cush's fifth or sixth drift, the white indicator stopped, then disappeared below the surface. Cush quickly flipped her right wrist up, raised her rod tip overhead, and hooked a trout far heavier than all three from fly school added together—even if you stuffed their tummies with D-size batteries.

The huge rainbow came hurtling out of the water and screamed floating gray line from her reel as it cartwheeled across the surface of the broad swift-flowing river.

Bird screamed when she saw it. "Oh my God!" she cried. "Bug all! Lookit 'im! He's one of those picture fish! My God, 'e's a bloody wall fish, Cush! Get 'im! Get 'im! *Get 'im!*"

Bird was so excited, she was leaping up and down, screaming with the loud, urgent fervor of a front-row rugby fan. "Bring him *in,* Cush!" she screamed again. *"Bring him in!"*

"Take your time," urged the guide. "Take your time. Not too much pressure. Gotta go slow. Can't muscle the big ones."

"What do I do if he swims down with the current?" Cush asked.

"Two choices," said the guide. "One is you can stay here and lose him. The other is that you run downstream after him."

Well, just then the monster trout finned out into the swiftest part of the Tongariro current, swirled behind the big mid-river boulder, and rocketed downstream toward Lake Taupo. Line screamed off the big fly reel as the distance between Cush and fish lengthened, actually doubling in less than a minute. The longer the line got, the greater the chance the fish would escape. Too many things worked in the fish's favor.

Cush went splashing after the giant trout, climbing and spilling over dry boulders and slippery moss-slickened rocks to keep up. She kept the rod tip high and the line taut the whole time, which kept the trout from breaking free.

Cush chased the fish 70 yards down the river and into a bend of deep, slow water. The trout slowed down to rest and concoct Escape Plan B while Cush splashed to a shoreside arrival 15 seconds later. This was the Bain Pool, or so read the sign on the riverbank.

Bird, meanwhile, ran back to the lodge as fast as she could, bursting into the lobby in search of Mrs. Haffield.

"Cush's got one! Cush's got one! Bloody big bugger! It's one of *those!*" Bird gasped, pointing to the big trout photos on the wall. "Big as that!" she added, pointing to a giant rainbow hanging on the wall by the fireplace.

"My heavens!" laughed Mrs. Haffield. "Here, honey," she said to Bird as she reached under the register. "Take this and bring me a picture." Mrs. Haffield handed Bird a small camera and Bird took off like a human motocross bike back to the action at the river.

Meanwhile, Paul unfurled his medium-sized rosewood landing net and held it at the ready in his right hand. He calmly urged Cush to bow her rod sideways toward the shallow pebble shoal and slowly sweep the rod tip—and the fish with it—toward shore. Cush did as she was told and the tired trout, a big jack male, slid on his side from the deep water toward the shallows.

The guide netted him quickly on the first try, head first, and struggled to one-handedly hold the big fish aloft. Through the black mesh of the net, both Cush and Bird could clearly see the trout's mouth was opening and closing, gasping for air. Paul quickly lowered the fish into calm shallow water while Bird scrambled across the rocks for pictures.

Cush just stared in awe.

"My word!" Cushla said excitedly. "I got 'im, didn't I? Fair and square? I bloody well got 'im!"

"Fair and square," smiled the guide. "This fish weighs ten pounds if he weighs an ounce. A beautiful fish. The trout of a lifetime for most."

"Ten *pounds!*" echoed Cush. "Ten *pounds!* He looks ten *tons* to me! How bloody beautiful—The Father of All Trout!"

Bird's scream announced the arrival of the paparazzi. She took six photos of Cush holding the trout, plus four more of Cush and Paul with the trout. The guide carefully kept the giant trout in the water and facing the current between shots.

After the photos, the guide asked Cush what she wanted to do with the fish. "Let him go, please," she said. "If we let him go, he can live forever. At least I hope he will."

Paul held the big trout with two hands, his right gently cradling the trout's belly behind its gills and his left wrapped around the base of the huge fish's tail. He pointed the old trout into the current to help flow resuscitating oxygen through its gills, and tail-swished the trout back and forth until a trout-supplied surge of power propelled the fish out of Paul's cradling hold and back to freedom.

"Bye, Mr. Fish!" waved Bird.

Cush gave the guide a hug and said, "Thank you." Paul appreciated that. Guides got blamed for losing a lot more fish than they got hugged for catching them.

The adventure now over, Paul squatted down to rinse and wash his hands in the clear, cold river water. He told Cush that trout was the biggest he'd seen come out of the Tongariro in the last six months.

With that, the happy trio trudged their way back to the lodge. Bird told Mrs. Haffield she'd go two miles into Turangi to get another roll of film so they could get these photos developed when they got to Wellington. Mrs. Haffield laughed and said the film was on the house if they promised to send an enlargement to hang on the lodge wall.

The deal was sealed and, within a week, dart champion and trout angler Cushla Wimsett and her smiling face adorned the wall of fame at the Tongariro Lodge. Cush co-starred in a beautiful photograph with her smiling guide and a trout so big, the Tongariro River's water level dropped three full inches when they finally netted him and hoisted him aloft. Or so Bird said whenever she re-told the story.

In the morning, the girls chugged on to Wellington.

And there, in the hotel room, they'd come fact to face with a two-year-old mystery.

"MWYADAETM"

When the girls reached Wellington the following day and started to unpack their suitcases, Cush put her clothes away and was ready to toss her travel bag under the nightstand when she felt something in the side zipper compartment. Curious, she unzipped the pouch.

Fishing around, she extracted a manila envelope holding a small white box no more than three inches square. She opened it, looked inside, breathed "Oh my *God*," and slowly pulled out a gold necklace with an inch-long gold rectangular charm. "Bird!" she called urgently. "Bird! C'mere quick, will ya?"

Bird rocketed out of the bathroom and saw Cush holding the necklace. She was also studying an inscription. Differing patterns of raised bumps were inside each of nine little rectangles, just like the ones Truck wrote on his business card the very first day they met.

"What does it say?" asked Bird. "I can't believe that self-centered boyfriend of yours would actually do something nice for a change. Jewelry, no less!"

"It was in my bag, and it doesn't say anything," Cush said. "It's just a bunch of letters. And it's not from Timothy."

"It's not?" asked Bird impatiently. "That's a relief. It's not Timothy. *Not Timothy?* But if it's not *him*, then who? And what're the letters? What's it say?"

Cush recited the letters, slowly and in order: "M, W, Y, A, D, A, E, T, M."

"Mwyadaetm?" asked Bird. "What the bloomin' bloody 'ell is a Mwyadaetm? Sounds like a bloody Maori Indian war chant."

"It's from Truck. I've seen the letters before. He sent me a carrier pigeon letter after the wedding with the exact same message. I'm just not sure what the bloody letters mean. It's an acronym for something, but I'm not sure what. I need to figure it out."

"*We* need to figure it out," corrected Bird. "It sounds Latin. Or pig Latin."

"Well, feel free to figure it out," replied Cush. "I welcome all assistance."

Bird held the necklace in her right hand and gently rubbed her fingers over the gold. "A carrier pigeon? You never told me about a carrier pigeon. He sent you a carrier pigeon letter? All the way from the States? That's one bloody determined bird!"

"Yes, it was," laughed Cush. "You should've seen it beg me not to send a reply!"

Bird laughed again as she studied the necklace, turning it over and over.

"No," Cush added, "it wasn't from the States. He sent it from Great Barrier."

Bird studied the raised bumps and looked at Cush. "What's this?" she asked. "What are the bumps?"

"Braille. It's the same message in Braille. Truck knows I know Braille. He knew my little brother went blind before he died. He's lost friends the same way, too. We even talked about it."

"Wow," said Bird. "Wait 'til Phoebe and Mitzi hear about this! How long you figure it was in your bag?"

"Two years," Cush sighed. "Two bloody years. Ever since Miami. Gloria Estefan's restaurant. The envelope was waiting for him. It even had his name on it."

"Two years?" asked Bird disbelievingly. "Two *years*? A guy gives you a handmade gold necklace and you don't thank him for two bloody *years?* Good luck *now,* princess. Can I listen in when you ring him?"

"My God, I can't call him," Cush said. "I'm supposed to know what this means. He must think I'm the rudest person on earth. No wonder he didn't call me.

"Oh, dammit! This is much too complicated," Cush continued uncertainly. "When we get home, maybe we can think of something."

Bird offered little sympathy. "Well, if it took two bloody years to *find* the silly thing, we'll die of old age before you figure it out. Figure out what the bloody thing means, will you?"

The tournament Cush had been so looking forward to suddenly seemed to be more of a distraction than a competition. Her mind was a whirling blender of convoluted thoughts, few of which related to competition.

After a lousy Friday opening round that dropped her into the challenge bracket, Cush wore the new necklace Saturday and threw much better. Sunday, she finished third overall, losing her semifinal match on a final-dart bounce-out.

By the time Bird dropped her off in Cambridge, Cush had a strong feeling that it was time to pull the plug and split up with Timothy. If it wasn't there, it wasn't there—and if it wasn't there *now,* it damn sure wouldn't be there five, ten, or 20 years down the road.

Cush arrived back at the farm still wearing the necklace. When asked what it meant, she simply replied, "It's a secret." And, she reasoned, technically it was.

As soon as she returned home to Auckland, Bird had the Posse's telephone lines sizzling. The gold necklace, and what to do about it, dominated several long-distance discussions. But after a week of detective work, the Posse members remained stumped. They didn't have a foggy clue *what* the bloody initials stood for.

Everybody but Cush wanted her to pick up the telephone, dial long distance, and find out. No *way* she was going to do that.

A couple of months later, about the same time Truck was at the Boise Airport buying a sack of spuds and mulling over quitting his job for the 10,000[th] time, Cush was back in the farm's observation tower watching pregnant mares. Eleven were in birthing paddocks surrounding her. All of them were fatter than hippos after a buffet lunch. It was a three-quarter moon and Cush had a hunch it would be a busy evening for the delivery team.

As Cush sat alone in the tower, she thought of many things: the ups and downs of her life to this point, the loss of her mother and brother, the pride she felt now that her father had booted the bottle and found a passion in life worth pursuing. She also wondered what would happen to her—how her future would unfold and how it eventually might even end.

Cush repeatedly fingered the Braille side of her necklace and silently mouthed each of the nine letters, in order. She felt strangely sure that if she rubbed the letters long and often enough, the message would come to her like a genie from a bottle.

As the sun set and temperature dropped, Sir Patrick climbed up the wooden steps to join Cush. He brought a blanket in case she'd forgotten her jacket, which she had. While the two sat there, Sir Patrick's visage ever vigilant, his intuition told him something was troubling his young charge. So, assuming he was right, Sir Patrick asked Cush what was on her mind.

She spent the next 29 minutes working Sir Patrick backward in time from when she had found the necklace in Wellington all the way back to the green-haired dart tossing in the Horse & Trap. She even told him all about the day in the meadow.

Midway through Cush's story, Sir Patrick blinked twice and looked cross-eyed at the point of his nose. He was almost rooting for a birthing incident, just to slow down this little girl's motor. But no mares obliged.

So, after listening to Cush for half an hour, Sir Patrick finally spoke. "If all of this is carrying on inside you," he said gently, "then perhaps it's time for you to decide what to do to make it go away."

"What do you mean?" Cush asked.

"Well, the way I see it, you have two choices. One . . . You can do *nothing*. Or, two . . . You can do *something*.

"If you do nothing, you'll regret it for the rest of your life. And if you choose to do something, regardless how it turns out, you will have lived your life the way you thought best. In my case, I can't imagine my life without Justine and our animals. I've made a lot of my own luck, but a lot of the courage along the way came from her confidence in me and in us and in our dream together.

"And I will add one more piece of fatherly advice since you didn't ask," Sir Patrick said with a smile. "Realizing the dreams of two is a lot more fun than chasing the lonely dreams of one."

Cush sat listening. She stared off at the far distant paddock, pretending to watch the mare Starflower Princess half-shadowed by a corner spotlight. She knew it was Starflower Princess, but couldn't really see her. Cush had too much water in her eyes— tears that wanted to flow south but hung undecided on her soft rosy cheeks.

"Want to know what I think you ought to do?" asked Sir Patrick, trying to jump-start the conversation again.

"What?" asked Cush quietly.

"I think that tomorrow morning you need to take a one-hour break—with the boss's permission of course—and drive into town, park at the corner of Victoria and Duke, and have a breakfast scone and a cup of coffee at one of the outside tables at the Coffee Pot."

"But what good will that do?" replied Cush. "How will that help anything?"

"While you're having your breakfast," continued Sir Patrick, "stare across the street at the travel agency. Your answer, whatever it is, will come to you by the second half of the scone. You'll know to either cross that street or come on back here and help deliver four-legged babies.

"Your answer, Cush, is in the scone."

"Will the scone tell me what to tell Timothy?" asked Cush ruefully.

Sir Patrick laughed. "You're overestimating the power of a scone," he replied. "But the way I see things concerning you and Timothy, again you've got two choices: You can either play a little poker and tell him as little as possible, or tell him what you've decided in your heart and why. Whichever you pick, you owe it to him to tell him in person, face to face. That way you'll be certain to make the right choice for all the right reasons. You'll also say the right thing.

"Just don't tell him you like him as a friend. Men hate that line."

With that, Sir Patrick climbed out of the tower to make a few phone calls and check on Zabeel and the other stallions. As he disappeared behind the tall row of border trees, Cushla remembered that the whole time she was growing up, she thought she had no dad. Here, in the cicada-buzzing semi-darkness of a peaceful Cambridge night, she suddenly realized she was lucky enough to have two.

Her mind clear, Cush went back to watching mares and thinking about how little of life was planned and how much of it was guided by chance. She sat wrapped in the warm blue wool blanket, not knowing what the balance of the night would bring. But Cush certainly felt much better about the morning. The sunrise, she thought, would deliver some answers.

— ◆ —

Cush awoke without her alarm at five o'clock and finished her early-morning chores by nine. She took an hour break and drove ten minutes into Cambridge.

She wasn't much of a scone person—after all, each little briquette weighed seemingly half as much as she did—but she'd been around Sir Patrick long enough to inherit some of his superstitions by sheer osmosis. So, that morning at the Coffee Pot, Cush took no chances. She ordered a coffee and a scone, sat at an outside table, and looked across Victoria Street to Harvey World Travel. She kept staring as she sipped her coffee and nibbled on the scone.

Sir Patrick was right. Cush knew her answer two bites into the first half of her jelly-topped scone. When the travel agency opened at ten o'clock, Jeffrey Franklin Wimsett was its first customer of the day and the only one to book a flight to the U.S.A.

"Oh, God, I hope I'm doing the right thing," she told her dashboard on the way back to the farm. "I've got to be out of my bloomin' mind, but oh, *God* do I hope I'm doing the right thing."

After Cush drove back inside the Cambridge Stud gates and parked in her usual spot, she walked past the full-bodied gravesite and memorial to Sir Tristram, then stepped inside the office. What Sir Patrick had done by taking a chance on Sir Tristram didn't make a lot of sense at the time, either—but it certainly worked out well in the end.

Then again, Sir Patrick had been a whole lot surer about Sir T than Cush was about her butterfly-driven shopping spree at the travel agency.

Sir Patrick was on the telephone as Cush stuck her head in his office doorway. Phone flush to his ear, Sir Patrick quizzed her with a wavering thumbs up, thumbs down motion. Cush paused, wiggled her thumb sideways with uncertainty, and dramatically jammed it high the air. Then she stepped quietly to his desk and placed a folded paper napkin next to Sir Patrick's adding machine. Unfolding it, Sir Patrick found a half-eaten scone. He broke into a huge grin and gave her a thumbs up right back.

Cush left without either one of them having said a word. She wished she had Sir Patrick's sheer blind confidence. He had it in everything he did.

As Cush walked through the back office door and over toward the broodmares, her breakfast-time bravado was rapidly giving way to doubt. Cush felt like fate was sucking her into a jet engine of vulnerability.

One way or another—for better or worse—*something* was going to happen.

$\mathcal{W}$indow Seat or Aisle?

If one plane flies east 550 miles an hour and another plane flies west 550 miles an hour, what happens when both land in the same place at the same time?

That depends. If they land at separate concourses, then nothing might happen. But if they land within minutes of each other at adjacent gates at Los Angeles International Airport, well, anything can happen. Fate intervenes and plays volleyball with destiny.

Determined to make some changes in his life, Truck Roberts made a long-distance call to New Zealand at noon on October 24. Mountain's phone rang at eight o'clock in the morning on October 25. He was face-first in a bowl of cereal, having kissed his lovely bride just minutes before as she left the apartment to go to work.

"Truck, baby! What it *izzzzzz!*" bellowed Mountain into the mouthpiece when he recognized Truck's customary "Yo, Buttwhistle" salutation. "What the hell's happenin,' buddy?" Mountain yelled back. "You comin' to visit?"

The men had a long talk for men—nearly four minutes. They spoke of married life, women in general, what a pain in the ass work was, the American and New Zealand sporting scenes, trout fishing, the pluses and minuses of life on foreign soil, world events, Mountain's daily craving for a good cup of his sadly missed Folger's coffee, and, in passing, mutual friends like Bird and Mitzi and the other remaining Posse member, Miss Cushla Wimsett, now of Cambridge.

"Cush? No, she ain't married," said Mountain. "I haven't had to wear a rented tux duct-taped together, so I know she ain't married. Last I heard, she was still engaged with no date to that horse-buyin' guy. She's still workin' at Cambridge Stud, too. That much I *do* know.

"Phoebe's got her number. You want it? No? Well, if you need it, she's got it.

"Oh. You're coming over? Hey man! Beautimous baby! That's great! When? Well, make your reservations and let me know.

"No. I won't. If you don't want her knowin' you were askin' about Cush, I won't mention it. She chews on that stuff like a cow and her cud.

"See you when you get here. Yo, brother." With that, he ended the call.

As sneaky as men tend to be from time to time, they rarely wake early enough to outfox their partners. And on this very morning, not an hour before while Mountain was lathering up in the shower, Phoebe answered a phone call from, of all places, Cambridge.

It was Cush. The girls exchanged ritualistic greeting squeals, then knuckled down to brass tacks. "I'm sure he's not married, Cush," said Phoebe matter-of-factly. "I'd know that for sure. And no, he's not that, either. Of *that* I'm certain. He's *definitely* not gay."

The girls talked until Phoebe heard the upstairs shower water shut off, signifying a clean Bigfoot was emerging to shake like a re-triever and obey the fashion commands she spread out on the bed. Phoebe didn't know until they were married that Mountain was col-orblind. No wonder he'd always dressed like a circus performer.

"Well," said Phoebe as she prepared to hang up, "call me if you need me. Nothing I'd like better than some international adventure and intrigue.

"No, I won't tell him. Good luck, OK? Love you. Bye."

A few minutes later, the heavy footsteps of Phoebe's squeaky-clean paramour lumbered into the kitchen and plopped down at the breakfast table. He poured some fiber-laced cereal. The stuff tasted okay with milk but, man, did it sometimes put up a fight on the other end. Phoebe told him to eat it, so Mountain just shut up and did.

And so, as Phoebe drove to town and Mountain laughed out loud at the comics in the morning newspaper, Truck Roberts began planning a trip to New Zealand. His million frequent flyer miles finally came in handy. The next day, he'd be on a United flight—two flights actually—headed west to Auckland.

And Cushla Wimsett, who'd booked her ticket at Harvey World Travel three weeks before and called Phoebe with hopes of learning a last-minute reason not to go, packed up her suitcase and plopped it by the door of her small apartment. Sir Patrick promised Cush he'd save her living quarters for her until she told him otherwise.

She exhaled deeply as she flopped backward on her bed. She stared vacantly at the ceiling. Again, she rubbed the Braille letters on her necklace and hoped for the one trillionth time she was doing the right thing.

The next day, she'd be on a United flight, two flights actually, headed east to Colorado.

Smogville

Cush couldn't believe L.A.'s blanketing layer of orange haze as her plane banked into its arrival slot behind a Delta jet in a long parade of landing aircraft. The air in New Zealand was so pure, she'd forgotten the rest of the world wasn't the same way. Hawaii, where she'd changed planes and cleared customs, was much better than this. Cush wrinkled her nose. She despised pollution.

Truck meanwhile, had made the Denver-L.A. connection a hundred times and didn't even bother looking out the window as the Boeing 737 banked and queued in line two planes behind a Delta jet from Atlanta. He was oblivious to the smog, which was as much a part of L.A. as the Dodgers.

Cush's plane landed and taxied to a halt at gate 78-A.

Two minutes later, Truck's plane landed and taxied to a halt at gate 78-B.

Since he wasn't trapped in coach, Truck was able to get off the plane quickly. He had a 50-minute layover before boarding his connection to Auckland and was long gone by the time people in coach finished jostling for position and clubbing each other with swinging baggage retrieved from overhead compartments. It was always a battling gauntlet back there, like a fight scene from "Braveheart." He would rather mow a lawn with his teeth than sit in coach.

Truck made a beeline from 78-B across the concourse and ducked into the men's room. While he was in there, Cushla karated her way out of coach, exited out of gate 78-A, quickly walked across the carpeted corridor, and ducked into the women's room.

And there the two sat, four feet apart, separated by a tiled wall.

Truck finished first, emerged, and paused, then veered to his right, opting to to kill time in the United 1-K frequent flyer lounge. He walked directly in front of the women's room entrance five seconds before Cush emerged—maybe even a count of just *a one-a, an' a two-a, an' a three-a* according to the old bandleader Lawrence Welk.

Cush paused at the women's room entryway, got her bearings, and turned left, cutting directly in front of the men's room entrance. She purchased a newspaper en route to her connecting gate and sat down to wait. Cush had half an hour before boarding. Her mind was flooded with a thousand things, none of which seemed related.

When it came time to reboard, Cush opted for another nervous pit stop in the women's room. While she was in there, in the same stall as before, Truck strode past the women's room en route to his Auckland connection at gate 82.

Truck passed by just as Cush stood in front of the sink to wash her hands and check her makeup. When she stepped back outside, Truck was on the blind side of the s-curve en route to his gate. He was 40 yards away, but might as well have been 8,000 miles.

So, as Truck Roberts climbed the steps up into the business class section of the mammoth Boeing 747 bound for New Zealand, less than 100 yards away Cushla Wimsett was kung-fuing her way back to the rear of coach and a window seat on a much smaller 737 headed for Denver.

Minutes later, after the planes waited one behind the other on the taxiway, both flights were airborne. Once over the Pacific, they soon peeled off in opposite directions.

Judging by the looks of things, Dame Fate the Puppeteer had just decided that a little more adventure remained to be sprinkled upon the lives of both.

The Courtship Dance of Two-Legged Mice and Stoats

Cush arrived in Denver with basically one thought on her mind. Over and over, she asked herself, "What the hell am I doing here?" Even her talking practice, where she rehearsed what she was going to say, wasn't going well. It was never good when an argument broke out and you were the only one talking.

Cush decided she had two choices. One would be to call Truck and tell him she was "just passing through town" and thought she'd just call to "say hi." This seemed to be the logical approach, the left-brained approach. He could then say "hi" back and hang up or invite her over for wild sex and the rest of her life.

The other option was more dramatic. She'd just show up at his door. Thank him for the necklace in person. Tell him she was no good at writing letters and thought a phone call too impersonal. Then he'd invite her in, they'd have lots of lighthearted talk over coffee and a perfectly wonderful time unless, of course, he had a girlfriend and she beat Cush up and left her in a puddle of blood on the living room floor.

This latter choice, obviously, took the courage of a thousand gladiators. And since Cush was exhausted from the trip and felt the courage of one midget gladiator trainee, she voted instead for a hotel room and a good night's sleep.

The same options would be waiting in the morning.

Truck, meanwhile, was snoring. Somewhere over the Pacific, the mental fatigue of all his talking practice—what he would say when he saw Cush—finally wore him out.

The way Truck saw it, he could do one of two things—three, if you counted chickening out and slithering back home. One was to just call Cush up out of the blue, tell her he happened to be in the country, was "just passing through," and thought he'd call to say "hi" and see how she was doing.

The other was to just show up at Cambridge Stud and spill his guts.

Right before he dozed off, Truck decided that the former strategy was the prudent thing to do and the latter required the bravery of a blindfolded rodeo bull rider. Since Truck's testicles tingled at the mere memory of his jaunt on Spartacus, he wasn't sold that just showing up at the farm was such a good idea.

His final thought before conking out was that maybe he could think up a better option in the morning.

The Next Day and Two Days Later

Cush checked out of her airport hotel, rented a car, and used the computerized kiosk to print out driving directions to Truck's house. She looked at this mission as an emotional root canal. Some days, you've just got to wake up, tug and tie your shoelaces tightly, and do what you've got to do. This day clearly fell into that category.

"The sooner this is over, the better," she thought to herself. Blind with determination, Cush followed the directions south on I-225 for 29 miles, went east on the Orchard Road exit, and two minutes later pulled up in front of Truck's house. She looked at the number by the door, the mailbox, the curb, and her directions. They all matched. Then she double-checked the address she'd gotten from Phoebe. It matched, too. For better or worse, Cush was here. For better or worse, she was doing what she knew was right. For better or worse, it was time to go headfirst to her destiny. She fingered her necklace for luck, exhaled deeply, marched up, rang the doorbell, closed her eyes, and courageously waited.

Nobody was home.

Cush rang the doorbell twice and no one answered. As soon as she pushed the bell the first time, she wanted to dive back in the car and squeal wheels, fleeing at full speed. But she stood there, forcing herself to wait for a door to open that never did. When she rang the bell the second time, she could clearly hear chimes echoing the hallways on the inside of the brown double-doors.

Nothing. No sign of life. No newspaper in the drive or mail in the mailbox. Maybe he was dead on the kitchen floor. Maybe he saw her through a curtain and did himself in with a steak knife. Maybe he saw her and escaped out the back door.

Cautiously, Cush skirted the outside of the home, trying to look normal while peeking inside each room. Still no signs of life. Better yet, no bodies on the kitchen floor. The furnishings looked dreadful, which meant there probably was no wife, girlfriend, or gay lover. Cush considered such awful design taste a moral victory in itself. At least she didn't have to worry about getting punched out by a girl like Ben did in Queenstown.

Stymied, Cush retreated, drove over to nearby Park Meadows Mall, and used a pay phone to call Mitzi at her office in Miami. Mitzi held the phone out and looked at it in disbelief when Cush told her where she was and what she was doing.

"You can't just show up!" Mitzi cried out.

"Why bloody not?" asked Cush defensively.

"Because people don't do that. Women don't do that. Black widow spiders don't even do that. They spin webs first," scolded Mitzi. *"Then* they invite the guy over."

"Oh yeah?" Cush retorted. "Well, I bloody well think that anyone who flies halfway 'round the bloomin' world is automatically entitled to do whatever they bloody well please!"

"Did it ever dawn on you that maybe he's at work? Look— you stay put in Denver. I'll find him and figure something out. In the meantime, go check in at the Brown Palace Hotel. I'll have

Emma make your arrangements. It's downtown—everyone knows it. Very nice, very famous. Been there a hundred years. We did a huge event in Vail last winter and I stayed there on the way home. Loved the place.

"Go to the Brown Palace, take a hot bath, and have some tea. Right now, you're delirious. I'll call you there later today when I know more." Then Mitzi said goodbye and quickly hung up the phone to avoid a debate.

On her way back out of the mall, Cush shopped the sale rack at Foley's department store, then got in the car and did as Mitzi instructed. She drove downtown, checked into the beautiful old hotel, hung around, had a hot tea and bubble bath—and waited. Maybe Mitzi *was* right. Maybe she had some sort of brain fever or delirium from a tick bite and could no longer think straight. Maybe that's what it was.

Truck, meanwhile, had landed in Auckland and picked up his rental car at the Hertz counter. He'd packed light, no fishing rods, and was able to roll off with his stuff and go quickly. He hadn't told Lloyd or Mountain what he was doing because explaining things that had no explanation was not one of his specialties.

Truck knew where Cambridge was, since he'd ridden past it several times on his various trips with Lloyd. He didn't have an address for the farm, but figured he wouldn't need one. Every local townsman knows where famous Thoroughbred farms are. Anybody in Lexington could tell you where Claiborne or Calumet or Overbook was. Anyone in Cambridge should be able to tell him where to find Cambridge Stud.

Cambridge proved to be a beautiful town, covered with shade-giving leafy trees down every side street. It was clean, too. A quiet and orderly little place, with many signs and references to the horse industry.

Truck opted for a bite to ease his nervous rumbling tummy and drove down Victoria Street. He stopped in front of Fran's Café where he grabbed a hefty sandwich and slice of homemade carrot cake thick enough to calm the Easter Bunny. He ate on the small patio out back, rehearsing his verbal script for the 10,000[th] time. His spiel sounded stupid, and he knew it. As he chewed, he wished he could fire his writers.

For the first time, Truck seriously doubted the logic of his actions.

What the hell was he doing here? *Really* doing here?

What did he want? What did he expect?

What made him think she gave so much as a possum's foggy bottom about what he thought or how he felt?

And what if he told her he had something important to say, spilled his guts, and she started laughing? Or even worse, what if she just sat there listening and cocked her head sideways—looking at him like a dog watching television? Then what?

"Too many questions," Truck muttered to himself. He stared at the potted flowers eight feet away as he slowly chewed his cake. "I must be nuts. I must be out of my friggin' mind."

But plutonium pebbles of courage can sometimes be found in anyone's shoe and Truck was no exception. He got directions. Sir Patrick's farm was close, just ten minutes away.

A jolting flood of nervousness washed through him when he drove up and saw the three-sided green and yellow Cambridge Stud sign above the thick hedgerow. It advertised four stallions, including Zabeel.

The electric gates opened slowly when Truck reached the wrought-iron double entryway guarding the farm's main entrance. Cambridge Stud's logo, a large *C* encircling a smaller *s*, was on the center of each half of the wrought-iron gate. The gates parted and peeled open. Truck waited, then slowly drove in. He was petrified.

The grounds were immaculate. It was a beautiful but short drive up the tree-lined black asphalt lane to the office. Truck thought it looked much like Magnolia Lane at The Masters golf tournament in Augusta, Georgia.

At the head of the drive, Truck saw a large horseshoe-shaped grave and monument to Sir Patrick's legendary stallion, Sir Tristram. A four-foot-high marble wall 40-feet long bordered the left side of Sir T's burial plot. Affixed were plaques with the names of all his champion racing offspring on one side and all his great broodmares on the other.

Truck parked to the left, inhaled deeply, and reminded himself the same thing he reminded himself every time he found himself in a nervous spot: No matter what happened, a billion Chinese just wouldn't care.

With stiff legs, he walked toward the office doorway, determined to stare his life's quixotic destiny right square in its astigmatismed eye. Halfway there, he'd already forgotten every word of what he was going to say.

Truck twisted opened the unlocked office door and stepped inside. He didn't think Cush worked inside, but figured he'd better announce himself first. Sir Patrick's office was just to the left. Hogan's door was open but he wasn't there.

A woman shuffling some invoices asked if she could be of assistance. Truck told her he was a friend of Cushla Wimsett and stopped by to say "hello."

"Cushla? Oh, I *am* sorry," the woman replied with a smile. "I'm afraid Cushla is out of town." The woman turned to another woman at a desk nearby. "Corrina, do you know when Cush will be back?"

"All I know is she went on a bit of a walkabout involving a young man she had a keen interest in," Corrina replied. "She'll be gone a week as I recall. Sir Patrick may know more of the details.

I could possibly find him for you if you wish. He's somewhere on the farm."

The moment Truck heard the words "involving a young man" the rest of the message faded to fuzzy background noise. Time froze like the crust of Antarctica and the air leaked out of Truck like a bike tire running over a box of spilled roofing nails. His sigh was nearly audible and his shoulders visibly sagged. Gone in a flash were the million hopes that fueled this trip.

His stomach hurt, too, but this was a new kind of hurt. A ball of confusion knotted tighter than it had ever been sat right where his carrot cake used to be. The knot had company, too. Those damn little butterflies fluttered in a thousand directions, every one of them looking for a one-way ticket out.

It had never dawned on him that Cush might not be there.

"No," Truck slowly replied with a forced smile. "That's OK. No need to disturb anyone. I apologize for interrupting your day. I should have called first. My mistake. Would've saved you the time and bother."

"No bother," said the first woman. "Sorry she's not here. I'm sure she'd love to say hello. Should I leave word on her return who called?"

"No need," said Truck. "She probably wouldn't remember even if you did."

And with that, Truck stiffly walked outside. He was alone again. More alone than all the other times added together. He was Novocain-numb all over when he dropped back inside the car. A billion Chinese might not care, but he sure as hell did. This was his life—and what a friggin' mess it had become.

A week. A whole damn week. He'd be back in Denver in a week. "Dammitall!" he hollered, pounding the steering wheel with an open right palm. "How the hell could I be so stupid? Stupid! Stupid! *Stupid!*"

Finding that point hard to argue, Truck left the farm and Cambridge. It was two more hours south to Turangi. Assuming there was room at the Tongariro Lodge, he could be knee-deep in the river by mid-afternoon. He'd sort it all out there. Maybe if he played his cards right, he could slip back home in a few days and no one would even know he'd been gone.

Cush grabbed the bedside telephone in her room at the Brown Palace on its third ring. It was five o'clock Denver time and Mitzi was calling from Miami. "I left a message for Ben to call me when he got in," Mitzi said. "Ben will know if Truck's in town or will be able to find out quickly enough. I'll just tell him I might be out tomorrow or the next day and was wondering if Truck would be around. As soon as I hear something, I'll call you back. And in the meantime, honey, don't do anything dumb, OK?"

Cush tacked into the wind with a little different question. "What day is today? The date I mean. What's the date?"

"The 28th. Why?"

"Even if he's out of town, I know he'll be home on the 31st," Cush said confidently.

"Why do you say that?" Mitzi asked.

"October 31st is Halloween in America, isn't it? He once told me his favorite day of the year was Halloween since it was the only day of the year you were allowed to make as many children happy as you chose. Every kid had a different birthday, and some had different kinds of Christmases, but all kids shared the same Halloween.

"Those were his exact words. I still remember them very clearly because they surprised me when I heard them. I had no idea he liked kids so much.

"Truck wouldn't miss Halloween," Cush added. "He'd never miss Halloween," she repeated. "I'm sure of it."

"Hmmm . . . you're pretty smart for a dart-thrower," laughed Mitzi. "But promise me you'll stay smart enough to not do anything crazy, OK? I'll call you later."

"Nothing stupid. Promise. Pinky swear and cross my heart. Thanks, Mitz. Love you."

Cush slowly returned the phone into its bedstand cradle. She flopped backward on her bed, arms wide on both sides, and stared at the ceiling.

"What the bloody 'ell am I *doin'!*" she yelled at the plaster. "*Aaaarrggggggghhhh!*" she screamed. "I gotta exercise or do something or I'll go flippin' *nuts!* I gotta get out of here and go for a friggin' run."

Six miles and one hour later, Cush had calmed down. She showered, changed, and went down for dinner alone in the Ship Tavern, a quiet pub tucked away in a corner of the hotel lobby.

It was there, fingering the Braille dots on her necklace for the thousand-and-twenty-ninth time, scribbling intently on a cocktail napkin during an after-dinner cabernet, that suddenly Cush smiled. Her smile broadened so wide, it nearly touched both ears. Happiness flooded excitedly throughout her whole body, from the tips of her freshly painted toenails to the auburn ends of her freshly blow-dried hair.

"*M, W, Y, A, D, A, E, T, M!*" she said aloud. She repeated the letters again, only this time a bit faster and louder. And finally, a third time—even faster and louder yet. Cush's left index finger jabbed the napkin in synchronicity with each letter's recital.

"*I've got it!*" she yelled out loud, excitedly laughing. "Bloody 'ell, *I've GOT it!*" Cush threw both arms high in the air, like a boxer winning a fight by knockout.

The Ship Tavern, filled with 16 tables of diners and another dozen railbirds at the bar, broke into a spontaneous cheer for the happy woman dining all alone.

"She got it, by God!" hollered one old man at the counter, hoisting his drink aloft.

"Here, here!" cheered the gang at the bar. "The little lady's got it!"

Flushed with two-thirds as much excitement as embarrassment, Cush re-checked her napkin again, letter by letter. "Bloody all, man, I've got it! *I have bloody well got it!*" she told herself in a husky whisper.

"OK, OK" she whispered softly, "I've got it. Now what? Now that I've got it—what do I do with it?"

Suddenly, deep in the recesses of her churning brain, tucked away in a file labeled "Common Sense & Good Advice," Cush's memory fingers thumbed quickly through the archive of her life's experiences before suddenly stopping at the sage counsel of Sir Patrick: "And if you do *nothing*, you'll regret it for the rest of your life," he'd said.

"And if you choose to do *something*, regardless how it turns out, you will have lived your life the way you thought best."

Cush broke into another big smile. She was going to do something, all right. She signed for her dinner, scooped up the three paper napkins covered with scribbles, rode the old elevator up to room 426, and spent the rest of the evening hatching her plan.

Things weren't going nearly that well for Truck. He finally arrived at the Tongariro Lodge, but it was full of corporate guys pretending to be working on an "executive retreat." Some might call it a businessman's safari where the men head into dangerous fishing jungles armed primarily with scotch and water.

The Tongariro suggested Truck overnight at the Creel Lodge, also on the river, about a mile and a half upstream. On the plus side, the famous Major Jones pool was out the back door. On the minus side, he'd have to go rent all of his fishing gear from the Sporting Life shop in Turangi Town Centre.

Under cloudy skies, Truck got in two hours of fishing before dark. He missed his only take when the trout chose the moment Truck lit his cigar to take the fly. "Dammit!" he fumed, as his fingertips fumbled and dropped a fat Cuban cigar into the swift river current. "I swear *to God* they do that on purpose!"

Truck opted back over to the Tongariro Lodge for dinner. He loved the place and the food was always great. Expensive, but great. Since the lodge was full, the dining room was crowded. Instead of getting to spread out at a table for four, Truck had to sit at a half-table set for two against the pine-paneled wall.

As luck would have it, Truck had just finished chewing his fourth venison medallion and was chasing it down with a robust Hawke's Bay merlot when he glanced at the framed fish picture hanging on the wall right above his head.

"Big trout," he thought as the wine swished around in his mouth. "Monster."

He looked closer. "Hmm," he mused, "caught by a girl. Good looker, too.

"Son-of-a-*bitch!*" he sputtered loudly as the wine choked his windpipe, "It's Cush! My God, *it's Cush!*"

Truck blinked twice and squinted at the photo again. It was still her. And it was still a big trout. A monster—far bigger than any he'd ever caught. From the looks of her, the photo looked recent. Truck stood up and scrutinized it closely from a foot away, his mouth as wide open as the trout's.

"What the hell was *she* doing here?" he thought to himself. "That must be her rich new boyfriend," he surmised, studying the handsome man in the photo with his arm happily around her.

"Dam-*nation!* First Timothy, now this guy. And this guy must be a skilled fly-fisherman, too! Money, horses, giant trout—no *wonder* she's gone off with him! Where the *hell* does she find these guys?

"Damn! Sheet, faddle, *duck!*" he ranted. "I can't friggin' believe it! That rich son-of-a-gun is probably proposing to her right now and handing over a diamond the size of a tennis ball."

Suddenly Truck wasn't hungry and wanted to leave. Quickly. "Check please," he called with a half smile and fake sophisticated pleasantry.

Truck drove quickly back to the Creel Lodge and didn't even turn on the television. Everything he touched was turning to methane and tonight more monsters were hiding under his bed than there had *ever* been when he was a kid. He even pulled the covers up over his head, praying the monsters of evil leave him alone until morning.

Truck had another day and a half to fish before driving back to Auckland to catch his airplane home. He awoke to a steady rain, which fit right in with the rest of the trip so far. Truck flipped on the morning weather report. Heavy rain showers blanketed the entire North Island.

"Figures," he said to himself. "Aw, hell—what's the point?" Truck bagged fishing and checked out. He had no clue what he'd say to Mountain or Lloyd, so he called neither. Truck drove slowly back to Auckland in the rain, through the steaming thermal mud pools and geysers of Rotorua, and north past Cambridge. There was no real reason to hurry. The windshield wipers were good enough company.

Meanwhile, back in Denver, Mitzi woke Cush at eight in the morning, calling from Miami to tell her Ben had called but didn't know where Truck was. Ben had reached Truck's message machine also, so Ben assumed he was out of town.

When Mitzi asked him when he thought Truck might return, Ben said it would definitely be by Halloween. "The guy is psychotic about Halloween," Ben said. "Never seen anyone like 'im. Carves a pumpkin, buys a ton of candy, stuffs piles of it into those little bags, and acts like John Barrymore every time the doorbell rings. Truck takes it *way* too seriously."

Cush, having stayed up 'til midnight concocting her plan, asked Mitzi to help get Bird and Phoebe to Denver as soon as possible. What she wanted to do required all four of them. They just had to arrive in Denver before Halloween.

"Why not?" was Mitzi's laughing response. "This sounds too good to miss."

An hour later, the phone rang again as Cush came back from breakfast.

"Done," Mitzi said. "They'll both arrive in Denver on the 31st on United 1278 from LAX at 3:57. I'll be in two hours earlier on United 1423, non-stop from Miami. See you then, kiddo. This'll be fun. And remember: Nothing stupid, OK?"

Cush laughed. "Promise! See you the day after tomorrow. I'll be waiting when you land."

Truck killed time in Auckland by shopping in the rain. He overnighted across the street from the Parnell Rose Garden, which featured a million roses of every blooming color and shade invented. He figured that staying across from a nice place would minimize his risk of swan diving off the balcony if one more thing imploded.

He also called United and tried to catch an earlier flight back. No luck, they told him. Not on a free ticket. Truck was still due out the next day on flight 842, at 6:35 p.m., to Los Angeles. He reconfirmed his seat in business class, again upstairs in the 400-seat 747. He was given row 15, aisle seat B. Same butt-lucky seat he flew out on.

Bird and Phoebe, meanwhile, were shopping for new clothes just two blocks from Truck's hotel. According to the itineraries Mitzi's office faxed them, the girls were scheduled to leave tomorrow, on United flight 842, at 6:35 p.m., to Los Angeles.

All Phoebe told Mountain was that Mitzi said it was a personal emergency and that Mitzi had paid for the ticket. That was music to Mountain's ears, all he needed to hear. Like all obedient husbands, he asked no further questions, especially since his wife was traveling on *OPM*—Other People's Money.

And so, at six the following evening, Truck, Bird, and Phoebe boarded a jumbo jet bound for America. Truck, boarding at first call, hiked up the staircase and out of sight. Downstairs, late to the gate, Bird and Phoebe took their seats in the center of the aircraft, two-thirds of the way back in coach. Truck was already buckled in by the time the girls boarded. He had no idea they were on the plane.

All three slept most of the way to Los Angeles.

Twelve hours later, the jumbo jet touched down. Truck, one of the first off the aircraft, quickly cleared customs and walked directly to the United 1-K lounge, the same place he'd foxholed during his layover earlier in the week.

The girls, meanwhile, cattle-carred their way through longer lines and had little time to do much except get their passports stamped before wheeling their roll-ons directly to the gate for Denver. Phoebe and Bird boarded the plane, a smaller 757, and stuffed their carry-ons into the overhead bins above row 23.

While the girls were adjusting their seat belts and getting settled, Truck walked across the tile floor from the 1-K room to the same airplane and boarded as the gate attendant made the flight's final boarding announcement. He had row 1, seat C. A front-row bulkhead with zero leg room. "Perfect, just perfect," he thought. This plane could fly Mach Four and it wouldn't end this trip soon enough to suit him. The only hideous tortures left to complete this global extravaganza were bamboo shoots under his fingernails served with some God-awful in-flight meal featuring couscous and tortured chicken.

Back in coach, Phoebe and Bird were pointing out the window at the L.A. smog, asking each other how people could even breathe that stuff, much less live in it.

The plane took off on time and headed for Denver. In two more hours, Truck Roberts would be back on the ground in his hometown. He'd be at the house by five—an hour or so before the Halloween trick-or-treaters started invading the community like ants at a picnic. "Thank God," Truck thought as he closed his eyes and leaned his head back against his seat rest. "Thank God for Halloween."

As he dozed off, Truck Roberts had no idea that, back in row 22, a pair of mischief-makers was chatting away, too excited to sleep. They knew nothing about the details of this top-secret mission, only that it was important. All Mitzi cryptically said when she called was that it was an emergency—and that the Posse needed to saddle up and head to Colorado immediately. In two more hours, they'd be there.

Whatever happened after that would come from an unchoreographed ballet starring four nutty women—and one very mixed-up man.

Happy Halloween

As Truck was returning to his seat from the toilet, Bird saw him from the back of the plane. He didn't see her and plopped back into his front row seat.

"My God, Phoebe. Look! It's bloody 'im!" Bird said, whapping a ribcage shot to her seatmate and pointing. *"He's on the bloody plane!"*

"Oh, my God," started Phoebe. "What if Mitzi's waiting for us? He'll be the first one out the door!"

"Wouldn't you love that?" said Bird. "And then *we* plow right into the both of them."

Both girls giggled loudly.

In first class, Truck was making a checklist of the stops to make on his way home. Halloween was Christmas practice with all the kids in uniform and Truck would never miss it. If you were a tiny chocoholic, his house was *the* place to be on October 31st.

Thanks to another little twist of luck—also known as inadequate parking—Mitzi and Cush were a few minutes late getting to the terminal as the girls arrived. After Mitzi's plane arrived, the girls decided to swap Cush's small rental car for a bigger one.

Switching cars wasn't that easy due to long lines at the rental counter. When Mitzi finally picked up her black Lincoln Town Car, there was nowhere to park it when they drove up to the terminal. Auckland didn't have these problems. There, it was much more civilized; you simply drove up, parked, and walked inside.

Since Mitzi and Cush couldn't meet the flight at the gate, they eagerly waited at the top of the escalators that passengers ascended after getting off the train connecting three concourses with the main terminal. People started to flood out into the foyer.

Mitzi hadn't taken a step when she saw a familiar face rising up the escalator.

Truck.

"Oh shit," she muttered. There was a time and a place for everything, and right now wasn't either.

Grabbing Cush by the elbow, Mitzi pivoted around and they both hid behind a large fat man.

When Cush peeked around and saw Truck, she simply closed her eyes and whispered, "Oh, my bloody Lord" to herself as she fingered the Braille side of her gold necklace. She felt her legs weaken like soda straws.

Meanwhile, Phoebe and Bird had intentionally hung back so they'd be the last ones off their plane. They took the underground tram to the main terminal and arrived several minutes after Truck had exited.

At the top of the escalator they they saw Mitzi and Cush. After a squealing group hug, the four girls decided to give Truck a much bigger head start.

In the meantime, Truck had rolled his travel bag directly to the top level of the parking garage and hopped in his car. He beat the worst of the rush hour traffic, ran his errands, and stepped inside his front door about five-fifteen. Quickly, he prepared the bags of Halloween candy for the kids, then lined up extra candy bars like grenades in a bunker in expectation of an invasion.

While Truck made last-minute preparations, all around town little kids suited up for one of the biggest nights of the year.

A similar costuming drill was going on in the back seat of Mitzi's Lincoln as it crept south in busy traffic on I-225 from the airport. Halfway to Truck's house, Mitzi pulled off the highway onto the shoulder of the road. All four car doors flew open and the two girls in the back, now in costume, giggled as they ran to the front and slid inside, while the two from the front dove inside the doors in the back seat so they could get changed, too.

The girls in back finished donning their costumes two blocks from the entrance to the street Truck lived on. Cush was driving, since she'd been there before and knew the way.

"Have we got plastic pumpkins?" asked Phoebe. She wanted to make sure she had something to put her candy in—just in case she got any.

"Yes," replied Cush as she slowed for a stop sign and clicked on her turn signal. "You have a bloody pumpkin. It's in the trunk. Can you wait 'til we stop or must you have it now?"

"This'll be fun," interjected Bird, trying to defuse the sparks from Cush's fraying nerves. "I've never done trick-or-treating in America before."

"I need you for just one house," Cush told her as she slowed the car to a stop and put it in park. "After that, you're on your own. Feel free to go all 'round the neighborhood and load up as necessary."

Cush parked the car two doors away from Truck's place in the shadows of a giant pine. All four just sat in silence. They felt like bank robbers armed with carved soap-pistols in those final moments before busting in and attempting the heist.

"Well," Cush finally said in a wavering voice, "we're here."

"Seems that way, doesn't it?" Mitzi replied dryly.

"The porch light's on," offered Bird. "He must be home."

"Look!" hissed Phoebe. "Those little kids are going up the walk."

"Oh my God, oh my God, *oh my God!*" chanted Mitzi excitedly. "Look! The door's opening!"

"There he is!"

Three of the four girls screamed but the car windows were tightly closed so none of the passing trick-or-treaters suspected a murder. Cush simply rested her forehead on the top of the steering wheel and closed her eyes. Suddenly she didn't feel so good.

Truck had opened the front door and did a deep knee bend to talk eye to eye with each small child. The kids selected a bag of candy from the large, outstretched wicker basket. After they turned away and headed down his walk, Truck stepped inside and shut the door.

Routine stuff—except for what was about to happen next.

"This is it," Mitzi urged. "It's show time, girls. Hands together," she said, putting her outstretched hand palm down for the others to pile theirs onto.

"One for one and all for all,

"Together we win, together we fall.

"Forever and ever, always friends –

"The Posse rides together again!"

Then they let out a loud whooping holler.

"*Now,*" Mitzi urged. "Let's go girls! *Let's go get him!*"

"Let's go!" cried Phoebe.

"Let's go!" cried Bird.

"Oh God, I'm gonna puke!" cried Cush.

"No time!" said Mitzi. "Save it for later! Let's go, girls!"

All four car doors flew open, the girls piled out and marched, in-step and in-costume, up Truck Roberts' front walkway. They halted in front of the door, Bird a bit too quickly since Phoebe plowed right into her, nearly knocking her into the shrubs.

"Dammit, Phoebe, watch it will ya?" hissed Bird.

"I'm gonna get sick," warned Cush.

"No time," Mitzi said. "But hold that thought. It's a good excuse to go inside and use the toilet."

Mitzi boldly pushed the doorbell and stepped back. The girls lined up and waited for the door to swing open. Cush closed her eyes, made a wish, and clicked her heels together three times. But the wish wasn't granted. When she reopened her eyes, she was still on Truck's porch and not safely under the covers back in her bed in New Zealand.

Truck was watching television in his easy chair when the doorbell rang. He got up and walked into his foyer, grabbing the straw basket full of candy. Without bothering to look out the peephole, he swung the front door open.

"Trick or Treat!" hollered three white-sheeted trick-or-treaters. As they stood there, shoulder to shoulder, Truck thought their greeting sounded a bit odd—a sort of accented harmony in a New Zealandish sort of way.

Plus, these were really big kids.

Truck wasn't sure what they were, either. They appeared to be disguised as either lumpy mattresses or ghosts. Truck decided they probably were ghosts. What looked like a fourth little goblin was hidden out of sight behind the three big blockers up front.

Truck said nothing. For a moment, he just stared. He wasn't looking at just their sheets—he'd seen ghost costumes with eyeholes cut out before. Nope, he was studying the Brown Palace Hotel logos stamped on all the sheets. These were well-heeled ghosts, whoever they were. These sheets had to cost 50 bucks apiece. Maybe even more. That's when Truck wondered if they really *were* lumpy mattresses.

But then he looked down at the front of each costume. The one on the left had three large and crudely drawn capital letters on it: MWY. The one in the center had three large and crudely drawn letters on it, too. It read: ADA. And the third, on the right, had the final three big block letters: ETM.

Together, side-by-side, the three ghosts—who'd yet to say another word since their opening chorus of "Trick or Treat"—spelled out "MWYADAETM."

The three front ghosts, prodded by jabs in the back by the little goblin in the back, started making wavy *"oooooo"* haunting sounds.

The front row parted and Jeffrey Franklin Cushla Wimsett stepped forward onto Truck Roberts' doorstep. She wore a white veiled wedding dress, with a blue ceramic pin attached to the lace near her left collarbone. The pin, in yellow block easy-to-read letters, simply said, "WYMM?"

Truck said nothing. He was hoping some little kids would parachute out of the darkness and rescue him from this Fellini-like film scene.

Cush took one more step forward. She carefully lifted the veil off her face and looked him straight in the eye. Never taking her eyes off his, she smiled softly and whispered loudly enough to hear, "Minutes with you are diamonds and emeralds to me."

"What did you say?" Truck asked, his eyebrow raised and head cocked slightly sideways.

"I *said*, Mr. Truck Roberts, 'Minutes with you are diamonds and emeralds to me.' You told me that the very first time we met. Years ago. In Auckland. At the Horse & Trap. You told me that as you shook hands and said goodbye."

"That *is* what it means, isn't it?" demanded a ghost that sounded a hell of a lot like Bird. "That *is* what the letters stand for, isn't it?"

"That *is* it, isn't it?" asked the shapeliest ghost who sounded like Mitzi.

"That's gotta be it," chimed in the Phoebe-sounding biggest ghost.

"I sure hope that's it or I'm going to walk back down this path and crawl back to New Zealand through that sewer grate over there," said Cush, pointing to the street. "And I shall do so immediately after I throw up."

Truck locked his eyes on Cush. He heard the others talking, but never looked away. At the moment, he felt no need to say anything. Around the world and back again, and all that mattered was standing right in front of him.

Overdressed, perhaps, but at least she was here.

Finally, he smiled. "Oh, really, Miss Wimsett?" teased Truck. "Did you bring a change of clothing in case you're wrong? It can be very nasty down inside that sewer."

"Would you hurry please?" urged the Bird-sounding ghost. "I've got to go to the toilet."

Cush stepped forward another half step to move her eyes even closer to his. Truck stepped down to the porch where she stood and gently placed his hands on her hips. He pulled her close. When their hips touched and their eyes were just six inches apart, Cush drilled into his soul and saw what she needed to see. Then she broke into the biggest, happiest smile of her entire life and leaped up into his arms, wrapping both legs around him in a vice-grip lock.

Truck fell backward into the house, onto the tiled foyer, with Cush on top of him. The rest of the Posse screamed with excitement.

"Must be it!" cried Mitzi in the middle of the noise.

"Gotta be!" yelled Phoebe.

"Thank God," muttered Bird after a break in the screaming let her step over the floor-wrestling lovebirds. "Finally I can go to the bloody toilet."

As timing and luck would have it, the women's screams terrified four little knee-high trick-or-treaters baby-stepping up Truck's walkway. What the little kids saw was a bride rolling around the floor beating the hell out of poor Mr. Roberts.

One of the kids, a yellow bumblebee, turned to the little fairy princess next to him and said, "He must not have any candy." And with that they decided to turn around and leave.

The largest ghost who looked like Phoebe ran after the children to tell them everything was OK and that there was plenty of candy for everyone. But when one of the parents saw an adult ghost chasing his kids, he started hollering and ran toward the ghost full speed. He leveled Phoebe with a flying gut-high tackle like an unblocked linebacker on a weak side blitz. His groin, however, was unprotected and mayhem ensued.

Mitzi immediately ran in and jumped on the bee's father. She started pummeling him for tackling Phoebe. Bird re-emerged from the bathroom, heard the kids screaming, and saw some man fighting and yelling and rolling around in Truck's front yard with her girlfriends. By now, the fist-flailing scrum was rolling down the lawn and toward the sidewalk—and directly toward the sewer Cush had mentioned earlier.

Whooping a native Maori Indian war cry, Bird zoomed down the walkway with her ghost arms flapping wildly and high-jumped a flying leap onto the top of the dogpile. Some of the other neighbors in the cul-de-sac saw the melee in Truck's yard and came running over to join the fray. Another looked out the window and called the cops.

Cush heard all the commotion, looked up from kissing her future husband, and decided to do the logical thing: She kicked the door shut.

Later that evening, Truck and Cush returned downstairs from a couple hours of looking at his coin collection, and there on the sofa, side by side, sat the rest of the Posse. Phoebe was holding an ice pack over her eye. Bird had a fat lip. Mitzi was sipping a glass of Perrier with a twist while trying to decide if she should phone the handsome policeman whose shift was nearly over.

Truck took one look at his bruised and battered ghosts and ordered a pizza. After the pizza, he emerged from his study with a box full of never-sent postcards. There were hundreds. "Here," he told Cush as he handed her the box. "I saved these for you. These are all places I've been where I was thinking of you. I didn't set out to do this—it just happened. I didn't know if I'd ever tell you about them, but now that you're here—if you like them— it'll save me a lot in postage just to hand them over."

Cush looked at Truck, trying to decide if he was serious. She picked up a handful and shuffled through them slowly, turning some of them over to read the notes on the back. She put the cards down for a moment. "This is wonderful," she said. "I haven't been to *any* of these places."

"Wrong," Truck answered. "You've been to *all* these places."

Cush leaned over and grabbed his neck, hugging him close and whispering, "I love you, Truck Roberts" in his right ear.

"I love you, too," he replied. Then Truck kissed her.

The Posse groaned. They were *afraid* this was going to happen.

When Pigs Fly, Again

It didn't take somebody who knew how to work a slide rule to figure out what happened next. Truck and Cush got married and, since Alma was the closest thing Truck had to a mom and Bonefish loved a good party, it only seemed right to get married in the Bahamas.

So they did, at sundown on a Saturday night at the tip of North Bimini by Casa Grande. Half of the island turned out to watch and Joe Shashaty flew over again to play the sax. Cush rode to the ceremony sidesaddle on Bonefish in the dry-cleaned wedding dress she almost puked on when she tackled Truck in the doorway at Halloween. According to Phoebe, it was Cush's good-luck gown. Bonefish, meanwhile, looked quite stylish with his custom-made lavender bow tie and black fedora with the ears cut out.

Truck arrived by bonefish skiff, a handmade wooden beauty whose varnished ribs shone like diamonds under a jeweler's bright light. On the stern of the boat in perfect hand-done lettering it read: *"MWYADAETM."*

The skiff was Anvil and Alma's gift to the bride and groom. Since every toothpick of it came from native island wood, it was one of the boat-builder's favorites.

Truck's cryptic MWYADAETM slogan was splattered all over the island for the whole weekend celebration. Some of the church ladies even made a giant sign with this message to drape over the second floor balcony at Casa Grande. But while the women loved it, a lot of Truck's pals told him to quit doing that kind of stuff because now all their women wanted diamonds and emeralds and jewelry, too.

The highlight of the reception was Joe Shashaty's saxophone wailing to the stars while Alma sang the song she wrote called *Minutes with You.*

Wearing the red dress Anvil bought her after the race Bonefish won, Alma let it fly. She was, in a word, magnificent. Truck didn't even know she could sing. When she cut loose, she sounded like a Bahamian Ella Fitzgerald.

Cush and the girls started crying as Alma belted out the last verses and refrain:

> *The stars make up my necklace,*
> *The sun my golden ring –*
> *Sapphires shine within your smile.*
> *My platinum when you sing.*
> *Your lips they are my rubies —*
> *Your eyes they are my jade.*
> *You are the greatest treasure*
> *That heaven's ever made.*
> *And minutes with you, my darling,*
> *Are diamonds and emeralds to me.*

When Alma finished, the applause and cheers were so loud that Bonefish looked around for the photographers and winner's circle. He thought he'd won another race. And minutes later, in a fitting conclusion to the ceremony, Elvis ate the bouquet.

After the wedding, life on the island pretty much went back to normal. Anvil and Alma are still there, grandparents now, and their son T-man is now a schoolteacher in Fort Lauderdale. The trophy Bonefish won at Gulfstream is still on the church mantle. Often visitors to the island go inside to see it. "Whatever it takes," commented Reverend Ossie Brown. "Whatever it takes to get them inside."

T-man and his beautiful wife have two young sons. With both, T-man kept track of all the diapers he changed on a scorecard held by a magnet on the refrigerator door. Both of his little guys prefer ocean fishing to the flats and laugh each time Grandpa gets sick over the side of the boat in deep water. T's oldest son Jordan caught a 20-pound mahi-mahi when he wasn't a lot bigger himself. He reeled it in on the very same reel T received as a gift from the folks at Manero's.

Anvil and Luther remained friends, good friends, long after Bonefish's racing days were over. Luther came over to the island to visit from time to time, and always brought pictures of the new horses he trained. He had even bought a few. In fact, Luther took the money he got from Bonefish's race and claimed a three year old with it. The colt hadn't done much, but Luther was either lucky or smart. He switched the horse from the dirt to the grass and son-of-a-gun if it didn't turn around and win the Grade II Pan American Handicap as a four year old.

Luther stayed off the bottle and carved out a nice living training a string of well-bred horses at Gulfstream and Calder. He still calls everybody "Gozzlehead," including the Governor.

Piso made out well, too. He kept riding, kept winning a few, and became the leading apprentice rider his rookie season at Calder. He married his girlfriend Isa and a year later they had their first son, Piso Jr. The next year they had their second, Luther Anvil Mojado, who proved to be a hellion in diapers. They live in the same condo complex in Hallandale as Hall of Fame jockey Jerry Bailey. Though Bailey lives upstairs and there are a whole lot of floors in between them, just being in the same building is close enough for Piso. And on his balcony stands a tripod and high-powered telescope trained on the sea. After dinner, he often relaxes by scanning the distant ocean way beyond the breakers for other rafters floating to freedom.

And, half a world away, that next splash you hear could be Lloyd gasping for breath as he flails downriver once again in the currents of the mighty Tongariro. He still steps like a novice ice skater through the simplest of streams in pursuit of a trout big enough to warrant a photo on the wall of the Tongariro Lodge. Lloyd has also taken up the clarinet, which sounds not unlike a wailing possum caught by the foot in a leg-hold trap.

Sir Patrick Hogan is still in Cambridge, breeding million-dollar yearlings and doling out advice to the hard-working young folks who toil under his relentless drive for perfection. And rare is the day Hogan spends more than he's earned, especially when those days are auction days.

As a wedding gift to the happy couple, Sir Patrick and Justine gave the two a breeding share in a stallion prospect they'd just bought off the track to stand at Cambridge Stud. A three-time Group I winner in Australia, Steamboat Springs proved to be a rock-solid sire, which came as no surprise to anyone. But getting a share in the stallion Cush had helped save as a newborn was especially frustrating for several horsemen willing to pay for the share Justine and Sir Patrick chose to give away.

"It's not about the money," Sir Patrick reminded those who called. "It's about the animals. And they will love the animals. Horseracing needs people like them."

And down on the South Island, in Glenorchy, life in the world's prettiest little hamlet rolls on much the same. It's still about a 25-possum drive from Queenstown and still only about 130 people live there.

The folks haven't changed much, either. Dangerous Dave, for example, is still dangerous. Last summer a German couple arrived in town searching for adventure and needing a guide. Dangerous learned this at their elbow in the Glen Roydon Lodge pub, whereupon he volunteered that he was, in fact, a guide—a true specialist of the great outdoors.

As part of their holiday wilderness experience, Dave chugged the Germans out to a remote island in the center of Lake Wakatipu, dropped them off on a Thursday morning, and told them he'd be back to pick them up in two days.

Four days later, on Monday afternoon, Dangerous Dave was in the same pub, riverdancing alone atop a table and drinking just a wee bit much. Word filtered through the bar that someone on an island in the middle of Lake Wakatipu was flashing S.O.S. signals with a hand-held makeup mirror. They also had kindled a crude fire by refracting the sun through some reading glasses and into a small pile of dry tinder. It was unclear from their smoke signals whether the stranded couple, Germans apparently, was signaling the letters "S.O.S." or the letters "S.O.B."

Dangerous Dave, clearly, remains quite dangerous.

But lovely Lizard, she of the lithe form and seven tattoos who rescued Ben and Bird from drowning during the wedding, has since moved on. At the Glenorchy Races one January, she walked out her front door to watch the horses run by and leaned up against the fence next to a chap named Crash Vanwell.

Crash had nine tattoos of his own and, two days later, had a tenth—a fine looking lizard. Crash was loaded—way beyond wealthy—having waited in line at a coffee shop in Seattle many years ago. He had struck up a conversation with a couple of tech-heads named Bill Gates and Paul Allen. The pair was convinced they could make money with computers and convinced Crash, too.

An original Microsoft investor, Crash took half a dozen paychecks he'd earned from stunt driving and bought company stock. Crash is now America's richest retired stunt driver and owns 70 Harley-Davidson distributorships around the world. He came to Glenorchy via Blanket Bay at the suggestion of Robin Williams, who had asked him to bring back some possum fur boot liners if he could please remember to do so.

Miss Piggala, Lizard's giant porcine companion, saw the writing on the arm once she noticed Crash Vanwell's new tattoo. And so, during Miss Piggala's annual May romantic foray to the farm of her intimate friend Big Jimmy, Miss Piggala decided, on her own, that she would not return to Glenorchy.

Miss Piggala wanted to be a family pig and dug in her hooves when first Lizard, then Lizard and Crash, tugged on her brass nose ring rope to load her in the truck. Miss Piggala stayed on that farm with Big Jimmy and lived happily ever after, especially each May. At last count, they had 177 children.

On the way back to Lizard's farm, Crash suggested that letting Miss Piggala bungy-jump off Hackett's Bridge on the way down to visit Big Jimmy hadn't been such a good idea after all. In some ways, it must have changed her.

"I could've sworn she enjoyed it," said Lizard firmly.

Chris Boddle, the same guy who'd ankle-tied Mountain at 361 pounds, body-suited Miss Piggala, weighing in at a svelte 362, into a corset-type jumping harness. Boddle hooked Miss Piggala up to "the big girl rope." The pig walked on her own out to the edge of the jump platform.

Miss Piggala looked to her left, looked to her right, oinked twice, and leaped, her hams fully extended toward all four compass points. She was squealing with delight all the way down—the same happy squeal she greeted Big Jimmy with.

Much to the terror of the guys in the raft below, Miss Piggala got a little excited when she jumped. They both leaped overboard for safety.

Sure enough, Miss Piggala bounced all the way back up to Boddle, just like Mountain did, oinked twice, and disappeared back down again. Boddle stood there and shook his head silently. "Man," he thought to himself, "one of these days I gotta get a real job."

Shortly after that, A. J. Hackett Bungy instituted its "No Giant Pig" rule.

— ◆ —

And as far as the Posse goes, well, Mitzi ended up becoming Cush's mother-in-law, which really complicated the holiday gift-giving season. Mitzi married Cleater, whose love for Italian Renaissance art led them to a small but beautiful vacation home in Florence as well as a condo in Key Biscayne near Mitzi's headquarters in Miami.

Cleater himself made a lot of money, a small fortune actually, buying and selling undervalued works of Renaissance art. By accident, he stumbled across one of Piranisi's works at a Florence rummage sale. Cleater paid a pittance in lira for a throw-out work— he wanted just its frame—and discovered the Piranisi in his kitchen that night beneath the outside canvas he was unframing. The Piranisi went for $2.1 million at a Sotheby's auction.

Things never really did work out between Ben and Bird. Ben got a job in the oil business and moved to Dallas a few years back. He is still single, still chasing girls. Occasionally he uses the hidden banana trick at dances and get-togethers, but now uses a wax one significantly larger than the one he bought from Cleater at Phoebe and Mountain's wedding reception. Party Patti also lives in Dallas now and dated Ben briefly before trading him in for a guy with a bigger banana. The night they split up, she told him she liked him as a friend.

Bird ended up dating Cush's ex-boyfriend Timothy, the horse buying-and-selling pinhooker. They were together for the better part of a year. For Christmas, Timothy gave Bird a stallion share in a big-money syndicate he put together. The two of them split up three months later, but she wrote him a thank-you note for her share of the horse. Each year, Bird breeds her stallion to one of Cush's mares and they split the money whenever the youngster sells at Karaka. In a good year, they split upwards of $100,000.

With her portion of the auction proceeds, Bird opened the first of her chain of popular coffeehouses near her home in the trendy Parnell section of Auckland. Her café is called the "The Bird's Nest" and sits in a beautiful corner location with a magnificent pohutukawa tree in the yard. There are now 32 Bird's Nests altogether, 20 scattered throughout New Zealand and ten in South Florida, including one on Key Biscayne across the street from where Cleater and Mitzi live. She also has a coffeehouse in Aspen and another in New York City near Central Park.

Bird is single, wealthy, and still most vulnerable romantically during the height of a full moon. She spends most of her time in New Zealand, but skis in Aspen each February, timing her visits with one eye on lunar positioning.

Phoebe and Mountain are still together, still happy, and the parents of five boy-crazy girls. The oldest got in trouble her first day of first grade for pinning a boy to the floor and kissing him against his will. They live in Queenstown, where Mountain designs and builds jet boat and engine prototypes. He did a lot of research on Shotover Jet's new kevlar-carborundum hull design for a whole new fleet of jet boats the company planned to launch. Mountain helped develop both the single and dual-engine variations. It's good work and he enjoys it.

Phoebe, meanwhile, has been dispensing advice as a Queenstown talk-show host on Chaz's radio station and has become very popular. Even Antonia calls in from the Bunker Bar occasionally.

And as for some of the others, well, the stoat never did figure out how all those birds got inside that box at the wedding nor did he ever catch the mice. The mice walked across the Routeburn River suspension bridge one night and lived the rest of their lives on the opposite side of the river where there was no stoat to worry about. The two brown trout lived near the mice in the Routeburn for years, until one day Carl got hungry and went fishing. Two more trout moved into the empty pool the next day.

And Bonefish? Well, Bonefish had a good long life and died in his sleep at the age of 22. He is resting in the church cemetery on North Bimini on top of a hill looking out across the Atlantic. And, like the great sire Sir Tristram half a world away, Bonefish is buried upright in a galloping pose with his tail to the sunrise and nose to the setting sun. Fittingly, his nose points to Gulfstream Park.

Elvis died four weeks after Bonefish and is buried right alongside his lifelong pal.

As for Mr. and Mrs. Roberts, they spend most of their time at their small farm outside Cambridge, about ten miles from Sir Patrick. They have a dozen horses—nine broodmares, two two year olds in training, and an old gelding Cush saved when he could no longer earn his keep on the track.

Mr. and Mrs. Roberts aren't rich, but then again maybe they are, since they have all they really need, which is each other. They have two daughters, Angelina and Angelica, and both could beat their father at darts before they turned five. He adores his children, just as he does their mother.

When Truck has the time, he trailers the wooden boat Anvil made him, *MWYADAETM*, down to the Waikato River and drifts downstream, catching an occasional trout. He doesn't catch as many as Mrs. Roberts, but he gets a few from time to time.

Every couple of years, the family travels half a world away to Miami and Bimini to visit their friends. They always stop by the racetrack to cheer for Piso to win his races. He normally does well, except when he races against Jerry Bailey.

Truck and Cush even took their two little girls to the Keys, where all four sat on the edge of Robbie's dock and tossed buckets of baitfish to hungry, swirling tarpon. Moss the Boss III ran back and forth at the end of the dock, barking and chasing the pelicans away.

Every trip over, before leaving Miami to fly back to New Zealand, Truck hops over to Bimini to visit with Anvil and Alma. He still goes bonefishing with Anvil, still hasn't caught anything close to a record fish, and always visits Bonefish's grave at sundown the night before the family leaves. It's a simple life, a good life—a very happy life.

Oh. And one other thing. Truck still listens to his old Louis Armstrong album, letting Satchmo remind him what he already knows.

What a wonderful world, indeed.